Romantic Times praises Connie Mason, winner of the Storyteller of the Year Award and a Career Achievement Award in Western Historical Romance.

SHEIK

'This is a story that will certainly keep you warm on a cold winter's night."

THE LION'S BRIDE

"This wondrous tale is a must read for the medieval fan and Ms. Mason's legion of fans!"

WIND RIDER

"A delightful, action-packed love story!"

TEARS LIKE RAIN

"Vivid . . . strongly written"

TREASURES OF THE HEART

"Connie Mason adds sizzling sensuality and a cast of unique characters to turn *Treasures of the Heart* into another winner."

A PROMISE OF THUNDER

"Once you pick up *A Promise of Thunder* you won't want to put it down."

ICE & RAPTURE

"*Ice & Rapture* is filled with one rip-roaring escapade following on the heels of another wild adventure . . . A delightful love story."

BRAVE LAND, BRAVE LOVE

"*Brave Land, Brave Love* is an utter delight from first page to last—funny, tender, adventurous, and highly romantic!"

CALL OF THE VALKYRIE

The first time he saw her she was clothed in naught but moonlight and mist and the midnight cloud of her lustrous hair. She moved as if she were made of shadow and vapor floating on a gentle breeze. He hadn't come for plunder or rape. Not this time. He'd been lured to the island by the whisper of the wind and the sultry call of a Valkyrie.

She was bathing in a narrow stream in a moon-dappled glen, her nude body shimmering like polished ivory, her shiny black hair falling to her waist in rippling waves. She was young and beautiful and exquisitely fashioned. Not large and strapping like Viking women, but small and delicately put together. A throbbing began in Thorne's loins.

He had to have her.

Other *Leisure* and *Love Spell* books by
Connie Mason:
WILD IS MY HEART
CARESS AND CONQUER
BOLD LAND, BOLD LOVE
DESERT ECSTASY
PROMISED SPLENDOR
MY LADY VIXEN
TENDER FURY
FOR HONOR'S SAKE
ICE AND RAPTURE
WILD LAND, WILD LOVE
BEYOND THE HORIZON
TEMPT THE DEVIL
WIND RIDER
TREASURES OF THE HEART
A PROMISE OF THUNDER
PURE TEMPTATION
TEARS LIKE RAIN
THE LION'S BRIDE
SIERRA
LOVE ME WITH FURY
SHADOW WALKER
FLAME
LORD OF THE NIGHT
PROMISE ME FOREVER
SHEIK

LEISURE BOOKS  NEW YORK CITY

Dedicated to my new grandson, Mason Robinson Osborn

A LEISURE BOOK®

July 1998

Published by

Dorchester Publishing Co., Inc.
276 Fifth Avenue
New York, NY 10001

ISBN 0-8439-4402-1

Printed in the United States of America.

Viking!

Prologue

The Isle of Man, 850 AD

The first time he saw her she was clothed in naught but moonlight and mist and the midnight cloud of her lustrous hair. She moved as if she were made of shadow and vapor floating on a gentle breeze. He hadn't come for plunder or rape. Not this time. He'd been lured to the island by the whisper of the wind and the sultry call of a Valkyrie.

Thorne the Relentless was not a superstitious man, nor one who acted recklessly, yet he had been lured to this dark shore by a powerful force more potent than his own survival instincts. His captains never questioned his orders to put ashore as his fleet of dragon ships scraped the shoreline. Nor did they stop him when he jumped into the water and waded through the surf to the sandy beach.

The firstborn son of the powerful jarl Olaf, Thorne had never led them astray. Thorne's vast knowledge of the sea and trade routes had made rich men of all his dragon ship captains and their crews.

"Wait here for me," Thorne ordered as the captains of his five dragon ships waded to shore behind him. "Find a river, fill the waterbags and set up camp while I explore. Tonight we will dine on fresh game."

"Shall I come with you, Thorne?"

Thorne dismissed Ulm, his most trusted captain, with a wave of his massive hand. "Nay, I go alone. Do not let the men stray inland. We are not here to plunder. Our ships are already filled with rich cargo from our latest raid upon the Norman coast."

Ulm wagged his head of shaggy, unkempt hair in reproof as Thorne disappeared into a thick forest of hardwood trees. Thorne rarely if ever acted precipitously, or without a valid reason, and his men knew it. Putting ashore now made no sense to anyone but himself, Thorne mused. True, they were low on water, but it was not yet a problem. Though Ulm might silently wonder about his decision, Thorne knew Ulm would never question orders from a man whose skill and carriage had kept them all alive during countless raids across treacherous seas and hostile lands.

A wary deer turned and fled at the sound of Thorne's leather-clad feet treading upon damp earth and dead leaves. Thorne paused, listening to the wind whispering in the trees, raising his face to the wedge of moonlight spearing through the lofty branches. Had he tried, Thorne couldn't have explained the mysterious, seductive urgency that had beckoned him to this place. If it was magic, he wanted nothing to do with it. Yet how else could he explain the bizarre circumstance that had lured him to the island? It was almost as if destiny had preordained his arrival on this deserted strip of beach. Why?

Then Thorne stepped into a clearing and saw a vision that made his heart thump within the confines of his chest. She was bathing in a narrow stream in a moon-dappled glen, her nude body shimmering like polished ivory, her shiny black hair falling to her waist in rippling waves. She was young and beautiful and exquisitely fashioned. Not large and strapping like Viking women, but small and delicately put together. A throbbing began in Thorne's loins.

He had to have her.

She turned slightly, as if sensing his presence. Thorne sucked in a ragged breath, captivated by the sight of a pair of perfect breasts crested by rosy nipples. His mouth went dry with longing. Thor's hammer! She was lovelier than the goddess Freyja, Thorne thought as his expression turned lustful. The throbbing in his loins was almost painful now as his shaft swelled and hardened.

His gaze slid past her breasts to linger on her tiny waist; he could easily encircle it with both his hands. Her hips were gently rounded, her legs long and shapely. The dark, mysterious patch between her legs seemed to beg for the touch of his hands and mouth. Her ankles were finely turned, her feet small and delicate. He must have groaned, for she looked in his direction, poised like a frightened deer on the verge of flight.

Thorne stepped from the shadows into the moonlight. The girl—she could hardly be called a woman—gasped, apparently frozen by fear as she spied the fierce Viking warrior, a man her people had learned to fear. Vikings had terrorized her island for years, but none had landed so close to her home before.

Never had Fiona seen so fierce a warrior. He was a veritable giant. His chest was thick and solid, his legs long and sturdy as the oak trees that grew in the forest. Golden blond hair escaped from beneath his iron helmet, sweeping over his massive shoulders. He was beardless. He wore a shirt of ringlink mail that reached to mid-thigh and a tunic beneath it that left most of his muscular arms bare. His flat-soled boots were made of leather and were laced up his legs to fasten at his bare calves. Her attention was drawn to the silver buckle adorning his leather belt, and to the assortment of weapons he carried.

His sword was long, its hilt finely carved and decorated with silver. A throwing axe, dagger and battleaxe were thrust into his belt. Even in the darkness Fiona sensed the violence in him, and fear shuddered through her. The shudder seemed to release her from her frozen stance and she turned to flee.

Thorne knew the moment the mystery maiden decided to flee and reacted swiftly. She had scarcely taken a single step before Thorne reached her, jerking her against him.

"Do not go," he said in a voice made rough with lust. "Who are you? Are you real, or a figment of my imagination?"

She stared at him, apparently stunned to hear him speak to her in her own Gaelic tongue. She had no way of knowing that Thorne the Relentless was not just a raider, but a trader who had learned many languages during his travels to distant lands.

"Who are you?" Thorne repeated.

She raised her eyes to his and the breath slammed from Thorne's chest. Her eyes! They were so vivid a violet that he dared not stare into them too long lest they bewitch him. But it was already too late. He was forever and irrevocably lost in those captivating violet depths. His gaze lowered slightly to her lips. Full and lush and enticing. If he didn't taste them he would surely perish.

Thorne was a man who took what he wanted, when he wanted, and he hungered for this woman. Unaccustomed to asking for what he wanted, Thorne crushed the entrancing maiden against his muscular chest and kissed her with all the fury and passion he was capable of.

Overwhelmed by this untamed marauder, the maiden uttered a protest and tried to defend herself against the obscenity this Viking intended for her. Rapine and plunder. Christians since St. Peter visited their island, the maiden and her countrymen prayed daily for deliverance from the fury of the Norsemen.

She whimpered, frightened and bruised as he plundered her mouth. Her breasts and stomach wore the imprint of his mail and her buttocks bore the marks of his large hands. She wrested her mouth free and cried out, "Nay!"

The husky quality of her voice sent shivers of awareness through Thorne. "So, you *can* speak. Who are you, lady?" He held her like a vise with one hand while caressing her breasts with the other.

She shook her head, determined to tell this fierce Viking nothing. She was frightened out of her wits at the thought that this brutal man may be the Viking the old Celtic wizard, Brann, had described from a vision he'd had many years ago. According to Brann, her future and that of a Norseman were intertwined. Surely this savage Viking wasn't the man fate had given her. God wouldn't be so cruel, so unfeeling, would he?

"I don't care who you are, lady," Thorne said roughly. "I will have you nonetheless." He lifted her in his arms and bore her to the ground.

She gazed into his fire-and-ice blue eyes and knew she had to escape. What he wanted to do to her was wrong and sinful. When he knelt above her to remove his mail, she gathered her wits and reacted with a daring she hadn't known she possessed. Bending her knees, she kicked him backward onto his rump and leapt to her feet while he was struggling to rise. Then she turned and ran into the shadowy forest.

Grunting in dismay, Thorne sprinted after her. But burdened as he was by his armor and weapons, he was no match for the fleet-footed maiden. She had escaped him.

"Odin take you!" His curse thundered through the forest, disturbing all manner of night animals. He ached with unrequited need, and he had a dreadful premonition that no woman would ever please him as the mystery maiden would have. One word came to mind. A word so frightening he dared not say it.

Witchcraft!

The maiden had cast a spell upon him. She had bewitched him. He had to flee now or risk his soul.

A short time later the five dragon ships slipped from shore and sailed into the dark mist rising from the sea.

Chapter One

Kaupang, a trading port on the Norwegian coast, one year later

"Loki take you, Thorne! You haven't been yourself since you went a-Viking last summer. You've all but lost your appetite for women. What happened during that voyage?"

Thorne sent his brother a quelling look, then glanced around to see if any of the thralls were lurking nearby to hear them. They were alone. The thralls had long since retired to their shelves and benches lining both sides of the hall. Thorne knew his brother wouldn't understand his reluctance to rut with just any woman, so he didn't attempt to explain.

"Nothing is wrong, Thorolf. I haven't seen a woman who appeals to me."

"I don't believe you," Thorolf scoffed. "Ulm said you haven't been the same since your dragon ships put ashore on the Isle of Man. He thinks something happened there. I know you haven't been sleeping well; I hear you pacing at night. You're short of temper and quick to lash out. You rarely take a woman anymore. Has Tyra ceased to please you? 'Tis not like you, brother."

"Naught is wrong," Thorne repeated, as if trying to convince himself.

"Tell that to someone who doesn't know you as well as I. 'Tis not like you to go so long without a woman, or to remain at home when you could go a-Viking."

"Perhaps 'tis because I'm now betrothed," Thorne opined.

Thorolf threw back his shaggy head and gave a shout of laughter. "Not you, brother. Marrying Bretta will not stop your wild ways. I've fought at your side, Thorne the Relentless. You're as fierce as any Viking berserker I've ever seen. 'Tis time you told me the truth."

"I agree." Thorne's father strode into the hall and stopped before his sons, hands on hips, legs spread wide. Olaf was even more massive than either of his two sons. His yellow hair and beard were shaggy and streaked with gray. His huge, brawny body was covered with battle scars, and he was missing two fingers on his left hand.

"Thorolf isn't the only one who's noticed your strange behavior," he told Thorne. "You've been acting like a man bewitched."

Thorne started violently. He knew Olaf's words were meant to be teasing, but his father had come too close to the truth for his liking. Thorne had long since decided he'd been bewitched. Since that night he'd been lured to the Isle of Man, he'd been unable to forget the beautiful, mysterious maiden. She continued to haunt his dreams and make his waking hours unbearable. Sleep was a luxury no longer allowed to him. The maiden was a witch, there was no other explanation. And he was doomed to live in misery for the rest of his days.

Olaf's eyes narrowed suspiciously. "Odin's balls! That's it! You're bewitched."

Thorne glanced down at his hands. They were strong hands, hands accustomed to wielding weapons, to slaying enemies, yet they rested uselessly in front of him now. A man of his awesome strength and determination should be capable of conquering his erotic dreams, yet he could not. It was almost as if the dark-haired, violet-eyed maiden had invaded his mind and was slowly seducing him to madness.

"Aye, Father," Thorne said with considerable anger. "There is no other explanation. I am bewitched."

"By Odin's beard! What are you saying?" Thorolf roared. "Someone must have bashed you on the head, else you would never make such an outrageous statement."

"I encountered the witch on the Isle of Man," Thorne explained. "She lured me to her shore, I swear it. She spoke to me through the wind and the waves, promising me a taste of Valhalla. She is as beautiful as a Valkyrie, with hair as black as midnight and eyes the color of the violets that grow upon the hills in summertime. She was naked, her body shimmering like ivory in the moonlight. And I wanted her more than I have ever wanted another woman."

Thorolf moved to the edge of his bench, apparently enthralled by Thorne's tale of witchcraft. "By Odin's beard! A woman such as you described would have to be a witch. What happened? Did she cast a spell upon you? A story like this is worthy of the most talented scald. He would sing it throughout the land."

"I spoke to her in Gaelic, but the witch refused to answer," Thorne said, delving deeply into his memory. "She uttered but one word."

"What word was that?" Olaf asked. He seemed surprised that the fiercer of his two sons would allow a woman to bewitch him.

"She said 'nay' as I bore her to the ground. I wanted to be inside her, could think of nothing else. I was hard and aching and wanted to ravish her. When I paused to remove my mail, she caught me off guard and escaped. I tried to follow, but she seemed to disappear into thin air. Only a witch could do that. Instead of searching the island for her, I panicked and ordered my men to their ships. I felt, nay, I *knew*, I had been bewitched, and it frightened me. Never have I been so utterly captivated by a woman. The beautiful witch I encountered on that misty isle that night has made my life miserable ever since."

Olaf's blue eyes, so like Thorne's, gazed with pity upon his son. He could tell that Thorne was suffering and he liked it not. He rubbed his bearded chin as he pondered Thorne's plight. Olaf had never believed in witchcraft, but he was not one to dismiss something he did not understand. If Thorne believed he was bewitched, then something must be done about it.

"You must go back to Man," Olaf decreed.

"For what purpose?" Thorne asked. "I never want to see that cursed place again."

"Since when have you ever turned down a chance to raid and plunder?" Thorolf jeered. "Heed our father, Thorne, for he is wise and will tell you how to break the witch's spell."

"Very well. I will take my dragon ships to Man, to raid and plunder the land. When I am through, they will curse my name for generations to come."

"Aye," Olaf said, obviously content with his son's response to his advice. "But there is more. You must find the witch and slay her. Her death will free you from her spell."

Thorne stared at his father, his eyes blazing with unholy light. Of course! It was all so clear now. He should have thought of it himself and ended all those months of erotic torture. Once the witch was dead she could no longer enchant him, or make him ache to possess her.

"I will gather a crew and undertake the journey," he said, anxious now to be off. "Every inhabitant on the Isle of Man will learn to fear the name of Thorne the Relentless."

Thorolf nodded sagely. " 'Tis a wise decision. You must kill the witch and break the spell. Besides, the plunder and captives will bring us new wealth. Byzantium clamors for fresh slaves to meet their demands."

"Will you explain to Bretta the Fair why our marriage must be delayed, Father?" Thorne asked. "I know you made arrangements for us to wed at the *althing* this summer."

"The wedding can wait. I will invite Bretta to stay with us while you go a-Viking. The wedding can take place upon your return. Once the witch is dead, you'll be able to concentrate on wedding Bretta and producing children.

"We will await your return, Thorne. May Odin the All Father see you safely to your destination, and Thor the thunder god give you strength to defeat the witch."

Chapter Two

Isle of Man, Summer, 851 AD

Cold gray waves washed the western shore. The land was silent and deserted. No peasants roamed the shoreline. No smoke plumed above the wooded hillsides.

Peasants native to the isle knew better than to build too close to the sea lest a savage Viking horde swoop down upon them in their sleep and slay them. They were wise enough to build well away from the sea to give them time to close the log gates of the palisades surrounding their villages and string their bows in times of peril.

No sound broke the silence on this summer morning except the lapping of the waves against the shore and the shrill crying of gulls as the rising sun broke through the morning mist.

At his post on a hilltop overlooking the sea, a young peasant boy wrapped in a heavy woolen cloak stretched and yawned and got stiffly to his feet. His job was to watch for any strange craft approaching their shore and warn the villagers in time to arm themselves. He had seen nothing since taking over from another boy the night before and was bored with scanning an empty sea. He reached into his greasy leather wallet for his breakfast of coarse black bread and cheese, but before he could take a bite, something far out in the swirling mist caught his eye. He blinked, then stared fixedly at a dark shape riding low in the water. Then he saw another, and another. Five altogether. Suddenly the sun caught the edges of sails and glinted from flashing oar blades.

Now he could see the fierce dragon heads rising above the graceful hulls. Flashes of light reflected off polished helmets, spear points and sword blades. Along each gunwale hung a line of brightly painted wooden shields, one overlapping the next, two shields to each oar hole. Each dragon ship was propelled swiftly by sixteen pairs of oars, seventeen feet long. From a yardarm slung across the forty-foot pole mast hung a single red-and-white striped square sail.

The young watchman stood frozen with fear as the five narrow, shallow draft ships scraped the shore below him. Thirty tall, bearded and moustached golden-haired raiders leaped ashore from each ship. One hundred and fifty in all. They wore mail shirts of interlaced steel rings that reached almost to their knees, over which were slung handsome fur-trimmed cloaks, fastened at the throat by jeweled gold or silver brooches. Their leather shoes were laced and crisscrossed around their bare legs, and conical steel helmets protected their heads.

Each man carried an assortment of weapons: a long, two-edged sword, battleaxe, spear, short knife and round wooden shield with a metal boss in the center. As the Vikings disgorged from their dragon ships, the lad finally found the courage to move his frozen limbs. But by then it was too late. He had already been seen from below. Two fierce Vikings charged up the hill and seized him before he could carry a warning to the village.

"We have the boy, Thorne," Ulm said as he dragged the struggling boy to the beached ships where Thorne was directing his men. "What shall we do with him?"

Thorne gave the lad a cursory glance, noting that he was young and offered no threat to them except for the warning he would have carried. "I will speak with him."

Ulm held the boy by the shoulders while Thorne fired off questions. "How far to the village, boy?"

The lad stared at Thorne, surprised to hear the savage Viking speaking to him in Gaelic. When he remained mute, Ulm gave him an ungentle shake. "Answer the question, boy!"

The lad gulped and tried to speak, but terror froze his throat.

"I won't harm you, just answer truthfully," Thorne said. "How far to the village?"

"N-not far. A league, no more."

"Does your village have a palisade?"

"Aye, but the gate will be open."

"I'm looking for a woman. She has hair as black as midnight and eyes the color of violets. She is a witch. Do you know of her?"

The boy's eyes widened. "A witch? Nay, there is no witch in the village. Only one woman matches your description. Fiona the Learned, but she is no witch."

Thorne's blue eyes narrowed. "Think hard, lad. The woman I seek is a great beauty, no mere peasant."

The boy licked his lips nervously. "I-I—nay, I know not of whom you speak."

Thorne didn't believe him. He would find his witch, and when he did he would force her to remove her spell. "Take the boy away. Tell the men who will remain here to guard the ships to watch him. We'll learn nothing more from the lad."

The morning was fine and clear as Thorne led his savage horde toward the village. When Ulm spotted a monastery situated atop a hill, he turned off the path with half the men, leaving Thorne to continue on alone. Monasteries usually held a wealth of gold and silver, much more than could be gleaned from peasants. Wielding their mighty swords, Ulm's men descended upon the unsuspecting monks. But

Thorne was not distracted by the promise of riches or slaves. He was here for one reason alone.
The witch.

Fiona the Learned wended her way through the forest to Brann the Wizard's cottage. As was her habit, she visited the old Celtic sorcerer daily, usually before her father stirred from his bed and the villagers began their day at morning Mass. Today she carried a basket filled with medicinal herbs such as St. John's wort, laurel, fennel, vervain and sage. Brann was a healer as well as a wizard. He concocted potions and brewed medicines that had mysterious healing powers. The villagers sought his help with everything from love problems, to impotence, to warding off danger.

Fiona trod the well-worn path to the tiny daub-and-wattle cottage sitting in a small glen not far from the village. She knocked once on the door, then let herself inside without waiting for an invitation. The cottage was dark and smoky, smelling strongly of herbs and medicines of which only she and Brann had knowledge. Before her untimely death, Fiona's mother had been a renowned healer and she had taught her daughter her skills.

Though Mairie the Healer had embraced the Christian religion, her Celtic roots ran deep. She was said to have mystical powers inherited from her Celtic forbears. Fiona's powers were not as strong as her mother's, but Brann had shown her how to use those she did possess, such as clairvoyance and healing, for the benefit of others.

Fiona peered through the smoky gloom of the room and saw Brann standing at the single window, staring toward the sea. He didn't stir as she approached him. She set her basket down on the table and gently touched his shoulder.

"Brann? What is it? Are you unwell?"

Several moments passed before the old man turned to acknowledge Fiona. Though his eyes were clear, they burned with a fervor that made Fiona shiver. They seemed to look right through her. She'd never seen Brann so distracted and it alarmed her.

"Brann? What's amiss?"

"Ah, Fiona," Brann said, suddenly gaining his wits. " 'Tis beginning."

"What? What is beginning?"

Brann glanced past her, his eyes unfocused as he began to recite in a singsong voice: "They will arrive on our shore in dragon ships to plunder and raid. You will know him by his name. He is called 'Relentless.' His sword is Blood-drinker and his ship is *Odin's Raven*. He holds your fate in his massive hands. He comes to take your life. Instead he will steal your heart."

His words fell off and his eyes cleared. But his expression remained grave.

"I've heard that prophesy before, Brann, why do you taunt me with it now? I no longer believe it to be so. Vikings visited our shore a year ago but nothing came of it, thank our blessed Lord, and they did not return. 'Tis an abomination to think that a Viking berserker will steal my heart. Besides, why would a Norseman come to our shore specifically to kill me?"

"The answer is unclear, but you will know soon. If you survive the day, you will travel to a far-off land and face grave danger."

Fiona knew better than to dismiss Brann's prophesy out of hand. She had cut her teeth on his teachings and trusted him implicitly. But this . . . this implausible prediction simply could not be true. She thought back to her encounter with the fierce Viking warrior that moonlit night a year ago and remembered the feel of his hands on her naked flesh. There wasn't a soft place on his hard body or a tender spot in his cruel heart. He had wanted to ravish her, and probably would have killed her afterward if she hadn't used her wits to escape.

Though she'd never admit it, not even to herself, she thought of the Viking far too often for her liking. She remembered him as a golden giant, with strong features. He was fierce and strong and could have been called handsome if his face weren't set in ruthless lines. Sometimes he tormented her dreams, but in those dreams he wanted to do things to her that had nothing to do with her death.

"What are you thinking?" Brann asked.

Fiona flushed. Could the wizard see into her mind? She prayed not. "How much time do I have before your prophesy becomes reality?"

Brann gave her a sad smile. "The day is at hand."

Fiona started violently. "Vikings are here? On our shore? Now?" Why hadn't she sensed this?

"At the village gates this very minute."

"Lord protect us! What am I to do? I must return immediately."

Brann nodded his shaggy white head. "Aye. We must make haste to the village. It may already be too late."

Fiona didn't stop to ask what Brann meant as she made a hasty exit and sped along the path to the village. Brann was hard on her heels, moving surprisingly fast for one so old.

"Hurry, Brann," she called over her shoulder. "I can sense them now and feel their anger reaching out to me. You are right. They want to kill me."

Thorne had surprised the villagers at their morning chores. A dirt wall topped by a stockade of pointed logs surrounded the village, but the gate had stood open. Few villagers had had time to arm themselves, and those who did were quickly cut down by the fierce marauders. After a short battle the peasants had laid down their crude weapons and surrendered to the raiders. Few pleaded for their lives, for most expected to die. By the time Ulm, fresh from his raid upon the monastery, rejoined Thorne, there was naught left to do but plunder, rape and fire the huts.

Thorne had no appetite for rape but he could not deny his men their pleasure. He watched with distaste as a man dragged a hapless maiden behind a hut. He shut out her screams as the remaining villagers were prodded at sword-point to the village green. Thorne was on a witch hunt. He wouldn't rest until he found and destroyed the woman who had cast a spell upon him.

"Who is your chieftain?" Thorne barked.

A slight man of middle age stepped forward. "I am Adair."

"You are the chieftain?"

"Aye. Kill me, Viking, but spare my people."

"No one will die if you give me what I seek."

Adair made a helpless gesture. "You have already stolen all that we own."

Thorne dismissed Adair's words with a wave of his hand. "I seek a woman. I know not her name, but she is a witch. She has hair as black as a raven's wing, eyes a stunning violet, and the body of an enchantress."

Thorne was surprised by the collective gasp that rose from the crowd.

Adair stared at him, apparently appalled. "There is no witch in our village."

Thorne's eyes narrowed as he waved Blood-drinker in the air. "You lie! I want her. Bring her to me."

"Why? What do you want with her?"

"The witch has placed a spell upon me." He waved his sword in the air. "Blood-drinker will slay her and free me."

"I do not understand any of this," Adair said slowly. "We are Christians. There are no witches in our midst. Where did you encounter this witch?"

"On your very shore," Thorne said. "She lured me here with her siren's song on my last voyage. 'Twas then she placed a spell on me. If you do not produce her now, you will all be made to suffer the consequences."

Adair knew the Viking was referring to his own beloved daughter, Fiona, for no other woman matched his description. But Fiona was no witch. She did have certain powers Adair did not understand, and he prayed that Fiona would sense her danger and remain hidden no matter what happened.

Adair hung his head. "Do to me what you will, Viking, for I know of no witch."

Exasperated, Thorne turned to the villagers, who were clinging to one another in abject fear. "Which one of you will speak out to save your chieftain's miserable life? Where is the witch I seek?"

Not one man, woman or child stepped forward.

Never had Thorne felt so thwarted, so helpless. These people had ample reason to fear him, yet to a man they were defending the witch. Was she so beloved that they would sacrifice their lives for her?

"You have sealed your own fate," Thorne thundered. "One man will be slain each hour until the witch is produced, beginning with your chieftain. When all the men are slain, your widows and children will be sold into slavery."

Thorne expected to see at least one person willing to trade information for his life and was stunned when his words were met with silent tears and quiet acceptance. Was everyone bewitched? What manner of woman earned such blind loyalty?

"You!" Thorne said, pointing Blood-drinker at Adair. "On your knees. Perhaps when these peasants see their chieftain's head roll, they'll come forward."

Adair fell to his knees and bent his head. Thorne stared down at the vulnerable place on his neck where his hair parted and felt scant liking for his task. Killing didn't bother him; he did it in the heat of battle with relish. But slaying an unarmed man was not his way. He had expected these ignorant peasants to break long before now. Unfortunately, there was no turning back. To rescind his order now would make him look weak. Instead of delivering the killing blow himself, he lowered Blood-drinker and motioned for Ulm to take over.

Ulm moved with alacrity into the spot vacated by Thorne. He raised his sword and prepared to bring it down upon Adair's bowed head.

Suddenly a woman darted through the parting crowd and flung herself upon the kneeling man. Her long black hair fell like a protective cape around Adair, and Thorne felt as if he'd been slammed in the chest with a battleaxe. His limbs trembled and he felt a hardness swelling his loins.

Thorne had found his witch.

"Hold!" Thorne cried when Ulm would have slain both Adair and the woman. Obviously disgruntled at the delay, Ulm lowered his sword. Thorne realized the thirst for blood still raged within Ulm, but it couldn't be helped.

Thorne strode to Fiona and pulled her away from Adair. Then he held her at arm's length and stared at her. He saw at a glance that she hadn't changed since that first meeting, except, perhaps, to grow more beautiful. Then he made the fatal mistake of looking directly into her eyes and was captivated anew. His lust was so powerful, he wanted to tear off her clothing and thrust himself between her legs, to lose himself in her sweet flesh, to rut until he was sated. Seeing her again was a shock to his system. He was convinced that he would not escape her spell as long as she lived and breathed the same air as he.

Fiona's eyes widened in dismay when she realized that this man was the same Viking she had encountered that fateful night a year before. She should have known it would be he. Brann's predictions were rarely wrong.

Thorne's expression did not change. "So you *do* remember me," he said when he saw her eyes kindle with recognition. "Do not deny it, for I can see it in your eyes. What are you called?" he asked roughly.

Fiona stared into the Viking's fire-and-ice blue eyes and saw her own death. She knew not why he wished her dead, but whatever the reason, she would not beg for her life. If it was meant to be, the Lord would deliver her from this heathen monster.

"I am called Fiona the Learned."

"Fiona the Learned," he repeated slowly. "Did you earn your name by practicing witchcraft?"

Fiona gasped. "Witchcraft? I am no witch. Whatever gave you that idea? I am a Christian. I was given the name because of the healing powers I possess."

Thorne gave a snort of laughter. "Do not lie, Fiona the Learned. I know you are a witch. You cast your spell upon me and I have not known a moment's peace since then. You have stolen my mind." He leaned closer, thrusting his face into hers so his words could be heard by no one but Fiona. "You threaten my manhood. Me!" He thumped his chest. "Thorne the Relentless. Women no longer appeal to me. I am possessed, I tell you, and 'tis all your fault."

His unfounded accusations seemed to appall Fiona. "You're mad. I am no witch. I did nothing to you. 'Twas you who assaulted me."

"Do not deny it. I know you are a witch. Even now I can feel your seductive pull upon my heart, squeezing the lifeblood from me. I won't be free until your blood is spilled upon my sword. Kneel, witch!"

Adair suddenly lurched forward, shielding Fiona with his body. "Nay! Do not slay her, Viking. Fiona is my daughter. In truth she is no witch. She is sweet and well-loved by all who know her. She has served the villagers since the day her blessed mother died and left her legacy of healing to Fiona."

Thorne shoved Adair aside. Though his heart wasn't in it, killing Fiona with his own hands was the only way he knew to escape her spell. A shudder went through him as he raised Blood-drinker. He'd expected Fiona to cower, to beg, to cringe, but to his surprise she stood her ground, her chin raised, her extraordinary eyes piercing through to his very soul.

Odin's balls, he couldn't do it! Fiona the Learned had stripped his soul bare and left him half a man, deprived of both his manhood and his courage.

Suddenly he felt a hand on his shoulder and he whirled on his heel, ready to strike down the man who dared to interfere. He very slowly lowered Blood-drinker as he stared into the dark, glowing eyes of an old man with flowing white hair and beard.

"You cannot slay her, Lord Viking," Brann said in a voice surprisingly strong for one so frail.

"Out of the way, old man," Ulm said, pulling Brann away. " 'Tis Thorne's mission to slay the witch."

"Fiona is no witch. She's a holy woman and a healer. Her knowledge of herbs has saved countless lives. Killing her will bring a curse down upon you and your family."

Thorne blanched. Curses were not to be taken lightly. "Who are you?"

Brann's eyes burned like twin coals in his wrinkled face. "I am Brann the Wizard, Viking. I honed Fiona's skills, making her as knowledgeable in the art of healing as I. Heed me well, Viking. Protect her, for she is your future. Your stars travel the same course."

"You speak in riddles, old man," Thorne jeered. "My sword is my future. When the Valkyries carry me to Valhalla, Blood-drinker will be at my side, joining me as I fight all day and feast all night. To a warrior, there is no greater glory."

"I will say it again, Viking. Kill Fiona and you will live to regret it."

Thorne stared in horror at Brann. Was he truly a wizard? Or was he a fraud who spun lies and practiced witchcraft? Thorne was superstitious enough to consider the consequences should he slay Fiona. He stared at her standing defiantly before him, her chin raised, her violet eyes as clear as the precious jewels that decorated Blood-drinker's hilt. They seemed to suck the very soul from him.

And he wanted her. Loki take him, he wanted her until he ached from it.

"The man is a charlatan, Thorne, do not listen to him," Ulm warned. "Give the order and we will slay every man over the age of ten, burn the village to the ground, and sell the women and children into slavery. 'Tis no more than the witch deserves."

Thorne didn't want to kill Fiona. Nor anyone else, for that matter. Killing peasants had never bothered him before, but something made him look at the village and surrounding land with an eye to the future. This isle was lush and green and rich with game and wildlife. Trade routes to the world could be easily reached from Man. Someday he might want to establish a holding for himself on this island. These people could conceivably become his karls. Intuition told him that killing or enslaving them would be a mistake.

"Halt the killing and raping, Ulm," he ordered. "I wish to leave the village intact."

Ulm grunted in obvious disapproval. "The woman has turned you soft," he grumbled. "You will never escape her spell unless you kill her."

Thorne's heated gaze settled on Fiona. He was surprised to see her return it boldly, neither dropping her gaze nor pretending submission. He had to admire a woman like that, even as he loathed what she had done to him. But the emotions boiling inside him were complex and went deeper than simple admiration for the witch. There was something volatile in the way their gazes met and clashed; an attraction so powerful, so omnipotent that intuition told him nothing short of death would set him free. Yet he could not kill her. That shocking thought decided the course he would take. He would make the witch his thrall and force her to remove the spell she had placed upon him.

With great difficulty, Thorne tore his gaze away from Fiona. "This land is fertile and will produce good crops," he said. "The forests are rich with game and the seas teeming with fish. Someday I may decide to settle here and I will need karls to till the land and pay taxes. With that in mind, it makes sense to spare the peasants and their village. I will ask for volunteers to remain on Man and rule in my name until I am ready to return.

"As for Fiona the Learned"—he gave her a smile that did not reach his eyes—"she will become my thrall. I doubt she will adapt well to slavery, but she will learn."

Fiona sucked in a startled breath. To become this Viking's slave would kill her. How would he use her? Would he expect her to share his bed? Would he rip away her innocence and make her whore for his men? She couldn't bear it. She faced him squarely, her expression grim.

"Kill me now, Viking. I do not wish to become your slave."

"Remove your spell and I will consider it."

"I have placed no spell on you. I am a Christian. Ask any of the good monks at the monastery."

Ulm gave a nasty laugh. "I fear the monks are in no condition to answer questions at this time. They were unwilling to part with their riches and we had to use force."

A shocked cry echoed through the throng of villagers gathered in the dusty street. Only Fiona was foolish enough to voice her opinion.

"Murderers! Berserkers! How dare you touch the holy ones?"

"Enough!" Thorne bellowed. "We will see how well you wear the chains of slavery. A thrall always obeys his master. I command you to remove your spell."

"The Devil take you!" Fiona spat. "Only a brainless idiot would consider me a witch. I am a healer, nothing more."

"An idiot, am I!" Thorne thundered. He turned away from her and shouted orders in his own language. Immediately a pair of hefty Vikings seized Fiona and dragged her away.

Fiona's father made a feeble attempt to stop them. "Do not take her, my lord, I beg you. Fiona is a good daughter. She is all I truly value in this world."

"You are young enough to sire another daughter," Thorne said. " 'Tis best you forget Fiona. She is my thrall now, to do with as I please. Be thankful that I have spared your village instead of destroying it and selling the people into slavery. My men will deal fairly with them so long as they obey the laws I set forth."

Fiona tried to keep panic at bay but the prospect of leaving her home was daunting. She sent a desperate look at Brann, even though she knew he could do nothing to save her.

"Hold!" Fiona was shocked when the old man stepped directly in front of Thorne the Relentless, his slight body dwarfed by the golden Viking. "Take me with you, Lord Viking."

"Why would I want a scrawny specimen like you," Thorne jeered, "when I could have my pick of sturdy peasants?"

"Because I have powers that none of your people possess. One day you will have need of me, Thorne the Relentless, this much I know."

"Witchcraft!" Ulm said, backing away from the bearded old man. "We do not need the likes of him."

"Aye, you *will* need me," Brann predicted. His dark eyes burned with inner fire, as if he saw things others did not. "I will retrieve my medicines and potions from my cottage and return shortly."

"Why do you wish to leave your home, old man?" Thorne asked suspiciously. "If you mean us harm, I will kill you myself."

Brann glanced at Fiona and his expression softened. "My reasons are clear, Lord Viking. No harm must come to Fiona. I cannot stop you from taking her, but I will do everything in my power to see that she is kept safe. And I tell you this with all certainty: the day will come when you will have need of my special powers."

"Very well, get your potions, magician. But heed me well, neither you nor Fiona will receive special treatment. You are both thralls, nothing more, and will be treated like my other slaves."

"Brann, don't sacrifice yourself for me," Fiona threw over her shoulder as Thorne's men led her away.

"Be at peace, Fiona, all will be well," Brann assured her. He sounded so utterly sincere that Fiona's trembling eased somewhat. "I will be with you anon," he said as he hurried away.

Thorne's face wore a worried frown as Fiona was hustled away to his dragon ship. Intuition told him he was making a grave mistake, that he was inviting trouble. The kind of trouble he'd never known before. Thorne realized his family wasn't going to be happy with this turn of events. They fully expected him to kill the witch and return home free from enchantment. That had not happened, however. If anything, he was even more captivated than before. He hoped enslaving Fiona was the answer, since he couldn't bring himself to kill her.

Then another thought occurred to him. Would taking her body and sating himself on her sweet flesh break the spell? It was worth considering. Odin and the gods knew how desperately he wanted her. The only thing that kept him from ravishing her was the certain knowledge that once . . .

Would not be enough.

He had a consuming fear that once he appeased his lust, his obsession with Fiona would grow until she owned . . .

His soul.

Chapter Three

Fiona huddled, numb with cold and miserable, on the planked deck of the dragon ship beneath the meager protection of the tent Thorne had ordered erected for her and Brann. Thorne's flagship was the largest of the five, being seventy-six feet long and about seventeen feet wide. There was sufficient room for sixteen oarsmen to sit on their sea chests on either side of the ship. Fiona had learned much about these fierce Viking warriors since being taken from her home and dragged aboard Thorne's ship.

She discovered that the Vikings stored their plunder and supplies in the space beneath the removable pine plank deck, some six and a half feet deep. Their meals while at sea consisted of dried and salted food, and they drank from leather waterbags stored beneath the planks.

Fiona hadn't known what to expect once she lost sight of land. She had never been so far from the coast before, or with men who both feared and hated her. She was grateful for Brann's company, for Thorne had all but ignored her once they set sail. She had expected to be set upon and raped, but no one had touched her, though sometimes she caught Thorne glaring at her as if he'd like to wring her neck. She'd greatly appreciated the tent and the measure of privacy it afforded her.

They had been at sea five days when the first storm struck. The ship was tossed about like a cork, blown hither and yon by the capricious wind. Fiona and Brann huddled together beneath the meager canvas shelter, praying that the wind and waves wouldn't rip them away from beneath it. Brann was pale as a ghost. During the height of the storm he had staggered to the side of the ship to vomit. When he returned he collapsed beside Fiona, moaning and clutching his stomach.

Though queasy herself, Fiona knew she had to do something to ease Brann's suffering. She searched through his medicine chest until she located a small vial containing valerian, a potion often given to ease distress. Then she left the shelter in search of fresh water.

Poised at the tiller of his wind-tossed ship, Thorne saw Fiona leave her shelter and experienced a moment of fear. He knew that Fiona's small body was no match for the violent elements and he watched in trepidation as she inched her way across the windswept deck. Then Thorne became aware of a great clamor that rose up among the crewmen when they saw her.

" 'Tis the witch! She has cursed us! Throw her overboard!"

One of the crewmen seized Fiona and lifted her above his head, intending to throw her into the sea. Thorne's heart pounded furiously as he left the tiller and shoved and pushed his way through to Fiona.

"Put her down," he ordered with cold fury. "The woman is my thrall, no one is to touch her but me. It does not please me to kill her."

Ulm stepped forward, his expression ruthless, hard. "The woman is a witch, Thorne. She has called Thor's fury down upon us. We will all die."

"We have all faced storms, some worse than this," Thorne scoffed. "Our ship is in no danger. *Odin's Raven* rides the waves with ease. Go back to your stations. Even as I speak the storm abates."

Fiona was lowered none too gently to her feet as the men returned to their chores, grumbling about witches and spells. Thorne grasped her arm and dragged her back to her shelter.

"What were you doing out there?" he demanded to know. "You could have been swept overboard. My men think you caused the storm." He eyed her suspiciously. "Did you?"

"Nay, I did not! Let go of me. I needed water to mix with a potion for Brann. He is ill."

"Stay here, I will fetch the water. The men are riled enough. Seeing you only makes it worse."

A few minutes later Thorne returned with a horn filled with water. He handed it to Fiona, then turned his attention to Brann. "What's wrong with him?" he asked.

"He's seasick. I found a potion in his medicine chest to ease his symptoms, but I needed water in which to mix it."

She poured a few drops of liquid from the vial into the horn. Then she knelt beside Brann, lifted his head and put the horn to his lips. After he took a few sips, his eyes closed and he appeared to drift off to sleep.

"What did you give him?" Thorne asked. "What manner of magic have you brewed?"

"No magic," Fiona returned. " 'Tis merely an infusion of valerian to ease his stomach. All healers know of the remedy."

Thorne stared at her. Even wet and bedraggled, she was lovely. Her captivating eyes seemed to have the ability to reach into his soul. He tried to look away but couldn't. His fingers itched to touch her face, her hair, to find the sensitive places on her body and memorize them. He'd tried to ignore her these past five days, with little success. He should take her down right now and ease his lust between her white thighs. The only thing that stopped him was the frightening knowledge that lust was but a small part of his attraction to Fiona.

Thorne watched in fascination as Fiona shifted uncomfortably beneath his intense perusal. "Why are you looking at me like that?" she asked.

"How am I looking at you?

"You're staring at me like you did that night you

found me bathing in the stream." She retreated a step but there was nowhere to go.

Thorne's gaze did not waver. This was the first time he'd been alone with her since he'd set eyes on her. Despite the fact that nearly thirty men were toiling against the storm a few feet away, and that the wizard was sleeping nearby, he felt as if no one else existed but Fiona.

"Do you fear me, Fiona?" he asked when he saw her retreat beneath the intensity of his gaze.

"N-n-nay."

"You should. Vikings are the most feared of all men. Many call us crazed savages. Berserkers. Pirates. We are all of those things and more." He stalked her into a corner. "I could squeeze your scrawny neck with one hand were I of a mind to."

He nearly laughed aloud when he saw Fiona raise her pointed little chin in blatant challenge. "What is stopping you?" she asked boldly.

"Those seductive violet eyes, for one," Thorne muttered. "If I kill you, I fear I will be damned forever. But I am stronger than you. One way or another I will force you to release me from your spell." He gave her a hard look. "You are my slave. I can gorge myself on your sweet flesh if it pleases me to do so. Once I am sated, perhaps the spell will be broken and I will be free of your enchantment."

"You're mad! If I were a witch I would never cast a spell upon a Viking, a man universally feared and despised."

Thorne's jaw tightened and his brows drew together in a fierce frown. "I don't think you despise me at all, Fiona. I remember the heat of your kiss, the provocative curves of your body. The memory seduces me even in my dreams."

To Fiona's horror, Thorne reached for her, dragging her against his powerful chest. He had removed his mail; she felt the remarkable hardness of sinew and muscles against her softness. The contrast overwhelmed her senses. Then all thought ceased as he grasped a handful of long black hair and pulled her face to his. His mouth came down hard on hers, bruising her lips. She opened her mouth to rage against the indignity and found it filled with his tongue.

Fiona felt helpless, completely and utterly possessed by this fierce sea raider. The assault upon her emotions stole her breath and sent blood pounding through her veins. She was surprised when she felt his lips soften and gentle; she had expected brutality but found startling pleasure instead. What manner of man was this fierce Viking? Tender one moment and intimidating the next.

Thorne thrust his loins against her, making her aware of his rampant lust. His staff was fully distended and throbbing. Fiona moaned as his hands slid down to her buttocks, pulling her flush against him. She offered resistance but he quelled it with the sheer strength of his determination. His hands moved upward, skimming her hips, her waist, finally settling on her lush breasts. He molded them in his palms, rolled the nipples between his thumb and forefinger.

Fiona could stand no more of his subtle torture.

She grasped a double handful of long blond hair and yanked with all her might. He broke off the kiss with a groan and a curse. She tried to break free of his arms. He was immovable, much stronger than she. A huge, hulking mass of muscle and brawn and tenacity. When he started to lower her to the deck, Fiona protested violently.

"God help me! Nay, Viking, cease!"

"You are my slave, Fiona. I will have you now."

God must have heard Fiona's prayer, for the deck heaved beneath them and water washed through to the tent, nearly sweeping them away. Lightning flashed. The wind howled and the sea surged. The ship traveled up one trough and down another, buffeted from every direction, sending men and sea chests sliding across the wet deck.

"Thor save us," Thorne cried, sending Fiona a dark look. " 'Tis true! You *are* a witch. Have you called your evil forces down upon us?"

Startled, Fiona had the good sense to realize that Thorne had just presented her with a way to protect her virtue. She prayed for forgiveness and lied. "If that is what you believe, then, aye, 'tis true."

Thorne paled, but was allowed no time to consider the implications of her reply. He was needed immediately at the tiller. He was the only man aboard with the experience to lead them safely through the storm.

" 'Tis far from finished between us, Fiona," Thorne promised in parting.

"You did well to resist him, Fiona."

Fiona glanced down at Brann. He wasn't sleeping

as she had thought. His eyes were open, his burning gaze fastened on her face. "You heard?"

"Aye. And saw, too. 'Tis as I predicted. The Viking believes you have bewitched him, but in truth 'tis much more. He is a hard man, Fiona. There will be difficult times ahead for you. But one day Thorne the Relentless will recognize your worth and open his heart to you."

"Nay! I do not wish it. Why, Brann? Why must it be the Viking? Is there naught I can do to change the course of fate? I do not want the Viking. He is too powerful, too big, too . . . male. He wants to make me his whore."

"In the fullness of time you will be everything to him, Fiona." Before Fiona could question his strange remark, sleep again claimed him.

Fiona mused over Brann's words. How could she be everything to Thorne when he believed her to be a witch? None of this made sense. The Viking had appeared from nowhere a year ago. After their brief encounter he had disappeared. Then he had returned to complicate her once tranquil life. What had brought him back? she wondered. Surely not some silly nonsense about witches and spells. She sighed and settled down beside Brann, listening to the storm rage around her, thinking it was nearly as fierce as Thorne's assault upon her senses.

A week later the dragon ships made landfall on the western coast of Scotland. They sailed up a river, erected tents on the beach, filled their water-bags, made an evening meal of wild game, then sailed away the following morning without encountering a single soul. Fiona and Brann had shared a tent. They were fed grudgingly by men who eyed them with fear and revulsion. She knew the Vikings blamed her for the frequent storms they had encountered and they wished Thorne had slain her.

Days passed. The sea was monotonous and unchangeable, except during intense periods of rain and storms. The dragon ships made brief stops on the Isle of Skye and the Orkneys to replenish their water supply and feast on fresh meat. On Skye, Ulm plundered a nearby monastery that yielded gold, silver and captives. The plunder was stored below the planked decks and the captives were divided among the other four dragon ships.

Fiona felt a pang of pity for the poor monks who would no doubt be sold into slavery by these fierce sea raiders. She tried not to dwell on their fate, for it only made her own future frighteningly unpredictable.

Before they left the Orkneys, Thorne informed Fiona that the next landfall would be his homeland. "Prepare yourself, slave," he warned. "My father and brother will not welcome you. They will think me crazed for bringing you to our home. I can only guess at what my betrothed will say."

"You are betrothed?" Fiona asked, wondering why she should be surprised. Most men Thorne's age were either married or betrothed.

"Aye. I am to wed Bretta the Fair. Why are you not wed? You are old enough to have several children tugging at your skirts."

Fiona flushed. It was true. Most girls married by thirteen, and by twenty, her age now, they had given their husbands several sons and daughters. But Adair had not insisted that she wed when Fiona expressed her desire to remain single and continue to learn from Brann. Besides, of all the men her father had paraded before her, not one of them had pleased her. Fiona thought Adair rather liked having her around to ease his loneliness after her mother had died.

"There was no one I wished to marry," Fiona explained, "and my father did not push me to wed. I am a healer. My powers are better utilized without a husband and children vying for my attention."

"Are you saying there has never been a man to whom you were attracted?"

Fiona gazed past him, recalling Dirk, the brave boy who had died while saving her during a freak winter gale that had blown in from the sea and nearly swept her away with the tide. He was gentle and kind and she might have married him had he lived, but he'd been carried out to sea and lost.

A surge of jealousy jolted Thorne. Fiona's expression had turned wistful and he wondered who had stolen her heart. "So, there was a man. Why didn't you wed him?"

"He's dead."

"Did you love him?"

"Perhaps."

"What kind of answer is that?"

" 'Tis all you're going to get."

"Are you a maiden still? Or did you gift him with your maidenhead before he died?"

"If I did, 'tis none of your concern, Viking."

He gave her a smile that did not reach his eyes and shrugged his massive shoulders. " 'Tis of no account. Soon I will find out for myself, won't I?"

"I think not, Viking."

"We shall see, witch."

That was the last time Thorne had spoken to her until the dragon ships sailed up the fjord and docked at the trading town of Kaupang. It was late summer. Fiona had no idea what she would encounter in Thorne's homeland, but she never expected to see a thriving town bustling with people and activity. The mesmerizing sight of towering snow-capped mountains outlined against clear blue skies captivated her.

"As you can see, the land is rocky and steep," Thorne pointed out. "Farming is confined to the coastline. Fishing and hunting grounds are plentiful, but winters are harsh and long and tillable soil is limited by the mountains and bogs containing iron ore. Many of our people are seeking new lands on which to settle."

"What about your family? Are they looking to settle on new lands?"

"Nay. My father is a jarl; his holdings are vast. I stand to inherit everything upon his death. But fortunately he is still hale and hardy. Summon Brann, 'tis time to debark. The homestead lies but a short distance from the town."

"I am here, Lord Viking," Brann said as he joined Thorne and Fiona.

"Fiona will ride with me," Thorne announced. "Brann can follow on foot with Ulm and the others. Most Vikings prefer to walk and use horses as beasts of burden. They do not ride well. But I find riding invigorating. Ah, here comes a slave with my horse now." He pointed to where a man stood beyond the dock, holding the reins of a spirited black stallion. "Father must have seen our sails and sent him down to meet my ships."

Fiona followed Thorne onto the narrow dock, gazing with interest at the assortment of houses and buildings hugging the bank of the fjord. The stream bed had been diverted and planked as the streets spread parallel and at right angles to it.

"Most of the wooden, straw-roofed buildings house craftsmen and merchants who trade in luxury goods such as jewelry and furs," Thorne informed her. "The landward side of the town is protected by a semicircular rampart constructed of earth and logs."

" 'Tis a fine town," Fiona said as she looked her fill.

When they reached the place where Thorne's mount awaited his master, Thorne lifted her onto its back and leaped up behind her. The horse reared and shot forward. Moments later they were racing through the countryside. Fiona found herself pressed between Thorne's massive thighs, his arms holding her tightly lest she be thrown to the ground. He rode with wild abandon, which didn't surprise

Fiona. Thorne the Relentless generated excitement. He did everything with vigor and passion and a zest for life that made everyone else pale in comparison.

Thorne was intensely aware of every curve of Fiona's body pressed so intimately against his. Heat suffused him. His loins stirred, blood pounded through his veins. He *had* to be under a spell, he reasoned, for he couldn't recall ever being so obsessed with a woman. His arm tightened around her, pulling her resisting body against the muscular hardness of his. He couldn't remember when anything had felt better than the warm body now pressed against him.

"You needn't hold me so tightly," Fiona complained. "Or ride so wildly. Are you trying to kill us both?"

Thorne gave a laugh of pure enjoyment. "Fear not, witch, I can control Thor's Hammer. Just as I will control you. Onc day I will break the spell you have placed upon me, and when I do, your magic and enchantments will have no teeth."

"I am no threat to you," Fiona claimed.

Thorne gave her a look that conveyed without words the unbearable fascination she held for him. For an entire year he had suffered her enchantment, her spells, the bedevilment of his mind and body. She had lured him to her island, bared her body to him, then cast her spell. Thorne knew he should have killed Fiona and freed himself, but something inside him had balked at slaying a woman with powers he did not understand.

Thorne was still lost in his thoughts when Fiona spied a collection of buildings built of rough pine logs sporting pitched roofs made of either straw or turf. There were so many buildings it looked like a small village. Fiona thought that Thorne's family must be very rich to afford so much. Though plain on the outside, Fiona could see that the buildings were of sturdy construction, built to last many years.

Several people stopped their work to hail Thorne as he rode into the yard, scattering pigs and chickens. Two huge men hurried forward to greet him. One man was a slightly younger version of Thorne and the other an older version, with graying blond hair and a thick beard. Both were veritable giants. Their steps slowed somewhat when they saw Fiona.

"Welcome home, son," Olaf greeted as Thorne dismounted and lifted Fiona to the ground.

"Was your mission successful?" Thorolf asked after giving his brother a bruising hug.

"There is sufficient plunder to satisfy everyone," Thorne said.

"And slaves, I see," Olaf said, nodding toward Fiona. "Does this one understand our language?"

"Nay, but she will learn. Her name is Fiona. She speaks Gaelic."

Fiona glanced at the men with misgiving. She knew they were talking about her but couldn't understand a word they said. Were they deciding her future?

"Are we to assume the witch is dead?" Olaf asked uneasily.

Thorne stiffened. His father wasn't going to be pleased with what he had done, but there was no help for it. "Nay, Father." He pushed Fiona forward. "Fiona is the maiden I encountered on Man, the one who has bewitched me."

Thorolf stepped back, his face a mask of fear as he placed his hands in front of him as if to ward off evil. "Odin's balls, why did you bring her here?"

"I had no choice," Thorne said in his own defense. "Her mentor, an old Celtic wizard, claimed she was a holy woman. He threatened eternal damnation if I killed her."

"And you believed him?" Olaf roared. "Heed me well, Thorne, trouble will come of this. What in the name of Loki are you going to do with her?"

"Fiona is my thrall. She will be as any other slave in our household, serving where she is needed."

"You will *not* take her to your bed, Thorne the Relentless!"

Fiona started violently, stunned by the swift approach of a statuesque beauty with angry blue eyes and silvery blonde hair woven into a coronet atop her regal head. She was nearly as tall as Thorne, but there was nothing masculine about her body. She was all woman, clad in rich silks and wearing gems at her throat and upon her fingers. And she was young, possibly no more than seventeen or eighteen.

"Bretta," Thorne greeted. "I had forgotten you were here."

"Obviously," Bretta said, glaring at Fiona. "I meant what I said, Thorne. Once we are married, I will not tolerate the witch in my home. Or in your bed," she added with a hint of menace.

Thorne's expression hardened. " 'Tis a wife's duty to obey her husband and accept whatever pleases him. I will take whomever I wish to my bed. 'Tis the way of things."

"You will take no mistresses once we are wed," Bretta proclaimed. She wrinkled her nose at Fiona, her distaste clearly evident. "Your slave stinks, Thorne. Her stench offends me. How can you stand her near you? She shouldn't be allowed in the house with civilized people. I understand she's a witch. Give her to me, I will make sure she casts no more spells."

"Fiona is mine, Bretta, do not forget it."

Bretta's lovely face turned almost ugly. "We shall see!" Then she turned and flounced off.

"You shouldn't have goaded her, son," Olaf contended. "Bretta brings a rich dowry. Her brother Rolo has accompanied her to our home. He intends to make sure the wedding goes off as planned. It seems Bretta has her heart set on this match and Rolo has indulged her shamelessly since the death of their parents."

"Fear not. The wedding will take place as planned, Father. I have just returned home after a lengthy voyage and wish to enjoy a long rest first."

"Is that all you wish to enjoy?" Thorolf asked, sending Fiona a disparaging glance. "Or have you already enjoyed your thrall?"

Fiona shifted nervously. She didn't like not knowing what was being said about her. "What's happening?" she asked Thorne. "Who was that woman?"

"That was Bretta, my betrothed. She took exception to your being here."

"Send me home," Fiona suggested hopefully. "I do not wish to anger your betrothed."

"Aye, send her home," Olaf agreed, speaking in Gaelic. "Or better yet, kill her."

"You speak my language," Fiona said, stunned.

"Aye. Like my son, I am a trader. I speak many languages. So do Thorolf and some of our kin, including Bretta and her brother Rolo. But I advise you to learn our native tongue if you wish to survive in our land."

"What I wish is to return home," Fiona said with bravado.

"You will speak only when spoken to!" Olaf roared. "You may have my son under your spell, but I am not so gullible. I rarely order whippings, for my slaves know their places, but I may be forced to make an exception with you."

"Father, Fiona is mine," Thorne warned him. "If punishment is warranted, it will be by my hand. There is something else I would tell you before I bathe and eat. Brann, Fiona's mentor, will arrive soon. 'Tis said he's a wizard. Both he and Fiona are healers."

Olaf looked aghast. "I cannot believe you've brought a wizard into my home. You are truly bewitched. Nothing good will come of this."

Thorne was inclined to agree. He must have been mad to bring Brann and Fiona to his homeland.

Alas, it was done and he must live with the consequences.

"I take full responsibility for my thralls, Father. I intend to take them to my new home when I marry."

From the corner of his eye Thorne saw Bretta's brother, Rolo, approaching. Bretta must have gone directly to Rolo to complain, Thorne thought with disgust.

"Welcome home, Thorne," Rolo said in greeting. "Bretta told me about your new thrall." He slid his gaze over Fiona, apparently liking what he saw. "She is lovely. Unfortunately, my sister is not pleased with your new thrall. I thought I'd come and see for myself what has riled Bretta. Now that I have seen the woman, I've come upon a solution that should appease Bretta. Sell the thrall to me. She pleases me. I will pay whatever you ask. I have just sent my latest mistress packing and I need another to serve me in bed."

Thorne felt the sharp rise of his temper. The vision of Fiona in Rolo's bed sent a rush of anger through him. His fists curled at his sides and his fire-and-ice eyes darkened. "Fiona is not for sale." He grasped Fiona's arm possessively and dragged her away.

"What was that all about?" Fiona asked as she stumbled after Thorne.

"That was Rolo, Bretta's brother. He wants to buy you for his bed."

Fiona glanced over her shoulder at Rolo and shivered. He was every bit as fierce looking and menacing as his fellow Vikings. His shaggy, unkempt hair was red instead of blond and his beard nearly touched his chest. His bushy eyebrows grew together across his brow, giving him a permanent scowl. He appeared strong enough to break her with his two hands.

Fiona dug in her heels. "You didn't sell me, did you?"

Thorne came to a halt, dragging Fiona against the hard wall of his chest. He looked down into her eyes and saw a flicker of fear. He should sell her, he thought. It would certainly solve a lot of problems. His family didn't want her, and his betrothed had declared her an enemy. But some perverse demon inside him balked at the thought of selling her. Aye, he was bewitched, all right, there was no other plausible explanation for his obsession with the violet-eyed beauty. It came to him suddenly that he could not wed Bretta until he had found a way to break Fiona's spell.

"Nay, I did not sell you, though 'tis still a possibility. If you do not remove your spell, I may be forced to sell you so that I may live in peace with my wife."

Fiona paled. "Nay, Viking. I am no witch. Look into your heart and see me for what I truly am."

His lips were very close to hers when he said, "When I look into my heart I see more than I wish to see."

Chapter Four

Fiona tore her gaze away from the seductive promise shimmering in the hot blue depths of Thorne's eyes. She recalled Brann's prophesy and wanted to run as fast and as far as her legs would carry her. It seemed inconceivable that her future was linked to that of a violent pirate and marauder. How could his hands, stained with the blood of innocent souls, make her flesh tingle and burn? How could she look at his hard mouth and want him to kiss her? God help her, for she was in danger of losing her soul to the Devil.

Thorne felt Fiona shy away from him and came abruptly to his senses. His mouth was so close to hers he could feel her soft breath against his lips. What in Odin's name was he doing? With a curse he pushed her away, aware that they were being watched.

"Bretta is right," he said harshly. "Neither of us is fit to enter the house. We will visit the bathhouse first."

He hailed a slave who was drawing water from the well. "Bring clean clothing to the bathhouse, Tyra, I would bathe before entering the house. And bring something for my new thrall to wear. Her clothing is too fine for a slave."

"Aye, my lord," Tyra said as she hurried off. "Welcome home," the pretty thrall threw over her shoulder.

"You have a bathhouse?" Fiona asked. She was of the opinion that Vikings never bathed.

"Aye, and a fine one it is." He pointed out a small, circular hut. "The tub is large enough for two."

Fiona's eyes widened. "For two?"

"Are you hard of hearing, wench? Come, your first duty will be to bathe me." He grasped her hand and dragged her toward the hut. The door was open and he shoved her inside.

The windowless room was dark and smoky. The only light came from the fire burning beneath the large cauldron of boiling water. A huge wooden bathing tub dominated the room. Fiona gazed wistfully at it, longing for a long soak . . . alone.

Moments later three male thralls entered the hut and began to fill the tub with equal amounts of hot and cold water. When the tub was sufficiently full, Thorne motioned them away. Then Tyra arrived with a stack of clean clothing. She laid Thorne's things out carefully on the bench and began to undress.

"I will bathe you, my lord."

Thorne gave an impatient wave of his hand. "Not this time, Tyra. Fiona will bathe me."

Suddenly Fiona realized that both Tyra and Thorne had spoken in Gaelic, and that Tyra must have come from her part of the world. "I will gladly relinquish the chore to Tyra," Fiona said, smiling at Tyra. Perhaps they would become friends. She would like that.

"Nay," Thorne said. "Tyra can attend my brother and father. Bathing me will be your job, Fiona."

Tyra sent Fiona a venomous look, dashing Fiona's hopes for a friendship with the pretty slave. "If she does not please you, my lord, I will be happy to attend you." Then she flounced out the door, her skirt swirling around her shapely ankles.

"Are you a nobleman?" Fiona asked. "Tyra addressed you as such."

"Aye. Father is a jarl, an earl in your country. He is a favorite of King Harald Fairhair. Help me to undress, the water grows cold."

"Nay, my lord," she mocked in a tone that was far from submissive.

"Do not try my temper, wench." He braced his foot on a bench and pushed her down on her knees before him. "Unlace my shoes."

Fiona gritted her teeth and complied. When she finished she stood up, her mouth gaping open when Thorne pulled off his cape and tunic and tossed them aside. A nude Thorne was far more intimidating than a clothed Thorne. Light golden hair covered his chest, thickening into a dense patch across his loins. His body was crisscrossed with scars, some old, some still puckered and healing. Thick, ropy tendons rippled beneath the tanned flesh of his arms and torso. His legs were long and sturdy, a masterpiece of strength and power. There wasn't an ounce of fat anywhere on his massive body. Then her gaze settled on his manhood and she blanched. He was in a state of full arousal. She tore her gaze away from him.

Thorne seemed not to notice the direction of her gaze as he eased into the tub and sighed audibly. "Come," he said, crooking his finger, "the water is fine."

"I'll wait until you're finished," Fiona contended.

"You can't wash me from there. I'll tear off your clothes myself if you do not obey."

Fiona feared he would do just that if she did not comply, so she started to climb into the tub, clothes and all.

"Nay, not like that. Remove your clothing. I won't have you fouling up the water. It won't be the first time I've seen you naked."

A trail of red crawled up Fiona's neck. That was one encounter she'd like to forget. "Perhaps Tyra—"

"Tyra won't do. Do not prolong what is inevitable. I am the master, you are the slave. Remove your clothing and get into the tub." His voice was hard, implacable . . . determined.

Fiona could turn and run, but what good would

it do her? She had the sinking feeling that Thorne would rise out of the tub stark naked and force her to do his bidding. Certainly no one in his household would come to her aid. A slave's lot was a hard one. If she didn't obey, she would be severely punished.

With shaking hands she removed the brooch from her shoulder. The tunic fell to her waist, revealing the thin linen shift beneath. Then she unclasped the belt around her waist and the tunic pooled at her feet. She stepped out of it and looked at Thorne, hoping he'd let her keep her shift. It was not to be.

"Everything. Take off everything. Hurry, the water grows cold."

Her lips thinned in resignation as she slipped her arms from her shift and let it fall to the floor. She entered the tub so quickly Thorne scarcely got more than a brief glimpse of white skin, rosy nipples and taut buttocks.

"You forgot the soap." His lips curved into a wicked grin as he glanced meaningfully at the bench against the wall.

"Why do you delight in tormenting me?" Fiona asked angrily. "Do you not fear my spells? Mayhap my next spell will render you impotent."

Thorne stared at her, his expression one of half fear, half outrage. "If I thought that, I would have killed you instantly. You are very good at bewitching a man, but I do not believe your powers to be evil or your heart black enough to do me harm. The soap, Fiona. I'm waiting."

Cursing the Viking beneath her breath, Fiona

climbed from the tub and retrieved the bar of soap and a cloth from the bench. Seconds later she was back in the tub. But not before Thorne had made a thorough perusal of her lush body. Her skin was smooth and flawless, her waist tiny and her legs long and shapely. Her breasts were round and perfect, with elongated nipples the color of ripe cherries.

"Wash my back," Thorne said, moving away from the side of the tub and presenting his back.

Fiona soaped the cloth, intrigued by the sweet fragrance of the soap. The soap on Man was made of lye and ashes and not nearly so fragrant. "I've never seen soap like this," she remarked.

"It comes from Byzantium. Our ships trade furs, amber, honey, swords and slaves for soap, spices, cloth of silk, gold and silver. We are not as savage as people like to believe."

Fiona thought otherwise but wisely kept her views to herself. When she had finished soaping Thorne's back, he held out first one arm, then the other. Then he sat in the water and presented his legs, one at a time. Next he dunked his head beneath the water and made her wash his long blond hair. Fiona felt like holding his head under the water until he ceased to breathe. Finally he took the cloth from her and washed his private areas while she turned her head and stared elsewhere.

"May I leave now?" Fiona asked, inching away from him.

Her request seemed to amuse him. "You must bathe first." He left the tub for a clean cloth and was back almost before Fiona realized he was gone. He turned her roughly and scrubbed her back.

Fiona fumed in embarrassment as he washed her arms and then her breasts. He was staring intently at her, as if he expected her to react in some special way to his ministrations. "I can wash myself," she said in a strangled voice as Thorne dragged the soapy cloth below her waist.

"It pleases me to do it," he said as he moved the cloth between her legs.

Fiona bit her lip to keep from crying out. No one had ever touched her there. It was wicked, yet the slow back-and-forth motion of the cloth was creating a clamor within her that made her legs tremble and her nerve endings tingle.

"Don't do that." Her voice was a parody of itself, weak and ineffectual. "My lord, please."

Ignoring her protest, Thorne dropped the cloth, replacing it with his fingers as he caressed and teased her soap-slick creases. Fiona could not suppress a cry of shock when his mouth found a pert nipple and he began to suckle her. When his thick forefinger thrust into her wet passage, her body jerked violently.

He probed her deeply, searching, and finally finding. His face rose from her breasts. He was smiling. "You're a virgin." His voice held a note of satisfaction.

She didn't answer. She couldn't.

Suddenly he lifted her from the tub and carried her to the bench. "I will have your maidenhead, Fiona. 'Tis the price I demand for my bewitchment." He dropped to his knees beside her, his burning gaze fastened on her rosy, full lips. His thoughts ran amok as he thought of the erotic pleasures she could give him with that lush mouth.

His hand returned to her secret place and his mouth to her nipples as he laved the taut buds with his tongue. His fingers stroked her inner flesh, thrusting and retreating, while his thumb found a place so sensitive she arched up violently against his hand.

"Don't do this terrible thing." Her voice was raw with fear. She didn't know what was happening to her.

"I've done naught yet but test your passion. Your breathless gasps and writhing body please me. You may be small of stature but you have passion in abundance. Aye, Fiona, I will have your passion, all of it," he said fiercely. "You will come to me now. I command it."

Fiona had no idea what he was talking about. She only knew she was falling apart, breaking into a million pieces while the sweetest pain she'd ever known shuddered through her. The shock of it rendered her nearly unconscious. She heard Thorne calling her name from a very long distance but couldn't summon the strength to answer.

Thorne sat back on his heels, dismayed by Fiona's reaction. He had taken countless women. Some in haste, some with considerable expertise, but seldom had he seen a woman who possessed more innocent passion than Fiona. He wondered how she would react when he entered her and brought her to climax with his staff instead of his fingers. He couldn't wait to find out. He couldn't recall ever being so hard or so ready to take a woman.

He would take her any time of the night and day, whenever the urge to have her came upon him, he decided. He would feast upon her sweet flesh until her spell lost its power to enchant; then he would sell her to Rolo. He moved aggressively over her, then went still as a frightening thought occurred to him.

What if her spell became stronger after he took her? What if he never tired of her? What if he remained in a perpetual state of enchantment? What if . . .

There were too many uncertainties and frightening consequences to consider. Common sense told him to resist her subtle seduction and fight to free himself from her spell. It would take considerable willpower, but only a weak man would allow her to tempt him with her sweet body and seductive violet eyes. With profound reluctance he struggled to his feet.

Fiona's eyes were glazed and unfocused. She knew what it was Thorne wanted and girded herself against the pain of the giant Viking's forced entry. Then she felt him shift away from her and she stared up at him in confusion.

"Get dressed!" he ordered harshly. "I nearly succumbed this time, but I'll not let you claim my soul." He plucked a single garment from the bench and tossed it at her.

Fiona looked at the tunic made of coarse brown

homespun and wrinkled her nose. "I'd rather wear my own clothing."

"You will wear the garment provided for my thralls." He dressed swiftly in rich clothing befitting a nobleman and waited for her to don the tunic. When she hesitated, he snatched it from her hands and yanked it down over her head. The coarse material hung on her small, slender form like a sack and chafed her tender skin. He found her belt from amid her heap of soiled clothing and clasped it about her waist. "Come, Tyra will coach you in your duties. None of the other thralls can speak or understand Gaelic. I suggest you cultivate her friendship."

Fiona doubted Tyra would ever accept her as a friend. She thanked God for Brann. Without him she would have no one. She followed Thorne out of the smoky bathhouse and into the bright sunshine. The first person she saw when her eyes adjusted to the light was Brann.

Brann's eyes lit up when he saw her. "Are you all right?" he asked anxiously as he rushed forward to greet her. He sent the Viking a censuring glance when he saw the rough clothing Fiona wore. "Has he hurt you, child?"

"Does she look hurt?" Thorne asked harshly. "We do not harm our slaves, they are too valuable. Unless," he added ominously, "they do something to deserve punishment. Come inside, both of you. Food and drink will be made available to you if you hunger. We do not starve our slaves, either."

The inside of the house surprised Fiona. All the

woodwork in the long hall was carved, painted, and touched with gilt. Brightly embroidered tapestries hung on the walls. The air was smoky and redolent with cooking smells. A fire burned in a hearth in the center of the hall; a long plume of smoke escaped through a hole in the roof. An enormous kettle hung over the fire, tended by a thrall whose duty was to make sure nothing burned. Other thralls bustled around a long table that was being set in anticipation of the evening meal.

Men sat on benches lining both sides of the hall, chatting and playing board games. All activity came to a halt when Thorne entered the hall with Fiona and Brann in tow. Thorne motioned to Tyra. She hastened to his side.

"I'm placing Fiona in your charge for the time being," he told her. "You speak her language; make sure she knows what her duties are." Tyra bowed her head in acknowledgment.

Thorne walked away to join his brother and father without a backward glance. It was as if he had already forgotten Fiona. But that was far from the truth. Thorne recalled everything that had taken place in the bathhouse. Never in all his years had he been so consumed with one woman, so intent upon taking everything she had to give. It had taken all the control he possessed to escape Fiona's powerful spell.

He'd have her, aye, but on his own terms. When his obsession had dulled somewhat and he could take her objectively, without losing a part of himself in the taking. He was a strong man, capable of standing firm against Fiona's witchcraft. Making Fiona his thrall had been a wise decision, he decided. With Fiona in his control, her magical allure would soon lose its power and her spell would be broken.

Fiona learned a lot those first hours of her servitude. The thralls treated their master and his sons with deference. For the most part, the women slaves kept their heads lowered and their bearing humble, but that wasn't to say that the more courageous of them didn't eye Thorne and his brother with admiration and sexual speculation. Fiona was well aware that her arrogant Viking master was an impressive man, and vowed never to willingly place herself in a position where she would be alone with him. What had happened in the bathhouse had shown her that she had no willpower where the Viking was concerned. Not that she'd been given much choice.

Thorne was too experienced for her. She must consult with Brann at the first opportunity. If Thorne was her future, she must teach him to respect her, to treat her not as a possession but as a woman to be valued for herself. Then again, how could Thorne be her future if he was betrothed to Bretta?

From the corner of his eye Thorne watched Fiona move around the hall. Her movements were graceful and fluid despite the crude tunic she wore, and Thorne felt himself harden as he envisioned the perfection of the body beneath the coarse homespun. He frowned when he saw Tyra prod and pinch Fiona to hurry her along. He could visualize the resulting bruises on her white skin and had to forcibly restrain himself from reprimanding Tyra. It wouldn't do to show partiality to a thrall.

A moment later Bretta entered the hall, and by unspoken consent everyone took their places at the long table. Mutton and beef baked in hot ashes were set out on large platters, accompanied by boiled eggs, smoked fish and bread spread with fresh butter and honey.

Thorne watched as Fiona carried a large pitcher of ale to the table and began to fill the drinking horns. As she poured ale into Thorne's horn, his hot gaze settled upon her and he saw her hand began to shake. He smiled, pleased that he could visibly affect her so.

Fearing Fiona would spill ale on him, he grasped her wrist and took the pitcher from her. "You're exhausted, take your meal with Brann. The journey from Man has been long and arduous. We do not mistreat our slaves. You can resume your duties on the morrow."

"Why must you coddle the woman, Thorne?" Bretta asked, glaring at Fiona. "She is but a slave and of no consequence."

"Slaves are valuable. She is worth a fortune should I decide to sell her."

Rolo learned across the table. "I want her, Thorne. Name your price."

Thorolf heard and joined into the discussion.

"Sell her to Rolo, brother. Let him deal with her magic."

"I do not believe in witchcraft," Rolo scoffed. A lewd gleam darkened his eyes. "Besides," he added crudely, "I could use a little magic in bed."

His remark drew raucous laughter from those seated at the table, and more than a few coarse remarks.

"I am not yet ready to sell her," Thorne said easily. "When I am, I will consider your offer."

Still held captive in Thorne's grip, Fiona had to force herself to look at Thorne. She hadn't understood the exchange, but she could tell by the way everyone was looking at her that they were discussing her.

"What did he say?" Fiona demanded to know.

"I will tell you," Bretta said, switching to Gaelic. "Rolo wants you, and Thorne promised to sell you to him."

Fiona's gaze swung to Thorne. Would he really sell her? Rolo was even more of a barbarian than Thorne. Her unspoken question remained unanswered as Thorne sent Bretta a fierce scowl and repeated his order for Fiona to take her meal and rest upon the bench. Fiona fled the moment he released her wrist.

"Why did you bring her here, Thorne?" Bretta asked. "There will be trouble, mark my words. By your own admission she is a witch. How long will it be before she works her dark magic on one of us?"

"Bretta speaks the truth, son," Olaf agreed. "Why

do you insist upon keeping the witch? She can only bring trouble down upon us."

"I will hear no more about Fiona!" Thorne roared, banging his fist on the table."

"Very well," Olaf said, sending his son a dark look. "Let us speak of your wedding. Name a date and I will send for an elder to perform the ceremony."

The last thing Thorne wanted was to talk about his wedding. He could marry no one until he broke the spell Fiona had placed upon him. "I will think on it," he hedged.

"Better make it soon," Rolo urged. "I cannot stay here forever. My own homestead demands my attention."

"The next meeting of the local *althing* takes place at the end of summer, before the first snowfall," Olaf said. "All the elders will be present. 'Twould be a good time to wed."

"I said I will think on it," Thorne repeated, bringing an end to the conversation.

"Can you understand their language?" Fiona asked Brann as she listened intently to what was being said. She could tell by Bretta's reaction to Thorne's words that the Viking woman was not pleased by the way the conversation had gone.

"Aye," Brann said. "I can make out some of their words. They argue about you."

Fiona flushed and bent her head over her plate. " 'Tis as I thought. Will Thorne sell me?"

" 'Tis not clear," Brann said, refusing to look at her. "There will be difficulties ahead, Fiona. You must prepare yourself for them. Thorne does not want to sell you, but sometimes a man is forced to do something he has no heart for because there is no other option open to him."

"I don't understand."

"Nor do I. I but read the runes and consult with the stars. They have never failed me. Even when I do not understand them myself, what they tell me always comes to pass. The prophesy I gave you many years ago has not changed. The Viking is your future. I know not how or why, just that it is so."

"I hate him!" Fiona said fiercely. "He tried to . . . He wanted to . . ." She hung her head, unable to continue.

"But he didn't," Brann reminded her.

Her face was ravaged by shame. Did Brann suspect the things that had transpired in the bathhouse? "Nay, but I wanted him to. What he did to me . . . I cannot explain, but it was wondrous, indeed. I wish I had a mother to advise me. Or a confessor. Aye, a confessor," she repeated, "to shrive me of my sins."

"Fiona, Fiona," Brann crooned, patting her shoulder with a gnarled hand. "Do not despair. I cannot tell you what lies between, but I do know the ending, and it is a happy one. In his own good time the Viking will come to value you, aye, even to love you. But you must be patient. Teach him by example that you are a woman like no other. Now eat your supper and lie down on the bench. These past weeks have not been easy for you. And they will grow more difficult before they get better," he added cryptically.

Fiona couldn't imagine an arrogant barbarian like the Viking loving any woman, let alone her. Could she learn to love him? she asked herself. He'd made her feel things she was sure were sinful. She had never pictured herself as a wanton, but she could find no other description for her behavior. Thorne had manipulated her body with an expertise that had left her needful and wanting. With her woman's heart she knew there was more than what she'd been given in the bathhouse. There was pleasure, certainly, but there was also a meeting of souls, something she doubted Thorne would ever give her. God forgive her, she wanted everything.

Thorne finished his meal and lingered behind with his father, his brother and Rolo after Bretta retired to her small quarters and the karls and thralls stretched out to sleep on the benches and shelves in the hall. He had seen Fiona and Brann speaking in hushed tones earlier and then watched avidly as she lay down on the bench and fell asleep with Brann watching over her.

"You cannot take your eyes off Fiona," Olaf charged. "I watched you during the meal and you had eyes for no one else."

"Bretta is a jealous woman," Rolo contended. "I do not envy you should you decide to keep Fiona. I'm inclined to believe you truly are bewitched. Perhaps you should listen to your father and kill Fiona."

"Killing Fiona will not end her spell," Thorne pointed out. "I must convince her to remove it of her own free will. I grow weary; sleep well," he said, rising. Then he strode from the hall, averting his eyes from Fiona when he passed the bench where she lay sleeping.

Fiona awoke with a start. She had no idea what had awakened her. She listened to the various night sounds of men snoring and muttering in their sleep and decided nothing was amiss. The bench was uncomfortable and she was cold. The fire in the hearth had burned down to coals and she hadn't been given a blanket. She looked for Brann and saw that he was sleeping soundly a short distance away, apparently oblivious to the cold. Suddenly a hand clamped over her mouth, frightening her out of her wits.

"Do not be afraid," a voice whispered into her ear. "Come outside with me, I wish to speak with you."

Fiona shook her head and tried to bite the hand stifling her cries. She recognized Rolo's voice and wanted to go nowhere with him.

Rolo ignored her wishes as he scooped her up from the bench and carried her past the sleeping thralls and karls and out the door. He didn't set her down or remove his hand from her mouth until they were safely away from the house.

"What do you want?" Fiona sputtered angrily. "You have no right to take me from my bed."

"Why aren't you in Thorne's bed?"

"Why? Why would I be in his bed?"

"If you were my thrall you'd be in mine. I couldn't sleep for thinking of you. You but lay across the room and I could hear the whisper of your gown across your limbs as you turned in your sleep. I knew I would not rest until I had you."

He dragged her against him. She was like a toy in his massive arms, powerless against his immense strength. Fiona fought and lost. Black despair settled over her as he bore her to the ground. She prayed for deliverance but feared none would be forthcoming. She was alone in this foreign world of giants and barbarians.

Thorne couldn't sleep. His mind kept straying to Fiona, asleep in the hall with the thralls and karls . . . and Rolo. He remembered that she hadn't been given a cloak or robe to keep her warm and sought to remedy the lack. Throwing his own fur cloak over his nakedness, Thorne found a spare in his chest and left the small cubicle that served as his chamber. He made his way through the hall to where Fiona had been sleeping and was perplexed to find her missing. He shook Brann awake.

"Where is Fiona, old man?"

Brann glanced at the empty bench, then back to Thorne. Worry furrowed his wrinkled brow. "I do not know, Lord Viking."

"I thought you were a wizard. Wizards know everything." He grasped the front of Brann's tunic in his huge hands, shaking him like a bundle of rags. "Where is she?"

Brann's eyes clouded as he looked past Thorne

toward the door. "Go, Viking, she needs you. Quickly."

Thorne stared at Brann, trying to make sense out of his words. A moment later his eyes kindled with understanding. He flung Brann away and hastened out the door. It was dark outside. He saw nothing at first. Then he noticed movement next to a building where tools were stored and swerved in that direction. Seconds later he broke into a run.

Fiona went limp in Rolo's arms, pretending submission. Once he let his guard down she intended to kick him in the groin and escape. She gagged when he gave a triumphant cry and clamped his mouth over hers. His kiss sickened her. She prayed for the strength to do him permanent injury and drew her knee back to strike.

Thorne, in the guise of her savior, appeared out of nowhere. "What in Loki's name is going on?"

Rolo released her so suddenly, she fell to the ground.

"You are a guest in my home, Rolo. One does not abuse the hospitality of one's host. I thought I made it clear that Fiona was off limits to everyone but myself."

Rolo shrugged. "I have no excuse, Thorne. I don't know what came over me. I beg your pardon."

Thorne appeared unappeased. Fiona picked herself up off the ground, backing away from Thorne's fury, which for some reason seemed to be directed at her as well as Rolo.

His potent gaze rendered her immobile. His

words stunned her. "I should have known you'd try to bewitch the brother of my betrothed, Fiona. Are my father and brother next? How many men do you want panting after you?"

Chapter Five

The ability to speak left Fiona. Thorne's accusation was so utterly ridiculous, her first inclination was to laugh. Then mirth was replaced by anger. Finally she found her tongue and decided to answer his ludicrous question with the kind of absurdity it deserved.

"What an interesting thought, Viking. I doubt I could have every man panting after me, but it would certainly test my powers to find out, wouldn't it?" she said sweetly, deliberately aiming her gaze above his waist.

Thorne went still. Nothing moved but for a muscle that twitched along his jaw. That should have warned Fiona, but she was too angry to notice.

"If you value your life, I suggest you limit your magic spells to one man. Luring Rolo out here wasn't a good idea. You're my property, Fiona. Until I release you from captivity, or you free me from your spell, do not set your sights upon another."

"Your arrogance is disgusting," Fiona said with considerable heat. "*If* I were able to work spells, I would change you and Rolo into toads. All Vikings are barbarians. Rolo carried me out here against my will. 'Twas only by the grace of God that I escaped his lecherous attack."

Thorne swung around to confront Rolo. "Is that true? Did you take Fiona against her will?"

"Nay. Fiona lured me out here, just as she lured you to her island. I awoke from a sound sleep and felt her gaze upon me. 'Twas as if I had no will of my own. I heard her siren's song and responded instinctively."

"He lies!" Fiona spat.

"Leave us, Rolo," Thorne said. "I will deal with my thrall."

Rolo made a hasty retreat, happy to escape Thorne's retribution.

"Come with me," Thorne said, grasping Fiona's wrist.

"Where are you taking me?"

"You can't be trusted to sleep in the hall with the other thralls. You would soon have my warriors fighting among themselves for your favors."

He dragged her into the house and through the hall to his bedchamber at the far end of the long building. Fiona hadn't been to the family section of the house yet and was surprised to see several doors, which she supposed led to separate bedchambers. Separate bedchambers were a luxury her own home on Man did not have. She and her father slept in tiny curtained alcoves off the hall and everyone else slept on benches or on the floor.

Thorne opened a door and pulled her inside the chamber. The windowless room was not large, but it was private and it did have a small hearth. A chest for clothing sat against one wall and a bed of furs rested on the bare floor. A tapestry hanging on one wall added a rich splash of color to the otherwise drab decor.

"You are fortunate to have a home with a bedchamber all your own," Fiona said to allay her nervousness. Why had Thorne brought her here? What did he intend to do to her?

"Father is a rich man and I have amassed a considerable fortune of my own. Father built this house to his own specifications. There are four bedchambers, one for each family member. Bretta has the fourth, until we marry, of course. Then she will share mine."

"Why am I here?" Fiona asked. "I wish to return to the hall. It will be time to rise and begin my duties soon."

"Your duty is to obey your master," Thorne said. "Father was right, you are proving to be more trouble than you're worth. The only reason you're alive is because your wizard convinced me that killing you would bring all manner of disaster to my family. But mark my words, Fiona, I will free myself from your spell. Now lie down on the bed and go to sleep."

Fiona glared at him. "I prefer to sleep in the hall."

"Nay. I cannot trust you around men."

"I won't be your whore."

"I did not ask it of you. I've already decided that bedding you is not a good idea. I would be playing right into your hands. You want to steal my soul, Fiona, and possibly my heart, which no woman shall ever own. Women bear children, keep a home, and often bring a rich dowry and land to a marriage, but a Viking's heart belongs to the gods that rule his life. There is no place in Valhalla for a woman."

"There is a place for everyone in Heaven," Fiona pointed out.

"I am not a Christian, nor do I intend to become one. Lie down, I need to sleep. I'm going hunting at first light with Rolo and Thorolf."

Fiona sat gingerly on the fur pallet, waiting to see what Thorne would do. She turned her head away from the daunting sight of his nudity, refusing to acknowledge it. He did not seem at all embarrassed as he stretched, yawned and lay down beside her. He pulled a fur blanket over them and turned away from her. Minutes later he was asleep, snoring softly. Inching away from the heat of his body, Fiona finally relaxed enough to embrace slumber.

Thorne awakened at first light with a painful erection. Fiona was flush up against his body. His arms were curled around her, one of his hands cupping a firm breast. The other hand rested on the curve of her hip. He released her as if she were a flaming brand and scooted away from her. He cursed beneath his breath. Even in sleep she had the power to seduce him. He should send her back to the hall to sleep upon a hard bench with the other thralls, but he enjoyed waking up with her in his arms too much. Odin help him, her spell was getting stronger. Or was he becoming weaker?

He rose and dressed quickly, then shook Fiona awake. Fiona groaned and opened her eyes. "Get up. 'Tis time to begin the day. Tyra will tell you what to do."

Fiona scrambled to her feet and made a hasty exit. The other thralls were already busy preparing the morning meal and setting out the tables, which had been taken up and stored after supper the night before. Tyra took her to a room built at a right angle to the house that served as a lavatory, and then showed her where she could wash her hands and face. When she returned she was put to work stirring oats while other thralls placed large pitchers of both fresh and sour milk and food on the tables. Rounding out the meal of cooked oats were smoked fish, hard-boiled eggs, bread, butter and honey.

Sleeping warriors and karls were awakening and moving to the table to eat. Soon Thorne and his father and brother arrived. Bretta was the last to be seated. She asked for soft-cooked eggs, toasted bread and buttermilk, and the thralls moved quickly to obey. Fiona bent to pour buttermilk into Bretta's pewter mug. As she leaned toward Bretta, the Viking woman hissed a warning into her ear.

"I know where you spent the night. When I am Thorne's wife you will not be so bold."

"Speak to your betrothed," Fiona returned. "I but obey his orders."

"Did he please you in bed?" Bretta asked crudely. "A man his size must surely possess a mighty weapon."

Fiona had readied a scathing retort, but then she saw Brann shaking his head in warning. So she swallowed her biting reply and hurried away. Did everyone in the hall either hate or fear her?

Suddenly Bretta spat out a mouthful of buttermilk, startling her table companions. "The witch is trying to poison me! The milk is tainted."

Fiona heard Bretta's cry of distress and whirled. She hadn't understood what Bretta said but she knew it must be bad, for everyone in the hall was staring at her in fear and outrage. Some were even clutching their stomachs and turning green.

"What nonsense is this?" Thorne roared, glaring at Fiona. "Have you poisoned the milk, wench?"

"Is that what Bretta said? I refuse to answer so ridiculous a charge," Fiona declared.

"You *will* answer," Thorne returned. "Did you poison the milk?"

"Nay! Had I thought of it, I might have," she added injudiciously. "Your betrothed has a fertile imagination, Lord Viking."

" 'Tis poisoned, I tell you," Bretta insisted.

To settle the matter, Thorne seized the mug and drank the contents down without stopping. Then he wiped his mouth on his sleeve and calmly returned to his meal. Truth to tell, Thorne didn't know if the milk was tainted or not, but he was willing to take the chance to stop the speculation about Fiona's powers. He was convinced that she had the power to bewitch a man, but he didn't believe she would use her powers to kill a man . . . or woman. When everyone saw that Thorne seemed to have no ill effects from the milk, talk resumed and the meal commenced.

Olaf was far from reassured. "Are you well, son?" he asked Thorne in a hushed voice.

"I am well, Father. I doubt that Fiona would harm a fellow human. She is a healer. She uses her powers for good."

"Do you consider being bewitched a good thing?" Olaf argued. "Have you convinced Fiona to remove her spell?"

"Nay, Father. Fiona continues to insist that she placed no spell upon me. But the fact remains that I am no less captivated now than I was the first moment I set eyes on her. I have to believe that in time she will free me."

Olaf muttered to himself but said nothing more. He'd wait to pass judgment.

Fiona went about her serving chores as if nothing had happened. But she knew in her heart that Bretta's accusation had planted seeds of doubt in the minds of these barbarians. She was surprised at Thorne's reaction, however. Was he finally ready to believe that she was not a witch? It was brave of him to drink the buttermilk if he still thought she had dark powers.

"Come sit with me a moment," Brann said after everyone had been served.

Fiona followed him to the bench where his own meal awaited him. He had filled a plate for her and placed it in her hands when she settled down beside him.

"The Viking is coming around," he said, nodding with satisfaction. "He alone believed you hadn't poisoned the milk. 'Tis a beginning. The stars did not lie, child. When I met the Viking I feared I had read the signs wrong, but now I know I did not. Everything I predicted will come to pass."

He stared at her intently, his eyes glowing. "Nevertheless, I fear for you, child. It will not be easy. Difficult times are ahead. Dark forces are at work. You must use your wits to survive. Danger lurks in unlikely places."

"Are you referring to Thorne?"

"The only danger Thorne presents is to your heart."

"Then who?"

" 'Tis not yet clear to me. I can but tell you to beware of Bretta and her brother."

"Will Thorne marry Bretta?"

"A match between them is not in the stars."

Suddenly a scream brought everyone to their feet. Men reached for their weapons. Fiona spotted the problem immediately. Tyra had gotten too close to the hearth and set herself afire. She ran around in circles, trying to escape the flames licking at her skirts. Fiona acted instinctively. Her gaze lit on a cloak one of the men had left lying on the bench.

While everyone stood by helplessly, Fiona grasped the cloak, sprinted toward Tyra, threw her to the ground and smothered her in the cloak. Then she rolled her over and over on the floor until the flames were doused.

A moment later Thorne was beside her, helping to stomp out the remaining embers from Tyra's clothing. Tyra was sobbing with pain when she was finally released from the cloak. A quick examination by Fiona showed that Tyra had suffered burns to both legs from ankle to knee. Though the burns were not severe, the skin was blistered and painful. Without a thought to her slave status, Fiona issued crisp orders to those milling about. She called for lard. No one moved until Thorne translated and nodded approval. Lard was quickly produced. Fiona mixed it with herbs she carried in a bag attached to her belt and applied the mixture to Tyra's burns. Then she asked for strips of clean linen for wrappings, and Thorne repeated her request in his own language.

"There will be no scarring," Fiona assured Tyra when she helped the thrall to sit up. "But you should stay off your feet for a few days."

Tyra looked at Thorne for confirmation. "Aye," he concurred. "Rest until you feel able to continue your duties, Tyra." He summoned a male thrall to carry Tyra to a bench where she could rest.

"You saved my life," Tyra said, touching Fiona's hand in gratitude. "It feels better already. I won't forget what you've done for me."

"I'll brew something to ease your pain and help

you rest," Fiona said, embarrassed by Tyra's gratitude.

Thorne stared at Fiona, stunned at the way she had taken control of the situation. If he had doubted Fiona's healing skills before, he no longer did. Unfortunately the knowledge did nothing to allay his other doubts about Fiona's powers. Bretta didn't help matters any when she sidled up to him and whispered, "Fiona is a witch, I tell you. Her healing powers are tainted with black magic."

"Nay, that is not true," Brann said. He was standing nearby and heard what Bretta said. "A healer cannot be a witch. 'Tis the difference between good and evil. Think on it, Lord Viking," Brann advised as he turned away.

"Why is that man here?" Bretta asked, turning on Thorne. "Have he and Fiona stolen your mind? Really, Thorne, weakness does not become you. I want them both gone before we marry." Head held high, she walked away.

"Bretta is right," Olaf said, nodding sagely. "She will be your wife; there should be harmony in your household. There can never be peace as long as Fiona is around. Everyone knows you took Fiona to your bed last eve. 'Twas a grave insult to Bretta. I do not blame her for being bitter. I want this marriage, Thorne; 'tis a good political move. Do not disappoint me."

"I won't disappoint you, Father," Thorne said before he turned and strode away.

* * *

After the accident Tyra shyly offered Fiona her friendship, an offer Fiona readily accepted. When Tyra whispered that she forgave Fiona for bewitching Thorne, no amount of denial on Fiona's part could convince Tyra that she wasn't a witch and had no special powers. Everyone in the household knew that Thorne was obsessed with Fiona, and witchcraft was the only logical explanation.

One day Thorne entered the hall and searched for Fiona with his eyes. When he found her he beckoned for her to follow him to his chamber. His stern visage should have warned her that something was amiss. She blanched and wanted to flee when she saw him take a length of silver chain from his pouch.

"Come here." His voice brooked no argument and she offered none. The Viking was her future and she must try to get along with him until she could convince him of her worth.

"Turn around."

She stared at him for the space of a heartbeat, then proudly presented her back. An instant later she felt cold metal slide around her throat. She raised her hand to tear away the offensive chain but Thorne had already clasped it together with a tiny lock.

"Why did you do that?"

"So that everyone will know to whom you belong. No man will dare touch you while you wear my badge of ownership around your throat."

"I hate it!" Fiona cried, trying to tear it apart with her hands. The despicable silver chain was a harsh reminder of her captivity. Was that what he'd intended? She would never forgive Thorne for this. The chain made her feel lower than his pet dog. How could she teach Thorne to appreciate her if he held her in so little regard? She must speak to Brann, tell him she could never consider Thorne anything but a heartless barbarian.

Thorne pulled her hands away from her throat. "Leave it be, you'll hurt yourself. You can go now. I'm sure you have chores to perform."

Still fuming, Fiona spun on her heel and stomped away. No one in the hall dared to mention the silver chain around her neck. The fierce look on her face was enough to convince those who noticed it that silence was the better part of valor.

At the evening meal that night, Fiona circled the table filling drinking horns and mugs. When she reached Rolo, he lifted his hand to finger the chain at her throat. The gesture turned into a caress. Fiona stiffened and would have pulled away, but Rolo's grip upon the chain tightened and she could not move.

"I see Thorne has presented you with his badge of ownership. My sister's betrothed is a jealous man when it comes to his possessions. I will still have you, lady. I have great faith in my sister's ability to control Thorne. When he banishes you, I will be waiting." His hand left her throat and slid over her breast in an intimate caress that sent shivers of revulsion down her spine.

"Fiona! Pour me some ale."

Fiona wasn't surprised that Thorne had been watching her from across the table. His eyes were narrowed, his fury apparent as he raked her with his fire-and-ice gaze. She felt Rolo's hand slide away as she hurried away to serve Thorne. No one seemed to notice anything amiss, for the jovial talk around the table continued.

"Did Rolo remark upon the chain you wear around your neck?" Thorne asked with deceptive calm as Fiona bent to pour his ale.

"Aye, he mentioned it."

"What else did he say?"

"Why don't you ask him?" Fiona said with asperity.

Thorne was about to chide her for her brazen behavior when Bretta spoke to him, diverting his attention. "Did you know the wife of one of your crofters had a stillborn babe today?" Bretta asked, speaking in Gaelic for Fiona's benefit. "The midwife said the birth was progressing normally until Fiona stopped by the cottage to ask if she could help. The midwife believes your thrall placed a curse upon the woman when her help was refused, and that the child was born dead as a result."

Fiona let out a strangled cry as heads turned to stare at her. Those who understood Gaelic had quickly translated for those who did not. She heard the Viking word for *witch* being passed around the table.

"Nay!" Fiona cried, appalled by the accusation. "I heard that Dagny was having trouble birthing her child and stopped by to offer my help. I am a healer, not a witch. Had my help been accepted, the child might have been saved."

Bretta said nothing more as she calmly returned to her meal. She had done what she'd intended and but waited for the next opportunity to cast doubts upon Fiona.

"I did nothing," Fiona said when Thorne continued to stare at her. "They wouldn't let me try to save the babe."

"Fiona treated my rash with her salve," a thrall named Eric said in Fiona's defense. "It's gone now."

"She cured my stomachache," a female thrall added timidly.

"If Fiona is a witch, she's a good witch," Tyra insisted. "My burns are already healed, and not a scar to show for them."

"Enough!" Olaf roared, ending the controversy swirling around Fiona. "Let the meal continue. Didn't I warn you there would be trouble?" Olaf said in an aside to Thorne. "Not only have you disregarded my advice, but your obsession with the woman has grown out of hand. I fear for you, Thorne. Give her up before 'tis too late."

"Nay, Father, Fiona is mine," Thorne hissed beneath his breath.

"What about Bretta?"

"Trust me to handle Bretta."

Olaf watched with a hint of fear as Fiona fled to join Brann.

"She has gone to the wizard," Olaf said to Thorne.

"See, they conspire together. 'Tis not good. The men grumble among themselves and wonder which of them will be the recipient of her evil."

"Nothing will happen to them," Thorne said with a conviction he didn't feel. "I will deal with Fiona. As for Brann, I will find him a place with the crofters."

Olaf nodded agreement. " 'Tis a wise decision."

Thorne tried to ignore Fiona as the meal ended and board games were brought out. Later a skald entertained with stories of brave deeds, great warriors, and the gods who influenced their lives.

Unable to understand anything but bits and pieces of the stories, Fiona left the hall for a bucket of water while the other thralls listened eagerly to the scald. She didn't see Rolo follow her outside. She had just pulled the bucket up from the well and was turning to carry it into the house when Rolo stepped out of the shadows where he had been lurking. The bucket slipped from her hand, spilling water over her feet and hem.

"You frightened me. What are you doing out here, my lord?" She didn't know if Rolo deserved a title but she was taking no chances.

Rolo grinned and leaned forward, pinning Fiona to the well with his mighty bulk. "I hoped for a moment alone with you."

"Let me pass. I'm needed in the house." She tried to duck around him. He stepped into her path.

"Not just yet. You must know I want you, Fiona."

She fingered the hated silver chain, almost glad

for its presence. "I belong to Thorne. He is very possessive of me."

Rolo chuckled beneath his breath. "Thorne fears you will bewitch me like you bewitched him."

"I have bewitched no one."

"Aye, I believe you. I do not believe in witches or spells. What you have done to Thorne goes beyond simple sorcery, but the poor fool is too besotted to realize it." He grasped her shoulders and pulled her against him. "Show me how you did it, Fiona. Give me a taste of what makes him desire you. Did your kisses enchant him? Or did he fall under your spell when you opened your white thighs to him?"

By the time Fiona gained control of her temper it was too late to stop Rolo. His mouth came down hard over hers, crushing her lips against her teeth with such force she tasted blood. When he thrust his tongue into her mouth she reacted instinctively, biting down on the offensive wedge of flesh with such force that Rolo cried out and jumped back. Free at last, Fiona ducked around him and ran toward the house, right into Thorne's arms.

"Going somewhere?" Thorne asked in a voice made rough with anger.

"Oh! Aye, my lord. I've duties to perform. Please let me pass."

"Is that Rolo out there by the well?" he asked with deceptive calm.

Fiona swallowed past the lump in her throat and nodded.

"Did you lure him out here with your sorcery?

Did you let him kiss and touch you? What other delights have you promised him?"

Suddenly Bretta appeared beside Thorne, a brittle smile stretching her mouth. "Thorne, there you are. The night is so lovely I thought you might like to join me for a stroll. We can discuss our new home, the one you're going to build on the land I bring with my dowry. Will it be a large house?"

Fiona started to ease past the pair, but Thorne stopped her with a single word. "Fiona."

Fiona went still. "Aye, my lord?"

"Wait for me in my chamber, I won't be long."

"My duties—"

"Your first duty is to me."

"Let her go, Thorne," Bretta coaxed, pulling on his arm. "I wish to speak in private with you."

Fiona darted away before Thorne could stop her. He appeared distracted when he turned back to Bretta. "What did you wish to talk about?"

"You and I, my lord. I want this marriage. 'Tis everything I could wish for. I'm willing to overlook this mild obsession you have for Fiona, but it must end on the day we are wed. I will share you with no other woman. Have you bedded Fiona yet, Thorne?"

"Nay, though 'tis none of your concern, for we are not yet wed."

"Your father wants this union. I bring wealth and land with me. They will greatly enhance your family's holdings. If you need a woman now, I would be most happy to oblige you. The contracts have been signed and need only consummation to become legal. Let me come to you tonight."

Thorne tried, he truly did, to desire Bretta. She was fair to look upon, tall, blonde and shapely. Everything a Viking could want in a mate. But she was not Fiona. He would do his duty and bed Bretta when they were wed, but not before.

"Not tonight, Bretta. I'm going hunting with Ulm and a few of my men at first light tomorrow. We'll be gone several days. Perhaps when I return . . ."

Bretta chose to read promise into his words though Thorne had meant them as a stalling devise. "I'll be waiting, my lord," she said coyly. "I think I'd like to go inside now. It grows cool out here. Just one more thing," she added in a voice too sweet to be sincere. "I may be young but I am a Viking woman. No enemy will prevail against me."

"You have no enemies here, Bretta," Thorne assured her. "Father wants this marriage and so do I. I will do nothing to jeopardize it."

"It would please me were you to send Fiona to sleep in the hall with the other thralls."

Thorne scowled. "Do not dictate to me, Bretta. I can be pressed only so far. If you are not pleased once we are wed, 'tis an easy thing to divorce. You have but to state your intentions before witnesses on our doorstep and again beside our bed. Until we are wed I will do as I please with Fiona."

Unappeased, Bretta sent him a scalding look and flounced away.

Fiona lingered in the hall, conversing quietly with Brann. "I cannot spend another night in his chamber," she said, shaking with anger. "Thorne values me as a slave and naught else. There is naught between us but dislike. Perhaps you should consult the stars again. Could you not have made a mistake?"

"There is no mistake, child. Did Rolo hurt you?"

"You know? How?"

"The same way I know that you must be on guard at all times. Rolo lusts after you, but Bretta's jealousy is just as dangerous. Until she is sent away you must be ever watchful."

"Bretta will be sent away? Why?"

" 'Tis complicated and I do not know the why of it." Brann looked over her shoulder and hissed a warning. "Thorne comes."

"Why aren't you waiting in my chamber as I commanded?" Thorne asked, halting beside her.

"I had duties," Fiona replied.

"Your duty is to obey me. Go to my chamber and await me."

He strode away without a backward glance.

"Arrogant barbarian," Fiona hissed.

"Aye, he is a Viking," Brann said as if that explained everything. "Fear not, Fiona. Thorne is fighting a losing battle. Fate and the Celtic gods will not be denied."

Chapter Six

Fiona had no intention of obeying Thorne. Others might quake at the sound of his voice but Fiona was made of sterner stuff. Instead of going to his chamber as he had commanded, she finished her chores in the hall. When the skald began a new tale, and everyone in the household was listening with rapt attention, Fiona slipped outside to cool off. The night was warm and she was flushed from working over the fire. She gazed with longing at the bathhouse, wondering if anyone was using it. She doubted it, not with everyone in the household crowded around the storyteller, listening to his stories.

The bathhouse was empty, just as Fiona hoped it would be. Muted light from the fire flooded the smoky chamber. Fiona slipped inside and bolted the door behind her. The room was hot. Water bubbled in a cauldron hanging over the fire, ready to accommodate the next bather. Fiona found a dipper and began ladling hot water into the tub already half full of cold water. When the bathwater was lukewarm, she peeled off her coarse homespun and climbed in. It felt wonderful. She sighed in contentment as she sank down into the water.

Fiona saw a lump of soap lying on the rim and used it to wash her hair. She scrubbed vigorously, then dipped her head into the water to rinse off the soap. As she dashed strands of wet hair from her face, she heard loud pounding on the door.

"If you're in there, Fiona, you'd better let me in."

Thorne. "Nay!"

"You weren't in my chamber," Thorne shouted through the door.

"I cannot be in two places at one time," Fiona said with asperity.

The door rattled. "Let me in, Fiona!"

"I'm not finished."

"You're finished if I say you are."

"Go away, my lord. I'm sure Bretta is looking for you."

"Bretta is already abed. If you do not open the door, I will break it down."

Fiona looked at the substantial door and decided it would take a battering ram to break it down. "I will come out after I finish bathing and not before."

Fiona felt a frisson of fear when she heard a loud crash against the door. She tried to tell herself that Thorne couldn't possibly break down the door, and even if he could, he wouldn't hurt her. Brann had assured her that Thorne would come to value her one day; she just prayed he wouldn't kill her before coming to that decision. An angry Thorne was a formidable foe. She knew that defying him was dangerous, but his arrogance was appalling.

It wasn't going to be easy to love a man like Thorne, she decided. She was nothing but a possession to him, to be used for his own pleasure. How could she teach him to love her when he didn't know the meaning of the word? She sighed heavily. It was going to take tremendous fortitude and patience on her part to fulfill Brann's prophesy.

Suddenly the door flew inward and Fiona stared in dismay at the giant who had all but ripped it from its hinges. He stood in the doorway, hands on hips, legs spread apart, a fierce scowl darkening his features.

"You dare to defy me?"

"I wished to bathe in private," Fiona said, scrunching down into the water. "We are going to live together a long time, lord Viking. You should learn to respect my wishes."

Thorne stared at her as if she were addled. "What nonsense are you spouting, lady? What kind of witchcraft are you brewing now?"

"No witchcraft, Viking. Brann says our destiny is written in the stars and Brann is a great wizard. 'Tis not the fate I would wish for myself, but I will have to make the best of it."

Thorne fit the door back into the gaping hole and slipped the lock into place. Then he approached the tub, anger and bewilderment were visible in his expression. Silent and tense, he stared down at her. "*You* will have to make the best of it? You try my patience, lady. Get out of the tub!"

Fiona thought to refuse but his scowl was still firmly in place and she decided it would be foolish to anger him further. It might take a while for him to accept the fact that Fate had already decided their future. Vikings, she had learned, were excessively arrogant, bullheaded and barbarous, and easily aroused to anger. Fiona couldn't imagine why Brann insisted that this violent man was the perfect mate for her when she wanted no mate at all.

"Hand me my tunic, Viking," Fiona said, "and I will obey you."

Thorne didn't move. "I have seen you before. You lured me to your island and bared your body to me. I can still picture you as you were then, clothed in naught but moonlight and mist, far lovelier than the Valkyrie maiden who will escort me to Valhalla when my time comes. I knew then that you were no mere mortal woman."

He shook his head to clear it of visions of Fiona as he had seen her on the island that fateful day. He hadn't been the same since. "Get out of the water, Fiona, I want to see you as you were that night."

Thorne wanted Fiona every way a man could take a woman. He wanted her aflame with the passion he could sense in her. He wanted her beneath him, with naught between his skin and hers. He wanted to thrust himself into her, forcing his strength into her softness. He wanted her soft cries of pleasure to fill his ears as he experienced the pure joy of her willing response.

"What are you going to do?" Fiona felt the searing heat of his gaze and knew she could no more stop what was likely to happen than she could roll back the tides. It was meant to be, even if Thorne did not know it and she did not want it. But the element of fright still existed. The threat of impending violence clung to him like a dark mist.

He gave a dry, brittle laugh. "I'm going to do what I should have done on Man when I first saw you. Had I taken you then, I wouldn't be mad to have you now."

Fiona couldn't stir, couldn't speak as Thorne moved relentlessly forward, gripped her shoulders and lifted her from the tub with a great splash. He set her on her feet and deliberately took a step backward without releasing her. His eyes traveled the length of her body, each sweep of his hard gaze like a burning brand upon her flesh. Fiona swayed and clutched at his tunic for support. Her skin was flushed. She felt as if she were turning to cinder.

Thorne started to lower her to the hard-packed ground. She sensed his dark desire and even darker determination and knew she couldn't let him take her like this, here on the hard, cold ground. Then his mouth was on hers. Hot, hungry, his tongue was thorough and wild as he tasted her. She was swamped by a great and unknown power sweeping her toward her destiny. There was about this man something intoxicating, something bold and magnetic, something powerfully primitive and compelling.

Resist, an inner voice warned.

Thorne released her mouth as he pressed her to the ground and straddled her, his knees holding her captive. At some point between the moment he started kissing her and when she lay on the ground beneath him, he had removed his tunic. The sight of his massive form sucked the breath from her. He was magnificent. Hard all over and bulging with muscles. Copper nipples stood out on the mat of golden hair that covered his chest. Firelight sharpened the bones of his face, giving him a feral look. Her gaze dropped to his manhood. It rose like a stalwart warrior from his loins.

She didn't move. Didn't dare to breathe as he trailed his fingertips lightly across her stomach, moving lower and lower until they sifted through the fine hairs between her thighs. She shuddered and tried to collect her thoughts. This ferocious Viking was making her feel things that were wicked. Things that only a wife should feel.

"Nay! Don't! We are not wed."

Thorne was too aroused to think clearly, but her words finally sank in. "Wed? Surely you jest, lady. I am betrothed to another. You are my slave. I am taking you for my mistress."

"I will not allow it," Fiona hissed.

Thorne gave her a slow smile filled with promise. "Do you think all Vikings are selfish lovers? I know how to make a woman want me," he whispered against her mouth. "Do not ask me to court you with compliments and sweet words, for 'tis not my nature. But I can give you pleasure."

"You cannot bed me if we are not wed," Fiona insisted. She knew Thorne wouldn't agree to marry her and felt safe making a statement that was as outrageous as it was improbable.

Thorne was burning inside and out. His flesh was on fire and his innards boiling. His brains had turned to mush and he knew he was being directed by his loins instead of his head. His was a hell he had not created; it was an inferno that had ignited the instant he had first set eyes on the tempting witch. There was no logical explanation. It had to be magic. He could deny it no longer. He'd do anything . . . *anything* . . . to have her lie willingly in his arms.

Except wed her.

"Do not fight me, Fiona, for I am determined to have you."

"Nay! Not here. Not like this. You will have to rape me if you want me. But heed me well, Viking. Take me against my will and I will place a curse upon you and your family that will follow you into eternity."

Of course Fiona had no idea how to go about conjuring up a curse, but the threat seemed to work. Thorne went utterly still, apparently evaluating her words and the threat they implied. He stared at her for a long, silent moment. Then his head dipped once as if in mocking acknowledgment.

"We will wed."

His expression was so fierce, his voice so feral

that Fiona recoiled in fear. "What did you say?"

"We will wed."

"But you are betrothed to Bretta."

"I will ask Father to betroth her to Thorolf."

"Your father—"

"—will not be happy but will honor my wishes." He rose to his feet and pulled her up with him. "There is an elder in the village. He will conduct the ceremony."

Fiona pulled away from him, alarmed by this unexpected turn of events. She needed to talk to Brann. She could not believe the Viking truly meant to marry her. It was too preposterous. "Nay. I am a Christian. Unless a priest blesses our marriage, I refuse to consider it."

He bit out a furious oath. "I do not need your permission to bed you, Fiona. Nor do I need it to wed you. I do not fear you as a woman, but must take your threat against my family seriously. If I must wed you to have you, then so be it.

"I want you, Fiona. Witch or no. I am convinced that you have cast a spell upon me. Therefore I will wed you in order to keep my family safe from your black magic and to slake this unbearable lust that consumes me."

Fiona was rendered speechless. It seemed ludicrous that Thorne would wed her simply to satisfy his lust. Surely that wasn't what Brann had meant when he'd said Thorne was her soul mate, was it? She knew that few women were fortunate enough to choose their husbands for love, and that most women had no choice in the matter, but she had always thought that if she wed it would be for love. Not only would she love her husband, but her husband would love her. This barbarian didn't know the meaning of love. Until he did, she would not wed him, no matter what the stars said about her future.

"I will wed no one without a priest," Fiona maintained. She felt fairly safe making such a demand, for she knew there were no priests in this heathen land. There was much Thorne had to learn about women before she'd agree to become his wife.

"What if I could produce a priest? Would you wed me and let me bed you without incurring a curse upon my family?"

"Aye," Fiona said easily. That was how sure she was that there wasn't a priest within a hundred leagues of here. "Perhaps you could take me back to Man. Our village priest could marry us. I would like to have my father present when I take a husband."

"There will be no one present but your wizard," Thorne said, sounding more pleased than he had a right to be. "Dress yourself. I will return shortly with Brann."

Fiona stared at him in consternation. She couldn't imagine what Thorne had in mind. Before she could question him, Thorne had pulled on his tunic and was already striding out the door. With shaking hands she donned her coarse homespun, her mind in a turmoil. She had no idea what Thorne intended and was determined to refuse whatever he suggested. She would—

"Fiona. Are you in there, child?"

"Brann! Thank God. Come in. Have you seen Thorne?"

"Aye, I am here at his order."

"I don't understand. Why does he wish to marry me? He believes I'm a witch and he doesn't love me. You told me Thorne would value me, would love me even, but 'tis merely lust he feels for me. I will not wed him unless a priest blesses our marriage. It frightens me to think what Thorne's father and brother will say when they learn of this. Nothing will convince them I haven't bewitched Thorne. And Bretta! Dear God! She'll be livid."

"Aye," Brann said, nodding thoughtfully. "There will be danger, just as I predicted.

"Why, Brann? I understand none of this."

Brann closed his eyes. When he opened them he appeared to be in a trance, seeing and hearing naught but the silent voices that spoke to him in an ancient tongue. Fiona had seen him like this before and she waited patiently for him to speak.

"The Viking is strong. A fitting mate for a woman of your courage and intelligence. No male on the Isle of Man was worthy of you. Your future was revealed to me before you were born. The Viking knows it in his heart but resists. Your combined strengths will produce strong children who will rule the Isle of Man and protect it against invaders."

"I want to be loved, Brann. Is that so wrong?"

"Love is already present."

"What nonsense is this?" Thorne said, striding into the chamber. "Love is for dreamers. Pleasure is all a Viking wants from a woman. Are you ready, Fiona?"

He moved into the light and she saw that he had changed his clothing. He was resplendent in a knee-length tunic the color of the blue flowers that grew upon the hillside above her village. It was woven of the finest silk and fastened at the shoulder with an elaborate jeweled brooch. A finely wrought sword was thrust into a scabbard attached to a leather belt cinching his waist. The buckle and hilt of the sword were made of gold and adorned with jewels. His cloak of fine wool dyed a vivid red was held together with a simple gold brooch. He was truly splendid.

"Nay, I am not ready. There is no priest."

"Come with me. Both of you."

"Where are we going?" Fiona wanted to know.

"To the village. 'Tis not far. My horse is waiting. I've brought a mule for Brann to ride."

Fiona followed him outside, her curiosity conquering her fear. "Here," he said, handing her a bundle he'd been carrying. "Hang on to this, you will need it later."

Thorne lifted Fiona onto the horse's back and mounted behind her. Brann got himself onto the mule and followed at a slower pace. Though it was well past the supper hour, there was still sufficient light to guide them. Daylight lingered long in the summertime in northern climes.

They reached the village without mishap. Thorne rode directly to the harbor, where several dragon ships were tied to stone piers jutting out into the fjord.

"Wait here," Thorne said, dismounting.

Fiona watched in puzzlement as Thorne approached a dragon ship and hailed its captain. Moments later a ferocious giant appeared on the deck. He was huge, bigger than Thorne even. Rust-colored hair streaked with gray hung down to his shoulders in wild disarray, and his beard all but hid his fierce features. He joined Thorne on the pier, where they spoke earnestly for several minutes. Then Thorne placed something shiny in the captain's palm and waited as the man strode back aboard his ship.

The wait was short. A man wearing the ragged remnants of a monk's habit and hobbled by leg irons stumbled down the gangplank to join Thorne. They conversed heatedly. Fiona saw the man shake his head several times before he was led under protest to where she stood. The sound of his voice sparked recognition, and she let out a gasp of dismay.

The ragged monk was Father Damien, a priest from the monastery on Man. He had offered Mass many times in their little village chapel. She had given him her confession shortly before the Vikings sacked the island. She was aware that the savage Vikings had pillaged the monastery and taken prisoners, but she'd never expected to see any of them again.

"Father Damien!"

"Are you all right, child?"

"Aye, I am fine."

She rounded on Thorne, her eyes shooting violet

fire. "Is this how your kind treat holy men? How dare you!"

"Ulm sacked the monastery," Thorne revealed. "When I came ashore on Man I sought but one person . . . the woman who had bewitched me. The priests were sold to the slave trader when we reached port. They are going to the Byzantine, where slaves are in great demand."

"But they are Christian priests. You cannot send them to a heathen country."

" 'Tis all right, child," Father Damien said. "I am resigned to my fate. God in his mercy will protect me. Perhaps He has a plan for me and the others from the monastery. We will go forth and convert the heathens. Do not lament my fate; 'tis you I'm worried about. The Viking told me he wishes to take you as his mate and wants me to perform a Christian ceremony. Is that your wish, child?"

Fiona shook her head in vigorous denial even as Thorne said, "Aye, priest, 'tis Fiona's wish for us to be wed according to Christian rites."

"Is that true, Fiona?"

Fiona could not lie to the priest. She had indeed told Thorne that she would marry him if he could produce a Christian priest. "Aye, Father, 'tis what I said but—"

"Hurry, priest," Thorne demanded. "If you refuse, I will take Fiona to my bed whether or not we are wed."

Father Damien decided it would be in Fiona's best interest to wed the Viking. "Have you a witness?"

Thorne glanced down the road and saw Brann approaching on the mule. "He comes now. Brann will stand witness."

Brann slid off the mule and limped over to where Fiona stood beside the priest. He peered closely at the monk and recognized him instantly. "Why, 'tis Father Damien."

"You're just in time, wizard," Thorne said. "We have need of a witness. I am taking Fiona to wife."

"Wait, please! I need a moment alone with Brann," Fiona cried.

"The slavemaster's ship leaves with the tide. There is scant time for conversation," Thorne said.

Then he surprised Fiona by taking the bundle from her hands, unwrapping it and removing from it a beautiful blue woolen cloak lined in scarlet silk. He shook it out, threw it around her shoulders and fastened it with his own gold brooch.

"Now we are ready, priest."

"No!" Fiona's courage reinforced itself. "We hardly know one another. The Viking wants to marry me for the wrong reason."

"Fiona," Father Damien said gently. "The Viking has already made known his intentions where you're concerned. In God's eyes, 'tis better to be a wife than a mistress. Be content that the heathen is honoring your wish to be married by a Christian priest."

" 'Tis meant to be," Brann intoned sagely.

"Is my future not my own to decide?" Fiona cried, confused by the swift turn of events.

"Your future is in God's hands," the priest reminded her.

" 'Tis a prophesy written by ancient Druids who walked the earth before Christianity existed," Brann chanted.

"Enough of this nonsense," Thorne roared. "Wed us, priest. Do it now else I take the woman right here on the beach."

Thorne knew it was a false threat but he wanted this over and done with. He wanted Fiona's soft body beneath his. He wanted to be inside her. The spell she had cast upon him was growing stronger instead of weakening. He would have had her a long time ago had he not feared her dark magic and what it would do to his family if he took her against her will. He had found a priest to marry them and was even flouting his father's wishes to have her. Everyone would think him mad, but nothing was going to stop him now.

Fiona the Learned had burrowed under his skin and festered like a sore that refused to heal. Odin help him.

They were married. Fiona was still numb. She had refused to answer when asked whether she took Thorne to be her husband, and Thorne had answered for her. It must have been good enough for Father Damien, because shortly thereafter he had pronounced them man and wife in accordance with God's law. What God hath joined together, he had quoted, let no man put asunder. Father Damien returned to the slave ship and Brann to the homestead.

"Say nothing about this, wizard," Thorne warned as Brann left for the homestead.

"Where are we going?" Fiona asked when she realized that Thorne was taking a different direction.

"Where we won't be disturbed. I've waited a long time for this, lady. I've lived it in my dreams so often during the past year I can almost taste your silken flesh. The vital element missing in my dreams was the pleasure of piercing your sweet flesh with my mighty sword. But soon I will know that pleasure, with the blessing of your God, of course," he mocked.

"I had always hoped to marry for love," Fiona said. "I had hoped that my husband and I would care for one another."

Thorne gave a snort of laughter. " 'Tis not the way of things."

The road they traveled ended abruptly at a fjord. Darkness blanketed the land. The mist was heavy, so heavy Fiona couldn't see the high cliffs rising above the fjord. The vaporous mass clung to the water's surface, swirling and shifting, changing from one shape to another. Fiona couldn't turn her gaze away from the enchantment of mist and water and the moon-drenched night.

"What is this place? Why have you brought me here?"

Summoning his patience, Thorne said, " 'Tis private. There's an unoccupied cottage nearby, abandoned when a widow remarried and moved into her new husband's home. I thought you would prefer to be bedded for the first time without others listening to the sounds lovers make. Maidens are shy creatures by nature." He sent her a heated look. "You were a maiden when I first brought you to my home. Are you still?"

Fiona's gaze flew upward to meet Thorne's. Was it possible that this fierce, violent man harbored tender emotions? Was he actually considering her feelings? More likely he was thinking of his own gratification and comfort.

"I asked you a question, Fiona."

Recalling Thorne's question, Fiona nodded. "Aye, I'm a maiden still."

"I thought so. You have naught to fear; I will treat you gently."

He turned down a well-worn path. The cottage was set back from the fjord, but still close enough to afford a spectacular view on a bright day. Thorne opened the door and guided her inside. A shaft of moonlight pierced through the mist and entered through the open door, revealing a single windowless room devoid of furnishings. The tiny hearth held naught but cold ashes.

"I'll start a fire," Thorne said when he saw Fiona shiver.

He disappeared outside and returned a few minutes later with an armload of dried grass and kindling. Then he knelt before the hearth, struck a flint and fed grass and sticks to the spark until a thin stream of smoke rose into the air. He nursed it until the kindling ignited, then he turned his attention to Fiona.

"It will be warm soon. Relax while I find us something comfortable to lie upon."

Fiona stared at his departing back. She couldn't imagine why Thorne was being so thoughtful. Had she misjudged the Viking? She thought not. Too many acts of violence and mayhem had been attributed to Vikings for her to be wrong. Thorne must truly fear her nonexistent magical powers to go to such lengths to make her comfortable.

Thorne returned shortly, his arms filled with pine boughs and soft moss. He spread the boughs on the ground and covered them with moss. Then he pulled off his cloak and spread it over the makeshift bed. Everything was moving so fast, Fiona's head was spinning. The Viking wanted her, he'd made that clear from the beginning. That he would wed her in order to have her in his bed both confused and shocked her. Then Thorne spoke, and she knew the Viking hadn't changed. He was the same arrogant raider she'd always known him to be.

"Remove your clothing, wife, and lie down on our bed. Spread your legs and welcome your husband inside you with a sweet smile of surrender."

His words produced the fury he'd expected. He'd deliberately used those words to kindle fire within her, fire that he could turn to sweet passion.

"Nay!"

He reached for her and she spun away from him. "Where is the docile wife I was promised?"

"I promised you nothing."

She darted toward the door.

"You'll have to do better than that." He caught her easily. She tried to pull away but he held her fast. "Do you seek to deny your husband? You swore before your God to honor and obey me."

"Don't touch me!"

"You act as though I'm going to eat you alive. Do you fear me, Fiona?"

"You are a Viking! Long before I met you I heard tales of Viking raids and vile attacks upon defenseless women."

He gave her a mocking grin. "Use your magic if you fear me. Turn me into a toad."

She buried her face in her hands, unable to answer such an absurd challenge.

He pulled her hands away. "Nay, look at me. I'm not going to hurt you. I will take you as gently as I know how. It matters not that we were wed in a weak moment of madness. You are my wife now. Vikings honor their wives. I want to love your body, Fiona. I want to be inside you so desperately I ache. Witch or no, spell or not, I *must* have you. I *will* have you!"

His voice was rough with passion yet his hands were surprisingly gentle as he removed the brooch holding her cloak together and lifted it from her shoulders. His gaze never left hers. Fire and ice, Fiona thought. She was awash in the sensations summoned by his words. Then she was lost in the heat of his smoldering gaze as he unfastened her tunic and it dropped to the floor.

Thorne thought she looked like a goddess. Licked

by firelight, she was all gold and silver and shimmering, sent to earth expressly to torment him. Thorne's breath caught on a gasp as a great shudder shook him. This moment was the culmination of an eternity of yearning, a year of obsessing over the glorious woman who had bewitched him. He had returned to Man to kill her, only to find himself trapped in her web of seduction, unable to hurt her.

Odin save him, for he knew the moment he entered her body, nothing in his life would ever be the same.

Chapter Seven

Thorne's patience came as a surprise to Fiona. She had expected him to fling her upon their bed of boughs and fall upon her like a savage. Instead, he held her and spent a long time kissing her and nibbling at her tightly closed lips. Hands that were powerful and callused caressed her neck and spine with exquisite tenderness. Fiona could feel her tension give way beneath his seductive stroking, could feel herself leaning into him, her lips half clinging to his.

His hands traveled over her burning flesh, and when he cupped her breasts, she gave a muffled groan. Apparently the sound released something primitive in him, for he bore her down onto the bed of boughs and kissed her violently. His lips were hard, urgent, demanding, his tongue hot and bold as he sought entrance to her mouth. It was the kiss of an aroused male, of a warrior who took what he wanted and allowed no quarter. When he lifted his head they were both breathing hard.

"I've thought of naught but lying between your sweet thighs since I first saw you. I imagined myself thrusting into you and sinking deep. In my dreams I heard your cries of joy ringing in my ears."

"Those are poetic words for a fierce Viking warrior," Fiona said, panting from the effort of making a coherent sentence.

He eyed her with fierce regard. "Have you not heard our Viking poems of love and war? They are passionate tales of our exploits. Vikings are warriors, aye, but we are other things as well; farmers, fishermen, traders, storytellers; lovers of sagas, poetry . . . and women. We work hard, fight even harder, and make love with a vigor and zest lesser men envy. You will soon learn this for yourself."

When she made no reply, he stretched out beside her and stared at her breasts. His eyes were dark and enigmatic and she shuddered, touched by an emotion she'd never experienced before.

"Your breasts are beautiful," he said as he rubbed his knuckles against her jutting nipples. He kneaded her breasts almost roughly, then lifted them to his hungry mouth and suckled her like a babe.

Fiona whimpered as he took a nipple between his teeth, bit it, then laved it with his tongue. The sudden burst of pleasure was almost unbearable; she wanted him to stop because she enjoyed it too much. He released that nipple and went to the other, drawing it deep into his mouth and sucking strongly as his hands began to stroke the length of her, over ribs and belly, hips and thighs. Then his mouth fastened on hers, his tongue delving deeply, tasting of her. His hands were everywhere at once as he sucked and nibbled on her lips, stroking, caressing, making her burn. What manner of man was he to make her feel such sinful things?

She pushed on his chest, fighting to maintain some semblance of composure. It was a losing battle, and she knew it. There was something intoxicating about this man. Something magnetic. A primitive, moving force that made him as compelling as he was irresistible. She had tried to deny her overwhelming attraction to the Viking, to disregard Brann's prophesy, but her efforts had been futile. Thorne had inexplicably touched something within her she never knew existed.

Her half-hearted protest seemed to strengthen Thorne's determination to make her want him. He tormented her flesh with his hands and mouth. One hand drifted down over her stomach, becoming entwined in the dark, curling hairs between her legs, and she shuddered uncontrollably. He traced the outer edges of the dark triangle, delving into the moist folds of her skin. Her legs tightened against his invasion, but he would not allow it. Deftly he moved between her thighs, spreading them with his own.

She wasn't expecting it when he thrust his fingers into her inner wetness, and her hips rose off the bed, shocked by the stabbing pleasure. He slid his fingers in and out of her repeatedly, until she felt possessed by madness, eagerly wanting something that had no name.

"What are you doing to me?" she cried out in agony and dismay. "I cannot bear it. Please . . ." Her whole being became one hard, pulsing point where he rubbed and teased with his callused thumb.

"Take your release, Fiona. Take it now before I bring you pain."

She felt his hardness nudging against her hip, heard the note of tormented impatience in his voice, and a frisson of fear sped down her spine. Then her fear receded as his fingers and thumb caused incredible sensations to lash through her. She shoved upward against his hand and drew her legs tightly together as pleasure rocketed through her, pulling a hoarse cry from deep within her. She shuddered violently, confused and frightened. What kind of demon could do this to her? Make her feel as if her soul were leaving her body?

Rolling over on top of her, Thorne flexed his hips and pressed down, grinding the hard ridge of his shaft against her pelvis. Grabbing a handful of her hair, he directed her to look at him. She did, and was sorry. His sex was huge, rising up thick, long and hard from the golden nest of hair below his belly. Her eyes flew to his.

"You'll kill me with that."

"Nay. You'll stretch to fit me. Touch me," he said.

She hesitated, staring at his sex with growing panic.

He grabbed her hand and wrapped it around his thick shaft. He was hard and painfully full. If he didn't have her soon he would burst. When her hand squeezed him, the violence in him erupted. He grasped her hips and thrust into her, impaling her with a single swift stroke. His powerful entry broke through her maidenhead cleanly, somewhat diminishing the agony he might have caused had he done it clumsily. She cried out in surprise and pain, then lay still. She felt as if she'd been ripped apart. Then little by little the pain of his entry eased, and she felt his incredible strength stretch and fill her.

"I told you we'd fit," he said, giving her a smug smile.

"You hurt me."

He moved slowly, creating a gentle friction. "Does it still hurt?"

"Aye. You're a beast."

His body was pulsing against hers with lust. His heart was pounding in his chest, and he was panting like the beast she had accused him of being. "I'm not going to stop. I've waited too long for this. You fit me like a tight glove. Your insides are hot and wet and I'm trying to control the violence building inside me. You are my wife; I don't want to harm you."

She felt as if he were touching her womb, and for all of the strangeness and shocking moment of pain, it was no longer unpleasant.

He began to move faster now, thrusting and withdrawing, pleased when she began lifting her hips to meet his thrusts. When her hands slowly rose to cling to his shoulders, he gave a shout of joy.

It didn't take him long to rekindle her desire. He heard her moan as she shifted positions so she could take more of him. He managed to retain a thread of control by sheer dint of will. When he felt himself begin to shatter, his hand moved between their bodies to stroke the very heat of her. Then passion took control of his mind and body. His loins pumped and his thrusts deepened. He felt her nails dig into his shoulder and knew her own passion was rising swiftly.

Fiona had no idea what was happening to her. The pressure building inside her was becoming unbearable. Just when she was certain she would die from the sheer intensity of her feelings, his thrusting became wild, uncontrollable, more demanding. The feeling terrified her. It felt as though her soul were being torn from her body.

"Thorne! I'm frightened!"

"Nay," he gasped through clenched teeth. "Just hold on and come with me. Trust me."

It was difficult to trust a man who had taken her captive. A man who had proclaimed his ownership by placing a chain around her neck. But in this she had no choice. Fiona surrendered to the magical moment that had no name. Bliss filled her. She arched against her husband and let ecstasy consume her.

Thorne felt her release and allowed his own. With a long, low groan he shuddered and surrendered his seed to her. Moments later he collapsed against her with a grunt of male satisfaction. He wanted to stay inside her forever. His heart hammered like a drumbeat, and the scent of their lovemaking filled the air around them. He could think of no experience that had been as sweetly rewarding as taking his virgin bride. And he wanted to do it again.

"Get off me," Fiona gasped, poking him in the ribs. "You're heavy, Viking."

Thorne frowned. Somehow he'd expected her first words to be ones of praise for his prowess, or at the very least awe at the passion he had unleashed in her. Her passionate nature had exceeded his wildest dreams. Had she nothing to say about it? His male ego had been wounded.

"I know I pleased you," he bragged as he shifted his body off of her.

Fiona blushed and pulled the cloak over her flushed body. "You hurt me."

"It was unavoidable. There was no pretense in your sighs and moans of pleasure. I know when a woman enjoys what I do to her. Your arms held me and your nails scored my shoulders."

Fiona ground her teeth in frustration. Such arrogance didn't deserve to be rewarded with an answer. Truth to tell, Thorne had taken her to a magical place where naught but bliss dwelled, and she couldn't bear to talk about it. She needed time to consider what it meant it terms of their relationship. She didn't dare label what they had just done. Making love wasn't the right word, for love held no meaning for Thorne. To him their coupling was a simple matter of lust. She sighed. It was going to be exceedingly difficult teaching the Viking to love her, and even harder for her to love a man who considered her a possession . . . when he considered her at all.

A worried frown marred Thorne's brow when Fiona remained silent. Had he mistaken her response? He thought not, but he usually wasn't all that concerned about the women he'd bedded. But Fiona was different. He'd *wanted* to bring her pleasure. And not because he feared her black magic. Nay, something he couldn't name compelled him to be as gentle as he knew how.

"Fiona, have you naught to say? Did I hurt you so much? I know I am big, but no bigger than many of my countrymen. As your husband, 'tis my duty to take care of you. Lie still, I'll be right back."

Fiona watched curiously as Thorne tore off the hem of his tunic and strode naked from the cottage. He returned a few minutes later with the scrap of wet cloth in his hand and knelt beside her.

"Let me see," he said, drawing the cloak away from her body. When he pulled her thighs apart, Fiona gasped out a protest.

"What are you doing?"

"I want to see if I tore your flesh."

"Nay, you didn't! You didn't hurt me all that much." She tried to clamp her legs together but he wouldn't allow it.

"Stop fighting. I'm just going to cleanse blood and seed from between your thighs. Relax, the cool water will soothe you."

A streak of red crawled up Fiona's neck. "You

shouldn't. It isn't right. 'Tis immodest."

His expression hardened. "Never say me nay, Fiona. I will judge what is right and what is not between us."

Fiona's hips jerked as the wet cloth stroked between her legs.

"You're not torn," Thorne said with satisfaction as he tossed aside the soiled cloth.

"I said I wasn't," Fiona said through clenched teeth.

He stroked her with his fingertips, staring at her with burning eyes. "I want you again, Fiona. What manner of witchcraft have you used on me? If you do not free me soon, I will go mad with this aching need I have for you."

"You accuse me falsely."

"Deny it if you will, but I'm not the same man I was before encountering you. Odin's beard! I'm a Viking! Vikings thrive on raiding and raping and pillaging. 'Tis in our blood."

"I have not changed you, lord Viking," Fiona retorted. "I have not that kind of power. I can heal your wounds but naught else."

His eyes gleamed. "Heal me, witch. Appease this insatiable lust that festers within me. Take me inside you again. Drain my body of your spell. I long to become myself again."

He slid upward, bracing his weight on his elbows as he came fully over her. His mouth clamped down over hers as he separated her thighs with one of his own. He kissed her long and hard, then dragged his mouth from hers to taste the fragrant valley between her breasts. His mouth moved eagerly from breast to breast, causing her to move restlessly beneath him.

"Thorne . . ."

"Open for me."

His manhood prodded the moist portal of her sex, and Fiona's legs fell apart. His hands and mouth were wreaking sweet torture upon her flesh. She couldn't think, could only feel. When he entered her this time she felt no pain, only incredible stretching as he filled her with himself. Then his leashed passion exploded as he began to thrust violently, taking her with him to sweet splendor.

Fiona didn't get much rest that night. Thorne's thrashing about on their bed of boughs kept her awake. She was so small, and he was so large, that each time he turned he dragged her with him, rousing her from a sound sleep. And just before dawn she awakened to the velvet touch of his lips and hands upon her body. By the time she came fully awake, she was wet enough to take him again without causing her pain. She was shocked speechless when he clasped her waist, stretched out on his back and pulled her on top of him.

Fiona slept until Thorne prodded her awake late the following morning.

" 'Tis time to leave."

She stared up at him. Somehow he looked different this morning. There was no sign of the tender lover he had been during the night. He was a Viking warrior. Hard, implacable, fierce. She sat up, holding the cloak to her breasts.

"I want to bathe." The tangy scent of their joining clung to her body and offended her nostrils.

"I already bathed in the fjord. 'Tis cold but you'll find it refreshing."

Wrapping herself in the cloak, Fiona hurried to the fjord and tested the water. Thorne was right. The water was indeed cold, but it felt wonderfully refreshing on her skin as she waded in. Skin that now had intimate knowledge of a man's hands and mouth. Despite the cold water, she felt herself grow hot with the memory.

"Come out now, Fiona. The water is too cold to linger."

Thorne stood on the bank of the fjord, holding the cloak out to receive her. Fiona waded out of the water and stepped into his arms. He wrapped the cloak around her, bringing her against him. She felt the hardness of his loins pressing against her backside and let out a small cry of protest.

"There is no time now," he said, releasing her with marked reluctance. "We must return to the homestead before Father sends out a search party for us."

"What will you tell him?" Fiona asked as she returned to the cottage for her tunic.

Thorne followed her inside. "The truth. That I have no idea what possessed me to wed you. 'Twas rash and irresponsible. I can only surmise that your magic spell drove me to madness." He shook his head. " 'Twas madness."

She donned her tunic and turned to face him. "Nevertheless, I *am* your wife. Properly wedded and bedded."

"Aye. 'Twould seem so."

"Then remove this chain from my neck. I am no longer your captive. As your wife I have certain rights."

"I will think on it," Thorne said evasively.

Fiona stiffened. She was determined not to be presented as Thorne's wife wearing the offensive chain. "Take it off now, lord Viking."

One blond brow shot upward. "Or what, wife? What will you do? Place another spell upon me? I doubt one more spell will make my life more difficult than it is now."

"Don't be absurd," Fiona chided. "You will remove the chain because it is the right thing to do. Do all Vikings place chains of ownership around their wives' necks?"

"Viking wives would not allow it."

"Nor will I. Remove it, Viking."

Fiona held her breath. She had no idea whether Thorne would do as she asked. She prayed that he would, for it would mean he was beginning to realize he could fight neither Fate, God's will, nor Brann's prophesy.

Thorne remained perfectly still, poised on the horns of a dilemma. To do as Fiona asked would be the same as admitting that he had wed her with the full knowledge and intention of treating her as a wife instead of a captive. Supreme folly or not, he had wed her. He couldn't explain why he had sought the services of a priest. Had he done it to please her or simply because he wanted her willing and hot beneath him? As hot as he was for her. The fear of her black magic had driven him to do something he'd never consider were he in his right mind. Loki take him, 'twas pure madness!

Fiona recoiled in panic when Thorne placed his hands around her slim neck. Had she gone too far? She closed her eyes and waited for his fingers to tighten, for him to squeeze the breath from her throat. Her eyes flew open when he grasped the fragile chain in his huge hands and snapped it apart as if the links were made of braided grass.

" 'Tis done," he said, sending her a look of wounded outrage as he stomped away. She found him waiting for her beside his horse when she was ready to leave.

Fiona didn't dare let him know how pleased she was with him. Perhaps being the wife of this fierce Viking wasn't going to be so bad after all.

The household was in a turmoil when Fiona and Thorne arrived. Olaf had already organized a search party and was giving instructions when they rode up. He took one look at his son, saw Fiona with him and flew into a rage.

"Loki take you, Thorne! Where have you been all night? We thought you had been taken by the enemy. Eric the Red has been raiding our lands and we feared you had fallen into his hands." His eyes narrowed upon Fiona. "Was the witch with you? Your betrothed is beside herself with worry."

Thorne dismounted, then lifted Fiona to the ground. "Send the men away, Father. I would speak privately with you, Thorolf and Rolo."

"Go," Olaf ordered, scattering his clan with a single word.

Fiona melted away with them.

They walked a short distance from the house and stopped beneath a shady tree. Olaf turned bright blue eyes on his son. "What is it you wish to tell us that the others can't hear?"

Thorne began to pace. His agitation was evidenced by the bunching of the muscles in his neck and shoulders. "In a moment of madness I did something I will probably live to regret." He lifted his massive shoulders and faced his father squarely. " 'Tis done," he said with finality. "Last night I sought out a foreign priest and wed Fiona."

Olaf's roar of outrage shook the tree beneath which they stood. "Tell me I did not hear you right! Tell me you are but jesting! Tell me anything but what I fear I heard. You wed the witch? 'Tis madness! Her spell is more powerful than I suspected. I swear I will free you, Thorne. I will slay her with my own sword."

"Nay, let me slay her," Thorolf declared, drawing his weapon. "Where is she?"

Thorne's startling revelation had rendered Rolo mute. When he finally regained his wits, he began to smile. "Hold, Thorolf," he said, restraining the fiery young Viking's enthusiasm with a hand on his arm. "Did Thorne not say he was wed by a Christian priest? We are not Christians. The marriage means less than naught to us. There is no need to destroy a ripe beauty like Fiona. I will take her as my mistress. When I tire of her I will sell her to a slaver. You need never see her again. But I strongly suggest we do not mention Thorne's indiscretion to Bretta."

"Take her!" Olaf roared. "And good riddance."

"Nay! No one touches Fiona. She's mine. I will keep her until she no longer pleases me."

"Madness," Olaf repeated grimly. "You know not what you do, son. The woman has bewitched you. Were you in your right mind, you would have slain her long ago."

"Perhaps I am bewitched, and perhaps there is another explanation. Until I learn the answer myself, Fiona remains my wife."

"What about Bretta?" Olaf demanded to know.

"Wed her to Thorolf."

Rolo frowned. "Bretta is set on wedding Olaf's heir, not a second son."

"Have you considered the consequences of your rash act?" Olaf asked Thorne. "Your own kinsmen fear the woman. Are you prepared to protect her from your own kind?"

"Do I need to protect her from you, Father? Or from you, Thorolf? Will Fiona be safe when I am not around to protect her?"

"I do not like this, Thorne," Olaf said sourly. "I do not know if Thorolf is willing to wed Bretta."

"Or if Bretta will wed Thorolf," Rolo ventured.

"You will change your mind about Fiona when you come to your senses," Thorolf said with conviction.

"Perhaps," Thorne muttered. "I am sure of nothing anymore, except that Fiona is mine and will remain mine until I decide otherwise."

"Then I will wed Bretta," Thorolf said. "If she will have me, of course."

"If it makes a difference to Bretta, Thorolf can inherit in my place," Thorne said, surprising everyone, even himself.

"Nay, you are my heir," Olaf argued. "Thorolf will have his share, but you are my firstborn. Speak to Bretta, Rolo. I will understand if she refuses."

"The match is a good one whether 'tis Thorne or Thorolf whom Bretta weds," Rolo declared. "Our lands march together and can easily be defended against invaders. I will speak to Bretta. She will obey me."

"I will never reconcile myself to this outrageous marriage, Thorne," Olaf said. "Tell your whore to keep away from me. I refuse to acknowledge her as your wife, or to honor your Christian marriage."

The stark planes of Thorne's face turned grim. "We will remove ourselves from your hall after I have built a new home for myself and Fiona." With heavy heart he strode away. It was the first time in his memory that he and his father had exchanged angry words or disagreed so vehemently.

"He's mad," Thorolf said as he stared at Thorne's departing back.

"Or bewitched," Olaf contended.

"Or neither," Rolo intoned dryly. "I will go now and speak with Bretta."

"What in Odin's name did Rolo mean?" Thorolf

asked after Rolo had departed. "If Thorne is neither mad nor bewitched, what else could he be?"

Olaf did not reply. He sent Thorolf a fierce scowl and strode away.

Fiona watched Thorne stalk through the hall. His steps were hard and angry. She wondered what words had passed between Thorne and his father and decided she didn't want to know. They couldn't have been pleasant, knowing how Thorne's family and friends felt about her. A moment later Rolo entered the hall. He gave her a hard stare, then went to join his sister. Fiona watched in trepidation as Rolo and Bretta spoke in hushed tones, then left the hall together. Fiona had no idea what the future held for her and Thorne and wondered if Thorne would give in to family pressure and divorce her. She wouldn't blame him if he did. He had arranged their marriage on the spur of the moment without a thought to the possible repercussions.

"What is this all about?" Bretta asked as she followed Rolo from the hall.

"Not yet," Rolo said as he led her to a place where they couldn't be overheard.

"Something has happened," Bretta said, digging in her heels. "If this concerns me, I demand to know now."

Rolo ground to a halt and swung around to confront his sister. There was no easy way to tell her what had taken place, so he decided not to mince words.

"Thorne and Fiona were wed last eve. By a Christian priest."

Bretta let out a loud screech. "Nay! I will not have it! He cannot do that to me!"

" 'Tis done. He proposes that you wed Thorolf. I want this alliance, Bretta. Elder or younger, it matters not."

"It matters to me! Thorne stands to inherit the lands and title from his father. Thorolf is a second son."

"Olaf says he will provide handsomely for Thorolf. Your own dowry is substantial; you won't go begging."

" 'Tis not the same. Nor is it enough. I want Thorne. Fiona has bewitched him; he isn't in his right mind. He wouldn't have wed her if she hadn't cast a spell upon him."

"Perhaps you're right. Nevertheless, Thorne stubbornly refuses to divorce Fiona, or to send her away."

"They were married by a Christian priest," Bretta said with a hint of malice. "Their marriage is not valid in our country. Is Olaf willing to accept Fiona as Thorne's wife?"

"Nay, Olaf likes it not. But Thorne is a grown man and does as he pleases."

"I will wait for Thorne to regain his senses," Bretta declared.

"You will take Thorolf," Rolo advised with quiet emphasis. "Consider my words carefully, Bretta. Thorne is fearless. A berserker. He always places himself in the thick of battle. Men die in battle. Men die at sea. Thorne will not be happy on dry land for long. He'll soon go a-Viking again and may not return.

"Thorolf is a farmer at heart. He is brave but has not Thorne's fighting soul." He paused dramatically. "Many things can happen. Thorne could sicken and die. Men do, you know. Should something *unforeseen* happen to Thorne, Thorolf stands to inherit everything. Then you will be mistress here."

Bretta's eyes narrowed as she considered Rolo's words and all they implied. "I begin to understand, brother. Our minds indeed work the same. 'Tis no secret you want Fiona. Without Thorne's protection she would have no place in this household. Olaf would gladly give her to you."

Rolo gave her a devious smile. "You were ever quick to grasp my meaning. Shall I inform Olaf that you will wed Thorolf?"

"Aye. I will wed Thorolf at the end of summer. Who knows what the future will bring? Should Thorne meet with an unfortunate accident, Thorolf will become Olaf's heir."

Chapter Eight

" 'Tis done, then?" Brann asked as Fiona joined him in the hall. His keen, penetrating gaze seemed to pierce through her. "Did your husband take your maidenhead?"

Embarrassed, Fiona lowered her gaze. "Aye. 'Tis done."

"Did he hurt you? Was he brutal?"

"Nay, he did not. He was quite gentle, considering."

"Does Bretta know?"

"Rolo is telling his sister even as we speak," Fiona said. "I saw them leave the hall together. I cannot believe Bretta will like this."

"If Thorne refuses to divorce you, she will make trouble. Beware, child." He saw Thorne approaching and moved away before Fiona could stop him.

Thorne spotted her and swerved in her direction. "Gossip already is circulating about our marriage," he said. He held out his hand to her. "Come, you will sit beside me at the table and share my meal."

Fiona shrank away from him. "Is that wise? Let your kin grow accustomed to our marriage before I sit down to a meal with them."

Suddenly Brann was beside them. "Join your husband, Fiona," he advised. "The Viking will protect you."

Thorne turned his fierce regard on Brann. "Are you pleased, wizard? I could not help myself. My wits were dulled and my judgment impaired by a pair of sorcerers. Fiona is my wife now, and despite my Father's wishes, I find I cannot set her aside. I hope you are satisfied."

Brann gave Thorne a complacent smile. "Aye, lord Viking, 'tis most satisfying. If you'd but look into your heart, you'd be surprised to learn 'twas not my doing, nor was it Fiona's. Man fulfills what God wills."

"Pah!" Thorne scoffed. "I do not believe in your Christian God. As for my heart, 'tis hardened against witches. You may cast your spells upon my mind, but my heart remains my own."

"Stubbornness is not a virtue, lord Viking. Listen to me and listen well. Danger exists. I cannot tell yet whether 'tis directed at you or Fiona."

"You speak in riddles, old man. Explain yourself."

"Would that I could. I sense danger, but neither its source nor to whom 'tis directed."

"You see naught, charlatan," Thorne bit out. He

grasped Fiona's arm. "Come away from the madman."

He drew Fiona toward the long table set up in the hall and found a place for them on the bench. Immediately those on either side of them left and found other seats.

"They do not like me," Fiona said.

"Can you blame them? They see what your black magic has done to me and fear you will turn your evil eye upon them."

"I have done nothing to you, my lord. Your blame is misplaced. I have no special powers."

"Do not your countrymen call you Fiona the Learned?"

"Aye, but—"

"Do you not have special powers that enable you to perceive things yet to happen?"

"Sometimes, but—"

"Then you are a witch."

"I am a healer."

While Thorne and Fiona bickered back and forth, Olaf walked into the hall, saw Thorne sitting beside Fiona and marched up to them. His fists were clenched in anger, his stance belligerent.

"What is *she* doing at my table? You insult your family and Bretta by parading your whore before us. Send her away to eat with the dogs."

Fiona felt her temper rising but held it under strict control. She wanted to see how Thorne would react to his father's harsh words.

Thorne turned and faced Olaf squarely. "First of all, Father, Fiona is my wife." Thorne's bold confirmation of the gossip circulating in the hall brought a collective gasp from those assembled at the table. "She will remain my wife until it no longer pleases me to keep her. Second, Bretta is now Thorolf's betrothed. What I do should not matter to her. Third, you will never call Fiona a whore again."

Olaf turned red with rage. Never had his son spoken to him with such disrespect. He directed his animosity at Fiona. It was his belief that she had stolen his son's mind. "Heed me well, witch. Bring harm to my son and you will rue the day you were born."

Fiona swallowed convulsively. Olaf's threats were not made lightly, nor did she take them lightly. As long as Thorne kept her as his wife, she would have an enemy. Suddenly Fiona sensed another potential enemy. She shifted her gaze to Bretta, who was glaring at her with such hatred that Fiona could not suppress a shudder. Fiona knew exactly where she stood with Thorne's father, but Bretta's hidden threat was far more dangerous.

"I mean no harm to Thorne," she insisted.

Olaf turned away without uttering another word. She glanced at Bretta and saw her exchange a secret communication with her brother. Fiona tasted little of what she ate after that and tried to ignore the buzz of conversation around her. She wasn't successful.

After the meal Fiona rose to help the women clear the table and put the food away. Tyra sidled up beside her. "I'm happy for you, Fiona. Thorne is a wonderful lover. He'll make you happy if his father and Bretta let him. Did you truly bewitch him?"

Fiona was momentarily taken aback. She'd suspected Thorne had bedded Tyra, but hearing it put into words unsettled her. She wondered how many other slaves and servants he had bedded. Would he continue to bed them? That thought made her physically ill.

"These Vikings will believe what they will, Tyra, no matter how often I deny being a witch. I can heal their illnesses and treat their wounds, but I have not the power to cast spells. Thorne wed me simply because he wanted to bed me, and I told him he'd either have to wed me or rape me if he wanted me. I'm surprised he chose to wed me."

" 'Tis said he sought a Christian priest to please you," Tyra reminded her. "I think he cares for you." She sighed dreamily. "You are fortunate, Fiona. Now that Thorne has cast me aside, I will become fair game for anyone who wants to bed me. I am a thrall and not allowed to say them nay."

"Is there naught you can do?" Fiona asked, feeling sympathy for the slave. "No one you can turn to for help?"

"No one but you. Ulm has been eyeing me with desire. I fear him. He is not a gentle man. I have known no man but Thorne. Oh, do not think he loved me, never that. But he is not a rough lover and I did not mind so much."

"I will do what I can for you," Fiona promised, though she knew she held little sway over her husband. "Is there a man you favor among these Vikings?"

Fiona glanced across the hall at Thorne. He must have sensed her eyes upon him for he looked up, meeting her gaze with the burning intensity of his. She looked away. "Besides Thorne," she added quickly. "Give me his name and I will speak to my husband."

Tyra blushed. "The young Viking called Aren seems kinder than the others. He is Thorne's cousin. I think he is smitten with me. He would never approach me while Thorne still wanted me, but I've caught him watching me of late. I would not mind a man like Aren."

"I will . . ." Her words trailed off when she saw Thorne heading her way. "We'll speak of this later."

"Come with me," Thorne said without preliminary. He turned away without bothering to see if Fiona followed. He went directly to his chamber, waited for Fiona to enter, then closed the door.

"What is it? Has something happened?" Fiona asked worriedly.

"Take off your tunic," Thorne said harshly.

Fiona's violet eyes widened. "Now? You want to bed me now?"

"Are you refusing?" He sounded almost as if he wanted her to refuse.

"Nay."

He bit back a ragged sound as desire rocked him. Then he grabbed her and literally ripped the coarse homespun from her body. Seconds later his own clothing lay in a pile on the floor.

"You have only yourself to blame for this," he charged. "One minute I was speaking with my kinsmen and the next I felt your gaze upon me. You beckoned me without uttering a single word. Yet I felt the summons, just as I did that long-ago day on Man. Your power is more potent than I feared."

"I did nothing," Fiona denied. "You have a vivid imagination. I was speaking with Tyra."

He shrugged her words aside. "I know what I saw. What I felt. You wanted me, Fiona, and I am but granting your wish." He took her down to the bed with him.

His kiss was not gentle as his mouth took hers and his tongue thrust past her teeth. His heat scorched her, his hard body was heavy with desire. She groaned into his mouth as heat coursed through her in heavy, liquid waves.

With a hoarse curse, he nudged the wet cleft of her womanhood with his shaft. Fiona dug her fingers into his back. And then his hard, straining length opened her, filled her. She arched upward, against the hardness of his chest, against the rigid line of his body. She cried out his name as he began to thrust and withdraw, taking her with him to that place where pleasure awaited.

She hovered on the edge of forever, spinning out of control as Thorne gripped her hips and thrust into her. Then she toppled into a dark void as bursts of light exploded inside her head and ecstasy filled her. Thorne joined her moments later, pouring himself inside her, his release hot, potent, violent.

The low, hoarse words he uttered were spoken in his own language, words she did not understand.

Much later Thorne stirred and raised himself up on his elbows so he could look into her face. His expression was fiercely condemning; his eyes held a note of puzzlement. "How did you do it? How did you manage to steal my mind and control my body? I shouldn't want you like this. You used your magic to make me marry you, and I like it not."

With a sigh, Fiona tried to control her temper. "I don't recall forcing you to bed me in the middle of the day. Or to rip my tunic from my body."

Thorne rose abruptly and started dressing. Fiona would have done the same but her tunic lay in shreds on the floor. "What am I supposed to wear?"

Thorne eyed the homespun with disdain. "Not that. You'll wear something befitting your new station in life. I'll send Tyra with an assortment of materials from the storeroom. She will help you fashion something appropriate for the wife of a future jarl." He turned and strode from the chamber before Fiona could form a reply.

Fiona appeared in her newly fashioned tunic and undertunic for the evening meal. She had chosen a deep purple silk from the three bolts of cloth Thorne had sent for her use. She and Tyra had worked all day to finish the sleeveless tunic and the linen undertunic fashioned with long, tight sleeves that ended at her slender wrists. From somewhere Tyra had produced a belt of hammered silver and a brooch to match.

When she walked into the hall that evening, conversation came to an abrupt halt. With her dark hair spilling down her back, Fiona was a vision of loveliness, far outshining the fair-haired Bretta. Thorne was struck speechless, but quickly recovered when he saw the way Rolo was looking at his wife. He realized immediately that he had made a grave error by allowing Fiona to dress in clothing that enhanced her beauty. Suddenly a thought occurred to him.

The only way he could escape Fiona's drugging spell was to withdraw from her both emotionally and physically.

If he allowed his lust to continue unabated, he feared he would fall deeper and deeper under her spell, becoming irretrievably lost. His soul would no longer be his own to claim. Even now, going a-Viking no longer held the same appeal or excitement it once had. He had lost his zest for everything except Fiona. His life was falling apart, and he had to take steps now to stop the downward spiral.

Fiona was alarmingly aware of the way Thorne was staring at her. Had she done something wrong? Was he angry with her? After he'd made love to her earlier he had seemed withdrawn and remote. It was becoming exceedingly difficult to believe that this man, of all the men in the world, was fated to be her mate for life. Sometimes she wondered if the stars hadn't lied. Or if Brann had read them wrong. Turning Thorne into a man she could love was going to take longer than she'd thought. Maybe a lifetime.

After the lengthy meal of fish, fowl, mutton, cheese and bread, Fiona joined Brann while the Vikings continued to drink copious amounts of ale and listened to the skald begin another saga of Viking adventure. She had barely settled down beside Brann when Thorne rose abruptly and strode in her direction. Fiona watched in wary silence as he stopped before her, his expression fierce. She couldn't imagine what had triggered his temper this time.

"Tonight and every night hereafter, you will sleep in the hall," Thorne said tersely. He gave her a hard stare, then rejoined the merrymaking.

Fiona was quick to note that Bretta sidled up to him the moment he returned to the table. Though Thorne appeared to pay her scant heed, Bretta continued to lavish attention upon him, ignoring Thorolf, who appeared to neither notice nor mind. When the men began drifting off toward their benches to bed down, Thorne headed to his chamber. Bretta remained seated for the better part of an hour before she followed Thorne. From her vantage point, Fiona saw Bretta bypass her own chamber and enter Thorne's.

"Trust Thorne," Brann advised when he saw the direction of Fiona's gaze.

"I'm not sure I can," Fiona replied. "He's as stubborn as a mule and twice as ornery. One minute he's acting as if he's beginning to care for me, and the next he's ordering me out of his chamber. He's arrogant, possessive and jealous. He married me merely to satisfy his lust, then he accused me of bewitching him. I'll not live long enough to turn him into the kind of man I can love."

"Have faith, child," Brann said complacently. "The Viking married you, didn't he?"

"Aye," Fiona admitted grudgingly. "But he doesn't intend to honor his vows. I just saw Bretta enter his chamber."

Brann stared at something unseen beyond Fiona's shoulder and smiled. " 'Tis but a test of your husband's character. I have great confidence in his strength."

"Aye, his strength is formidable," Fiona agreed sourly. "I'm sure Bretta will appreciate his endurance and prowess in bed."

Thorne paced his small chamber like a caged lion, already regretting his decision to banish Fiona from his bed. Despite having bedded her once today, his body wanted her again. Was there no respite for him? Would his torment never end?

Thorne heard the click of the doorlatch and whirled abruptly, stunned to see Bretta leaning against the closed door. "Bretta! What in Odin's name is the meaning of this? Does Thorolf know you're here?"

"I care not about Thorolf," Bretta said in a low, seductive purr. "The hall is abuzz with gossip. 'Tis said you banished your wife from your bed because you're already displeased with her. That pleases Rolo greatly. He wants her, you know. Will you divorce her and marry me? I still want you, Thorne. You have always been my first choice."

Bretta pressed herself against Thorne. His heat surprised her and a small groan slipped past her lips. She was nearly as tall as he and they fit perfectly, breasts touching, loins meshing together. When she wound her arms around his neck, Thorne stared down at her impassively.

"I am married, Bretta," he said coolly. "You are my brother's betrothed. I would not betray him."

"You need not betray Thorolf if you divorce Fiona. You were wed by a Christian priest. No one would blame you if you abandoned Fiona. Let me free you from the witch's evil spell. Once you ease yourself between my thighs you will never want Fiona again."

Her nimble fingers moved to unfasten the brooch at his shoulder but Thorne caught her hand, stopping her. "You're a beautiful woman, Bretta. Until I met Fiona I was satisfied with my father's choice of bride for me. Unfortunately, only Fiona can free me, and she insists she cannot remove a spell that was never cast. I may be displeased with my wife but I am not of a mind to take a mistress. And that's all you would be to me. Go and be happy with Thorolf."

"Never!" Bretta spat, pulling away in anger. "You have dealt me an insult I cannot forgive. Beware, for you will pay the price of betrayal."

Head held high, Bretta whirled on her heel and left in a huff.

Thorne felt a frisson of apprehension slide down his spine, but immediately dismissed it. He feared no woman. Not even Fiona. What he feared was that which he could not understand.

* * *

The following day Bretta made a point of observing Brann. When Brann opened his medicine chest to treat a thrall's boil, she questioned him about the use of some of the vials stored inside.

Distracted, Brann named a few and mentioned their properties without thinking as he treated the slave. After a few minutes Bretta appeared bored and walked away. But she had gained valuable knowledge. Later, when Brann was away from the hall and no one was about but a few slaves who were busy with meal preparations, Bretta opened Brann's chest and removed a small vial the wizard had identified as a potent drug that could be deadly unless administered judiciously and with caution.

Two days later Brann was called away to the village to treat a man suffering from an ailment of the digestion. In his absence, Bretta seized the opportunity to act upon the plan she had devised.

A short time later Brann returned from the village in a dither. While he was treating the sick man, an intense premonition of danger had swept over him. He assumed the danger was to Fiona and had hurried back to warn her. He had no idea what form the danger would take but he told Fiona to practice caution. Fiona took Brann's words to heart and touched very little on her plate at the evening meal. Nor did she drink from her cup.

Unaware of danger, Thorne quaffed deeply from his own cup, trying to drown his unquenchable need for Fiona in ale. When the flagon in front of him was empty, Bretta quickly snatched it up before a servant could be summoned to refill it. "I will bring you another," she said as she moved off toward the ale barrel.

Bretta's hand began to shake. This was the moment she had waited for. If all went as planned, Thorolf would soon be Olaf's undisputed heir.

No one saw her pour a murky liquid from a vial into the flagon and replace the vial in her pocket. Brann was so concerned about protecting Fiona that he failed to perceive the danger to Thorne. Bretta placed the brimming flagon before Thorne and left the hall. Thorne remained at the table long after everyone had left, drinking until the flagon was empty. No one was around when he tried to rise several hours later and fell flat on his face. He remained there until morning, when Olaf found him and raised up a cry loud enough to awaken the entire household.

"Thorne is dead!"

Fiona sat up, roused from a sound sleep. It took her several moments to focus, but when she did, her heart nearly left her chest. Thorne dead? Nay, it couldn't be.

Despite his great age, Brann hurried past Fiona and knelt beside Thorne. "He still breathes," he announced.

"What is wrong with him?" Olaf demanded to know. "He was hale enough last night."

Brann raised Thorne's lids and saw that his pupils were dilated. His pulse was weak and thready and his skin had a bluish tinge. He cursed himself for a fool. Last night's danger was not to Fiona, but to Thorne, and he'd failed to sense it. "I'll have to examine him more thoroughly to discover what is wrong with him, Lord Olaf. Your son is in grave danger of dying. He must be treated immediately."

"Dying!" Olaf hissed in disbelief. " 'Tis the witch's doing." His eyes blazed with tormented fury. "She has cast a fatal spell upon my son."

"Let me examine Thorne, I beg you," Brann pleaded. "If there is a cure, I will find it."

"Nay! Neither you nor the witch will touch my son."

"My lord, please," Fiona begged. "Brann can save Thorne if you but allow it."

"Your concern is touching," Olaf spat. "But beyond belief. You seduced my son away from his betrothed. Then you used witchcraft to bring on this mysterious illness. Did you think he would leave you a rich widow? Or is it merely your nature to perform evil deeds?"

"You think I harmed Thorne?"

"You or the wizard, 'tis the same. There is a healer in the village. Thorolf will fetch him." He motioned to Ulm, who was standing nearby. "Lock the witch and her mentor in the storage shed," he ordered. "I'll deal with them later." He bent to lift Thorne and two karls hastened to help him.

"There is no time to waste," Fiona cried in growing panic. "Thorne will die if he isn't treated properly. Brann and I are the only ones with the knowledge to save him. If you don't trust me, at least allow Brann to help him."

Olaf remained stubbornly opposed to allowing either Brann or Fiona to touch Thorne, let alone treat him. Bretta, who had been observing the scene in smug silence, now said, "You are wise, Lord Olaf, not to let the witch near Thorne. She is evil."

Fiona protested violently when Ulm and two cohorts dragged her and Brann from the hall. The men were not gentle. By the time she and Brann were locked inside the storage shed, both were covered with scrapes and bruises.

Fiona sank down on a sack of grain and stared at Brann in despair. "Will he die?"

"I should have seen it," Brann said with remorse. "The danger I perceived was not to you. It never occurred to me that someone would want Thorne dead."

"Who do you suspect? What brought on his illness?"

Brann's eyes were bleak. "An overdose of a potent drug. A skillful healer can save him, but I fear these heathens know little about the art of healing."

"Dear God. Who would want Thorne dead?"

"Someone who would benefit from his death."

"But who—" Her eyes widened as a sudden thought came to her. "Oh, no. Both Bretta and Thorolf would benefit. Thorolf would become heir if Thorne died, and Bretta would be Thorolf's wife."

" 'Twas Bretta," Brann said with conviction. "And the drug she used to poison him most likely came from my chest. She must have stolen it while I was occupied elsewhere. The chest is always beneath the bench where I sleep. I should have been more vigilant."

" 'Tis not your fault." She swallowed a sob at the

thought of Thorne lying near death in his chamber. "How can we save him if Olaf refuses to allow us near him?"

"We pray for a miracle, child."

The miracle did not appear. The next morning Fiona and Brann were dragged from the shed to receive their punishment. The entire household was gathered around Olaf and Thorolf. Olaf stepped forward, his expression grim. Fiona's heart plummeted.

"Is Thorne . . . is he . . . ?" She could not say the word. If Thorne died, so would something inside her. When had she begun to love him?

"Thorne still lives, but there is naught the healer can do for him. He lies there unmoving, unfeeling, a man about to begin his journey to Valhalla. You both will die for what you have done to him. A warrior should die with a sword in his hand. A straw death is humiliating to a man like my son."

Brann struggled forward, his eyes dark with ominous warning. "Killing Fiona will solve nothing. She is your son's wife."

"She is my son's whore."

"Kill her and you'll be damned forever."

"You speak nonsense, old man!" Olaf roared.

"Fiona and Thorne belong together. Their future together was revealed to me before Fiona was born."

Olaf laughed harshly. "You're a lunatic as well as a purveyor of evil. Fiona must die." He grasped her wrist and shoved her to her knees. Then he drew his sword.

"Wait!" Rolo rushed forward, placing himself between Fiona and Olaf. "What if Brann is right? What if Thorne's life depends upon the witch's well-being? It might not be in Thorne's best interest to kill Fiona."

"I cannot bear the sight of her," Olaf said. "Because of her, my son has suffered through months of torment. He became obsessed with her from the first moment he set eyes on her."

"Give her to me," Rolo suggested slyly. "I desire her for my mistress. I will take her away and you will never see her again."

"Nay!" Fiona cried, distraught. "Kill me now, for I refuse to become Rolo's mistress. I am Thorne's wife, not his widow. Thorne still lives, does he not?"

"He breathes but does not live," Olaf said. "I do not recognize your Christian marriage."

"Kill Fiona at your own peril," Brann warned. His voice resounded ominously as he stabbed his arms into the air. To onlookers it appeared that he was imploring the gods to wreak vengeance upon the Vikings.

The threat affected Olaf just as Brann hoped it would. There was little that lived and breathed that Olaf feared, but witches and curses were things he could not fight with sword or battleaxe. He flung down his sword in disgust.

"She's yours, Rolo, take her! If I ever set eyes on either of you again, I will kill you both."

Rolo didn't wait for Olaf to change his mind. He swept Fiona from her feet and tossed her over his shoulder as if she were a sack of grain. He shoved her at Thorolf and asked him to watch her. Then he strode back to the hall for his belongings and to bid his sister good-bye.

Bretta met him at the door. "Soon you will be mistress here," Rolo said in a hushed tone. "Thorne is as good as dead."

"Aye, and you will have Fiona in your bed. I wish you joy of her, brother." Then they parted.

Fiona could not believe this was happening. Thorne would die unless Brann was allowed to treat him. No punishment could be as terrible as knowing that Thorne no longer lived. She saw Thorolf staring at her and realized her only hope was to appeal to him. She began speaking to him but he ignored her. Then curiosity won out and he listened to her pleas.

"Please listen, Thorolf. If you love your brother, you must convince your father to let Brann cure Thorne. Brann is the only one besides myself who can save him. I beg you, Thorolf, do not let Thorne die. He is my husband; I would never harm him."

That was all she was allowed to say, for a moment later Rolo returned with his bundle of clothing and dragged her away. She didn't even have time to plead for Brann's life. If Olaf had his way, Brann would be put to death.

Chapter Nine

Thorne hovered near death. Olaf struggled with hopeless anger at the sight of his son lying wan and helpless in his bed. Though the Viking healer from the village had given up on Thorne, Brann still claimed he could save him. Olaf entertained such fear and doubt over Brann's and Fiona's part in Thorne's illness, however, that he couldn't bring himself to let the wizard touch his son. Oddly, Olaf's anxiety did not ease after Fiona had been taken away. He feared that sending Fiona away had been a terrible mistake.

Days passed and Thorne's condition did not improve. Olaf and Thorolf sat in the hall after the others had sought their beds and spoke in hushed voices.

"It looks hopeless," Olaf said, pounding his fist on the table in frustration.

"Perhaps another healer . . ." Thorolf suggested.

"To what purpose? He will but concur that Thorne's condition is beyond help."

Thorolf had agonized long and hard about speaking out. Now he could wait no longer to unburden himself to Olaf.

"Let the wizard try to heal Thorne, Father. What harm can it do? I am certain my brother will die if Brann does not treat him."

"I cannot bear the thought of that wizard touching Thorne. How do we know Brann won't hasten Thorne's death?"

"We don't know, but I'm willing to take the chance. There is naught else left for us."

Olaf frowned as he pondered Thorolf's words. He was still meditating when Bretta approached them.

"I could not sleep," she said, sitting down beside Olaf.

"None of us can," Olaf muttered. "Not with Thorne so close to entering Valhalla. I ordered his dragon ship readied for his pyre. We will send him off in a style befitting his station. 'Tis sad he won't die a Viking death, with a sword in one hand and a battleaxe in the other. Dying a straw death upon his bed is not what Thorne would want."

"I suggested to Father that we should allow Brann to treat Thorne," Thorolf told Bretta.

"You jest!" Bretta cried in mock horror. "I feared mentioning it before, but I saw Brann and Fiona conspiring together the night Thorne fell ill. And I just now recalled that I saw Brann slip Fiona a vial from his medicine chest. 'Tis obvious to me that she fed Thorne poison."

Olaf's face turned dark as a thundercloud. Bretta's claim added fuel to his hatred for Fiona and Brann. "Nay, I'll not let Brann touch my son! Do not ask it of me again, Thorolf." He rose and stormed from the hall.

"Why didn't you tell me what you saw before now, Bretta?" Thorolf asked curiously.

"I was frightened Fiona would do me harm if I told," Bretta lied. "Now that she is gone, there is no longer a reason for me to remain silent."

"Aren't you afraid Fiona will harm your brother? Rolo didn't seem at all worried about taking Fiona into his home or making her his mistress."

"Rolo is resourceful. He can take care of himself. He will not allow Fiona to bewitch him as she did Thorne."

"Go to bed, Bretta," Thorolf growled. "I need to think."

"About what? When Thorne dies, you will become your father's heir. Have you never envied that which belongs to your brother?"

"Thorne is the future jarl," Thorolf contended. "I've never envied his position as our father's heir. Do not speak of Thorne as if he were already dead."

Bretta merely shrugged. She thought she'd given Thorne enough of the drug to kill him. That he still lived was due to his immense size and strong constitution. She decided not to belabor the subject of

Thorne's demise. Rising, she left Thorolf to his morose thoughts.

Thorolf's mood did not improve that night. Nor did it the next day when he looked in on Thorne and found him comatose and as near to death as a man could get. He decided not to approach his father again about allowing Brann to save Thorne. He had reached a decision on his own.

That night Thorolf bided his time, waiting until the household slept before leaving the hall. He stepped into the purple shadows of night and strode through the ground mist to the storage shed where Brann languished in solitary confinement. Olaf had been too distraught to make a decision where the wizard was concerned and had kept him locked in the crude cell. Thorolf hoped the old man had been given food and water, for he truly felt Brann held the secret to saving Thorne's life.

Thorolf unbarred the door and threw it open, seeking the wizard in the dank, dark corners of the shed. He saw Brann lying upon a sack of grain, his frail body shaking from cold. "Can you hear me, wizard?"

"Aye, I hear you, Thorolf. I've been waiting. It took you long enough to seek my help."

Thorolf swallowed the fear he felt rising within him. His brother's life was at stake; he couldn't let superstition sway him. "How did you know I'd come?"

" 'Tis not time for Thorne to die. Thus I knew someone would seek my help."

"Father is against using your skills, but I cannot

allow my brother to die. Can you cure him? *Will* you cure him?"

"I can and I will," Brann assured him. But when the old man tried to rise, Thorolf was shocked at how weak he'd grown. Obviously he had been ignored during the past few days. Thorolf moved with alacrity to help Brann to his feet.

"Are you sure you're able to do this?" Thorolf asked worriedly. "I'll have to sneak you into the hall and past the sleeping household."

"I'll survive," Brann said tersely. "Once we're inside the hall, find my medicine chest and bring it to Thorne's room. I am ready, Viking. We must save Thorne for Fiona's sake."

Brann tottered out of the shed behind Thorolf. He stopped at the well to drink deeply, then found the strength to continue. All was quiet inside the hall. Brann went directly to Thorne's chamber while Thorolf retrieved the medicine chest from beneath the bench where Brann normally slept.

"Bring me a flagon of hot water," Brann said when Thorolf entered Thorne's chamber and set the chest at the wizard's feet. Thorolf left and returned a few minutes later with the water. "Go now. Leave me so that I may save Thorne."

"I will stay," Thorolf insisted.

"Nay. Go to bed. There is naught you can do here."

Thorolf hesitated, then left the room with great reluctance. The moment the door closed behind him, Brann set to work to save his beloved Fiona's husband. Brann needed to cure Thorne so that he might rescue his wife from Rolo. In the meantime, Brann had no doubt that Fiona would be able to handle Rolo. Brann even managed a smile at the thought of what Fiona could do to Rolo without the man's knowledge.

Brann checked the thready cadence of Thorne's pulse, listened to the faint beat of his heart, and lifted his eyelids to inspect his dilated pupils. Thorne's condition was so grave that Brann feared he might be too late to reverse the effects of the drug Thorne had been given. It was then that Brann noted the missing vial of foxglove from his medicine chest. An herbal remedy used to treat those with weak hearts, foxglove worked well if used cautiously, but an overdose could be fatal. Aware now of the kind of drug that had caused Thorne's illness, Brann measured herbs from several jars into a cup, filled it with hot water and allowed the mixture to steep.

When he deemed the infusion ready, Brann painstakingly spooned it into Thorne's mouth. Then he massaged Thorne's throat to make him swallow. He repeated the procedure until Thorne had gotten down a quarter of the liquid that had been prepared. Then Brann sat back and waited. Shortly before daylight he began the ritual all over again. When he had exhausted all his considerable knowledge of healing, he pulled a bench close to the bed and prayed to the ancient Druid gods.

When Thorolf entered the chamber a short time

later, he found Brann sleeping upright on the bench and Thorne stirring restlessly in his bed. It was the first sign of life Thorne had exhibited since he had fallen ill.

Thorolf shook Brann awake. "What did you do to him, old man?"

"I treated him with the antidote of the drug he had been given," Brann explained. " 'Tis a powerful poison when used injudiciously."

"Poison!" Thorolf gasped. "Bretta was right. Fiona poisoned Thorne. Will he live?"

Visions danced before Brann's eyes and he drifted into a trance. Then darkness lifted, allowing him a glimpse of the future. "Aye, Thorne will live," he said slowly. "His sons will become great chieftains. When their time comes they will rule the Isle of Man with wisdom and courage."

"Speak not of the future, old man. Thorne will have no sons if he dies."

Brann came slowly from his trance. "I have seen what I have seen. Fetch Olaf. Tell him that his son will recover."

Thorolf hurried to get his father.

While Brann was feeding Thorne more of the antidote, Thorne opened his eyes. He tried to speak but could not. He was struggling to form the one name he wished to speak above all others when Thorolf and Olaf burst into the room. Olaf saw that Thorne's eyes were open and caught his breath in surprise.

"When Thorolf told me he had allowed you to

treat Thorne, I feared you would kill him and I was prepared to retaliate in kind. But now, my son is awake and I am inclined to be lenient. If Thorne lives, your life will be spared."

"Thorn will live," Brann said with conviction. "But he has a long way to go before he is well. He needs the special care that only I can give him."

"Why can't he speak?" Olaf asked as he watched Thorne struggle to form words.

"His throat has been paralyzed from the effects of the powerful drug he ingested."

"Are you saying my son was deliberately poisoned, old man?"

"Aye, that is my belief."

Olaf's fists clenched at his sides. "Bretta's accusations were correct. I should have killed the witch while I had the chance. Why did you give Fiona the poison when you knew she would use it on Thorne?"

Brann sank back in helpless dejection. "You think Fiona did this?"

"I *know* she did it," Olaf retorted. "No one else in this household had access to or knowledge of the poison. No one else had reason to want Thorne dead." His eyes narrowed. "Did you encourage her, wizard?"

"Brann would not have offered to cure Thorne had he wanted him dead," Thorolf claimed. "Nay, I doubt Brann is the culprit. This is strictly Fiona's doing."

Brann said nothing. Until he was able to prove

that Bretta had stolen the foxglove from his chest, he could not accuse her.

Olaf sent Brann a threatening look. "I demand that you restore my son to his former health. Meanwhile, you will not leave this room. If Thorne dies, you die."

Brann turned back to his patient after Olaf and Thorolf left the chamber. He would save Thorne, but not because he'd been ordered to. Nay, he'd save Thorne because Fiona needed the Viking.

Thorne made a slow recovery. Little by little, as paralysis left his body, he regained mobility in his arms and legs. The day he spoke his first word, both Olaf and Thorolf were in his chamber with Brann.

"What happened?" His voice lacked strength and was rusty from disuse.

Relief swept through Olaf. He'd begun to think Thorne would never regain the ability to speak. "You were poisoned."

It took a moment for Thorne to understand the ramifications of Olaf's reply. "Who?"

"Fiona," Olaf bit out.

Brann shook his head in vigorous denial. "Nay, do not believe it."

" 'Tis true," Olaf said firmly.

For the first time in days, Thorne's brain began to function clearly. Fear for Fiona shuddered through him. What had Olaf done to her? Knowing his father as he did, Thorne could imagine what Fiona's punishment would be for perpetrating such a dastardly deed. Death. He shuddered again.

"What is wrong, lord Viking?" Brann asked with obvious concern. "Are you in pain?"

"Fiona. What happened? Is she . . . Did Father . . . ?"

"The wizard convinced me to spare the witch," Olaf said sourly, "though 'twas not my intention. Fear not, son. She is gone from your life forever. Rolo has taken her for his mistress. He will deal harshly with her should she attempt to practice witchcraft on him."

Thorne closed his eyes as the agony of loss washed over him. It hurt to think that Fiona had fed him poison, but she was the only one besides the wizard with knowledge of such things. And he doubted that Brann would have bothered to save his life if he had wanted him dead. Nay, it had to have been Fiona. Nothing else made sense. Why did the knowledge pain him so much?

"We will speak of this later," Olaf said, sensing Thorne's exhaustion.

"Bretta has been eager to visit you," Thorolf said in parting. "Do you wish to see her?"

Thorne shook his head. He had no desire to see Bretta. Across time and distance Fiona's magic spell still claimed him. He knew without the slightest doubt that her memory would continue to torment him even beyond death.

Rolo's Homestead

Fiona knew the moment Thorne had begun to recover. She had closed her eyes and "seen" him speaking with Brann. Joy welled up inside her. Thorne lived! Nothing else mattered. She had searched deeply within herself for the power to use her special gift and was rewarded with the vision of Thorne. She and Thorne would be together; she believed in her heart that it was so. Destiny would prevail. There were still obstacles to overcome, including Thorne himself, but in the end she and Thorne would find happiness together.

"Fiona, where are you!"

Fiona started violently. Rolo had found her. His voice held an ominous ring and she shivered in response. She supposed he was going to try to bed her again. Several days had passed sincc her arrival at Rolo's homestead, and Rolo's anger was quickly turning to rage.

Fiona touched the bag of herbs she carried in a pouch beneath her tunic and smiled. She never went anywhere without her herbs, and with good reason. Without them and her knowledge of their special properties, Rolo would have ravished her that first night.

"There you are," Rolo said as he entered the small chamber she'd been given. "Take off your tunic and lie on the bed. I feel strong as an ox today. When I finish with you, you won't be able to walk for a week."

Fiona merely stared at him, which seemed to increase his anger. "Do it now!" he roared as he gave her a clout alongside her head.

Reeling from the blow, Fiona moved to comply. She knew the ritual by now. She was to lie naked on the bed and await Rolo. Once he shed his own clothing he'd fall atop her like a ravening beast. Then he'd try to put his massive organ inside her. But he would fail, just as he had failed each time he'd tried to penetrate her. She thanked God for giving her knowledge of the herbs she used to render him impotent.

As was his habit, Rolo carried a flagon of mead to his chamber each night, and each night she managed to mix certain herbs with the mead that made him unable to perform sexually. Should Rolo miss a night or two of imbibing, there would still be enough of the herbal mixture remaining in his system to keep his member limp.

Fiona grimaced with distaste as Rolo shed his tunic, baggy trousers and shoes. His body was enormous and beginning to run to fat. His chest and back were crisscrossed with battle scars, all clearly visible through a matted nest of reddish-blond hair. His full beard flowed down to his chest, and his arms and legs were thickly muscled. Despite the obvious strength of his massive body, his shaft hung limp between his legs. It was all Fiona could do to keep from laughing.

Anger, hot and volatile, boiled inside Rolo, threatening to explode into violence. This had never happened to him before. His nature was to take a woman hard and fast and keep on rutting for hours without tiring. Normally he had the staying power of ten men. When a woman left his bed she could barely walk; he'd always prided himself on his sexual stamina. It was all Fiona's fault, he thought, his expression thunderous. She had cast a spell upon him, rendering him incapable of functioning as a man in bed.

The thought that one slim woman could work black magic on him was infuriating. Thus he kept trying to bed her despite his failure. He desperately needed to prove to himself that no woman could steal his manhood.

"Spread your legs," Rolo ordered as he fell atop Fiona's slender form. "No woman is going to defeat me."

His oppressive weight nearly suffocated Fiona. She could scarcely breathe, let alone obey. Rolo cursed and pried her legs apart with his knee. Then he flexed his hips and tried to enter her. Nothing. His member was shriveled and flaccid, unable to penetrate her dry passage. With a roar of outrage, he flung himself off of her.

"What have you done to me?" he thundered. " 'Tis witchcraft! Olaf was right. But I will defeat you, wench. I will have you yet." He snatched up his clothing and strode naked from the chamber.

The same scenario was repeated the next night, and all the following nights. Then Rolo tried to bed one of his female slaves and failed miserably. After that he truly began to fear Fiona and her witchcraft. When he threatened to beat her if she continued to use black magic on him, she merely smiled and said, "Do so at your own peril, Lord Rolo. It would take little effort on my part to render you impotent for life." That horrifying thought apparently frightened Rolo so thoroughly that he left her alone after that.

Thorne's Homestead

Thorne was well enough now to leave his bed. Though wan and weak and thin from lack of proper nourishment, he was determined to regain his former strength. To that end he forced down huge amounts of food and began practicing with sword and battleaxe. Jousting with his friends provided an outlet for his frustration. Knowledge of the terrible thing that Fiona had done to him plagued him. No matter how hard he tried to forget her, he couldn't banish her image from his mind.

The first night Thorne sat down to share a meal with his family and friends, Olaf encouraged him to publicly divorce Fiona. It nearly choked him to do so, but after the meal Thorne did as his father requested, loudly proclaiming his divorce in his bedchamber and then by the front door. The divorce seemed to please the entire household. Except for Thorne himself. But after what Fiona had done to him, he felt he had no choice but to divorce her. Unfortunately, divorcing her did not guarantee that he would forget her.

Thorne obsessed constantly over Fiona's status as Rolo's mistress. He visualized her naked beneath Rolo's hulking form, imagined her making love with Rolo as sweetly as she had with him. In the darkest part of the night he even imagined he heard her cries of ecstasy as Rolo brought her to climax.

Thorne's life was unraveling and he didn't know what to do about it.

His misery was complete when Bretta slyly suggested, and his father concurred, that she and Thorne should honor their original betrothal. Thorolf offered no objection, but Thorne did.

"Let Thorolf marry Bretta, Father," he stated emphatically. "I have no wish to take a wife." What he did not say was that losing Fiona was a festering wound still too raw to be healed simply by taking another woman. He hadn't come to grips yet with the knowledge that Fiona had tried to kill him. He'd probably be haunted by Fiona's memory for the rest of his life.

Bretta hid her fury well. Thorne's rejection had hurt. She couldn't believe Thorne hadn't succumbed to the poison she'd given him. The man had the constitution of an ox. Nothing had worked out as she'd planned. Now Thorne had the gall to refuse to wed her. She hoped Rolo was beating Fiona regularly.

Thorne remained in the hall that night after everyone else had sought their beds. Something made him look toward the benches lining the hall. He frowned when he saw Brann staring at him with condemnation. He crooked a finger at Brann, and the old man shuffled over to join him.

"I'm curious, wizard. Tell me, why did Fiona poison me? 'Tis tearing me up inside."

"Fiona did not poison you, lord Viking."

"I should have known you would lie for her."

"You must look to another for the cause of your illness."

Thorne scowled. "There is no other. If you know something I do not, you had better tell me."

"You would not believe me. And I have not the proof to substantiate my claim."

"Who!" Thorne said in a low hiss. "Name the villain who wanted me dead."

"Very well, if you insist. 'Twas Bretta. She stole a potent drug from my chest and slipped it into your ale."

Thorne went still. Then he burst into laughter. "You speak nonsense. Bretta has no reason to kill me."

"Does she not? Think, lord Viking. The answer will come to you. I have read the runes and consulted the stars. You will know the truth when you seek it. Good night, lord Viking. I will take my rest now."

Thorne stared at Brann's bent back as the old man hobbled off to his bench. Should he believe the wizard? he wondered. It was ludicrous to think Bretta had poisoned him, yet he couldn't help recalling the night he had rebuffed Bretta's advances and the implied threat she had left hanging between them. But would the woman go so far as to try to kill him? The answer to that question nagged at him like a bad dream. He made a silent vow to learn the truth for himself.

Brann's sage words nagged at Thorne the following day, and the day after that. He watched Bretta closely. On the outside she seemed content with her betrothal to Thorolf, but there were times when he caught her looking at him with a mixture of loathing and longing. Thorne decided that he'd never really known the complex woman dwelling inside the calm beauty.

Thorne's confused thoughts had led to a single conclusion. Brann had hinted that evidence existed to substantiate Bretta's guilt. If there was such proof, Thorne vowed to find it.

The next day Bretta walked to the village with Thorolf to inspect the new dragon ship Thorolf had commissioned to be built. Thorne was invited to go along but he declined, thinking Bretta's absence would offer him an opportunity to do some snooping. First he sought out Brann and asked him to describe the vial that had been stolen from his chest. Then he slipped into Bretta's chamber to search for conclusive proof of her guilt.

There were few places in which to search. The chamber was small, furnished simply with a bed of furs, two chests for clothing, a table and a long bench. Thorne searched through one chest and found nothing but women's fripperies. The second chest held an assortment of folded tunics and little else. He was about to lower the lid on the chest and give up this wild goose chase when a bulge in the pocket of the tunic lying on top caught his attention. Without hesitation he searched the pocket and removed a vial identical to the one Brann had described to him.

Blood rushed to his head. His heart pounded. The meaning of his find made him want to shout with joy. Fiona had not poisoned him! The refrain sang through his veins and warmed his heart.

At that moment, Olaf passed the open door of Bretta's chamber and saw Thorne standing beside her clothes chest.

"What in Odin's name are you doing in Bretta's chamber?" Olaf asked from the doorway.

"Discovering something that will surprise everyone," Thorne replied.

"I don't understand. Are you ill again?"

"Not ill, Father. Merely wiser." He stuck out his hand, revealing the vial in his open palm. "I found this in the pocket of Bretta's tunic. 'Tis the vial stolen from Brann's medicine chest. It contained the drug that paralyzed me and nearly stopped my heart. 'Twas Bretta who poisoned me, not Fiona."

"How do you know 'tis the same vial?" Olaf charged, refusing to believe Bretta could be guilty of committing so grave a crime.

"Brann described it to me."

"Someone other than Bretta placed it in the chest."

"Nay. Bretta put it there herself."

"What is going on?" Bretta demanded as she walked into her chamber, surprised to see Thorne and Olaf there.

Thorne thrust the vial under her nose. "Do you recognize this?"

Bretta blanched. She had meant to get rid of the vial but hadn't found the opportunity to do so. "Where did you get it?"

"In your tunic pocket," Thorne replied grimly.

Bretta licked moisture onto her suddenly dry lips. Thorne looked ready to kill. " 'Tis medicine a healer gave me before I left home. I take it for headaches that come upon me suddenly."

Olaf gave Thorne a smug look. "See, I knew there had to be a plausible explanation."

Thorne popped the cork and held the vial to Bretta's lips. "Drink, Bretta. There's a small amount left in the vial."

Bretta tried to turn aside but Thorne grasped her head in his big hand and held it steady. "I do not have a headache," Bretta cried in desperation.

"Drink!" Thorne repeated harshly as he pressed the vial to her lips.

"Nay! I do not want to die!"

Olaf's chin dropped to his chest as Thorne stared at Bretta with loathing. The proof was indisputable.

"Why, Bretta?" Olaf wanted to know.

"I wanted Thorne but he did not want me. The insult was too much for me to bear. He bedded Fiona despite my offer to share his bed. Forgive me, my lord. I was not in my right mind. I was mad with love for Thorne and wanted to make him suffer for giving me to his brother. I never meant to kill him."

She fell to her knees, the perfect picture of humility and remorse. She knew Olaf had every right to kill her for what she'd done and she feared for her life.

"On your feet, woman!" Olaf roared. "I'm sending you back to your brother. There will be no betrothal. It pains me to think I harbored a viper in my home. Be ready to leave within the hour. Let Rolo deal with you now."

Olaf strode from the room. Thorne sent Bretta a hard look and followed close on Olaf's heels. Thorne knew if he remained a moment longer in Bretta's company he wouldn't be responsible for his actions. He accompanied Olaf through the hall, out the door and into the sunshine, leaving all that was dark and evil inside.

"I'm going after Fiona, Father," Thorne said. His words brought Olaf to an abrupt halt. "She did not hurt me."

"Fiona is Rolo's mistress now. You divorced her, remember? Everyone in the household heard you renounce her. Why would you want another man's leavings?"

"I don't know why," Thorne said honestly. " 'Tis an obsession. I am tormented when we're apart." He gnashed his teeth in frustration. "When I visualize her in Rolo's bed it makes me want to kill him."

Olaf snorted in disgust. " 'Tis obvious you're still bewitched. I'm standing firm on this issue, Thorne. I vow I will disown you and make Thorolf my heir if you bring Fiona back into my household. Forget her. We will find you another bride, one suitable to your station."

Thorne went still. His father's ultimatum both shocked and angered him. He'd always been his own man and made his own decisions.

"I once offered to relinquish my place as your heir in Thorolf's favor and you refused to accept," he said. "I need neither your wealth nor your title. I have enough wealth of my own to do as I please."

"So be it," Olaf said in a voice that would leave most men quaking.

Chapter Ten

Rolo's Homestead

Rolo continued to torment Fiona. Since he couldn't bed her, he was making her life miserable by taunting her with cruel words. The taunt that hurt the most was Rolo's claim that Thorne was dead. Fiona did not sense his death. She had probed her inner self and had been rewarded with a glimpse of him alive and well.

"What makes you think Thorne still lives?" Rolo asked after another frustrating attempt to ravish Fiona. He wanted to hurt and humiliate her as she was hurting and humiliating him. What she was doing to him was evil and he wanted to punish her. But he feared her threat to render him permanently impotent. Vikings took great pride in their sexual prowess.

"I *know* he is not dead," Fiona said with vehemence. "I have seen him alive and well."

"If he is alive, why doesn't he come for you?" Rolo challenged. "You're his wife."

"He blames me for his illness," Fiona said sadly.

" 'Tis a valid claim," Rolo charged. "Look what you've done to me." He glanced down at his flaccid manhood, then yanked down his tunic to cover his shame.

Fiona pulled down her own tunic and leapt from his bed. "We both know I had naught to do with Thorne's illness."

Rolo blanched beneath his beard. "You know naught!"

"I know everything."

Rolo recoiled in fear. He'd thought himself capable of controlling Fiona's black magic, but his formidable strength was naught compared to her dark powers. He slowly backed away from her. "If I promise not to touch you again, will you restore my manhood?"

"I will think on it," Fiona said complacently.

Rolo pulled open the door and nearly tripped over a servant in his haste to flee. "Get out of my way!" he roared.

"Master, your sister has returned," the servant said, trembling beneath Rolo's fury.

"Bretta is here?" He strode through the hall to greet his sister. Curious, Fiona followed.

"Why are you not with Thorolf, your intended husband?" Rolo wanted to know.

"Thorne lives," Bretta said by way of explanation.

Rolo's eyes narrowed. "But I thought—"

"You thought wrong. The man has the constitution of an ox."

"Do they know, then?"

"Aye, they know. They found the vial in my room."

Fiona gasped in outrage. "What manner of woman are you? What did you hope to gain by killing Thorne?"

"Thorolf would have become Olaf's heir upon Thorne's death. I had everything to gain," Bretta snapped. "I have been banished forever from Olaf's home with no prospect of gaining a husband."

"You were careless!" Rolo exploded. " 'Tis a wonder Olaf didn't slay you."

"I had to plead for my life. All is lost now." She sent Fiona a venomous look. "You're as much to blame as Brann, witch! Would that I had been here to hear you cry and beg for mercy when my brother made you his whore. Rolo is not a gentle man, I'm told."

Ashamed to admit he'd been emasculated by Fiona's witchcraft, Rolo said gruffly, "Fiona has learned to submit. I am well pleased with my whore."

Fiona gave him a startled look, opened her mouth to voice a denial, and found her lips sealed with Rolo's large hand. The fierce look he bestowed upon her warned her that not even her threat to render him permanently impotent would stop him from harming her if she revealed the truth to his entire household. He'd risk emasculation before he'd reveal to the world that he was half a man. At Fiona's slight nod of compliance, her mouth was released.

"What was that all about?" Bretta wanted to know.

"I'm trying to teach Fiona respect," Rolo claimed. "She's not to speak unless spoken to."

"I doubt you will succeed, brother," Bretta jeered. "However, I don't care what you and your whore do as long as it doesn't interfere with my plans for finding a new husband at the *althing* next month. 'Tis my hope that you beat Fiona severely and regularly." She turned to leave, then spun around. "By the way, Fiona, you may be interested to know that Thorne divorced you before the entire household. You are no longer his wife." Her laughter floated behind her as she made a regal exit.

At first Fiona was shaken by the news. Then she became angry. Thorne was a fool. Obviously he didn't know that Christian marriages were forever. Vikings might treat marriage lightly, but Christians did not. Then a terrible thought occurred to her. If Thorne no longer wanted her, what was to become of her? Where would she go? She had succeeded in making Rolo fear her powers, but what would happen when the herbs she fed him were gone? She had no idea if that particular kind of herb grew in this harsh climate, or where to find it.

Nay, she decided. She could not stay here in Rolo's home. Somehow she must find her way back to Man. She longed to see Brann, to be comforted by his presence. Brann had insisted that Thorne was her chosen mate and she had begun to believe it.

Because she had begun to love him.

Thorne's Homestead

Dawn was breaking as Thorne thrust his battleaxe in his broad leather belt and sheathed Blood-drinker. His face was taut with purpose. He was going after Fiona and no one was going to stop him. He had traveled all the way to the Isle of Man for Fiona, and no man was going to take her from him. She belonged in *his* bed, not Rolo's. It mattered not that he had divorced her before witnesses. If he couldn't have her as his wife, he'd take her as his mistress.

Nearly all of Thorne's warriors had volunteered to accompany him to Rolo's homestead. Not because they believed Thorne's cause a just one, but because they relished a good fight. Most still believed that Thorne was possessed, but the likelihood of a rousing battle overcame their reservations.

Thorne was anxious to be off. He'd been vacillating for days, until he realized he could not bear life without Fiona. He couldn't sleep. Had no appetite for food or drink or women. Fiona's image appeared before him constantly, plaguing him with her sweet smile and seductive gaze. Her spell had been a fatal one. The only antidote was to gorge himself on her sweet flesh until she was purged from his soul or he died from overindulgence. His obsession for her was driving him mad.

Thorne had just shoved his knife into his leg lacing when he saw his father and Thorolf striding toward him. He straightened and waited for them to approach.

"You're going after her, then," Olaf said harshly.

"Aye. I cannot let Rolo have Fiona."

"I meant it when I said I'd make your brother my heir in your stead if you deliberately defied me."

"Aye, I know that."

"And you're still determined to commit this folly?"

"I have no choice. I want Fiona."

Olaf sighed. "I had hoped you'd find the strength to break the witch's spell, but I was mistaken. You leave me no recourse, Thorne. I am a man of my word."

"Do not do this, Thorne," Thorolf urged. "You are Father's heir. The only way you can break Fiona's spell is if we remain united against her."

"I'm sorry, Thorolf. I cannot abandon Fiona, not for you or anyone. You are as worthy as I to become Father's heir."

"Is that your last word?" Olaf asked gruffly.

"Aye."

Olaf turned his back to Thorne and spoke in a voice loud enough to command attention. "Hear me! I hereby declare before witnesses that Thorne is no longer my heir. After I am called to Valhalla, my title and wealth are to go to Thorolf, my second born. Word will be carried to the king so that none may challenge my decision after my death."

Then he turned back to Thorne, his face etched in sadness. " 'Tis not that I love you less, 'tis just that I fear you are possessed."

"I'm sorry, Thorne," Thorolf said. " 'Tis not my doing. For your own salvation, I cannot wish you success."

Moments later Thorne mounted his horse and rode off. His men trotted on foot beside him. Few Norsemen rode with any degree of skill.

Not too many leagues separated Rolo's homestead from Olaf's. Their lands adjoined, making them natural allies. They had come to one another's defense against invading Danes many times in the past. But none of that mattered now to Thorne, for Rolo had something he wanted.

Rolo was practicing swordplay with one of his men in the yard when he saw a small army of warriors approaching. At first he thought he was being invaded by Danes in search of plunder and new lands. He bellowed a warning, and his men scurried for their weapons. But it was too late, the enemy was already upon them. A man on horseback stepped out from the pack and raised his battleaxe in challenge.

"Rolo! Can you hear me?"

Rolo blanched. It was worse than he'd thought. "Thorne the Relentless, is that you?"

"Aye. I've come for that which belongs to me. Give it up peacefully or meet me on the battlefield."

"If you're referring to Bretta, take her."

" 'Tis not Bretta I want and well you know it. 'Tis Fiona I've come for."

"Ah, I assume you mean my whore," Rolo taunted. "Mayhap she prefers me for a lover. She's a passionate little morsel. I'd hate to part with her."

Rolo was deliberately goading Thorne. It wouldn't do to let Thorne know how eager he was to be rid of the witch. He was convinced that once Fiona was out of his life, his manhood would be fully restored.

"Then prepare to fight for her," Thorne said, gripping his battleaxe with purpose. "I intend to send you to Valhalla."

"Hold!" Rolo cried. "We have been allies and friends too long to let a woman come between us. I have thralls more beautiful than she. Take Fiona. The more I know of her, the more I am convinced that she is capable of evil. She has been practicing witchcraft on me and I will not allow her to possess me as she has you. I will send her out to you."

"I will not tolerate trickery," Thorne warned, wary of Rolo's easy compliance. What had Fiona done to him to make him willing to give her up?

"No trickery intended," Rolo promised. "I am a man of my word."

Fiona was in her small, windowless chamber at the opposite end of the house and heard nothing of the exchange between Thorne and Rolo. Nor did she have any idea that Thorne had come for her. Thus she was surprised when Rolo flung open the door to her chamber and ordered her out.

Fiona stared at him in open defiance. "What do you want?"

"Your lover has come for you," Rolo sneered. "And welcome he is to you. Hurry, else he becomes restless and attacks."

"Thorne is here?" Fiona asked, her eyes wide with wonder.

"I was a fool to make light of your powers," Rolo remarked. "Thorne is a hard man, not given to fanciful notions or sentiments. Only a man possessed would want a woman as badly as he seems to want you. Fetch your cloak. 'Tis glad I am to be rid of you."

Fiona turned back to get her cloak, then hurried after Rolo. Bretta stepped in her path, bringing her to an abrupt halt.

"Go to your lover," Bretta sneered. "You can be nothing but his whore now. 'Tis unlikely he will marry you a second time."

Fiona gritted her teeth and stepped around Bretta, her head held high. Thorne might think they were no longer married, but she knew better. Nevertheless, she wasn't going to make things easy for him. It had been reprehensible of him to divorce her. If he didn't want her for his wife, then he could only want her for his whore. By the time she stepped through the door, she was seething with rage. How dare Thorne reduce her to the roll of leman!

She had to admit, however, that she was thrilled to see him restored to his former strength and vitality. She thanked God that someone had had the intelligence to seek Brann's help, otherwise Thorne might not be here today.

"Go, Thorne awaits you," Rolo said, shoving her forward. "But first, remove your spell from me. Restore my manhood."

Fiona struggled to contain her mirth. "Very well." She waved her hand. " 'Tis done. Wait a fortnight before taking a woman and I vow your vigor will be fully restored."

Rolo almost collapsed with relief. If Thorne hadn't come for Fiona, he didn't know what he would have done with her. He was so desperate, he had even considered sending her back to Man.

"Fiona!" Thorne's voice held a note of relief. He dismounted and strode forward to meet her.

Fiona wanted to run into his arms but refrained, still angry at him for ending their marriage. Instead, she waited for him to come to her.

Thorne practiced admirable restraint when what he longed to do was to sweep her into his arms, carry her away to a private bower and make endless love to her. "Are you unharmed?" His gaze swept over her with an intensity that made her skin tingle and burn.

"Aye. I am well."

Thorne's expression hardened as he searched her face. Fiona looked amazingly well for a woman who had suffered Rolo's rough loving. He'd heard that Rolo was a cruel lover, had seen proof of it himself, and he feared Fiona carried bruises that didn't show on the outside.

"If he mistreated you I'll kill him," Thorne said. "My men are eager to do battle."

Fiona shook her head. "Do not fight on my account. Rolo willingly gave me up; 'tis enough."

"Aye, 'tis enough," Thorne concurred without enthusiasm. Then he surprised her by sweeping her off her feet and carrying her to his mount. He settled her astride his horse and leaped up behind her. The steed leaped forward at his command.

They didn't speak again until Thorne called a halt for the night. They could have gone on but the men were tired, having marched that day to Rolo's homestead without respite. Thorne dismounted and lifted his arms for Fiona. She slid into them effortlessly, but immediately pulled away.

"You appear angry," he said, puzzled by her mood. He had rescued her, hadn't he?

Fiona stared into his fire-and-ice eyes and felt herself being drawn into the maelstrom of his dark desire. It seemed as if every event of her life had brought her to this moment, to be held captive by her need for this man. She looked away quickly, before her anger turned into fierce desire.

"What did you expect?" she challenged. "We are no longer wed. Will you make me your leman now?"

"So Bretta told you. I should have known. I had no choice but to divorce you. I was convinced that you had tried to kill me."

"Where does that leave us, Viking?"

He searched his mind but found no answer to her question, so he adroitly changed the subject. "What did you do to Rolo? He hinted that you practiced witchcraft on him. He appeared relieved to be rid of you."

"I did nothing to Rolo that he didn't deserve," Fiona sniffed.

Thorne nodded sagely. " 'Tis as I suspected. You *are* a witch. I am possessed. My mind and body are no longer my own. What manner of magic will you work on me next?"

"I have not yet decided," Fiona said with a hint of devilment. She started to walk away.

Thorne grabbed her arm and swung her around to face him. The broad planes of his face were set in rigid lines. "Did you enjoy Rolo? Is he a better lover than I? Does he have more stamina? Is his prowess to your liking?"

Fiona looked directly into the burning centers of his eyes and said, "I don't know. Rolo never bedded me."

Thorne laughed harshly. "Do you fear me so much that you would lie to me? No man in his right mind could resist you. Rolo has never denied that he wanted you in his bed."

His words filled her with cold anger. She tried to pull away from his grasp but he held her fast.

"Answer me! Did you enjoy what Rolo did to you?"

Put that way, Fiona could not withhold the truth. She'd hated everything Rolo had done to her. He'd been unable to complete the ultimate humiliation, but just having his hands on her body had sickened her.

"Nay, I did not like what Rolo did to me!"

Thorne released her abruptly and she stepped away from the fury she saw gathering in his tormented blue eyes. "I should have killed him."

"Do you enjoy killing so much?"

"I am a Viking," he said proudly. "It is what we do."

Fiona walked away while she still had the strength to do so.

The Viking warriors lay sleeping around the dying fire. Fiona wrapped herself more tightly in her cloak and tried to ignore Thorne's big body curled around her, protecting her from the night chill. Except for his warmth, he'd offered her little else. But she wouldn't have accepted it no matter what he offered. Her anger and his unyielding nature and lack of faith in her were like swords driving them apart. The stubborn fool would rather believe that Rolo had bedded her than accept the truth.

Fiona closed her eyes, trying to find sleep. Suddenly she tensed, her mind whirling as visions began forming behind her eyelids. The feeling was powerfully oppressive, so strong that her entire being ached from it. Succumbing to the supernatural power claiming her, she relaxed and allowed the vision to overtake her.

She saw Thorne's homestead being besieged by fierce invaders. She sensed desperation. Thorne had taken most of the warriors with him, leaving Olaf dangerously undermanned and vulnerable to attack. Then she sensed the cold presence of death, and the scream building in her throat burst forth.

Thorne jerked upright, reaching for his weapons. "What's wrong? Are we under attack?"

By now the sleeping Vikings were on their feet, alert and prepared to face their enemy.

"We must leave immediately!" Fiona cried, leaping to her feet. She was trembling so violently she could scarcely speak.

"What is it?" Thorne asked after he satisfied himself that no immediate danger existed.

"Viking invaders from the north," Fiona gasped in a rush of words. "Your homestead . . . We must hurry before everyone is slain."

Thorne grasped her shoulders, giving her a little shake. "Slowly, Fiona. Tell me how you know this."

"Sometimes I see things. Not very often, but I've learned to take my visions seriously. We must hurry, Thorne. I . . . I sensed death."

Thorne merely stared at her, trying to decide whether to believe her or treat her vision as a bad dream. His men were looking at her as if she were possessed. A few were even backing away in fear. Yet the longer he looked at Fiona, the more he believed that she had indeed experienced some kind of supernatural revelation. His skin crawled and his heart pounded. Mayhap he was mad, or as possessed as Fiona appeared to be, but he believed her. He shouted orders and tossed Fiona astride his horse. By the time he had mounted behind her, his men were already on the move.

They reached the homestead just as the sun was peeping over the mountains. The entire place had been turned into a battleground. The metallic clash of battleaxes and swords resounded like thunder across the land. Thorne gave Fiona a puzzled look, as if trying to understand the frightening power she possessed. Then he lifted her to the ground, told her to wait there with his horse, gave a Viking war cry and rushed to join his men, who were already hacking away at the invaders.

The enemy saw reinforcements pouring in to join the battle and slowly began to retreat. Thorne and his warriors had turned the tide of battle, and the Northmen were wise enough to know it. They melted away, routed but undefeated, and Thorne knew they would regroup and return another day.

Thorolf thumped Thorne's back when they met after the battle. "You couldn't have arrived at a better time, brother. We lacked the men to defeat the invaders without you."

"You can thank Fiona for my timely arrival," Thorne replied. "She had a vision and woke us from a sound sleep. Thor was with us, for we arrived in time. Where is Father?"

Thorolf glanced around the yard littered with bodies. "He was fighting at my back a moment ago. Perhaps he—"

They spotted Olaf nearly at the same time. He was lying face down in the dirt, a battleaxe imbedded in his back and blood pooling beneath him.

"Nay!" Thorolf cried, dropping to his knees beside his father. Gingerly he turned the older man over, saddened to see that his eyes were open but glazing over fast. It wouldn't be long before the Valkyries arrived to carry him to Valhalla.

Thorne knelt in the dirt beside Olaf. "Father, can you hear me? 'Tis Thorne. We've driven away the Northmen."

" 'Tis the witch's doing," Olaf gasped, convinced even at the moment of death that Fiona was to blame for every evil that had befallen them.

"Nay, Father," Thorne said. "Fiona warned me of the attack. My men and I arrived in time to save the homestead."

Olaf remained unmoved by Thorne's words. "I'm dying," he gasped with his last breath. "I name Thorolf my heir."

"Father . . . I—" Thorolf began.

"Nay, do not speak. Listen, for I have little time left before I begin my journey to Valhalla. The witch . . . Kill the witch . . ."

Blood gurgled in his throat as death claimed him.

"He's dead," Thorolf said with cold finality.

"Thorolf is the new jarl," Ulm said, thrusting his fist into the air to punctuate his words. He'd been standing beside Olaf when the dying man had named his heir.

"Aye," Thorolf acknowledged, finding no joy in it.

" 'Twas what Father wanted," Thorne acknowledged.

Suddenly Thorolf spied Fiona standing behind Thorne and said, "I will honor Father's last wish." He drew his sword. "Stand aside, Thorne, I must slay the witch. Your soul will not be your own until she lies beneath the ground for your feet to tread upon."

Fiona did not move. She was paralyzed with fear. She guessed that Thorne was too astonished to react quickly enough to save her and she prepared herself to meet her God.

Thorne was indeed stunned. He was still on his knees beside his father as Thorolf drew his sword. He saw the downward sweep of the blade before he began to move. He groaned in frustration and fear when he realized he would not reach her in time. He made a desperate lunge but fell short as the sword continued its deadly arc. Then, from the corner of his eye he saw Brann dart out from behind Ulm and throw himself in front of Fiona, shoving her out of danger's path as he took her place.

Thorolf's blade bit through flesh and bone, felling Brann with one mighty stroke. Fiona screamed and scrambled to Brann's side, cradling his head in her arms.

"Do not leave me, Brann, I beg you," she sobbed piteously.

"I knew ere I began this journey that I would never see my homeland again," Brann whispered in a voice so thready it could scarcely be heard.

"What am I to do without you?"

"Cling to your Viking. He is your future. You may doubt that now, but it will be. Let me go in peace, child."

"God be with you, Brann," Fiona whispered as the last breath left his body.

Brann's death did not appease Thorolf. He was his father's son in more ways than one. "See what Fiona has done now, brother? Nothing good has come of her being here. Our luck turned the day you were lured to her island and returned to us obsessed with a woman you'd seen only once. I did not want to kill the wizard, for he saved your life. Father was going to send him home to Man. The witch rewards her friends with death. Is that what you wish for yourself?"

"Had it not been for Fiona, you would have all been slain by the Northmen," Thorne bit out. "Do not lift your sword against Fiona again."

Thorolf sheathed his sword with a snarl of contempt. "I cannot fight witchcraft, but I can dictate who lives in my home. You are welcome, Thorne, but not your leman."

"I would do nothing to cause dissension between us," Thorne said. "Summer is waning but the seas are still calm. I cannot let you kill Fiona. I will take her home to Man."

He glanced at the circle of faces surrounding them, men he'd known since boyhood. "Many of you are landless," he continued. "Those who choose to fill my five dragon ships will find rich new lands to settle and comely women to bed. From Man you can sail to all the ports of the world and gain riches aplenty. Who is with me?"

Most of Thorne's crewmen from previous voyages were eager to sign on for this new venture. Replacements were quickly found for those who declined because of family obligations or other reasons. Aren, Thorne's cousin, volunteered, but Ulm elected to remain as Thorolf's lieutenant.

Thorne was pleased with the results. "We will begin preparations after my father is sent to Valhalla in a manner befitting his rank." He turned to Thorolf. "Does that meet with your approval, brother?"

"Aye. Just keep your whore confined in your chamber until you leave. 'Tis not too late to change your mind if you have second thoughts about this journey."

Thorne said nothing as he pulled Fiona away from Brann's body and dragged her into the house. He didn't stop until they reached his chamber.

"Thank you for taking me home," Fiona said once the door closed behind them.

"I am mad, or possessed, or both," Thorne muttered darkly.

"I'm sorry about your father."

"He died as he would have wished. A Viking could ask for no better death. You must not mourn Brann; he was an old man who had lived beyond his allotted time."

"I will miss him, but I am glad I'm going home. How long will you remain on Man?"

Thorne shrugged. "At least through the winter. Perhaps by then I will tire of you and be eager to go a-Viking again. Or mayhap you'll see fit to release me from your spell."

"How can you still accuse me of being a witch?" Fiona asked, furious at him for being so stubborn.

"How can I not? You see things others do not. You have knowledge of medicines and potions. You have done things to Rolo that make him fear you. And yet I still want you. My father lies dead and I can think of naught but tossing you down upon the bed, shoving your legs apart and sheathing myself in your heated center."

Without warning he grasped her shoulders and dragged her up against him. He was still wearing his mail, and she felt the pressure of every polished link digging into her tender flesh. But that slight pain disappeared as he lifted her chin and pressed his mouth against hers. She whimpered in protest as the hard stab of his tongue parted her lips and thrust past her teeth to explore her mouth. He kissed her until she grew dizzy, until breathing became a distant memory, until she went limp in his arms.

His hand went to the back of her neck in a caress so subtle, so tantalizingly tender, that Fiona feared her lack of breath was making her imagine tenderness where none really existed. Vikings were barbarians; they knew nothing of gentleness. Then she recalled that Thorne had never been rough with her, which was a contradiction of everything she had learned or ever been told about Vikings.

"Fiona, sweet Fiona, bewitching Fiona," he murmured against her lips. "I am obsessed with you. You own my soul. Even though I'll doubtlessly suffer a life of torment, I cannot let you go. I care not that you were Rolo's whore, for I will make you mine again."

His words were like a dash of cold water to Fiona. As he bore her down to his bed of furs, she rolled from beneath him in one agile motion. He sat up, bewildered, as she leaped to her feet and glared at him.

"We are no longer wed," she stated, waiting for him to confirm it.

" 'Tis true. It matters not. Our Christian marriage was never binding."

Her eyes narrowed. "We are no longer husband and wife, is that correct?" she repeated.

"We never really were."

"What am I to you? Your thrall? Your whore?"

Thorne frowned. "I have seen nothing to deny that you're a witch. Even Rolo has come to believe you have magical powers. I have seen proof of it myself. I do not want a witch for a wife."

Anger exploded inside Fiona. No matter what Thorne believed, she was still his wife in the eyes of her Christian God. Nevertheless, she did not want a man who considered her a witch, or one who would make her his whore. Deliberately she gave him her back.

"I am no man's whore," she declared. "Our Christian marriage is still valid."

Thorne's expression turned mutinous. Was she deliberately goading him? Did she think he feared her witchcraft? Nay, he feared no man or woman. To prove it, he said, "I am going to keep you. If you believe we are still wed, so be it." He knew the words had come from his mouth but couldn't believe he'd said them.

Madness!

Chapter Eleven

Fiona was confined within Thorne's chamber when Brann was buried later that day. Because Thorolf wanted her nowhere near him, she was forced to mourn her friend and mentor in private. At eventide Tyra crept into the chamber with a tray of food. She kept her head turned away and would have left without uttering a word, had Fiona not addressed her.

"I'm sorry I wasn't able to speak with Thorne about what we discussed before I was sent away."

Tyra lifted her head and Fiona dragged in a ragged breath. The left side of Tyra's face was bruised and her upper lip swollen, as if it had been bitten.

"Dear God, what happened to you?"

Tyra lowered her gaze. " 'Tis naught."

Suddenly the answer dawned on Fiona. " 'Twas

Ulm, wasn't it? Only an animal would treat a woman so."

Tyra shrugged. "Aye. I made the mistake of resisting. I won't do it again."

"Oh, Tyra, I'm so sorry. I'll talk to Thorne. I'll tell him I want to take you to Man with me."

Tyra's eyes brightened. "You would do that? I wouldn't ask it of you. I feared for you after you left. I know you suffered the same abuse as I as Rolo's leman. Bedding him couldn't have been pleasant for you, not after Thorne."

"Rolo didn't bed me," Fiona said, summoning a grin.

Tyra's eyes grew round. "But how—" She clapped a hand over her mouth. "You cast a spell on him! Would that I could do the same to Ulm."

"Not a spell, Tyra. My knowledge of herbs saved me. Rolo believes I stole his manhood, and in a way I did. He was much relieved when Thorne came for me."

"I must go before I'm missed," Tyra said, casting a furtive glance toward the door.

"Try to avoid Ulm tonight. I'll do what I can to help you."

"Thank you, Fiona. The Isle of Man is close to my own home; I know I could be happy there."

She slipped out the door, leaving Fiona to wonder how in God's name she was going to help Tyra when Thorne was being so hardheaded and contrary.

* * *

Fiona fell asleep beside Thorne's cold hearth. She had pulled one of the fur pelts from his bed and curled up on the floor. She was sleeping soundly when Thorne entered his chamber. The candle had burned down to a stub and he lit another, holding it aloft as his gaze wandered around the small chamber, looking for Fiona. He saw her huddled in the fur pelt and the tension left his body. He knelt beside her and brushed her pale cheek with his knuckles. Had Fiona been awake, she would have been surprised by his gentle gesture. His lips grazed the soft ebony hair at her temple. The tenderness he was displaying puzzled him and he sat back on his heels to delve deeply into his heart for the reason behind his tender feelings.

Fiona didn't even have to be awake to bewitch him, he reflected. He'd been captivated, beguiled and lured by powers beyond his understanding. He feared he was already beyond help, but he didn't really care as he scooped her into his arms and carried her to his bed. Moments later he was naked and lying beside her, working feverishly to remove her tunic and shift.

Fiona awoke with a start, holding back a shiver when she realized Thorne was undressing her. Her sensitive nipples tightened and contracted with a will of their own as he bared them to his hungry gaze. Then he bent his head and gently suckled her until her hands caught in his hair. He lifted his shaggy head and gazed into her violet eyes.

"Are you going to stop me?" he asked. "I've been

deprived of your sweet body too long." His gaze returned to her nipples, frosted by candlelight and the wetness of his tongue.

"I couldn't stop you even if I wanted to. You're twice my size. You could easily snap my neck with your hands."

"I can think of more pleasant things to do with my hands."

She caught her breath as his callused fingers slid between her legs to caress and stroke. Thorne watched her face, captivated by the fleeting glimpses of pleasure she could not withhold. Her body stiffened and she cried out as he dipped one finger into her tight sheath. Then his hand left her as he bent his head and placed his mouth where his hand had been.

Fiona nearly flew off the bed. "Thorne, nay! You can't. You don't mean to—"

"I want to taste you, Fiona. Don't deny me."

She could deny him nothing as his mouth created a clamoring in her body that was like nothing she'd ever felt before. The maddening rhythm of his tongue delving into her intimate flesh and lapping against the sensitive nub nestled between her thighs caused her to shudder and arch beneath him. Her lashes fluttered against her flushed cheeks. Her head rolled from side to side as her mouth crooned a silent tune.

Thorne felt her muscles convulse and he lifted his head to observe her. The stark planes of his face were cast in ruthless lines by the flickering candlelight. "I want to watch your face when I bring you pleasure. I want you to know 'tis me and not Rolo making your body sing." Then he thrust his finger deep into her one last time, smiling with satisfaction when she screamed and jerked violently. Before the last shudder left her body, he nudged her knees apart and thrust upward inside her.

His fingers laced into hers, pinning her hands on either side of her head as his mouth closed on hers. She moaned, tasting the musky, sweet flavor of herself on his lips. Then he began to move inside her, long, steady strokes that pierced her very soul.

When she thought she would perish from lack of breath, he finally broke off the kiss. She buried her face in his throat as he filled her so deeply she didn't know where her body ended and his began. She heard his breathing quicken as he rocked between her thighs. A guttural groan left his throat as he brought her to climax again.

"Come with me, love. Follow me to Valhalla."

Fiona arched against him as he poured his seed into her, impaling her against the bed with the force of his driving need.

The candle had burnt down to a tiny stub when Fiona awoke. She lay warmly clasped in Thorne's arms, her face nestled against his throat, his hand cupping her breast. He stirred and opened his eyes. She wondered if he'd been sleeping, so quickly did he waken. His hand tightened on her breast, then moved down to toy with the downy nest between her legs.

She tensed, then relaxed, letting him have his

way as her body warmed to his touch. How could a man as big and fierce as her Viking husband be so gentle? she wondered. Then suddenly she remembered his last words to her. He'd called her his love. A small sigh left her lips.

Thorne heard Fiona's breathy gasp and his hand froze on her thigh. "What is it?"

"Do you realize what you said?"

"When?"

"When we were . . . coupling."

"I probably said many things, most of which I don't remember."

Fiona frowned. Why must men be so unfeeling? "You called me your 'love.' Do you love me, Thorne? Was it love for me that sent you to Rolo's homestead to claim me?"

"Love? The word is foreign to me. Vikings have no time for sentimental gibberish. Viking warriors marry to beget children, to have someone to run their homes, and for political and material gain. We respect our wives, but rarely do we love them. Sometimes Viking women fight beside their men, wielding swords and battleaxes with dexterity and purpose.

"Divorce is a simple matter for Viking couples should they not suit. They have merely to announce their intention before witnesses. Most men take mistresses, and few wives complain."

"Christians marry for life," Fiona claimed. "Sometimes they do not love one another at first, but love comes with time. Viking women might allow their men to dally with their mistresses, but *I* will not."

"You will learn to accept the Viking way."

Fiona heaved a sigh. "You're making this difficult for me, Viking."

"How so?"

"How can I love you when you are too stubborn to accept my love? Or return it?"

Her question so unsettled him that he was rendered speechless. When he finally found his voice, he asked, "Who said I had to love you? I never asked for your love. Nor did I ask to be bewitched. Your siren's song lured me to your island, then you stole my soul."

"You're a fool if you believe that. I knew about you from the time I was old enough to understand. I knew not your name, but the knowledge that a Viking would come to Man and claim me has always been a part of my life. I didn't want to believe Brann's prophesy until the day you carried me away."

"How do you explain it?" Thorne asked as he began to stroke her body. "Was it the wizard who lured me to Man? I think not," he said, answering his own question. "Nay, 'twas no man's voice I heard summoning me over the sound of the waves and splash of the oars. Why do you believe we are fated to be together?"

"Because God has willed it. God and Brann's Celtic deity. Brann said we would love one another unto eternity, Thorne, but you are proving exceedingly difficult to love."

"I asked you to marry me, didn't I?"

"Then you divorced me."

"You said your God didn't recognize our divorce."

"True. But I will only be your wife if you love me."

This talk of love was making Thorne nervous. "I will never let you go; isn't that enough for you?"

"Nay."

"If I am willing to keep you as my wife instead of my whore, why must you ask more of me? If I admitted I loved you, I'd never know if 'twas my heart speaking or the result of witchcraft."

"Do you have a heart, Viking?" Fiona challenged.

"I believe I have exposed my heart to you."

"You have shown me your lust. 'Tis not enough, Thorne."

" 'Tis enough," Thorne said, pulling her beneath him. "I have given you more of myself than I've given any other woman. I've been obsessed with you so long I don't even recall when I was not. Now I'm going to possess you."

He spread her legs and thrust himself into her. She fit him like a glove, a very tight glove, and he groaned with pleasure.

"Why must you be so obstinate?" Fiona gasped as she moved in rhythm to his long, hard strokes.

"Why must you demand love when you already own me?" Thorne shot back as his mind shut down and his body began to take over.

"Because without love, what we're doing now has no meaning," Fiona whispered as Thorne stoked her passion into searing flame.

Thorne did not hear her. His body had stiffened

in anticipation of his climax, and moments later he spewed forth his seed. His last stroke sent Fiona over the edge.

Thorne rose from bed with the dawn. Fiona awoke when she felt him stirring. She hadn't had time to talk to Thorne about Tyra and intended to do so now, before Ulm hurt Tyra again.

"Thorne, I must speak to you about Tyra."

Thorne lit a fresh candle and hunkered down beside the bed. "I thought you'd sleep longer. Can't this discussion wait? Has Tyra done something to anger you? There is nothing between us. She was my mistress long before I brought you here."

"Tyra has not angered me. I want to take her to Man with us. She is your thrall, is she not? 'Tis for you to decide what becomes of her."

Thorne's eyes narrowed suspiciously. "Why this concern for Tyra?"

"She is being mistreated by Ulm. Without your protection she has become prey to men who would abuse her."

Thorne shrugged. " 'Tis the Viking way. Some men are rough lovers. Tyra will learn how to please him soon enough."

Fiona flew into a rage. "Tyra is a defenseless woman! Why would you leave her here for Ulm to mistreat? You have never mistreated me. Not all men are alike, not even Vikings. She belongs to you. Are you going to leave your property behind for others to enjoy?"

"You are my property and I'm taking you," Thorne retorted.

Foolish man, Fiona thought. In the eyes of God they were man and wife, not man and slave. "How can I remain with a man who doesn't love me?"

"The same way I can wed a witch who stole my soul." He gave her a sly smile. "How badly do you want to bring Tyra with us to Man?"

"Very badly. She and your cousin Aren are smitten with one another."

"So that's the way of it. Very well, she can come with us."

Fiona's face lit up. "Oh, Thorne, thank you!"

"There is a provision, of course."

"Of course," Fiona said warily.

"I will do this for you only if you willingly remain with me."

"As your wife?"

Thorne was silent so long Fiona feared he wouldn't answer. At length he said, "Aye, if that is your wish. We will remarry. You're mine, Fiona. No other man shall have you. When I think of Rolo possessing you, I want to kill him."

"Men are strange creatures," Fiona mused. "I doubt I will ever understand their perverse natures. I suppose there is naught I can say to convince you that Rolo never bedded me, so I won't bother. There is no need for us to remarry, for I've never stopped being your wife. My Christian religion doesn't believe in divorce and makes no provisions for it."

Thorne tilted his head back and laughed. "Then we are in agreement. You will remain in my bed and I will try to forget that you were Rolo's whore."

Fiona sputtered in frustration as he rose abruptly, forestalling her angry retort. "I must go. Today we are sending Father to Valhalla. All is in readiness. We have but to set a torch to his bier and cast his dragon ship adrift. He will be carried to Valhalla with all his possessions. The next day we will set sail for the Isle of Man. All my property and wealth has been stored in the holds of my five ships in preparation for our journey. If we don't leave now we will be stranded here until next summer, and I don't suppose you'd care to spend the winter months confined to my chamber."

"I'll be ready," Fiona said. "Will you tell Tyra?"

"Aye, on my way through the hall." He strode away.

"Thorne."

He paused, then turned to face her. "Aye?"

"If you ever mention Rolo to me again I will do to you what I did to him."

"What is that?" he asked curiously.

She gave him a sweet smile. "Why, steal your manhood, of course."

Thick mist hung over the harbor as five dragon ships carrying 150 men and all of Thorne's worldly goods slipped their moorings and moved with the tide and winds out into the fjord. Fiona sat huddled beneath a canvas tent erected for her privacy aboard Thorne's ship, *Odin's Raven*. The air was damp and cool, and she pulled a fur pelt around her to ward off the chill. She was feeling unwell this morning and blamed it on the excitement of returning to her homeland.

It would be wonderful to see her father again, she thought wistfully. The poor man must be sick with worry about her. She hoped the men Thorne had left behind on Man had ruled kindly in Thorne's absence and prayed that her people were prospering under the Vikings.

As the day wore on, Fiona began to suffer bouts of seasickness. It was a surprising turn of events, for she hadn't been seasick on the journey from Man to Thorne's homeland. She forced herself to swallow the bile rising in her throat and concentrate instead on her uncertain future with a man who wanted her but refused to admit that he loved her. Deep in her heart, Fiona believed Thorne loved her. She sensed it with every breath she drew, felt it each time he made love to her. She wondered if Thorne realized that she loved him.

Three days out of Kaupang, Fiona sat dozing in the late summer sunshine as the dragon ship cut smoothly through the water. Suddenly she lost all sense of time and space as a vision began forming in the dark void that opened up before her. She saw hordes of neighboring Norsemen swarming down the hillside to attack Thorne's homestead, catching Thorolf unprepared and undermanned. It was like the previous attack, only worse. This time Thorne wasn't nearby to come to the rescue.

Fiona's scream brought Thorne rushing to her side as his crewmen stared at her in fear. Her eyes were glazed and she was shaking violently. He dropped to his knees and brought her against him. "What ails you? Odin's balls, you're scaring the men with your odd behavior."

Fiona regained her wits slowly. "We have to turn back."

"What? Are you mad? We're three days at sea, woman."

"Thorolf needs you. Raiders from the north have returned and your homestead is under siege. Heed me, Thorne, I would not lie to you about this."

Thorne regarded her solemnly. "Nay, you would not lie. Tell me what you saw."

" 'Tis as I described. I saw little else."

"You would have me turn back even after Thorolf threatened to lop off your head?"

"Thorolf is your brother. You love him well. You must save him."

Thorne couldn't pull his gaze away from her as he barked out an order. The men obeyed without hesitation. The man at the rudder slowly turned the ship back toward land while the change of course was relayed to the other ships. In a short time all five ships were scudding before the wind.

Three days later they docked at Kaupang. Ulm was on hand to meet them. The warrior's head was bandaged and he favored his right leg. He'd taken refuge in the village after the homestead had been sacked and had seen Thorne's ships returning.

"The homestead was attacked three days ago and your brother taken prisoner. He's being held for ransom," Ulm told Thorne.

"Word has already been dispatched to the king,"

he added, "but 'tis doubtful he will strip his coffers to pay the ransom."

"Where are the invaders now?" Thorne asked tersely. "Is the homestead under their control?"

"The house is gone," Ulm said. "Burnt to the ground. The enemy is camped upon the banks of the fjord, awaiting word on the ransom. They've already claimed the slaves and Thorolf's property, but 'twas not enough. They sent me to the village with their terms. The villagers have no wealth to part with and sent a messenger to the king."

"How many strong are the invading Norsemen?"

"At least one hundred and fifty warriors," Ulm said. "They slipped up the fjord under the cover of night and attacked at dawn while we were still abed. Rolo has already been notified. Even as we speak he is rallying friendly jarls to Thorolf's defense. They will come. Thorolf's land will not be enough for the invaders. They will surely want to seize and claim all the surrounding land."

"Rolo is our ally," Thorne allowed grudgingly. "Despite our past grievances, 'tis to our mutual advantage to join forces. He will come to our aid to save his lands."

Ulm sent a dark look in Fiona's direction. "How did you know to return? Did the witch warn you?"

" 'Tis enough that I am here," Thorne said. "Leave Fiona out of it. There's no time to waste. I'm taking my men to Rolo's homestead so we can plan Thorolf's rescue together. Are you well enough to join us?"

"Aye. As long as I have one good arm to wield my

weapon and one good leg to stand upon, I can fight."

Fiona thought she had left Rolo's hall forever, but here she was, in the same house in which Rolo had tried without success to ravish her. Rolo had not been pleased to see her when she'd arrived with Thorne. He gave her a sour look and all but ignored her. Fiona tried to make herself inconspicuous as she moved about the hall, helping the servants prepare food for the vast number of men who were expected to arrive to defend their land against invaders.

The initial meeting between Thorne and Rolo was cool, but Thorne set his enmity aside for his brother's sake as he and the neighboring jarls made plans for a surprise attack upon the enemy. Thorne suggested that they leave at midnight and attack before dawn. It was agreed that no ransom would be paid to the enemy. It was not their way. They would fight for Thorolf's freedom, and succeed because Thor was on their side. The strategy meeting broke up and the jarls left to inform their warriors of their plans.

Inside the crowded hall, Fiona settled down on a bench to await Thorne. She saw him enter the hall, then she saw Bretta, whom she'd managed to avoid thus far, sidle up to him and whisper something into his ear. Fiona fumed inwardly. Would the woman never give up? To his credit, Thorne brushed aside with an impatient gesture the woman who had tried to kill him. Then he spied Fiona and headed in her direction.

"All is in readiness," Thorne said, dropping down beside her on the bench. "I don't like the idea of leaving you here with Bretta but I'm confident you can hold your own against her. Just remember," he said, bringing her up against him, "you belong to me. I've made arrangements with Aren to take you back to Man should I perish in battle. I won't leave you here for Rolo to enjoy."

He searched her face. "Have your visions forecast my death, Fiona?"

Fiona shook her head. "I have seen naught save what I told you. I can't force a vision. They come on their own and are rarely about myself."

He grasped her hand and pulled her from the bench. "Come outside with me. I wish a private moment with you before I leave to fight the Danes."

Fiona could feel Bretta's eyes boring into her back as she and Thorne left the hall hand in hand. They walked past snoring men to an orchard a short distance from the house. Thorne halted, leaned against a tree and fit Fiona into his arms.

"What did you wish to talk about?" Fiona asked. Moonlight reflected in the turbulent blue pools of desire his eyes had become as she searched his face.

"Thorne, I—" Her words ended in a gurgle of surprise when his mouth claimed hers in a wild and tempestuous kiss. She felt his shaft stir and swell against her. She moaned against his lips as his hands explored her body, moving sensuously over her breasts, hips and thighs.

He was driving her mad; her flesh burned, her heart pounded. Then his hands were cupping her bottom, lifting her against him. "Put your legs around my waist," he urged hoarsely as he impatiently shoved her tunic up around her waist. "I want you now. Battle lust fills my veins and you are the only woman who can appease it."

Fiona wound her arms around his neck as he lifted his own tunic and meshed their bodies together. "Are you sure, Thorne?" she asked. "Am I the only woman who can assuage your need? Did Bretta not offer herself to you tonight?"

He held her steady and thrust into her tight sheath, groaning from the pleasure she never failed to give him. "Bretta tried to kill me; I want nothing to do with her. You are my obsession, Fiona; no other woman appeals to me. When you cast your spell upon me, little did you know how effectively it would work."

He began to move slowly, thrusting and withdrawing, shifting her body to meet his strokes, stretching and filling her with his massive erection as he seized her mouth, kissing her breathless. Then she was soaring, her body trembling as he plunged and withdrew, driving her to a frenzy of pleasure so intense she thought she would die of it. He broke off the kiss, burying his head between her breasts as she climaxed around him. Then he unleashed the fury of his own passion, pounding relentlessly against her, stiffening and crying out her name as ecstasy claimed him.

Fiona clung to him with a desperation born of fear. What if Thorne should fall in battle? What if he should die? How would she go on without him? She searched for a vision, but it was denied her. What good was her gift if she couldn't use it at will? She mewled in protest when Thorne set her on her feet and settled her tunic down over her hips.

" 'Tis almost time to leave," Thorne said, squinting up at the position of the moon in the sky.

"Be careful, Thorne, I beg you."

Thorne gave her a mocking smile. "Do you care so much? Or have you decided I'm a better lover than Rolo?"

"The Devil take you! I don't know why I care so much," Fiona spat disgustedly. "You're arrogant, pig-headed and stubborn beyond belief. Mayhap I feel pity for a man so lacking in wit and wisdom. Or perhaps 'tis merely dislike I feel."

He grasped her shoulders and stared deeply into the violet pools of her eyes. "The truth, Fiona. Tell me the truth. Do you care what happens to me?"

She dragged in a shuddering breath. "Aye. I care. We are meant to be together whether you believe it or not. You are the only man who has ever . . . bedded me." She was going to say *touched* instead of *bedded*, but technically that wouldn't be the truth. Rolo had touched her and she'd hated it.

Thorne frowned. "I never asked for your love. I wouldn't know what to do with it. I don't know why, but your caring matters to me. It never mattered before what a woman thought, but for some unexplained reason it pleases me to know that you care."

Fiona gave him a blissful smile. "Really?"

"Truly. I'm beginning to enjoy being bewitched."

"Does that mean you believe I was never Rolo's mistress?"

"Leave well enough alone, Fiona. Don't ask questions to which you'll not like the answers. I still want you; let that be sufficient. I don't care if you're a witch. When I'm inside you, nothing matters but loving you and making you mine. The thought of another man having you brings on a violence I can't control."

"You love me, Thorne," Fiona said complacently. "One day, I vow, you'll admit it. Brann said that day would come, and I suppose I'll just have to be a little more patient. Come back to me soon, Viking."

Rising to her tiptoes, she planted a kiss on his lips. Then she spun on her heel and fled back to the hall.

Thorne didn't try to stop her. He touched his lips with the callused pad of his thumb and smiled.

Chapter Twelve

"I suppose you're feeling quite smug right now."

Fiona started violently. She should have expected Bretta to be waiting for her to return to the hall.

"I don't know what you're talking about," Fiona retorted.

"If not for your interference I'd still be Thorne's betrothed. Our marriage would be taking place very soon."

"You tried to kill Thorne," Fiona spat.

" 'Twas a mistake," Bretta argued. "I never intended to kill Thorne. I was angry at him for caring so little for me, and for giving me to his brother. I meant only to make him mildly ill."

Fiona knew better, but decided to hold her tongue as long as she was a guest in Bretta's home, vowing to eat and drink nothing that she hadn't prepared or served herself. And to remain vigilant. She hated being here but had to make the best of it until Thorne returned for her.

Fiona was grateful for Tyra's presence. Bretta had put the slave to work immediately, but it was still comforting to see a friendly face in the crowd. Fiona recalled with a shudder how she'd been subjected to Rolo's crude pawing in this very house. But God had been kind. Thorne had lived, and Rolo had been rendered impotent by her herbal concoctions. She shook her head as if to rid it of unpleasant thoughts and turned her mind to prayer.

Thorne and the combined Viking forces crept through the forest toward the enemy camp. Thus far they had encountered four sentries, and all were dispatched with speed and finesse. The invaders were sleeping. Thorne could see them stretched out on the ground, wrapped in their fur pelts, their weapons lying within reach. Their numbers were daunting, but Thorne had great faith in the strength of his Viking warriors.

"Do you see Thorolf?" Rolo whispered as he knelt beside Thorne on the mossy ground.

Thorne's gaze made a thorough sweep of the campsite. He spotted two guards walking along the perimeter of the camp but he failed to locate his brother.

"Nay. 'Tis too dark to see beyond the small campfire."

"Perhaps they took him aboard one of their longships," Rolo offered.

"Aye," Thorne agreed. "I'll take ten men and circle around to the fjord. If Thorolf is on one of their ships, I'll find him. Can you and the others handle things here?"

Beneath his droopy mustache, Rolo's lips flattened in a parody of a smile. "The invaders will rue the day they set foot upon our land. Find your brother, Thorne. I'll take care of things here."

Thorne nodded and silently disappeared into the darkness to select the men who would accompany him. He chose Ulm and Aren and several others from among his own warriors. They circled around the sleeping Norsemen and were headed toward the fjord when sounds of a fierce battle broke out behind them. Thorne spared but a glance back at the ensuing battle, concentrating instead on finding and freeing Thorolf.

Thorne saw four dragon ships bobbing in the surf and counted about twenty men left behind to protect the ships. Thorne considered his own ten warriors an even match for the twenty invaders.

Hoisting Blood-drinker in one hand and his battleaxe in the other, Thorne bellowed a Viking war cry and advanced toward the enemy, wielding his weapons with equal dexterity. The Norse raiders heard the cry and advanced to meet the Viking savages. The battle was fierce and bloody. Skulls were split and flesh skewered. Arms and legs were severed with a single stroke of a sword.

Aren fought at Thorne's back; Ulm was at his side. Aren sustained a minor head wound but kept on slashing, ignoring the blood dripping from his wound. Ulm deflected a lethal blow and dealt a killing thrust of his own. Thorne fought like a berserker, as relentless as his name implied. Aren dashed blood from his eyes, momentarily blinded to the danger threatening Thorne's back. With a triumphant cry, the man thrust his sword past Aren's guard and into Thorne's unprotected back.

Pain and surprise registered on Thorne's blood-splattered features as he swung his sword around and neatly gutted his attacker. It was his last act before he slid to his knees and fell flat on his face.

Ulm saw Thorne fall and gave a bellow of rage as he rallied the surviving men to even greater effort. The raiders retreated beneath the renewed onslaught but were given no quarter as they were slain to the last man by the fierce Viking warriors. Thorne saw nothing of the enemy's defeat as he lay on the ground, his lifeblood draining from his body.

" 'Tis done, Thorne," Ulm said as he knelt in the soft dirt beside Thorne. "They are all dead."

"Thorolf?" Thorne gasped.

"Aren is searching the ships. If he's there, we'll find him."

Aren found Thorolf bound and gagged, lying in the stern of the flagship. He was weak from being starved and beaten, but except for a wound on his thigh that was already crusted over, he appeared unhurt.

"How can you be here? I thought you went with Thorne," Thorolf said when Aren removed his gag.

"We were three days at sea when we turned back," Aren said, helping Thorolf to his feet.

"What made you return?"

"Fiona warned us. She saw Norse invaders attacking the homestead and urged Thorne to turn back. Ulm met us in the village and told us what had happened."

"There are Norsemen camped nearby," Thorolf warned. "It will take a Viking army to defeat them. Where's Thorne?"

"Rolo and neighboring jarls joined forces with Thorne. They're waging a battle against the raiders even as we speak. Thorne is gravely wounded and is in danger of dying if we don't get him help. Can you walk?"

"Aye. My wound isn't serious. What about you? There's blood all over your face."

" 'Tis nothing. It's Thorne I'm worried about."

Thorolf spotted Thorne immediately. He was lying on the ground, surrounded by Ulm and those of his men who had survived the battle. Thorolf pushed his way through to his brother's side. He dropped to one knee, wincing when he saw the enormous amount of blood pooled beneath Thorne's body. Moments later, Rolo and the rest of the Vikings came crashing through the forest, their jubilant cries attesting to their victory.

Thorne was still conscious, though fading fast. He saw Thorolf bending over him and forced a grin, which quickly turned into a grimace of pain. "I'm glad we arrived in time," he gasped from between gritted teeth. "Rolo and the others are—"

Rolo appeared at Thorolf's side. "The surviving raiders have been driven away."

"Hang on," Thorolf said. "We'll find a healer to treat you."

"Fiona," Thorne whispered with his remaining breath. Fiona was the only person with the knowledge to save him.

"Make a litter," Thorolf ordered. "We'll take my brother home."

"Your homestead is gone," Rolo reminded him. "Take him to my hall. Fiona and Bretta can tend him."

Thorolf spit out an oath. "I like not the idea of entrusting my brother's life to a witch and a murderess."

"You have no choice," Rolo said, annoyed. "Fiona is a healer. She has knowledge of herbs and medicines that can save Thorne's life. And Bretta regrets her rash act. She never intended to kill Thorne."

"Very well," Thorolf allowed grudgingly.

"Cast aside your doubts. Your brother is welcome to Fiona. I'm inclined to concur with your estimation of her. She is a witch."

A litter was made and the Vikings began the slow journey to Rolo's hall. Thorne's wound was packed and bound to prevent further bleeding, but he was so deathly pale few believed he would survive the journey.

Fiona knew the exact moment Thorne was struck down. She felt an excruciating pain pierce her back and cried out, falling to her knees and wailing in despair as she hugged her arms about her body and rocked to and fro.

Tyra saw her and came running to her aid. "Fiona, what happened? Are you ill?" She attempted to help Fiona to her feet.

Fiona brushed Tyra's hands aside as she wove back and forth, her pain fierce and overwhelming. "Thorne. Something has happened to Thorne. Oh God, he's dead." She lifted her tear-stained face. "Nay, not dead, but close. Too close."

"You don't know that," Tyra said. "Sit down. I'll fetch you some ale. You're so pale it frightens me."

Fiona allowed Tyra to help her to her feet and settle her on a nearby bench. Then the slave hurried off to fetch ale.

"What did you see this time, witch?" Bretta asked with scathing disdain.

"There are many wounded," Fiona said, ignoring Bretta's sarcasm. She searched beneath the bench for her medicine chest, which she had carried with her from Thorne's dragon ship, and breathed a sigh of relief when she found it with ease. "Thorne will need a chamber to himself. I can treat the others in the hall."

"What in Odin's name are you talking about?" Bretta asked. "Old Matilda has always treated our wounded; you needn't trouble yourself."

"I will treat Thorne myself," Fiona insisted.

Bretta frowned. "What makes you think Thorne is among the wounded?"

Fiona shuddered and closed her eyes. "I know."

Bretta slowly backed away, her face tense with fear. Then she turned and ran.

* * *

The wounded arrived the next morning. Fiona was shaken but in control of herself when she ran out to greet them. She took one look at Thorne's white face and knew there was no time to lose.

"A chamber has been prepared for Thorne," she said, directing the litter bearers to an empty bed-chamber. "Handle him gently."

"There's nothing you can do for him," Thorolf said harshly. "Thorne has neither moved nor spoken since we began our journey back."

"How could this have happened?" Fiona rounded on him. "Thorne is a magnificent fighter. He's too canny to be struck down by his enemy."

"No man is immortal," Thorolf responded. "Thorne will die a warrior's death, just as he would want it. Cut down in battle, a sword in one hand and a battleaxe in the other. 'Tis a valiant way to die."

Fiona raised herself on her tiptoes and faced Thorolf squarely. "Do not speak as if Thorne is already dead. I will not allow him to die, do you hear me? See to your other wounded; I will take care of Thorne." Whirling on her heel, she followed the litter-bearers into Thorne's chamber.

Thorne made no sound as he was placed on the bed on his stomach. Fiona borrowed a knife and skillfully cut his blood-soaked clothing from his body. Tyra appeared with a basin of hot water and clean rags. Fiona rummaged in her medicine chest, found the packet of herbs she sought and sprinkled them in the water. She waited a few minutes for the herbs to steep, then used the mixture to clean and disinfect Thorne's wound.

"You're not going to die, Viking," she whispered in his ear as she washed away blood and grime. She shuddered in dismay when she pressed lightly on his torn flesh and saw pus seeping from the ugly wound.

Fiona worked feverishly, pressing out all the pus and using various herbs to disinfect and cleanse. Then she sprinkled the open wound with dill seeds to hasten the healing process. In a day or two, God willing, after all the infection was gone, she'd sew the torn edges of flesh together. Meanwhile, she covered it with a clean cloth slathered with marigold salve and prayed for Thorne's recovery.

The following day produced little improvement in Thorne's condition. He had lost a great deal of blood, and Fiona decided he needed something to replenish the loss. She sent Tyra out to find yarrow and brewed a tea known to revive the spirit. She fed Thorne small doses until he'd swallowed enough to satisfy her.

When fever raged through his body, she demanded that leaves and bark from the willow tree be brought to her so she could extract the juice and give it to Thorne to ease his fever and the aches accompanying it.

Two days later the dill seeds and marigold salve had worked their magic upon Thorne. Miraculously, the infection was gone and the wound was pink and clean. With meticulous care Fiona sewed together the gaping edges. Thorne would now have another scar to add to his vast collection. But even though she had used all the skill and knowledge available to her, Thorne remained unconscious.

When Fiona had done all she could, she left Tyra to watch over Thorne and went to the hall to treat the other wounded. Most had already been tended by Matilda, an old crone with limited skills in healing who probably did more harm than good. Fiona did what she could to undo the harm Matilda had done, then returned to Thorne's side, so exhausted that she fell asleep sitting on a bench beside his pallet.

Fiona awoke with a start when Thorolf entered the chamber. "I'm leaving with Rolo to attend the *althing*," he told Fiona as he regarded Thorne's still features with sadness.

"You should at least wait until Thorne awakens," Fiona said with a hint of censure.

" 'Tis unlikely he'll awaken," Thorolf said, "but I'll return after the *althing* to give Thorne a proper sendoff to Valhalla. He was a dead man before we left the battlefield. You are but prolonging his journey to Valhalla with your witchcraft." He made an impatient gesture with his hand. "Leave me alone with my brother. I wish to bid him good-bye in private."

Fiona waited outside the door while Thorolf spoke in his own language to Thorne. He didn't stay long. Moments later he departed without a word or a glance at Fiona.

A short time later Bretta entered the sickroom, wrinkling her nose in distaste at the sight of the bloody bandages that Fiona had just changed.

"Will he live?" Fiona asked. "Thorolf doesn't seem to think so. Even Rolo expects Thorne to die. My brother left with Thorolf to attend the *althing*. If not for you, I'd be marrying Thorne at the *althing*. Instead, Rolo must now find a new husband for me."

Fiona opened her mouth to make a scathing reply but was distracted by Thorne's moan. She hurried to his side, her brow furrowed with concern. The single moan had been the first sound to escape Thorne's lips since he'd arrived.

"Can you hear me, Thorne? 'Tis time to wake up."

"You're wasting your time," Bretta said as she moved regally toward the door.

Exhausted, worried, and angry at Bretta's flippant manner, Fiona lost control of her temper.

"You're a vindictive bitch, Bretta. You care for no one but yourself, and when things don't go according to your wishes, you use devious methods to get revenge. You have no conscience. You care not whether Thorne lives or dies."

"Why should *you* care?" Bretta taunted. "Thorne made you his slave, then his whore. He cares not what happens to you. He was already becoming bored with you. Everyone knows 'tis your witchcraft that keeps him bound to you."

Fiona's face turned red with rage; veins bulged at her temples. She was so angry she was shaking. Suddenly the room began to spin, taking Fiona with it. Dizziness and nausea swirled around her as she made a slow spiral to the floor.

Bretta stared at Fiona's prone form dispassionately. Then she called Tyra to see to her mistress.

"Fiona needs rest," Tyra declared, fanning Fiona's face with her apron. "In a real bed. She's exhausted herself trying to save Thorne's life."

"Take her to Rolo's chamber," Bretta said, staring at Fiona oddly. Her mind worked furiously as she considered various reasons for Fiona's sudden weakness. If her suspicions proved correct, she had already thought of a way to use Fiona's condition to her advantage. "I'll send Matilda to tend her."

"I will take care of my mistress," Tyra said pugnaciously. She didn't want that dirty old woman touching Fiona.

"Nay, Matilda is knowledgeable in these things. Stay with Fiona. I'll send someone to carry her to Rolo's chamber."

Tyra was forced to leave the chamber while the old crone examined Fiona. Tyra knew Fiona wouldn't allow the woman to touch her were she conscious, but Fiona was blissfully unaware of the brief but invasive examination performed by Matilda. When the old woman left, Tyra awakened Fiona by waving a burnt feather beneath her nose.

Bretta summoned Matilda to her chamber. When the old woman joined her, Bretta sent her an inquiring glance.

"She's breeding," Matilda said sagely.

"Are you certain?"

"Aye. Her womb is quickening with child."

"You may go, Matilda," Bretta said dismissively.

Once the old crone left, Bretta remained in her chamber, pondering. She wondered to whom the babe belonged. Did Fiona even know? Bretta believed that since Fiona had been intimate with both Rolo and Thorne she couldn't possibly know who had sired her child. Her lips parted in an ugly sneer. She'd just been given a valuable piece of information and she intended to use it wisely.

Fiona wrinkled her nose and turned her head away from the noxious scent of burnt feathers. "Wake up, Fiona," Tyra urged anxiously.

Fiona's eyelids fluttered. "What happened?"

"You fainted."

Fiona frowned when she realized she was in Rolo's bed. She shuddered in revulsion. "What am I doing here?"

"Bretta had you carried to Rolo's chamber. She ordered me away and sent Matilda to examine you."

"Oh, God." Fiona couldn't suppress a groan when she thought of the old crone's hands upon her body.

A short time later Bretta walked into the chamber, her skirts swishing around her ankles. "Leave us," she ordered Tyra. "I wish to speak to Fiona in private."

Tyra looked at Fiona, saw her slight nod, and reluctantly left the room.

"Do you know why you fainted?" Bretta asked harshly.

"I have a pretty fair idea," Fiona said evenly.

"Whose child is it?"

Bretta's brash question rendered Fiona speechless.

"You were whore to both Thorne and Rolo,"

Bretta claimed. "I know for a fact that Rolo bedded you regularly while you were here. The servants confirmed it and so has Rolo. I wonder how Thorne will take the news, should he live."

Fiona jerked upright, then fell back against the pillow as her head spun dizzily.

"Stay in bed," Bretta ordered imperiously. "Tyra can see to Thorne until you're able to return to the sickroom."

Fiona had no choice in the matter. She was too weak and exhausted to leave the bed. She lay back with a sigh and closed her eyes. After a good night's sleep she'd be better able to cope with Bretta's devious machinations. The woman was acting far too complacent to trust.

Thorne opened his eyes to the light of day. He was in too much pain to be in Valhalla, so he knew he still lived. His mouth was bone dry and tasted like sin. He saw Tyra dozing on a bench nearby and opened his mouth to ask for a mug of ale. All he could manage was a growl that sounded more animal than human. But it was enough to alert Tyra, who rushed to his side and held a mug to his lips while he drank thirstily.

"So, he lives after all," Bretta said as she slipped inside the chamber and approached the bed. "I thought I heard a commotion in here. You may leave, Tyra. I can handle things now. After all," she lied smoothly, "my expert care has brought Thorne from the brink of death."

"But—" Tyra protested.

"Go," Bretta ordered, pushing Tyra from the room.

Once Tyra left, Bretta approached Thorne with an ingratiating smile on her face. "Praise Odin you've awakened," she said, smoothing a lock of hair from Thorne's forehead. "I've been terribly worried."

"You took care of me?" Thorne croaked. His mind was still fuzzy from his illness, otherwise he would have known Bretta possessed no healing skills.

"Aye," Bretta said. "I was the only one who believed you would live. Thorolf had already planned your entrance into Valhalla. What can I get for you, Thorne? I want to make amends for all the grief I've caused you. Can you ever forgive me?"

Thorne frowned. He couldn't think straight, nor could he believe Bretta had nursed him during his darkest hours. Where was Fiona? Had she refused to use her skills on him? He wished his memory was not so vague.

"Fiona," he finally managed to gasp out.

Bretta's smile became brittle. "Fiona is ill."

"Ill? How . . . ? Why . . . ?"

"She's expecting Rolo's child," Bretta said in a gloating voice.

Thorne thought he'd heard wrong. Had Bretta said that Fiona carried Rolo's child? "Nay . . ." His eyes closed and he drifted off to sleep.

"Oh, aye, Thorne the Relentless," Bretta said with slow relish. "I know you. You are too proud to accept another man's child. What will you do now, my arrogant Viking?" Her laughter drifted over the sleeping man like a noxious cloud.

Fiona rushed into Thorne's chamber minutes after Bretta's departure. Tyra had informed her that Thorne had awakened, and she pushed her exhausted body out of bed to see for herself. Unfortunately, he had fallen back to sleep by the time she'd arrived. But Fiona wasn't about to leave his side this time. While she waited for him to awaken again, she fetched hot water and washed and shaved him. When she finished, she sank down on the bench to rest. Thorne opened his eyes a short time later, his gaze finding her immediately.

"What are you doing here?" he gasped in a voice rusty with disuse.

His accusatory tone startled her. "You're welcome," she said sweetly. "If not for my healing skills, you'd be feasting in your Valhalla now."

Thorne looked thoroughly confused. "Bretta said you were too ill to care for me. She led me to believe that her skills saved my life."

"You're addled if you believed her," Fiona scoffed. "Does Bretta look like a healer? She didn't even come into the sickroom to inquire about your health until yesterday."

The truth of Fiona's words hit him forcefully. He had indeed been addled to think that Bretta possessed healing skills. That he lived now was due entirely to Fiona and her vast knowledge of healing. What else had Bretta lied about?

"Do you think you could eat something?" Fiona asked, her gaze roaming over his gaunt frame. "I've been spooning liquids down your throat, but little food has passed your lips."

"I could eat a horse," Thorne said, meaning it.

"We'll start with broth and bread and see how well you keep that down." She turned to leave.

"Fiona, wait."

She turned back expectantly. "Aye?"

He searched her face, noting her paleness and pinched features. "Bretta said you were ill."

Fiona flushed and looked away. " 'Tis naught." She intended to tell him about the babe, but not until he was in full control of his senses.

Thorne's gaze slid down her body, lingering on her flat stomach. "Are you carrying a babe?"

Fiona went still. What had Bretta told him? No one but Bretta could have known such a thing. Her chin tilted defiantly. "Aye."

"Am I right in assuming the child belongs to Rolo?"

Fiona sucked in a startled gasp. Bretta had already spread her poison, she reflected bitterly. How could Thorne believe Bretta's lies? Thorne didn't deserve an answer and she wasn't about to give him one. Perhaps if she ignored him, he'd realize how foolishly he was behaving.

"I'll return shortly with your broth," she said curtly.

"Aren't you going to answer my question? Whose child are you carrying?"

"Yours."

"She lies!" Bretta entered the chamber in time to hear Fiona's answer to Thorne's question. "Fiona was Rolo's whore. The child belongs to my brother. Rolo told me himself that he bedded Fiona, and he wouldn't lie to me."

Thorne closed his eyes to escape the pain of Bretta's words. He was fair-minded enough to realize that Fiona had had no choice in the matter, but still it hurt. She'd been given to Rolo against her will to serve him in bed. What really hurt were Fiona's lies. Why did she continue to deny she'd been Rolo's leman? Despite the knowledge that she'd taken Rolo inside her body, he still wanted her. Neither pride, nor disgust, nor anger had changed his need for her. He'd been truly bewitched. It was going to take magic even stronger than Fiona's to break the spell she'd woven around his heart.

"Bretta's lies are dipped in poison," Fiona charged. "Believe her if you want, Viking, I no longer care. Just grant me one boon. Take me home to bear my child."

"I'm in no condition to take you anywhere," Thorne said sourly. "I know you saved my life. For that I thank you."

Fiona shrugged. " 'Tis what I do best."

Thorne searched her face, recognizing her exhaustion and feeling guilt for being the cause of it. "Let someone else get my food. Go to bed. You look ready to drop and I need to think. My mind's been inactive too long."

"Very well," Fiona said, heaving a sigh. "Brann said it wouldn't be easy, but I never realized how difficult it would actually be."

"What is difficult?" Bretta demanded to know.

"Making Thorne realize he loves me," Fiona said as she flounced from the chamber.

" 'Tis witchcraft!" Bretta accused, drawing her skirts away as Fiona strode past her. "She has cast a love spell upon you."

"Aye," Thorne mumbled with weary resignation. " 'Tis exactly what she has done."

Chapter Thirteen

Thorne's recovery began the day he awakened from his stupor. Each day was an improvement over the last. Fiona continued to treat his injury despite his sullen and uncommunicative mood. Fiona knew Thorne's dark temperment was due to his belief that she had lied about sharing Rolo's bed. Unfortunately, her refusal to discuss it with him hadn't improved his disposition. She'd already said all she was going to say on the subject. The stubborn man was going to have to work it out for himself.

Meanwhile, Fiona wallowed in misery. The father of her child was acting like a jealous fool, and his former betrothed was trying to undermine her at every turn. Not a day went by without Bretta reminding Thorne that Fiona had been Rolo's mistress and claiming that Fiona couldn't possibly know which man had sired her child. Complicating matters was the morning sickness plaguing Fiona. Her stomach simply refused to accept food.

Fiona was surprised one morning when she went into Thorne's chamber to change his bandage and found him standing beside the bed, testing his legs.

"You shouldn't be out of bed yet," she admonished.

Thorne sent her a fulminating look. "I'm not a weakling. It won't be long before I'll be practicing with battleaxe and sword."

"Men," Fiona said, exasperated. "Do they think of naught but fighting?"

"We think of other things," Thorne said, sending her a guarded look. "You should be well acquainted with men's needs and desires by now."

"Aye," Fiona agreed evenly, "you taught me well, Viking."

His gaze lingered on her lips, then lowered to settle on her flat stomach. "How fares the babe?"

"Do you care?"

"He could be mine, you know."

"Aye, he certainly could be yours," Fiona agreed cheerfully.

"You look pale. Are you eating well? Is Bretta plaguing you? You're much too thin for a woman breeding a babe."

Fiona stifled a smile. Thorne could pretend all he wanted. He *did* care about her. He was just too obstinate to admit it and too pig-headed to believe that Rolo hadn't bedded her.

"I'm well, except for nearly constant nausea. As

for Bretta, I try not to let her upset me."

"Unfortunately, we're stuck here for a while. I won't be able to attempt a long sea voyage yet, and with winter coming on 'twould be unwise to begin one. We've nowhere to go right now. Thorolf will probably rebuild the homestead, but he won't have you in his hall."

"Are you certain we cannot travel before winter? I want to have my babe at home."

" 'Twould be difficult to find men willing to undertake a long voyage this time of year," Thorne informed her. "We could be blown off course. Any manner of things could go awry." His mouth flattened. "Perhaps you should ask Rolo if he wants to risk his child's life on an ocean voyage."

Fiona paled. Thorne's words were like a blow to the gut. She clasped her hand over her mouth and ran from the chamber. She just made it through the hall and into the lavatory, where she spewed out her breakfast. When she turned to leave, she found Thorne standing behind her, offering her a cup of water. She took it gratefully and rinsed out her mouth several times.

"How long will this continue?" Thorne demanded to know.

"Not long," Fiona said. " 'Twill pass eventually." She tried to move past him but he planted himself solidly in front of her.

"Where are you going?"

"Anywhere you're not."

"Come back to my chamber." He seemed to stagger a bit, and Fiona realized he wasn't as strong as he would like everyone to believe. "I want to speak to you."

"You've already said more than I wish to hear, but I will help you back to your chamber. You've been active enough for your first day out of bed. Lean on me."

Thorne stifled a grin. "You can't begin to hold my weight upon your shoulders. I can make it on my own."

To demonstrate his returning strength, he grasped her arm and literally dragged her into his chamber.

"I may as well change your bandage and remove the stitches while I'm here," Fiona said crisply. "Take off your tunic."

Thorne stripped off his tunic. He wore nothing underneath, neither a cloth wound around his loins nor braies. And he was magnificent. Her gaze slid the length of his body, still powerful despite his injury and lack of exercise. His waist was narrow for such a big man, and his muscular thighs and calves bulged with corded tendons. Her eyes settled on his fully distended manhood and her gaze flew upward.

"What did you expect when you look at me like that?" Thorne asked when he noted her flaming cheeks.

"How is it possible? Just days ago you lay near death."

"I have amazing recuperative powers. Either that or your magic has empowered me." He reached for her.

Fiona backed away. "Nay. You're not well enough. Your back—"

"I don't make love with my back. I want you, Fiona. Nothing has changed. Not the fact that Rolo may be the father of your child nor the knowledge that you lied to me about sharing Rolo's bed. I had you first; nothing will change that."

"I don't want *you*, Viking," Fiona insisted. "I have never lied in my life. Turn around so I can get to your wound."

Thorne spit out a curse and presented his back. He didn't flinch once while Fiona meticulously removed the stitches and covered the wound with a clean bandage.

"You can put on your tunic now," she ordered crisply.

He spun about and reached for her. Fiona neatly slipped from his grasp. "You are my wife," he reminded her. " 'Twas you who insisted we were still wed according to Christian law."

"Why would you still want me when you believe I'm carrying another man's child?"

Thorne's expression grew fierce, as if he was displeased with his answer. " 'Tis insanity. I can't help myself. Wanting you is akin to breathing, I can't seem to do without either."

Fiona exhaled sharply. The Viking never ceased to amaze her. With one breath he all but admitted his love for her, and with another he accused her of lying. She'd been infinitely patient with him, but if he didn't change his ways soon, she was going to challenge Fate and try to forget that Thorne the Relentless was her soul mate.

"I have duties," Fiona said, ducking out the door before he could make another grab for her. "I'll accept your apology when you come to your senses."

"For what do I need to apologize?" Thorne called after her.

"For being your usual intractable self," she returned as she closed the door behind her.

Thorne pulled on his tunic and sank down onto his bed. He had used the last of his reserves but hadn't wanted to admit it to Fiona. It was difficult to acknowledge weakness when he'd been a strong man all his life. He smiled to himself. Somehow he would have dredged up the energy to bed Fiona had she allowed it. Odin's balls, but she was beautiful, Thorne thought. The shadows beneath her eyes and hollows in her cheeks enhanced rather than detracted from her fragile beauty. Her violet eyes would haunt him into eternity. Everything about Fiona was pure enchantment.

Thorne wondered how she would look with her belly round with child. Doubtless her cheeks would fill out as well and her face would glow with the special beauty granted to expectant mothers. That thought gave him pause. Would the child look like Rolo? he wondered. If Fiona would but admit she had been Rolo's mistress, he could forgive her. And should the babe look like Rolo or Bretta, he could always give it to Rolo to raise.

He almost laughed aloud at such a ludicrous idea. Fiona would never give up any child of hers no matter who the father. He pictured Fiona holding the babe to her breast and was shocked at the jolt of longing he felt. Then the image faded, replaced by a vision of Rolo suckling at Fiona's ample breast, making her cry out in ecstasy. Rage festered within him and there was nothing he could do to ease it. He still wanted Fiona. Witch. Enchantress. Rolo's leman. It mattered not. Fiona was his. The old wizard Brann had told him so.

Fiona wanted him to love her.

Could he? Did he have the ability to love a woman who might or might not carry another man's child? He truly didn't know. But he would have no problem bedding the bewitching wench.

Thorne continued to gain strength. He saw little of Fiona except when they met in passing, or when she came to his chamber to change his bandage. One morning he was still abed when Bretta slipped into his chamber.

"Are you awake, Thorne?"

"Aye."

"We really haven't had a chance to talk in private since you've regained much of your strength. That witch is always about, listening to every word we say."

"I didn't know we had anything to discuss," Thorne said. "I'm grateful to you and Rolo for the roof over my head, but I can't forget that you once tried to kill me and almost succeeded."

Bretta fell on her knees beside the bed. "I was out of my mind with jealousy. I wanted *you* for a husband, not Thorolf. Then you brought that witch home and cast me aside. I swear I never wanted you dead."

"You fed me poison," Thorne said harshly.

"I know nothing of drugs. It was a mistake. I had no idea so small a dosage could kill a man. You insulted me as a woman when you gave me to Thorolf. I merely wanted to punish you, to make you sick, but never to kill you. You're a strong man, Thorne, I never expected you to be so ill. Can you ever forgive me?"

Thorne sighed wearily. "Forget it, Bretta. I'm alive. You have generously offered your hospitality, and for that reason I forgive you, but I will never trust you again."

"I swear I would do nothing to harm you ever again," Bretta said heatedly. "Can we not return to where we were before Fiona? I want to be your wife, Thorne."

"I already have a wife."

Bretta gave a snort of laughter. " 'Tis not like you to take another man's leavings. Will you feel the same when you see Fiona swollen with Rolo's child?"

"The babe could be mine."

"True," Bretta agreed, "but I doubt it. Fiona didn't quicken with child until after Rolo finished with her. Did you ever wonder why Rolo gave her up so easily?"

"Rolo didn't want to fight me," Thorne guessed.

"Rolo not want to fight?" Bretta hooted in derision. "Rolo never turns down a good battle. Nay,

Thorne, Rolo tired of Fiona. The servants said he bedded her whenever the urge came upon him, night or day. Rolo's previous whores told me he is not a gentle lover. But none heard Fiona complain. Fiona liked Rolo's roughness, that's why she didn't protest when he bedded her. If you do not believe me, ask the servants. Rolo hinted that Fiona tried to practice black magic on him. I believe he wanted to be rid of her because he feared her spells."

"What did Fiona do?" Thorne questioned. "Did she bewitch him? Enchant him?"

Bretta shrugged. "Rolo did not say. Sell her to a slave trader now, Thorne, before bad things happen again. Your father is dead and your homestead destroyed, all because of Fiona. She brings naught but disaster and death."

Bretta's words made too much sense. Almost everything she said was the truth, or close to it. "I cannot sell the woman who may be carrying my child."

"You will never know for sure," Bretta said with sly innuendo. "You don't need Fiona." She leaned down, touching his mouth with hers, running the tip of her tongue along the seam of his lips in a teasing manner.

Thorne went still as she slid her body atop his. He didn't want Bretta but he was willing to find out if she could arouse him to the same fever pitch he attained with Fiona. When Bretta's tongue demanded entrance, his lips parted to accept her offering. His hands began to roam her body, mutely comparing it with Fiona's gentle curves.

Bretta was a tall, raw-boned woman, full-busted and generously endowed. She was a robust blonde beauty, the kind of woman every Viking warrior admired. She would bear children with ease and be willing to fight at his side should the need arise. But she was not a raven-haired, violet-eyed witch named Fiona.

Bretta reached down between their bodies to grasp his staff. Thorne moaned as he thickened and filled her hand. He might not want Bretta but he was a man. A man who hadn't had a woman in a very long time. His body reacted without volition, and Bretta was smart enough to take advantage of his forced arousal.

"You don't have to do anything," she whispered into his ear. "Let me do it for you." She lifted the hem of her tunic and pressed herself against his loins.

Thorne felt the heat and wetness of her but could summon none of the excitement or enthusiasm he experienced with Fiona. It was as if Fiona had bound him to her with a magic thread of enchantment, one that would endure forever.

"Help me raise your tunic," Bretta panted into his ear. "I want to present you with my virginity."

Before Thorne could reply that he didn't want her virginity, didn't want her at all, he saw Fiona standing in the doorway, her eyes round and despairing.

Thorne bellowed a curse as he lifted Bretta off of him, but it was too late. Fiona had already fled. "Don't ever try that again," he roared as he shoved Bretta away. "I don't want you."

"Why would you prefer my brother's whore to me?" Bretta screeched, venting her spleen. "You wanted me, I felt you stir against me. I held you in my hand. I know what it means when a man swells and hardens."

Thorne leaped from the bed, forgetting his wound until he felt something pull and tear. He ignored the pain as he took off after Fiona. The hall was empty save for servants. He spied Tyra and asked if she'd seen Fiona.

"Nay. I was in the storeroom. Has something happened to her?"

Thorne didn't bother to answer as he rushed out into the brisk September air. He found Fiona leaning against an animal pen, vomiting into the grass. He fetched her some water from the well, remaining watchful as she rinsed out her mouth and spat. When his arms came around her to steady her, she slapped them away.

"Don't touch me! Let me go!" She sounded almost frantic. "I can't remain in the same house with your mistress." She began to shiver, and not just from the cold.

"You're cold. Come inside."

"Nay! How could you?"

"I did nothing, Fiona. 'Tis not what you think."

She regarded him with silent condemnation. "Isn't it? Did you summon Bretta to ease your lust when I refused to rut with you?"

"Nay, I did not summon Bretta. She is not the woman I want. The spell you have cast upon me is too potent, Fiona. I want no woman but you. Had you arrived a moment later, you would have seen me sending Bretta away," he explained.

He pulled her against him. Fiona struggled, pounding on his shoulders with her fists. Suddenly Thorne released her, staggering backward, pain contorting his face. When he turned to steady himself against the animal pen, Fiona saw blood dampening his tunic.

"Dear God, what have you done?"

" 'Tis naught," Thorne said dismissively.

"Your wound is bleeding again. What did you do to aggravate it?"

"I said 'twas naught," he bit out.

"Come inside. I'll need my medicine chest."

Thorne didn't move. He wasn't a child to be ordered around. But when Fiona put her soft little hand into his callus-hardened one and pulled him toward the house, his belligerence fled. She led him to his chamber, pushed him onto the bed and turned to inspect the contents of her medicine chest.

"Take off your tunic," she said brusquely.

When she found what she wanted and turned back to Thorne, he was sprawled on his stomach, naked. This time, she vowed, she wouldn't allow herself to be beguiled by the sight of his nude body. She pulled a pelt over his legs and buttocks and let her eyes stray no further than his wound.

"You've opened your wound. 'Tis bleeding again, but it doesn't look too serious. A layer of marigold salve and a fresh bandage should take care of it."

"I told you 'twas naught," Thorne said with a hint

of impatience. He started to turn over but she pushed him back down.

"Hold still."

Thorne felt the slick coolness of salve touch his skin and then the slightly rough surface of the bandage as Fiona wound a strip of cloth around his chest to hold it in place.

"There," she said, sitting back and inspecting her handiwork. She let out a startled yelp when Thorne turned abruptly and pulled her down on top of him.

"What are you doing?" Her voice rose on a note of panic. She was all too aware of her lack of control where Thorne was concerned. She couldn't bear for him to touch her now, not after what she'd seen in his bed earlier.

He brought her beneath him with practiced ease. He was as solid as a rock and as unmovable as a mountain. "Don't," she whispered against his mouth moments before his lips claimed hers.

His kiss was wild and ravenous and so full of need, Fiona's thought processes shut down completely. His hands were rough yet oddly gentle as he tore her clothing away, baring her body to the torment of his mouth and hands. He kissed her until she grew dizzy, until a trembling need began low in her belly and she could no longer remain still beneath him. Then his hands found her breasts, kneading and molding, teasing her nipples until they grew painfully erect. When his lips finally abandoned her mouth to claim her nipples, Fiona strained against him, riding the heavy, liquid waves of heat flowing through her.

With a hoarse curse, he nudged the hot cleft of her womanhood with his sex. Then his hard, thick length opened her, filled her.

A jolt of blinding pleasure broke free inside her, sending her arching upward into the rigid line of his body. She cried out his name, writhing beneath him as his powerful hands anchored her in place.

She gazed up into his fire-and-ice eyes, mesmerized by the vivid spheres of passion claiming her.

"If this is enchantment," Thorne groaned against her mouth, "then I welcome it."

His eyes closed as he sank deeper inside her, his body a thrusting blade moving in a primitive rhythm of power and invincible heat, teasing, withholding just enough to make Fiona mad with wanting.

"Thorne, please." Her hands twisted in his long hair, wanting more of his hot, impaling length than he was giving her.

He arched his back and stiffened his flanks, driving her deeper into the soft fur pelts with each powerful thrust, effortlessly giving her everything he had, all she needed.

Pleasure raked her as she took all of him. When she thought there was no more, he proved her wrong. He drew out her pleasure, leaving her trembling on the edge, then he slowly cast her over the brink of forever. Blindly she wrapped her arms and legs around him, her hands clutching, urgent. She could not hold back the bursting climax rocketing through her. Thorne grabbed her hands, pinning them on either side of her head as he shouted her name and poured himself inside her.

Thorne leaned on his elbow and brushed a dark strand away from the pale curve of Fiona's cheek. Fiona felt his feather-light touch and her eyes blinked open in confusion. Her gaze roamed his stark features. "How could I let this happen? Isn't Bretta enough for you?"

"I've never bedded Bretta and have no desire to do so. You're the only woman I've bedded in longer than I care to remember."

His deep voice wrapped itself warmly about her, making her almost believe he truly cared. She didn't know what had happened in this chamber with Bretta, but she felt certain now that Thorne hadn't initiated it. He was a strong man, but he was still recovering from a serious wound and she doubted he had sufficient strength to exert himself with two women. And he had certainly exerted himself with her, she recalled with a sigh.

"Are you all right?" Thorne asked when he heard her sigh. "Did I hurt the babe? He may not be mine, but I'd never willingly hurt him."

"I'm fine. Why must you be so stubborn? Why is it so difficult to believe that Rolo never bedded me?"

" 'Tis no secret Rolo wanted you. He offered to buy you more times than I can count. 'Tis inconceivable that a virile man like Rolo would leave you untouched. If you need more reasons, there's Bretta and the servants. They all agree that Rolo bedded you regularly."

"Does my word count for naught? If you believe I am a witch, why can't you believe a witch would find a way to keep a man she did not want from bedding her?"

Thorne recoiled in confusion. "*Did* you find a way?"

"Aye."

"What did you do to him? I recall how eager Rolo seemed to be rid of you. He said you practiced witchcraft on him."

"I have knowledge of herbs and medicines. It didn't take witchcraft to accomplish what I did to Rolo."

"Odin help me," Thorne muttered. "What is it you did to him?" His eyes narrowed suspiciously. "Or is this another of your lies to convince me that the babe you carry is mine?"

"Pig-headed fool," Fiona hissed. "If you make me angry enough, I'll render you impotent, just as I did Rolo."

Thorne went still. "You made Rolo impotent?" His lips twitched, his eyes crinkled at the corners. Moments later he burst into raucous laughter. "Rolo is impotent?" he repeated. "No wonder he was anxious to be rid of you. Odin's balls, Fiona, what kind of witchcraft did you use to accomplish so great a feat?"

"I told you. I have knowledge of herbs. I merely mixed certain herbs in his mead. 'Tis not a permanent condition. Without the daily dose of herbs he soon returned to his former state of potency."

"Why didn't you tell me this before?" Thorne demanded.

"You weren't ready to hear it."

"So you let me go on believing the babe you carry might not be mine."

"Nay, 'tis you who believed it. I tried to tell you otherwise, but you were too stubborn to listen."

"But Bretta—"

"—Hates me. Besides, she doesn't know the truth. Rolo led her to believe he bedded me, and I was wise enough to realize he would do me serious harm had I denied it. He was too prideful to admit he'd lost his virility."

Thorne flattened his hand on Fiona's stomach. "The babe is mine." His voice held a note of awe. Suddenly a frown worried his brow as he visibly measured the space between her hip bones. "You are not built like Viking women and I am a large man. Mayhap my babe will be too big for you."

Fiona had had the same thought but tried not to dwell on it. "I will survive. Brann said I will bear many sons and daughters."

"What else did Brann say?"

"He said our sons will become the future rulers of Man. He told me our meeting was fated, that we were meant to be together and to live a long and happy life. I've known this since I was a very small child. The day you arrived on Man, I knew you were the one who would fulfill the prophesy."

"Only witches and wizards know such things," he contended. "The first time I saw you, I thought you were a faerie spirit. You appeared to move like mist through time and space, and I couldn't forget you. The memory of you summoned me from across the sea. From the moment I first saw you, your image tormented me. I had to return to Man."

"To kill me," Fiona reminded him.

"Aye. I was desperate to break the spell you cast upon me. You stole my heart and claimed it for your own. Healer you may be, but 'tis a witch's soul you possess. I believe everything you've told me about Rolo, but nothing can convince me you're not an enchantress. You bewitched and beguiled me. I no longer recognize the man I have become. 'Tis no wonder my brother fears you. He knows what you are capable of."

Thorne's words both thrilled and disconcerted Fiona. She drew upon her courage and asked, "Do you love me, Thorne?"

Thorne remained silent so long, Fiona feared he wasn't going to answer. Finally he said, "I truly cannot say. My obsession with you may be the result of witchcraft."

"Tell me how you feel," she probed. Would the foolish man never say the words?

"I feel bereft without you," he admitted somewhat hesitantly. "The need to make love to you is like a constant ache inside me. No other woman appeals to me. The thought of life without you torments me." Another lengthy pause ensued. "If love is what you call this strange churning inside me, then perhaps I do love you."

Fiona's heart swelled with incredible joy. She was about to throw her arms around him when his next words sent her plummeting back to earth.

"But this unnatural feeling could be the result of witchcraft. Remove your spell, Fiona, and let me become myself again. 'Tis the only way I will know for sure whether my feelings are pure and not the result of black magic."

"Very well," Fiona said, thoroughly exasperated. She waved her hand in the air. " 'Tis done. The spell is removed. What do you feel?"

Thorne closed his eyes and breathed deeply. When he opened them, Fiona was startled by the depth of emotion visible in their brilliant blue centers. "I do not know what I feel. Confusion, certainly. I *want* to believe I've been released from your spell, but I still feel enchanted. I need to test my feelings."

He turned on his back, grasped her waist and settled her on top of him. Her legs straddled him, bringing her heat in intimate contact with his loins.

"You shouldn't be doing this again," she gasped as his staff nudged her cleft. "Your wound—"

" 'Tis naught," Thorne murmured distractedly. "Open to me, Fiona. Perhaps my confusion will cease when I'm inside you again."

He raised his hips, prodded between her legs with the hard tip of his sex, and found the slick opening. He slid inside easily, imbedding himself so deeply Fiona shuddered and bit back a moan of pleasure. Thorne was the only man with the power to move her emotionally and physically. Never before had she considered sexuality as something to be desired. Now she gloried in the way Thorne made her feel, in the pleasure he brought her.

"You're so tight," Thorne groaned against her lips. "You make me wild. No woman has ever fit me like you do."

He began to move, thrusting upward, retreating, slowly at first, then picking up the rhythm. Until Fiona couldn't tell when one stroke ended and the next began. His big hands raised and lowered her hips to meet his strokes as he lifted his head to suckle her nipples.

Fiona felt her bones melting as Thorne drove her higher and higher. Then she lost her grip on reality and screamed his name.

Thorne stiffened as her contractions sent him careening over the edge. He thrust hard, then again, flooding her with his seed.

Chapter Fourteen

Fiona rested in Thorne's arms, breathing erratically as she slowly regained her wits. She could tell by his harsh panting and the loud pounding of his heart that he was similarly affected. Neither she nor Thorne was aware that Bretta had been spying on them through a crack in the door. Nor did they see the look of uncontrolled fury on her face as she retreated in silence.

"What are you feeling now?" Fiona asked, recalling Thorne's words shortly before his lips and hands had made her forget her own name. He'd said he could better explain his feelings after he'd made love to her again.

Thorne sent her an inquiring look. He knew Fiona was probing for a specific answer but he couldn't recall what the question had been. Then he remembered. She'd asked if he loved her. "I feel as though I'm still possessed," he hedged. "As though you own me body and soul."

Fiona felt a sharp pang of disappointment. The stubborn man was impossible. Moments ago he had all but admitted he loved her. Now he attributed his feelings to witchcraft. Were she naught but a simple woman with no special skills, perhaps Thorne would accept her love and return it.

"I want you in my bed every night," Thorne demanded. "I'll have no more of this coldness between us."

"What about Bretta?"

"What about her? She is nothing to me. If I wanted her in my bed, she would be in my arms now instead of you."

"Soon I'll grow large with child. Some men take a mistress when their wives are increasing."

Thorne's blue eyes settled on her stomach. She felt their scorching heat and tried to cover herself, but he would not let her. "It will take more than a bulging stomach to keep me from having you. There are ways to accomplish things without hurting you or the babe. I still find it difficult to believe the child is truly mine."

"Believe it," she returned tartly.

"I'll want a son, Fiona," Thorne said with typical male arrogance. "You may have a daughter after you've given me several sons."

"You'll take what you get." Fiona bit back a smile. Thorne sounded like a man who intended to remain with his wife forever. The one thing that would make everything perfect was Thorne's unconditional love. But that would never happen until she could prove she wasn't a witch and hadn't used magic to enchant him.

Thorolf returned from the *althing* the next day. He was alone. Rolo hadn't returned with him. Thorolf's joy at seeing Thorne alive and well and jousting in the yard with one of his men was overwhelming. The brothers pounded one another's backs in cheerful greeting.

"I thought I was returning to send my brother to Valhalla," Thorolf said, choking on the words.

"We have Fiona to thank for my recovery," Thorne answered.

Thorolf frowned. "I will thank the witch for naught. She has brought adversity upon us since her arrival. You owe your life to your own determination to live and your strong constitution. Her influence over you frightens me, Thorne. You should try harder to resist her magic."

"Fiona is carrying my child. 'Tis not magic that put my seed in her belly."

"Nay, 'tis Loki's mischief," Thorolf said sourly.

"What is Loki's mischief?" Bretta asked as she strolled over to join them.

"Fiona carries Thorne's child," Thorolf repeated.

"Nay, she carries Rolo's child," Bretta said with firm conviction. "Where is my brother? Ask him. He will confirm my words."

"Rolo did not return. He arranged a marriage for himself while attending the *althing*," Thorolf said.

"He is to marry Rika, youngest daughter of Garm the Black. She is fourteen and ripe for marriage. Rolo traveled to Garm's homestead to meet the girl. If she meets with his approval, he will marry her there. He said to tell you he will return before winter with his new wife."

"What about me?" Bretta cried. "He was to find a husband for me at the *althing*. Did he succeed?"

Thorolf shrugged. "He tried, but word of your evil deed spread throughout the gathering. It wasn't long before everyone knew that you had tried to kill Thorne. No man would even discuss a betrothal to you."

"Who told them?" Bretta asked, sending Thorolf a look that suggested he was the guilty party.

"I suspect it came from my own household. Men talk. 'Tisn't easy to suppress gossip about an act that nearly ended in tragedy."

"What am I to do?" Bretta wailed. "I cannot live in my brother's home forever. His new wife might object to having another woman underfoot."

"You should have thought of that before you fed me poison," Thorne said harshly. "Unless Rolo can find a man who has never heard of you, chances are you'll remain a spinster."

She turned on him, her eyes wild with rage. "*You* were to be my husband! I was blinded by jealousy. I knew not what I did. I vow you will still be mine, Thorne the Relentless," she hissed. "When the babe Fiona carries turns out to resemble my brother, you will come to your senses." Spinning on her heel, she marched away.

"I'd be careful of that one," Thorolf warned. "Come home with me. I need your help. I have to build a new hall before the snow flies."

"I will help, and gladly, Thorolf, but I won't leave Fiona behind to bear the brunt of Bretta's hatred."

Thorolf stared at him. "Bretta swears the child belongs to Rolo. You have only Fiona's word that it is yours."

"According to Fiona," Thorne said, recalling Fiona's explanation of how she had rendered Rolo impotent with herbs, "Rolo never bedded her."

Thorolf's face registered his disbelief. "And you believed her? Only Rolo knows the truth."

"He will deny it, of course," Thorne observed. "No virile man would willingly admit he had been rendered impotent by a woman."

"Is that what Fiona told you? That Rolo was impotent with her?" Thorolf's laughter was loud and raucous. "We both know that is a lie. We have seen him take women with the blood-lust of battle still upon him. He's had several mistresses. The claim is ridiculous."

Thorne frowned. His brother's observations made sense. Fiona's claim did not seem as reasonable as it had when she'd told him what she'd done. Could a few herbs render a powerful man like Rolo impotent? It certainly gave him pause for thought. Had he been too quick to believe Fiona?

"Well, brother, will you come back home with me?" Thorolf asked again. "Without Fiona, of course. I've not changed my mind about her. Babe or no, she is not welcome in my hall."

"I'll make no decisions until Rolo returns to either confirm or deny Fiona's claim."

"So be it," Thorolf said. "If you need me, you know where to find me. I'm pleased there was no need to dispatch my brother to Valhalla to join our father. I must go now, Thorne. There is much work to accomplish."

They clasped arms, and then Thorolf took his leave. Fiona watched the exchange from the edge of the forest near the house. She had gone to collect medicinal plants before frost withered the usable herbs that were available in this cold land. Her basket was full as she strode briskly toward Thorne.

"Where have you been?" Thorne asked as she joined him.

"Collecting herbs. Some are strange to me, but others I recognized immediately. Is Thorolf gone?"

"You heard?"

"Aye. I was surprised you didn't go with him. It will take many hands to build a new hall before winter."

"He will send for me if I'm needed."

"I'm not comfortable staying in Bretta's home. I sense danger. We must leave, Thorne."

"There is nowhere else to go," Thorne said. "I've already checked the village and no dwelling is available. We have no choice but to accept Rolo's hospitality."

Fiona shuddered. She did not like it. Danger surrounded her; she could feel it closing in on her.

* * *

Some of Thorne's men elected to remain with him, sleeping in Rolo's hall and taking their meals with Rolo's household. It was apparent to all that Tyra and Aren were becoming closer. Fiona rejoiced that someone could find happiness amidst the turmoil. Despite their closeness in the privacy of their bed, Fiona still didn't know where she stood with Thorne. He refused to let her sleep anywhere but in his bed. Yet there were times she caught him looking at her as if in judgment. In her heart she felt he wasn't entirely convinced that the child she carried was his. But he was still concerned enough about her welfare to suggest that she take stock of her medicine chest each morning to make sure nothing was missing. Evidently he trusted Bretta even less than he trusted Fiona.

One day Bretta drove the pony cart to the village. Fiona watched her leave with relief. The odd sensation of impending doom continued to plague Fiona, but no vision appeared to reveal what or whom she had to fear.

Bretta returned from the village later that day wearing a smug expression. No one seemed to know the nature of her errand, but Fiona did not like it.

During the following days, Fiona concentrated on gathering herbs and hanging them from the ceiling to dry. The days had become extremely cold and nights were almost bitter. Sharing a bed and body warmth with Thorne these nights was comforting. Thorne continued to make love to her, but Fiona knew he still harbored grave doubts about the child she carried. Though he hadn't voiced them, the uncertainty was there, clearly visible in the icy blue depths of his eyes.

One bitterly cold night Thorne made love to her with the heat and passion of a Viking berserker. He bared her body to his hungry gaze, then kissed and teased his way down her belly to the soft nest between her legs. When he lowered his head and took her with his mouth, she shrieked and went rigid. He parted her with his fingers, then slid his tongue along the slick membranes to her heated passage. The guttural sounds that escaped her throat urged him on without words as he dipped a finger inside her and thrust it deeply.

Fiona was shaking violently. His finger was driving her wild. When he placed his mouth where his finger had been, she shattered, crying out his name as she climaxed violently. Thorne waited until she calmed before bringing her on top of him and sliding inside her. Fiona thought he had taken all she had to give but Thorne proved her wrong. He deliberately withheld his own pleasure, thrusting and withdrawing until she began to respond. Together they strove for the top, reaching for the splendor and clinging to it in breathless ecstasy.

Thorne held Fiona close as sleep claimed her, his thoughts diverse and complex. He was known as Thorne the Relentless, a title he'd earned honestly. And relentless he'd been in his determination to make Fiona his own, and to keep her with him despite his grave reservations. Call it witchcraft, call it obsession, call it anything but what he dared not name, the fact remained that there was magic in their loving. The kind of magic Thorne wanted to experience forever.

Rolo returned with his new bride on a gray, dismal October day, appalled to learn that Fiona was still present in his hall. He hadn't consummated his marriage to Rika yet and feared that Fiona would work her evil on him again and render him impotent with his new wife. He gave Fiona a wide berth as he greeted Thorne.

"I never expected to see you again in this life, Thorne. Apparently Valhalla was not yet prepared to receive you."

"I owe my life to Fiona's skill," Thorne replied. "We are both grateful for your hospitality. Currently I have no home and nowhere to go. In early summer I will take Fiona to her home on Man. I hope your wife does not object to guests."

Rolo shrugged. "Rika will do as I say. She is very young and uncertain of her duties. I have waited to consummate our marriage tonight in my own home. Tell Fiona to stay away from Rika. I do not trust your leman. My hospitality extends only so far. You may remain in my home until weather permits you to begin your journey." His eyes narrowed as he sent a furtive glance in Fiona's direction. "Take heed, friend. If I suspect your woman is practicing witchcraft, I will turn her out into the cold to fend for herself."

From where she stood a short distance away, Fiona could not tell what they were saying. They were speaking in their own language, and though she had learned enough to understand and reply simply in their tongue, she couldn't follow their exchange. Rolo spoke at length and Thorne's answers were short and angry, but somehow she knew they were talking about her.

Fiona's gaze shifted to Rika. The girl appeared frightened of Rolo, and with good reason, Fiona supposed. Rolo was not a gentle man, and Rika was too young and inexperienced to stand up to him. Fiona bit back a grin. Perhaps she should give Rika instructions on how to handle Rolo. Fiona's heart went out to Rika, but there was little she could do at the present time to ease the girl's lot in life . . .

Unless Rika sought her help.

Rolo's return brought an end to the privacy Thorne and Fiona had enjoyed in their own bedchamber. With only two private bedchambers available, Rolo had reclaimed the room for himself and his bride. Fiona was obliged to stretch out on a bench and pull a fur pelt over her while Thorne curled up in his cloak before the fire.

The first night of Rolo's return was a nightmare. Fiona tried to close her ears to Rika's pitiful cries but she could not. The following morning the girl was subdued and visibly hurting. Fiona vowed to wait until Rolo left on some errand or other and then offer Rika medication to ease her discomfort. Her opportunity came later, when both Rolo and Thorne went outside to tend to the animals. She found what she needed in her medicine chest and approached the girl.

"I'd like to help you, Rika," Fiona said, speaking slowly in Rika's language. "I know you're hurting. I'm a healer. I can give you a special salve to ease your pain."

Rika, a stately blonde whose beauty and body had not yet attained their full potential, drew back in alarm. "Rolo said you're a witch."

"Nay, I am a healer. Here," she said, holding out a small jar of yellow salve. "Use this on your tender parts. I swear 'twill not harm you. If you'd like to keep Rolo from bedding you for a few days, I can give you something to bring on your woman's time."

"You can do that?"

"Aye. Come to me if you need it."

Rika nodded and limped away.

"What did you tell my wife?" Rolo wanted to know. He had entered the hall in time to see Rika speaking with Fiona.

"I was but offering her some womanly advice," Fiona ventured. "She is young; you were too hard on her last night. A woman's first time should be accomplished without violence."

"Do not tell me what to do, witch. And leave my wife alone. I do not trust you."

"Has Fiona done something to offend you?" Thorne asked as he joined them.

"She has been putting ideas into my bride's head," Rolo said crossly. "I cannot believe that I ever wanted the witch in my bed."

Thorne went still. "But you *did* have her in your bed, didn't you, Rolo?"

Rolo's gaze swung to Fiona, his brow lifted. "What did Fiona tell you?"

"Fiona said you were impotent with her."

Though seething with anger, Rolo threw back his head and howled with laughter. "Me? Impotent? Ask my bride just how impotent I am." He laughed again. "She'll tell you that I took her four times last night. Does that sound like a man lacking in vigor?"

"Fiona is carrying a child," Thorne said evenly. "Could it be yours?"

Fiona stifled a cry of dismay, hurt and appalled by Thorne's question. She'd thought that issue had already been resolved. Apparently something or someone had raised new doubts in Thorne's mind.

Thorne's words stunned Rolo. He had no intention of claiming the witch's spawn, but admitting that he'd been rendered impotent by Fiona's black magic was equally abhorrent to him.

"I relinquish all claim to the child," Rolo vowed. " 'Tis yours, Thorne, and you are welcome to it."

Rolo's disclaimer did not assuage Thorne's lingering doubts. "Are you saying you bedded Fiona while she was with you?"

"What do you think? You knew I wanted her."

"Nay!" Fiona cried. "He lies! Do not believe him, Thorne. Rolo's pride is wounded, the truth embarrasses him. My skin still crawls when I think of his hands upon me. He tried to take me, but that vile thing between his legs refused to harden after I fed him herbs to make him impotent."

Rolo lifted his hand to strike Fiona, but Thorne stepped between them. "Do not touch her."

"You heard what she said. Would you let a woman slander you in such a manner?"

"I heard, but I am not sure she lies. Fiona has knowledge of herbs and medicines that can do strange things."

"You do believe me, don't you, Thorne?" Fiona asked hopefully. "The babe is yours. I've known no other man."

"Perhaps I believe you," Thorne said after a long pause.

Rolo snorted in disgust. "You're a besotted fool, Thorne the Relentless." Then he turned and strode away, satisfied that he had adequately defended his manhood. A man had his pride. No woman was going to make a fool of him.

Several days later Ulm arrived with a plea from Thorolf. Foul weather and illness had slowed the building of his hall, and Thorolf wanted Thorne to bring his men to help complete the building so that they might have shelter from the harsh elements. Of course, Thorne could not refuse and made plans to leave the following morning.

"How long will you be gone?" Fiona wanted to know.

"I have no idea," Thorne said distractedly. "It depends on the weather and the speed with which we rebuild the hall."

Fiona's heart skipped a beat. "You *will* return, won't you?"

He gave her a hard look. "Do you think I'd leave you to Rolo?"

She regarded him solemnly. "I don't know. I cannot see into your heart."

"Fear not, Fiona. I have your future well in hand."

His words hung between them like a dark, ominous cloud. What kind of future did Thorne have in mind? she wondered. She watched in growing apprehension as Thorne turned away and spoke at length with Rolo. She knew they were talking about her, for Rolo kept sending her sidelong glances.

Fiona dreaded the thought of remaining in Rolo's hall without Thorne. Bretta hated her and Rolo feared her magic power. It was disheartening to be trapped in a country where people hated and feared her. She longed for Man, for her father and the people she knew and loved. But most of all she missed Brann, the wizard who had taught her to accept the gift God had given her and to use it wisely.

That night there was no private farewell for Fiona and Thorne. The hall was crowded with men and women sleeping on benches and on the floor, making privacy impossible. Thorne had seemed distracted and on edge during the evening meal, and Bretta didn't help matters when she sweetly asked Thorne if he still intended to claim Rolo's child as his own.

Rolo forestalled Thorne's answer. "I want nothing to do with Fiona or the child. I relinquish my claim to the little bastard."

Thorne's jaw clenched and Fiona felt the pressing weight of his confusion. She opened her mouth to fling out an angry retort, but Thorne's silent warning stopped her.

"Don't say it, Fiona," Thorne bit out. "I've heard your explanation before. I'm inclined to believe you, but . . . Thor's beard, what is truth and what are lies? Both Rolo and Bretta want me to believe you are carrying Rolo's child."

"And I say Rolo never bedded me," Fiona declared. "I've never encountered a man as stubborn as you. Perhaps we don't belong together."

"Perhaps you're right," Thorne returned without enthusiasm. He would never give Fiona up. The spell she had cast upon him would endure until he drew his final breath. But it wouldn't do to let Fiona know just how besotted he was with her.

Fiona could feel Bretta's burning gaze pierce her as she rose from the table and went in search of Tyra. Tyra was her only friend in this household of vipers. Fiona sensed danger closing in, and there was nothing she could do about it.

That night Fiona was awakened by a terrible, wrenching cry that came from Rolo's room. Thorne must have heard, too, for he sat up on his pallet and reached for his weapon.

"What is it?" Thorne asked, rubbing sleep from his eyes.

" 'Tis Rika," Fiona said. "Rolo is an animal. I think he hurts the child on purpose. Is there nothing we can do?"

" 'Tis none of our concern. Rika is Rolo's wife."

"There is something *I* can do," Fiona muttered beneath her breath.

"What did you say?"

"Nothing. Why doesn't Rika divorce Rolo? 'Tis an easy thing to do in your country."

Thorne shrugged. "Perhaps she will. But it is not our place to interfere. We are guests here. Come here," he said, holding out his hand to her. "The night is still young. I wish to hold you in my arms before I leave."

Fiona thought to refuse, then changed her mind. A voice inside her whispered that it might be the last time for a long while that Thorne would hold her like this. She rose from her bench and joined Thorne on his pallet. He covered them both with his fur cloak and curved his body around hers. She sighed in perfect contentment and started to doze off when the sound of Thorne's voice roused her from sleep.

"Your breasts have gotten larger," he whispered as he weighed a breast in his large hand. His hand slid down to her stomach. "Not much difference here, though."

Fiona tensed as his hand pressed into the indentation between her legs. "Have you missed me, Fiona? Do you crave my manhood inside you?" He began inching up her tunic, baring her legs. "Will you seek Rolo's bed after I leave?"

Fiona gasped in outrage. "How dare you! Rolo is a pig."

The hem of her tunic was up around her waist now as his hand sought her heated center beneath the fur robe. Around them men stirred in their sleep but did not awaken.

"What are you doing?"

"We cannot indulge our passion as we wish, but I can still give you pleasure." He turned her on her back and probed his finger upward into her moist heat. He stretched her with his thumb and inserted a second finger. When he began to thrust and withdraw, Fiona nearly screamed aloud. But his mouth covered hers, swallowing her cries.

His tongue began a rhythm inside her mouth that mimicked the movement of his fingers below. Fiona felt her bones melt, felt her tender passage expand and grow taut beneath the frantic thrusting of his fingers. And she felt heat rising inside her, burning, scalding through her veins.

"Now, Fiona, come now," Thorne panted into her ear. Then his mouth took hers again, muffling her cries as she arched sharply upward and climaxed around his fingers.

"Why did you do that?" Fiona asked once her breathing had returned to normal.

"I didn't want to leave without a proper good-bye." He paused, then said, "Only the gods know what the future will bring."

Fiona thought he sounded oddly distant, as if he had already removed himself from her. She sighed but did not voice her fears. No matter what Thorne did or said, nothing would change the course of Fate. The road might be fraught with trials and tribulations, but they were fated to be together forever. She closed her eyes, snuggled deeper into Thorne's arms and slipped easily into slumber.

Thorne listened to the even cadence of Fiona's breathing and knew she slept. Unfortunately, sleep eluded him. He feared that Fiona would turn to Rolo in his absence. He knew he was acting like a jealous, besotted fool and blamed it on Fiona's spell. He didn't want to leave but he could not in good conscience deny Thorolf's request for help. Fiona would be waiting for him when he returned, of that he was certain, but would she still want him? Only time would tell.

Thorne and his men were gone the next morning when Fiona awakened. Tyra told her they had left at first light.

A short time later Rika emerged from Rolo's room, sobbing hysterically. She ran to Fiona and fell to her knees. "I beg you, Fiona, please help me. I cannot bear Rolo's abuse another night. My mother mentioned nothing about this kind of pain when she told me what takes place between a husband and wife."

"Not all men are like Rolo," Fiona said, raising the girl from her knees. "Some are gentle and giving with their wives."

"Can you help me?" Rika asked as she perched gingerly on the edge of the bench beside Fiona.

Fiona cast a furtive glance around her, saw no one within hearing and said, "Aye, I can help you. But you must do exactly as I say."

"I'll do anything, Fiona, *anything*, to end this nightly torture."

Fiona smiled and drew her medicine chest from beneath the bench.

Chapter Fifteen

"You want me to mix this into Rolo's mead tonight?" Rika asked curiously as she accepted a small packet from Fiona.

"Aye. Sooner, if he wishes to bed you again before nightfall. But don't let him see you do it."

"What will it do to him?"

"Render him impotent. He won't be able to hurt you."

Rika regarded her solemnly. "He will beat me."

"I will threaten him with dire consequences if he tries. Would your family take you back?"

Rika nodded vigorously. "Oh, aye. They would be angry if they knew I was being mistreated. My father was reluctant to give me to Rolo at first, but Rolo convinced us that he would be a gentle and loving husband. I realize now that he put off bedding me until we reached his homestead so my family wouldn't hear my cries."

"Then you must divorce Rolo and return to your family. I will threaten him with a spell if he won't let you go or attempts to harm you. Rolo already fears me. It wouldn't be difficult to make him believe I will make him permanently impotent."

"You would do that for me?"

"I would do it for any woman in your position. I have learned something of your laws here. Viking women have rights and exercise them often. Divorce is a simple matter in your land. I believe Rolo married you because you are young and inexperienced and he could subjugate you to his will."

Rika looked puzzled. "Does not Thorne subjugate you to his will?"

"Perhaps he *thinks* he does. I was a captive. He could have bedded me any time he pleased, but he married me first. Does that sound as if he dominates me?"

"Bretta says you bewitched Thorne. He was to marry Bretta until he saw you on Man and fell under your spell."

"Bretta is a bitter woman. Believe her not."

Fiona would have said more but she fell silent when Rolo strode into the hall, a fur cloak thrown over his nakedness. "There you are, Rika. Why did you leave our bed? I am not finished with you. Bring a flagon of mead with you when you come. And be quick about it. Since you are still too inexperienced to satisfy me, I must spend more time teaching you how to please me."

He turned and strode away without waiting for a reply.

Rika paled and began to shake.

"The herb, Rika, use it," Fiona hissed. "Mix it in his mead now and make sure he drinks it all before he tries to bed you."

Rika nodded jerkily and went to fetch the mead.

Fiona fidgeted nervously after Rika entered Rolo's chamber with the flagon of mead. She hadn't wanted to frighten Rika, but this endeavor could turn ugly. Rolo was a brutal man prone to violence. If Rika's situation weren't desperate, Fiona wouldn't have suggested so dangerous a ploy.

Matters came to a climax later that day when Rolo let out a roar that reverberated through the hall and stormed out of his chamber, stark naked, dragging Rika by the hair.

"This is your fault, witch!" he shouted, pointing a condemning finger at Fiona. "You have done it again." He dragged Rika forward. "This whining child possesses neither your power nor your skills, and I detect your fine hand in this."

Feigning innocence, Fiona said, "I know not what you're talking about."

"Don't you?" Rolo shouted. He tossed Rika aside and advanced on Fiona. "Take a good look, witch." He thrust out his loins. Fiona saw his limp organ dangling between his legs and wanted to laugh. Fortunately, she was astute enough to display no emotion whatever.

"Remove your spell, witch!" Rolo demanded.

"Cover yourself, brother," Bretta hissed as she

tossed a cloak over Rolo's shoulders. The commotion had drawn her into the hall. One glance at the unfolding scene warned her that her brother was close to violence. All of it directed at Fiona. Her mind worked furiously as she sought a way to turn her brother's fury to her own advantage. She'd been waiting for the opportunity to get rid of Fiona permanently, and the gods had provided it.

Abruptly Rolo turned his rage on Rika, who was cowering at his feet. "Bitch!" he screamed, kicking her in the ribs. "You and Fiona have conspired together to rob me of my manhood."

Rika scrambled to her feet, holding her side, her face stiff with resolve as she sought Fiona's support for what she was about to do. Fiona nodded encouragement. It was exactly what Rika needed. Her jaw firmed beneath her trembling lips as she limped toward the bedchamber. Curious, Rolo and Bretta followed. Soon a crowd had gathered at the door.

Rika paused at the foot of Rolo's bed, turned resolutely to face her husband and his household and said, "I divorce you, Rolo the Bold." Then the small assemblage parted as she walked past them and through the hall, stopping at the front door. Once again she turned and said before witnesses, "I divorce you, Rolo the Bold."

Silently applauding Rika's courage, Fiona went to stand beside the young girl, lending her support. She had no idea what would happen next and feared she had unleashed a demon within Rolo.

Bretta gave a brittle laugh. "Well, well, the infant has claws. I wonder how much of this newfound courage was inspired by Fiona. And I wonder if Fiona would have acted so rashly had she known that Thorne had instructed Rolo to get rid of her before he left to join his brother."

Fiona went still. "What did you say?"

Rolo immediately seconded his sister's lie. " 'Tis true. Thorne told me to do with you as I please. He wants you gone from his life, for he doesn't intend to return. Why do you think he took his men with him?"

"Thorne doesn't want me?" Fiona repeated stupidly. "I don't understand."

" 'Tis simple," Bretta explained. "Thorne cannot live with the knowledge that Rolo sired your child. He wants you out of his life but didn't trust himself to tell you of his decision. He fears that your spell is still too strong for him to openly defy you in a face-to-face confrontation."

"I don't believe you," Fiona said, shaken to her very core.

" 'Tis true," Rolo concurred. "After the foul thing you have done to me, I wouldn't allow you to remain in my home even if Thorne hadn't wanted you sent away. You will leave immediately."

Fiona heard the wind howling outside and shuddered. "Where will I go?"

"I made arrangements some time ago for your departure," Bretta revealed. "Even before Thorne expressed his desire to be rid of you. I knew he would tire of you sooner or later."

"I'll take Fiona with me to my father's hall," Rika said, finally finding her voice.

"I suppose your father will demand the return of your dowry," Rolo said nastily.

" 'Tis the usual custom," Rika returned.

"Allowing you to associate with Fiona was a terrible mistake," Rolo said bitterly. "The witch has corrupted you. Go, go now, before I change my mind and kill you."

Bretta laid a hand on her brother's arm. "Do not be so hasty, brother. I said I had made prior arrangements for Fiona's departure. My plans could also include Rika and Tyra. If I may have a private word with you . . ." She urged Rolo toward his bedchamber, where they could speak without being overheard.

"Do not attempt to leave until I return," Rolo ordered harshly as he closed the door behind him and his sister.

"What does Bretta intend?" Rika asked once they were alone.

"Nothing good," Fiona answered.

Fiona was still reeling over the bitter knowledge that Thorne wanted her out of his life. Could it be true? She had known Thorne was upset and confused over her pregnancy but she hadn't once thought he would wish her harm. Had Brann's predictions and prophesies been naught but figments of his fertile imagination?

Her mind spun with the painful truth. She had forced Thorne to marry her, and he had obliged because he thought himself bewitched by her. And to satisfy his lust. Apparently his lust had been sated and he no longer wanted her. The stubborn Viking cared not at all that she carried his child. What was she to do now? What vile plan for her future had Bretta hatched?

"You and Tyra will accompany me to my home," Rika said with the innocence of one who failed to recognize the potential danger they faced.

"Where do your parents live?" Fiona asked.

"Down the coast. Near Bergen. A six-day journey on foot."

" 'Tis winter," Fiona said, "and I am carrying a child. I will not survive a six-day journey."

Rika looked as if she wanted to cry. But being a Viking woman, she merely shrugged her shoulders and said, "I will carry you if I must. I am twice your size. Your slight weight will be easy to bear."

Rika's selfless offer brought tears to Fiona's eyes. "Perhaps Rolo will lend us horses and enough food to carry us to your home," she suggested hopefully.

Fiona's hopes were dashed when Rolo and Bretta returned to the hall, their expressions far too smug for Fiona's liking.

" 'Tis settled," Bretta said. "Arrangements have already been made with Roar the slave trader. One of his ships will transport you to Byzantium. I have but to inform him when to come for you."

Fiona's expression registered her shock. "Was it Thorne's wish that I be sold?"

"Aye," Rolo lied.

"Will you send Rika home to her father?"

"And part with her dowry? Not likely," Rolo muttered loudly enough for Fiona to hear. "If Roar is agreeable, I will sell her along with you and Tyra."

"I demand to be returned to Man," Fiona said.

"You have no right to demand anything, witch," Bretta crowed. "When Thorne deserted you, he left your fate in our hands. Roar's clients in Byzantium clamor for fair-skinned slaves to warm their beds. He will take all three of you off our hands."

Rika gasped in dismay. "Nay! You cannot do this to me. I am a free woman."

"I can do as I please," Rolo said nastily. "You are in league with the witch. No one would blame me."

"I am with child," Fiona said, clutching her belly.

Bretta shrugged. "It matters not. Roar has assured me that he can find a place for the child in some foreign potentate's household should the infant survive the journey. All the better if the child is a boy, for many Eastern men enjoy boys in the same way most men enjoy women."

Baring her nails, Fiona flew at Bretta. How could one so young and lovely be so heartless? she wondered. Though quickly subdued by the larger woman, Fiona nevertheless managed to scrape five raw lines down Bretta's face. Bretta screeched and flung Fiona aside.

"You'll be sorry, witch," Bretta promised.

"Nay," Fiona said, her violet eyes flashing with anger. "You and your brother will be the sorry ones." She turned to Rolo, her eyes darkening to murky purple.

Rolo recoiled in fear as her gaze pierced through him, promising dire consequences. "Listen well, Rolo the Bold. I am called Fiona the Learned with good reason. I possess powers that can make your staff shrivel up into your belly. Never again will you bed another woman if you and Bretta do this terrible thing."

Fiona had no idea if her bold tactic would work, but it was worth a try. Rolo couldn't possibly know she had no powers beyond that of her knowledge of herbs and medicines.

Overwhelming fear caused Rolo's eyes to bug out. The ability to speak left him. He could do naught but stare mutely at Fiona, his jaw working soundlessly as his panic mounted.

Bretta had no such problem. "Seize them!" she cried out to Rolo's warriors. "Do not let them escape. I will send for the slave trader directly."

One man grabbed Tyra while others quickly surrounded Fiona and Rika and herded them toward the back of the hall. When Fiona felt the back of her legs collide with a bench, she sat down hard. Once they were subdued, Rolo approached them, his face mottled with rage.

"Remove the spell, witch!" he roared. He was so distraught, he appeared to be foaming at the mouth. "Take it away, I say! I am a man. A Viking. I will not allow you to turn me into a eunuch."

Fiona's eyes narrowed. "I will make a deal with you, Rolo. Send Rika back to her father and release Tyra and I will remove the spell."

"Nay! I am not stupid. Rika will spread malicious gossip throughout the land about my . . . my . . . failure." He shuddered. "Better that all three of you end your lives in Byzantium."

"Think, Rolo," Fiona said in a voice meant for his

ears alone. "Imagine yourself wanting a woman so badly you ache from it, and yet you cannot rise to the occasion. Think how your puny, shriveled flesh will look hanging useless between your legs, unable to bring you pleasure. You're a young man, Rolo. Is restoring your manhood not worth a woman's life?"

"Not if the entire kingdom ends up laughing at me," he bit out harshly.

"Rika will promise not to breathe a word of this to anyone if you send her home to her father," Fiona vowed. "Perhaps she can even convince her father to let you keep the bulk of her dowry."

"Aye," Rika said, echoing Fiona's vow. "I promise to say naught."

Rolo stroked his bearded chin as he considered Fiona's request. He cared nothing for Rika. If she could convince her father to let him keep her dowry, he had no objections to sending her home. He could always say she'd proved inadequate as a wife. At this point he was willing to do almost anything to restore his manhood. The last time Fiona had worked her spell on him, he had remained impotent for nearly a fortnight. Being permanently unmanned was unthinkable.

"Do you promise to remove your spell if I agree to send Rika home to her father?" Rolo demanded.

"Aye. Send Rika home with a proper escort and I will remove the spell. What about Tyra?"

"My benevolence extends only to Rika. Tyra will share your fate. Thorne wants naught to do with you and neither do I. You and Tyra will be sold to the slave trader according to Bretta's arrangement."

"Very well," Fiona said. "I will remove the spell the moment Rika is on her way with the escort. By tonight you will be fully restored and as vigorous as ever."

"If I am not, I will kill you." He turned abruptly to make arrangements for Rika's departure.

"So," Bretta said, her eyes narrowed thoughtfully. "You were telling the truth about rendering Rolo impotent. Your child actually does belong to Thorne."

"I did not lie to you," Fiona said wearily. "I used my knowledge of herbs to keep Rolo from bedding me."

Bretta's laughter was harsh and grating. "I can well imagine my brother's rage when his manhood failed. He's not one to be denied. I've known him to take three different women in one night."

"I pity them," Fiona muttered beneath her breath.

"Aye, I agree. Rolo is not an easy man to please. None of his mistresses remain long with him, and the slave women all fear his heavy hand. Little Rika doesn't know how lucky she is to be rid of him."

Rolo, his instructions completed, turned back to them. With a stroke of his knife he freed Rika's arms and legs. "Gather your things, Rika. You'll leave within the hour with your escort. As for you, Fiona," he said, giving her the full benefit of his harsh glare, "your life will depend upon my prowess in bed tonight. If all goes well when I bed one of the slave women, your life will be spared. I pity the potentate who buys you to warm his bed. I fear he will get more than he bargained for."

Having given his final word on the subject, Rolo returned to his bedchamber. Bretta flashed Fiona a triumphant smile, then flounced off.

"I can't leave you like this," Rika said, reluctant to abandon the woman who had saved her from a terrible fate.

"You must go," Fiona replied, "else all we did was for naught. Go home to your father. Tell him that you divorced Rolo because he was a brutal husband. If your father loves you, he will understand."

Her gaze wandered somewhere past Rika's shoulder. Her eyes glazed over. "There is another man in your future. I cannot see his face but I know he will love you and you will love him. One day your new husband and your father will join forces and recover your dowry. Rolo will receive just punishment for his acts of brutality." The vision disappeared as suddenly as it had begun, and Fiona shook her head to clear it.

"You can see all that?" Rika asked, awed by Fiona's psychic ability. "What about *your* future? What will become of you and your child?"

Fiona shook her head. Her own future was less clear to her. She sensed danger and sadness but little else. "I don't know. I once thought Thorne was my future but now I'm not so sure. Thorne doesn't want me, Rika. He cares not what happens to me. Somehow I will find a way to return to my home on Man."

"May the gods protect you," Rika said as she placed her hand on Fiona's shoulder. "If ever I cross paths with Thorne, I will tell him exactly what I think of the way he has treated you."

Just hearing Thorne's name brought unbearable pain to Fiona's broken heart. Her people feared and hated Vikings for their brutality, but for a short time she had believed Thorne was the exception. To her misfortune she had learned that Thorne was as cruel and heartless and vicious as any Viking she had ever seen or heard about. He couldn't have been more brutal had he shoved a blade through her heart and twisted.

An hour later, swathed in warm furs and boots, Rika was escorted from Rolo's homestead. By nightfall, Roar the Trader had arrived, accompanied by three warriors who acted as bodyguards. Roar looked Fiona and Tyra over, grunted his approval and went off with Rolo and Bretta to haggle over price.

"What's going to happen to us?" Tyra asked fearfully. She no longer feared slavery, if that was to be her lot in life. It was the unknown she dreaded. And the thought of never seeing Aren again.

"I wish I knew." Fiona sighed. "We'll think of something. Ships can't travel in winter, so the trader will have to keep us somewhere nearby. Perhaps we can escape and seek shelter with Rika's father. She told me how to reach her home."

"Perhaps," Tyra said with little enthusiasm. Fiona knew she was thinking of Aren and the possibility that she might never see him again.

After negotiations for the two women were concluded, Roar was invited to spend the night in the hall. Rolo looked over the women slaves in his household, grabbed a pretty one named Mista and dragged her into his bedchamber immediately after the evening meal. Fiona and Tyra were untied and allowed to eat and visit the lavatory before being trussed up for the night.

Fiona spent an uncomfortable night stretched out on the bench without benefit of blanket or warm robe. Nothing made sense to her. It wasn't like Thorne to let others take responsibility for his decisions. Had he wanted to be rid of her he would have done so himself, or so Fiona assumed. How could Brann's prophesy be fulfilled if Thorne cast both her and their unborn child aside without a thought for their well-being? When sleep finally came, nothing was settled in Fiona's mind.

Early the following morning Rolo charged out of his bedchamber grinning from ear to ear. Apparently his manhood had been restored and he had rutted the entire night. He strode directly to Fiona and shook her awake.

"I won't have to kill you, after all, witch," he said, puffing out his chest with masculine pride. "My vigor has been restored, and I am satisfied. After you are gone I will have naught to fear again. Thorne was wise to send you away. He is better off without you."

Fiona closed her eyes, the bitter betrayal of Thorne's abandonment cutting through her like a thousand sharp knives. She squared her shoulders and vowed to rise above the crushing defeat of Thorne's cruel dismissal. She had more pressing problems right now, including finding a way to save herself and her child from slavery in Byzantium.

Roar the Trader was ready to leave after he had broken his fast. Fiona had few belongings besides her medicine chest, and Tyra had even less. A heavy fur cloak and thick, fur-lined leather shoes were welcome additions to their wardrobe. The heavy clothing had been provided by Roar, who strove to keep his slaves healthy for greater profit.

The day was as cold and bleak as Fiona's heart when they left Rolo's homestead. Though the village was but a short distance away, the trip could have been arduous had there been wind and heavy snow to contend with. Between them, Fiona and Tyra shared the weight of the medicine chest. As Fiona trudged across the frozen tundra, she recalled Bretta's parting words. They were meant to be hurtful and had succeeded only too well.

"Do not worry about Thorne, Fiona," Bretta had said in a cutting aside. "I will do my utmost to make him happy. He was always meant to be mine. Soon he will forget you ever existed."

"Are you all right, Fiona?" Tyra asked as Fiona stumbled and then caught herself before she fell.

"As well as can be expected under the circumstances."

"This isn't like Thorne, Fiona. I'm not convinced he is aware of what is happening to us."

Fiona shrugged wearily. "Convinced or not, it makes little difference. Even if Thorne didn't ask

Rolo to get rid of us, by the time he learns what has happened it will be too late. Besides, I'm not sure he cares enough about me to want to find me."

"Save your strength for walking," Roar warned as he prodded them forward. " 'Tis threatening to snow and I don't want to be caught out in it."

Though he saw that the medicine chest was heavy, and that the two women struggled with it, he did not offer assistance. Late that afternoon they arrived at Roar's homestead located just beyond the ridge that circled the village. Fiona was so cold her feet felt like blocks of ice and her flesh was chilled beneath the fur cloak.

The blast of heat from the open door felt wonderfully welcome as Fiona and Tyra stumbled inside. A tall, thin woman of middle years met them at the door.

"Welcome, master," she said, ushering them inside.

"The heat feels good, Morag," Roar said, shaking the snow from his cloak. "This is Fiona and Tyra, two new thralls bound for Byzantium. I want them kept healthy enough to withstand the journey. Fiona is increasing. I was fortunate enough to get mother and child for the price of one. The child will bring a good price if it's born healthy."

Fiona gasped and hugged her stomach. "No one is going to take my child from me."

Roar regarded her coolly. "You have no choice, slave. Go with Morag. She has prepared a chamber for you and Tyra. If you resist, I will beat you. I am skilled in plying the whip without causing lasting scars." His threat hung in the air like heavy smoke as he walked away to join his men at the ale barrel.

When Fiona would have challenged his authority, Morag touched her arm and said, "Do not argue, lady. I felt the bite of the lash many times before I learned to accept my lot. 'Tis not pleasant. Follow me. 'Twill not be so bad, you'll see. Byzantium can't be half as bad as suffering Roar's heavy hand."

Fiona saw the wisdom of her words and followed her meekly through the hall to the bedchamber she and Tyra were to share. "Does Roar travel to Byzantium often?" Fiona asked.

"Aye, each summer he carries new slaves he has purchased throughout the fall and winter. He recently took Christian priests all the way to Baghdad. Roar is a very rich man. He eats from gold plates and adorns his walls with priceless tapestries."

Morag opened the door to a small chamber and motioned them inside. "I'll bring food later. Warm yourselves. Few houses can boast of a hearth in the bedchamber, but Roar is very careful of his female slaves. Male slaves are kept in a compound, but the women are housed in luxury. You'll not be starved or beaten here, unless you do something foolish. Roar does not tolerate disobedience."

Tyra said something to Fiona in Gaelic. Morag's thin face lit up as Fiona answered in the same language. "You speak Gaelic," she said with a hint of surprise. "Are you both from Ireland?"

"I am," Tyra said. "Fiona is from the Isle of Man. Did you understand what we said?"

Morag's expression grew wistful. "Aye, I understood, though it has been many years since I've heard or spoken my native tongue. I come from Ireland. I was taken in one of the first Viking raids upon our coast. Roar bought me for his bed and soon tired of me. He said I wasn't beautiful enough or young enough to please another master, so he kept me to run his household. Rest now; I will return soon."

After Morag left, Fiona and Tyra discussed a possible escape. "Perhaps we can convince Morag to help us," Fiona said hopefully. "She seems very sympathetic."

"She fears Roar," Tyra argued. "He would kill her if she allowed us to escape."

"Perhaps you're right," Fiona concurred. "We will just have to bide our time and plan our escape carefully. God willing, we will never reach Byzantium."

Chapter Sixteen

Thorne and Aren blew in with a ferocious storm a fortnight after Fiona had been sold to Roar. They were alone. Their warriors had remained with Thorolf, preferring Thorolf's newly constructed hall to Rolo's, where they did not feel welcome.

Bretta hurried to take Thorne's heavy fur cloak as she bid him welcome. Thorne had no time for Bretta as his gaze swept the hall for Fiona. Aren had already hurried off to find Tyra.

"Warm yourself by the fire," Bretta urged as she handed Thorne's snow-encrusted cloak to a servant. "A hot drink will warm your insides," she said, offering him a horn filled with hot mulled wine.

Thorne sipped the wine, all the while searching for the only person he truly cared to see in Rolo's hall. "Where is Fiona?" he asked as a pang of foreboding pierced through him. Something felt wrong. Very wrong.

"Forget Fiona for now," Bretta said. She wanted her brother to be the one to tell Thorne the story they had concocted together.

Suddenly Aren appeared beside Thorne, distraught, his eyes wild. "They're gone, Thorne! Fiona and Tyra are gone."

Thorne appeared bewildered. "Gone? Gone where?"

"No one seems to know. Or is willing to say," he added.

Bretta suppressed a smile. The thralls and karls had been threatened with severe punishment should they reveal what they knew about Fiona and Tyra.

Thorne turned, pinning Bretta with his gaze. "Is this true?"

"Aye," Bretta said, feigning regret. "I tried to stop them but they wouldn't listen."

"Odin's balls! Where could they have gone? And why? 'Tis the middle of winter and Fiona is with child."

"Ah, here's Rolo," Bretta said with relief when she saw Rolo enter the hall from his bedchamber. "He will explain what happened."

"Did you send Fiona away?" Thorne roared, rounding on Rolo.

"Nay. The witch left of her own free will. She took her medicine chest and her servant and announced her decision to leave my hall."

"Why would she do such a foolish thing?"

Rolo shrugged. "A jarl from the North arrived after you left, seeking shelter for the night. Fiona became friendly with the man, if you take my meaning," he hinted slyly. "When the jarl left the next morning, Fiona and Tyra accompanied him. 'Tis my belief that he promised to take Fiona home to Man when he went a-Viking next summer. Since Fiona wasn't my slave, I could do naught to stop her."

Thorne stared at Rolo in disbelief. "You lie! Fiona would never go off with a stranger."

"But she did," Bretta assured him. "We tried to stop her but she was determined. You know how stubborn the witch can be."

"Give me the jarl's name!" Thorne roared. "I will split him from gullet to groin."

"Be reasonable," Bretta cajoled. "The witch made her bed, now let her lie in it. Fiona made it clear that she was leaving you. She's probably already warming the jarl's bed. 'Tis no great loss to you."

"I cannot let her go," Thorne claimed. The pain in his heart became so sharp he nearly doubled over from it. Though there was a good possibility that Fiona carried Rolo's child, he still wanted her. Would his enchantment never end? Was he destined to spend the rest of his life under a spell so strong it could not be broken by either absence or betrayal?

"The name, Rolo. Give me the jarl's name."

Rolo and Bretta exchanged frantic glances.

Bretta raised an elegant brow, signifying that Rolo should handle the matter.

"Despite our differences we are still friends and neighbors," Rolo said. " 'Tis for your own good that I withhold the jarl's name from you. You cannot wage a battle in the winter. Should you feel the same in the spring, I will give you his name.

"Look around you, Thorne." He gestured expansively. "I have many comely slaves. Any one of them will help you to forget Fiona the Learned. Bretta is still eager to become your bride. She regrets that small episode with the poison. 'Tis time you forgave her and married her as your father and I planned."

Thorne heard none of what Rolo said. His mind whirled with the implications of Fiona's defection. Why had she left? Had she suddenly realized that the paternity of her child would always be in question? Had she bewitched the jarl in the same way she had bewitched him? He pitied the poor, unsuspecting wretch if that was what Fiona had done. His own life hadn't been the same since he'd first spied the enchantress.

"Thorne, what are you thinking?" Bretta asked when Thorne remained uncommunicative.

"Murder wouldn't be too far from the truth," Thorne returned. He was angry enough to kill. At first his anger had been directed at the jarl who had captured Fiona's fancy. But the longer he thought about it, the more convinced he became that the jarl wasn't to blame for what had happened. His rage toward Fiona grew in leaps and bounds. Were she standing before him, he'd wring her beautiful little neck.

"Come share our meal," Bretta urged. "Things will look brighter tomorrow. In time you'll realize how lucky you are to be rid of the witch."

"I'll share your meal but not your hall," Thorne said. "I will return to my brother's hall, for I can no longer abide this place."

During the meal Thorne noticed that Rika was not present and succumbed to curiosity. "Where is your wife, Rolo? Is she ill?"

Everyone in the room grew quiet, waiting for Rolo's answer. "Rika divorced me," Rolo said easily. "I sent her home to her father. 'Tis no great loss. The wench and I didn't suit."

Thorne promptly put Rika from his mind as he contemplated his own woes.

As luck would have it, a fierce blizzard arrived before Thorne could leave, and his rage continued to simmer as he waited for the weather to moderate. Rolo's refusal to reveal the name of the jarl whom Fiona had accompanied did nothing to ease his bad humor. Thorne suspected that Rolo and Bretta had lied, but he couldn't prove it. Something did not smell right. He didn't buy Rolo's claim that starting a war over a woman was not worth a man's life. Why wouldn't Rolo reveal the name of the man who had stolen Fiona's affection? Was it because there was no such man?

Thorne bided his time, aware of the air of mystery pervading the hall. He remained watchful and vigilant. One night he bedded down in his usual place on a bench close enough to the fire to absorb its warmth. He longed for Fiona with every fiber of his being, then railed at himself for being weak where Fiona was concerned. He even dreamed about the child she carried. Some deep, warm place within his heart believed that the child was his, conceived of the passion they had shared. Aye, and love. The love he felt could be only the result of Fiona's spell, but it felt very real to him. Unfortunately, he had come to that realization too late.

As Thorne lay beside the fire thinking of Fiona, he heard a rustle and tensed, his hand reaching for Blood-drinker. The banked fire in the hearth cast a dim circle of light. Beyond that circle the hall was dark. A woman's voice whispered to him from out of the darkness. Thorne relaxed his grip on Blood-drinker and strained to listen.

"Stay your sword hand, my lord," the woman hissed in his ear.

"Who are you? What do you want? I'm in no mood to fornicate tonight."

The woman gave a muted snort of resentment. "I just came from Lord Rolo's bed. Fornication is the last thing on my mind."

"You're a thrall?"

"Aye, but ask no more questions of me."

"What do you want?" Thorne demanded.

"I have information for you. Do you wish to know the truth about Fiona?"

Thorne stiffened. "Speak, wench. What is it you wish in return? I cannot free you."

"I want naught but Fiona's safety. What I tell you must remain between you and me. If Lord Rolo learns of this, he will kill me."

"Why are you telling me this if it endangers your life?" Thorne asked suspiciously.

"Because I hate him!" the slave said with a vehemence that startled Thorne. "He is not a gentle lover. He and his sister betrayed you, and you should know of it."

Thorne started to rise but a small hand pushed him back down. "Nay, do not move. I fear discovery."

"Tell me what happened to Fiona and Tyra."

"They were sold to Roar the slave trader."

It was all Thorne could do to keep from bellowing in outrage.

"Rika would have suffered the same fate had not your lady pleaded her cause. She threatened Rolo's manhood if he did not send Rika home to her father. Apparently Rolo feared Fiona's power, for he sent Rika home, but he did not extend his mercy to Fiona and Tyra. They were sold to the slave trader."

"Sold," Thorne hissed, caught between the urge to kill Rolo and the need to go after Fiona. Rescuing Fiona was more urgent; he could always return and kill Rolo at his leisure. "How long has Fiona been gone?"

"Since shortly after you left."

"Odin's balls! Do you know where Roar took her?"

"Nay. He cannot sail in winter so he could have taken her to his home near the village. I must go now, before Rolo awakens and finds me gone. I hope you find your lady."

"Wait!" Thorne said. "Don't go yet."

When he turned to peer into the darkness he found nothing but shadows. Quietly he moved to where Aren slept and shook him awake. Then he revealed everything the woman had told him. Aren's anger was as great as Thorne's. They whispered together for several minutes; then Thorne crawled back to his bed beside the fire.

Roar's Homestead

Fiona and Tyra bided their time, waiting for the right moment to escape. Unfortunately, the recent spell of bad weather put a temporary hold on their plans. Then something happened that changed their fortune.

One day Roar went out with some of his warriors to hunt for fresh game. He was borne home on a makeshift stretcher. He'd been gored by a wild boar he had cornered in the forest. The wound was high on his thigh and serious enough to cause grave concern.

"You are a healer," Roar said to Fiona when he was settled in his bed. "Heal me. I am in great pain."

Fiona studied the wound, which had started to crust over, and shook her head. " 'Tis a serious wound, Master Roar. Mayhap the leg will have to come off. If it isn't treated, it will fester and you will die."

Roar's face contorted with fear. "Nay! Save me,

lady. Ask anything and it will be yours."

"Freedom, Roar, mine and Tyra's," Fiona demanded. "I will save your leg if you will free us and allow us to leave in peace afterward."

"Aye, anything, anything . . . But if you let me die, my men will kill you."

"Will you swear before witnesses?"

"Aye, but hurry. I cannot stand the pain."

Fiona called Roar's thralls and karls into the chamber. All heard Roar swear to free Fiona and Tyra if Fiona saved his leg and cured him. Then Fiona shooed them away and set to work.

She called for boiling water and brewed an infusion of mandrake root to ease Roar's pain. While it steeped, she wet a clean cloth and carefully soaked the wound until the bloody crust washed away. She changed the water three times before the gash was clean and the heavy bleeding stopped. Then she fed the mandrake infusion to Roar. Later she called for strong red wine and poured a generous portion directly into the wound. Roar made a strangled sound but did not pass out.

"The wound must be cauterized," Fiona determined. "Fetch a knife," she said to Tyra, who hovered nearby, "and place it in the fire."

Tyra obeyed without question. She found a short, broad blade, moved to the hearth and plunged it into the fire. When it glowed a dull red she removed it and brought it to Fiona. Fiona hesitated but a moment before placing the flat of the blade against the wound. The stench of burning flesh permeated the air. Roar howled and finally passed out. Fiona worked quickly after that. She sent Tyra to her medicine chest for a salve made of marigolds and spread it over the wound. Then she applied a bandage, winding it around the seared flesh to hold the salve in place.

"Will he heal?" Tyra asked hopefully. "Are we going to be free?"

"God willing," Fiona prayed. "I'll brew an infusion of herbs to fight the fever that's sure to come. I feel confident that Roar will live, and keep his leg in the bargain. He's lost a lot of blood, but I will prepare a remedy to strengthen and renew him."

"We can leave now, Fiona. Roar is in no condition to stop us."

"I promised to heal him and so I shall. God willing, we will soon be free."

By the time the storm abated and the weather turned unseasonably mild, Roar was well on his way to recovery with his leg intact. He was so grateful, he didn't try to stop Fiona when she announced her intention to leave the next day.

"Where will you go, lady?" he asked curiously.

"Have you heard of Garm the Black?"

"Aye. His daughter is married to Rolo the Bold."

"Rika divorced Rolo. Tyra and I intend to seek shelter with Rika's family."

" 'Tis a long journey. You'd be better off taking your chances in Byzantium. I will see that you have the best of masters. One who will allow you to keep your child."

"I will be no man's slave," Fiona said with firm resolve. "Is your word not good? Is your honor so lacking that you will rescind your vow to free us?"

Roar was indeed thinking along those lines. But mindful of everything Fiona had done for him, he quickly discarded thoughts of monetary gain where Fiona was concerned. A pity, he reflected, for he knew many Eastern potentates who would give a king's ransom in gold for a woman with Fiona's beauty and skill.

"Nay," he said sourly. "You and your serving woman are free to leave. 'Tis a foul time of year to travel, but I can see you are determined."

" 'Tis not far to Rika's homestead. I will pray for six days of moderate weather," Fiona said, fearing Roar would change his mind. "There is naught more I can do for you. Your limb and life are no longer in danger. I will leave instructions and medicine for your care."

A weak sun broke through the clouds, dispelling the gloom as Tyra and Fiona took their leave the next morning. Morag gave them sufficient food to last to their journey's end. Since Fiona's heavy medicine chest would hinder them, Fiona and Tyra each filled a pouch with dried herbs and salves and attached it to their belts. Clothed in woolen tunics, fur cloaks and high, fur-lined boots, they set out on their long trek south.

Thorne and Aren had left Rolo's hall before the household stirred. The blizzard had ended during the night and a weak sun shone through the clouds. It went against Thorne's nature to let Bretta and Rolo go unpunished, but he'd promised not to betray the confidence of his informant. He vowed to return and confront Rolo and Bretta once he rescued Fiona from the slave trader. Their vile deed wouldn't go unpunished; Rolo and his sister would pay dearly.

Thorne knew exactly where to find Roar's homestead. He'd visited on more than one occasion when he'd had dealings with the slave trader.

They reached the spacious house late that day. "Be prepared for anything," Thorne warned Aren as he pounded on the door. "I'm determined to get Fiona back no matter what it takes."

"I will be right beside you fighting for Tyra," Aren vowed.

Morag opened the door and Thorne pushed inside, followed closely by Aren.

"Where is Roar?" Thorne bellowed when a visual search of the smoky hall failed to reveal either Roar or the two women he sought. Several karls sprang forward to defend their master's hall. Thorne waved them back. "I mean no harm to your master if he cooperates with me."

"Roar is abed," Morag said, "recovering from a serious wound."

"Where are the two women he recently purchased from Rolo the Bold?"

Morag wrung her hands. "Gone, my lord."

"Gone!" he shouted. "What nonsense are you spouting?"

Roar heard the commotion and hobbled out of his bedchamber to learn the cause. "Who in Thor's name is doing all that bellowing?" He recognized

Thorne from previous dealings, noted the fierce look on his face and came to an abrupt halt. "Thorne the Relentless. What brings you to my homestead?"

"Call off your men. I seek but a private word with you."

Roar motioned his men away and led Thorne to a bench at the back of the hall. He sat down with a sigh, stretching out his leg to ease the pain. "What is it you want? Do you have more Christian slaves for me? The foreign priests I purchased from you last summer greatly pleased my clients in Baghdad."

"I'm not selling slaves this time. I'm looking for two women you recently purchased from Rolo the Bold."

Thorne could tell by the wary look on Roar's face that the trader knew of whom he spoke. "There are no female slaves here besides my own."

"One of the women you purchased from Rolo is my wife."

Roar's eyes nearly bugged out of their sockets. "I would never knowingly buy a man's wife, unless it was the husband's wish for the woman to be sold into slavery. It happens sometimes." He shrugged expansively. "I am a slave trader. I do not look too closely into a slave's background. I was led to believe the women in question were slaves. Lady Bretta approached me weeks ago about purchasing a pair of beautiful Christian slaves."

"Bretta!" Thorne spat. "I should have known she'd be involved somehow. Produce the women,

Roar, and you will be amply reimbursed for your time and trouble."

"I cannot," Roar lamented. "The women are no longer with me."

"You lie!" Aren shouted, taking a menacing step toward Roar.

"Nay. I speak the truth." He pointed to his leg. "As you can see, I'm recovering from a serious injury. I was in danger of losing my limb as well as my life. Fiona saved both and was rewarded with her freedom. She and Tyra left this morning."

"Left! I cannot believe you'd allow two defenseless women to leave in the dead of winter. Where did they go? They could both be lying dead in a snowdrift."

"They had a destination, my lord," Morag offered timidly. She'd been hovering nearby and heard the conversation between Thorne and Roar.

Thorne rounded on her. "Speak, woman! Where did my wife go?"

"Fiona believed you didn't want her, my lord. She said you had Lady Bretta sell her to my master. Rika, daughter of Garm the Black, offered her shelter."

"Rolo's wife?" Thorne questioned.

" 'Tis my understanding that Rika divorced Lord Rolo. Your wife and Tyra were dressed warmly and carried sufficient food for a six-day journey."

"My wife is with child," Thorne said, his voice taut with concern. Though late in coming, he'd finally realized that Fiona had not lied to him. The child was indeed his. If Rolo feared Fiona would render him impotent, he must have good reason to believe such a thing.

"What do we do now, Thorne?" Aren asked with a hint of desperation.

"We follow." He turned to Roar. "Can you give me directions to Garm's homestead?"

"I've done business with him a time or two. He lives south along the coast, near the town of Bergen. 'Tis late. Share our meal and sleep tonight in my hall. You can begin your journey tomorrow, when you are refreshed."

Thorne was eager to be off but he recognized the wisdom of Roar's advice. "Aye, we accept your hospitality, Roar. We were both duped by Rolo, so I do not hold you accountable for my wife's captivity."

Thorne tossed and turned most of the night. He was desperate to find Fiona before a new winter storm or brigands threatened her. When he found her he would beg for her forgiveness, though he knew he didn't deserve it.

The first few miles had presented little difficulty for Fiona and Tyra. The coast road was nearly deserted this time of the year and they'd encountered little traffic. That night they found shelter with a farmer and his family. The large one-room house was cozy and warm and the weary travelers shared it with the couple, their four children and three dogs. They also shared their simple but ample meal.

Vikings were renowned for their hospitality. The family who gave them shelter asked no questions despite their curiosity and sped them on their way the next morning after a substantial breakfast of cooked oats, warm bread and milk.

Thorne and Aren started out early, munching food Morag gave them to eat along the way. Thorne was desperate to catch up with Fiona so he set a hectic pace, jogging when the road was clear enough to do so and walking as fast as humanly possible when it was not. It was Aren's idea that they stop and make inquiries at a small homestead they passed along the way. Thorne was glad that they did, for they learned that two women had indeed sought shelter with them the night before. They declined the farmer's hospitality and moved on.

"If the weather holds, we can catch up with them tomorrow at the latest," Thorne determined. He glanced up at the lowering sky. "It doesn't look promising. Snow will fall before nightfall."

Aren's anxiety was nearly palpable. "We're traveling twice as fast as the women. Perhaps they will seek shelter early because of the threatening storm." As he spoke, large flakes of snow drifted down upon their heads. Exchanging worried glances, they broke into a brisk trot.

Both men were in excellent physical shape, possessing extraordinary strength and stamina. They covered an impossible amount of ground in a very short time. By nightfall the snow was coming down faster, and Thorne knew they had to find shelter for the night or perish in the thickening storm.

* * *

The second day of travel had been difficult for the women. A light snow had hampered their progress, and Fiona had begun to show signs of exhaustion, despite frequent rests along the way. A nagging pain in the middle of her back had plagued her off and on during the day. As night fell, they'd spied a deserted homestead nestled amid a copse of trees. Fiona was so grateful she offered a prayer of thanksgiving. Something was happening inside her body, and she knew she could go no further.

"Look, Fiona, there's a stack of wood beside the door," Tyra said excitedly, "and I have a flint in my pouch."

"I'm sure the owners won't mind," Fiona allowed. "It's threatening to storm again. Thank God we won't have to spend the night outside."

The small house was indeed deserted. It was a simple one-room dwelling containing a tiny hearth, two rickety benches pushed up against a wall, a stack of straw in one corner that served as a bed, and two rusted cooking pots turned upside down beside the hearth. There was nothing else, but it was enough.

Tyra carried in wood and used a handful of straw for tinder. The straw caught and in a short time a tiny flame set the wood afire. Once the fire was going well, they ate sparingly of the food in their pouches and made a bed in the straw, rolling in their cloaks for warmth. They both slept soundly despite the early hour.

A few hours later, sharp, knife-like pains roused

Fiona from a deep sleep. Tyra awakened to her cries.

"What is it, Fiona? Is it the babe?"

"Oh, God," Fiona sobbed. "My baby! My poor baby."

Aren had been the first to see the thin spiral of smoke rising from a copse of snow-draped trees. The snowfall was so heavy now that they had failed to notice the ramshackle hut until Aren spied the smoke.

"We'll ask for shelter," Thorne said, heading for the hut. "They look like poor people, judging from the condition of the house. They may not have extra food to share, but the fire will warm our bones."

"Aye," Aren agreed, pulling his fur cloak closer about him. "Mayhap they've seen Fiona and Tyra. We should have caught up with them by now. The pace we've set has been grueling, and we've made excellent time. You don't suppose—"

"Nay! Don't even think it. We will find them tomorrow. They probably sought shelter along the road with another farmer."

Thorne heard the scream as he stepped up to the door, followed by moaning sobs. He didn't bother to knock as he grasped the door latch and flung open the door.

Fiona was sick with despair. The babe was lost. Too tiny even to have formed within her. The violent pain and rush of blood between her legs was all the proof she needed to know she had miscarried. The scream that had escaped her lips was a furious protest against nature's cruel punishment. Fiona sobbed piteously, inconsolable. Her babe. Her precious babe, Thorne's child, was gone.

Suddenly the door was thrust open and two snow-shrouded apparitions burst into the room. Tyra screamed and hovered protectively over her mistress.

Thorne shook the snow from his cloak and pulled the hood from his head. With his beard grown shaggy, Tyra didn't recognize him at first.

"Please, kind masters, do not hurt us. My mistress just lost her babe."

Aren stepped forward. "Tyra, 'tis Aren and Thorne. We've been searching for you and Fiona."

"Aren?" Tyra appeared dazed and confused. "Oh, Aren! Thank God you've come."

Thorne was already on his knees beside Fiona, noting with horror her bloodstained skirts and pale features. Her eyes were closed, and immediately Thorne thought the worst. The blood froze in his veins as color drained from his face.

"Odin help us, she's dead!"

"Nay, Lord Thorne, she is merely sleeping," Tyra informed him. "Fiona has just lost your child and is exhausted." She sent Thorne a look of intense dislike. "What did you expect? You sold your wife and unborn child to the slave trader without a thought to her well-being. She loved you well, and you betrayed her."

Thorne cradled Fiona against him, paying scant heed to Tyra's words. He couldn't lose Fiona, not now, not when he had finally accepted that his love for Fiona had naught to do with spells and enchantments and everything to do with his heart.

The warmth of Thorne's body broke through Fiona's exhaustion, and she opened her eyes. She searched his face for the space of a heartbeat, recognized him, then beat weakly against his chest.

"Go away! I hate you! I hate you!"

Chapter Seventeen

"I don't blame you for hating me, but it wasn't my doing," Thorne argued. "I believed you had left me. Rolo and Bretta deceived us both. A courageous slave who hated Rolo told me what really happened. If not for her, I might have gone on believing that you had left with another man."

"Just leave me alone, Thorne," Fiona said on a sob. "I cannot bear the sight of you. Our child is lost. I do not even know if it was a daughter or a son."

"You're upsetting Fiona, Thorne," Tyra said, pulling Thorne away from Fiona. "She has suffered a great tragedy and needs time to heal."

"Do you think I'm not suffering?" Thorne challenged. " 'Twas my child she lost."

"This is the first time you've ever admitted that

the child is yours," Fiona charged. She turned away from him. "I'm so weary. So very weary."

"Will she recover?" Thorne asked worriedly as Fiona seemed to drift into unconsciousness.

"She's sleeping, Thorne," Tyra said. " 'Tis what she needs right now."

"How long before she can travel?" Thorne wanted to know.

"Several days, I would think. She needs rest and nourishing broth to sustain her. Perhaps you and Aren can catch a fat rabbit or two. I found two usable iron pots, and there's still plenty of firewood. I'll prepare something nourishing to sustain her when she awakens."

Though reluctant to leave, Thorne welcomed the opportunity to be useful. He felt helpless in a situation like this, and helplessness wasn't a state he enjoyed.

"I'm sorry for your loss," Aren said as they left the hut. "I will enjoy watching you wreak vengeance on Rolo and Bretta. 'Twas a vile thing they did."

"Aye," Thorne said, thinking of all the ways he'd make Rolo and Bretta suffer for what they had stolen from him and Fiona.

It rankled him to think that he was partly to blame for what had happened. Had he not left Fiona with Rolo and Bretta to fend for herself, she would still be carrying his child. There were so many obstacles to overcome that sometimes Thorne wondered whether he and Fiona would ever surmount them. Even his own brother feared and disliked her.

Then Thorne saw a fat rabbit outlined against the snow and his mind shut down as his hunter instincts took over.

Fiona's dream seemed to take on shape and substance before her closed eyes. She saw Brann standing beside her, a tender smile upon his face. She reached out to him. He grasped her hand and crouched down beside her.

"I've lost my child," Fiona said in a voice made hollow with grief.

"Do not despair, child," Brann replied, squeezing her hand. "There will be other children. Many other children. I have always known that your first son would be born on Man. He will have the strength of his father and the wisdom of his mother."

"Nay. I will bear no more of Thorne's children. I cannot bear the rejection, nor the pain of loving him and being unloved in return."

Fiona must have cried out in her sleep, for Thorne was beside her instantly, clasping her hand. Still lingering in that hazy place between sleep and full awareness, she opened her eyes, expecting to see Brann. She saw only Thorne. She blinked repeatedly, but her beloved friend and mentor did not reappear. Then she became aware of the tempting smell of cooking meat and tried to sit up. She flinched as a sharp pain pierced her innards. Then reality intruded. She had lost her child, and it was Thorne's fault. Had he not wanted to be rid of her, she'd still have her child safely beneath her heart. She didn't understand what he was doing here.

"Are you all right?" Thorne asked when her eyes focused on him. "Are you in pain?"

"The pain is in my heart," Fiona whispered. "You could have told me yourself that you didn't want me instead of having Bretta do it for you. I would have returned to Man long ago had you allowed it."

Thorne recalled everything he had said and done to earn Fiona's distrust. He remembered accusing her of enjoying her role as Rolo's mistress. He recalled how he had stubbornly refused to believe the child she carried was his, listening instead to Rolo's and Bretta's lies.

"I'm guilty of many things but not the sin of selling you," Thorne denied.

"Admit it. Had our child lived, you would have always wondered to whom it belonged," Fiona charged.

Thorne had nothing to say to that. Lying didn't come easily to him. Though he regretted it with all his heart, Fiona's words were partly true. The notion that Fiona carried Rolo's child had festered and grown until Thorne hadn't known what or whom to believe.

"Perhaps," Thorne admitted. "That is something we will never know for sure. Forgive me for causing you such grief. I don't care if I'm bewitched. 'Tis no longer important. You're mine, Fiona. We are still husband and wife according to your Christian God."

"Continue your conversation later, Thorne," Tyra said, shooing him away. Aren was right behind her, carrying the pot of broth Tyra had made. He set it down beside Fiona.

"We have no dishes but we do have our spoons," Tyra said, removing a spoon from her pouch and handing it to Fiona. "We will eat after you have had your fill."

When Fiona would have taken the spoon from Tyra, Thorne moved to intercept. He grasped the utensil in his hand and patiently spooned the broth into Fiona's mouth, feeding her bits of cooked rabbit between each mouthful of broth. Despite the lack of salt, the broth was rich and filling, and when she'd eaten her fill, Thorne helped her to lie down.

While she rested, Thorne, Aren and Tyra shared the remaining broth and rabbit and discussed plans.

"Fiona isn't fit to travel," Thorne said in a low voice.

"What are we going to do?" Aren asked, anxious to do anything to help Thorne and Fiona.

"I think you and Tyra should continue on to Garm's homestead. Fiona and I will follow as soon as she's able to travel."

"Can you survive here that long?" Aren asked worriedly.

"Aye. I've done it before. There is plenty of wild game to fill our bellies, and wood to feed the fire. We have fur cloaks to keep us warm and a bed of straw to lie upon. The hut is in fair condition despite its neglect. We will manage."

After the meal, Aren and Tyra moved a portion of straw to the opposite corner and bedded down for the night. Thorne lay down beside Fiona, pulling his cloak over both of them. When he took her into his arms, she stiffened but did not protest. A few minutes later he heard her even breathing and knew she had fallen asleep. Holding her tightly against him, he joined her in slumber.

When Fiona awakened the following morning, it was so quiet she feared she had been abandoned. The hut was empty save for herself; there was no sign of Thorne, Tyra or Aren. Then the door swung open and Thorne entered, filling the room with his dynamic presence. His arms were piled high with firewood, which he proceeded to stack next to the hearth. Fiona was quick to note that he had scraped the beard from his face with his blade while she slept.

"Where are the others?" Fiona asked, surprised that her voice was so weak.

Thorne whirled at the sound of her voice and strode over to her makeshift bed. "You're awake. How do you feel?"

Fiona's hand went to her stomach. "Empty." She felt like crying.

"Fiona, I—"

"Nay, I do not wish to talk about it." She turned her face away from him.

Thorne dropped to his knees beside her. "Don't turn away from me, love. I'm consumed with guilt over this. 'Tis my child you lost."

"I don't care what Brann said," she said wistfully, "this child will be sorely missed."

"Brann? Brann is dead." Was she hallucinating? Thorne wondered as he placed a hand on her forehead, testing for fever. She was cool to his touch.

"Aye, Brann is dead, but there is a special bond between us that defies space and time, even death."

"Brann spoke to you? What did he say?" Thorne was curious now, despite his lack of faith in Fiona's ability to speak to the dead. But Fiona had proved him wrong so many times, he thought it best to hear her out.

"He told me not to despair, that there would be other children."

"And there will be, Fiona. I will give you all the children you want."

Fiona shook her head. " 'Tis too late, Thorne. I do not want your children."

"I know you're hurting now, but—"

"You know naught of how I feel!" Fiona charged. "No man can know how a woman feels after losing a child. Perhaps I will have other children but they will not be yours, Thorne the Relentless."

Thorne wisely decided not to argue the point. Fiona was too weak to waste energy exchanging angry words. "I sent Aren and Tyra on to Garm's homestead. We will follow in a few days."

"Why didn't you go with them? I can take care of myself without your help."

Thorne scowled at her. "I would never leave you, Fiona. I'll take care of you until you're well enough to travel."

"Is that what you truly want, Thorne? Or are you

staying with me merely to salve your guilty conscience?"

"Remember when I said I felt bereft without you, that I want you with me always? Naught has changed. I missed you. I couldn't wait to return to tell you that I loved you, that I'd been a fool to doubt you. When Rolo told me you'd left with another man I wanted to kill someone. I apologize for believing you capable of such deceit. What will it take for you to forgive me?"

"I'm not sure I can ever forgive you. Perhaps if our child had lived . . . but 'tis too late now."

"I'll make you love me, Fiona, I swear it."

Fiona sighed and closed her eyes. She felt broken, as if the pieces of her life had been shredded and trampled upon. Before, there had always been Thorne to cling to, but now she felt abandoned and lost. She wanted to go home, to see her father, to enjoy the soft air and rolling green hills of her jewel-like island. She wanted to forget all the unhappy times with Thorne, as well as the happy ones, and return to her simple life as a healer.

When Fiona remained mute, Thorne moved determinedly to the hearth and carefully removed the iron pot from the fire. He had filled it with snow earlier and placed it over the fire to melt.

"I heated water in case you'd like a good wash," he said as he set the steaming pot of water beside her. He didn't wait for a reply as he removed the brooch at her shoulder and lifted her so he could remove her tunic and undergarments.

"I can do it," Fiona protested weakly.

"Let me," Thorne said firmly, pushing her hands aside.

With deft hands he removed her clothing and covered her with her fur cloak. Then he tore a piece of her tunic, dunked it into the warm water and pulled back the cloak, baring her upper torso. With gentle strokes he washed her face, neck, arms and breasts. When he finished he covered her upper body and bared her lower extremities. He winced at the sight of her bloodstained thighs but set to work with grim purpose.

"There," he said, rinsing the cloth one last time. "Now I'll see about getting you some breakfast. The rabbit I caught and cleaned this morning is simmering over the fire. Can you smell it? After you've eaten, you can take a nap while I wash out your clothes and dry them before the fire."

Watching Thorne perform feminine duties was an awe-inspiring sight. Vikings weren't known for their domestic skills. Thorne was special in so many ways, she thought dimly, but that still didn't alter the decision she had made. He'd have to earn her trust before she relented.

Thorne sat beside Fiona, watching her sleep. The numbness that had set in after he'd learned that Fiona had been sold was just beginning to wear off. She had suffered enormously because of Bretta's jealousy and Rolo's pride. He'd almost lost her. The loss of their child had been heartrending, but losing Fiona would have been the final blow. She'd be shocked if she knew how desperately he needed her, how very much he . . .

Loved her.

Fiona insisted upon moving about the hut the next day. She was growing stronger but wasn't strong enough yet to attempt a journey. Thorne began to fret when he noticed signs of a new storm gathering over the horizon. Fearing they might be snowed in for a while, he went out that day, trapped several rabbits and brought down a young buck.

Thorne knew that he and Fiona wouldn't starve as long as he had his weapons, nor would they freeze to death with a roof over their heads and plenty of wood nearby for burning. He was grateful to the previous occupants of the hut for the iron pots, thankful for his weapons and for the various implements he'd had the foresight to carry with him. And for the bag of herbal remedies Fiona carried with her. Thorne had little doubt that her rapid recovery was due to the herbs she steeped in hot water and drank three times a day.

Fierce and relentless, the expected storm struck the following day. Wind howled and pellets of icy snow struck the sides of the hut with daunting force. There were times when Thorne feared they would be blown away. But they were surprisingly warm and cozy huddled together beside the blazing fire, wrapped in their fur cloaks. With enough food to last them for several days, Thorne felt strangely at peace. There was no one he'd rather be snowbound with than Fiona.

Fiona, on the other hand, was restless and melancholy. The loss of her child still filled her with grief and she felt as if she had been cast adrift. Even as Thorne's captive, her life had had a purpose . . . making Thorne love her. She had begun to believe that she and Thorne belonged together. Then just when she'd found love, her whole world had fallen apart.

The storm dumped two feet of new snow on the countryside. Thorne stomped a path to the latrine so that Fiona could visit it without getting lost in a snowdrift. With little to do but wait out the storm, a tentative peace formed between them. It might be days, or weeks even, before they could continue their journey. And little by little, Fiona's stamina was returning.

Thorne was able to go out hunting again and returned more often than not with enough fresh meat to keep them from going hungry. When Fiona spent too much time staring moodily into the hearth, brooding and grieving, Thorne did his best to distract her with tales of his adventures in Byzantium and other foreign countries.

Compared to her rather mundane existence, Fiona thought he had lived a fascinating life. The more time she spent with him, the more she realized that no other man would ever measure up to Thorne.

One day, after they had been cooped up in the hut for two weeks, Fiona expressed a desire to bathe. Thorne stretched his cloak between two wooden pegs in the wall in order to make a private place for her. Bathing and washing her hair in an iron pot wasn't the ideal way to bathe but it sufficed. When she stepped out from behind the makeshift curtain a short time later, her face shiny and her hair hanging in loose waves down her back, Thorne was so struck by her beauty he could not have stopped what happened next had he wanted to.

Paying scant heed to Thorne's passion-glazed eyes, Fiona knelt before the hearth combing her fingers through her hair. She was surprised when Thorne knelt behind her and pulled her against him. Through the barrier of their clothing she could feel the overwhelming heat emanating from his body.

She stiffened. "Thorne, don't." She feared her response to this unique man, feared the way her body tingled and her heart pounded when he touched her.

"I need to hold you, Fiona. I could have lost you for good. One day I hope to identify the thrall who told me the truth about your disappearance and reward her." He turned Fiona about to face him.

He knew his reputation as a ruthless marauder instilled fear in men and women alike, but with Fiona he had found a place within him that was soft and nurturing. Should his brother or comrades learn of this defect in his character, they would surely laugh at the way one small woman had accomplished what no man had ever dared.

"I'm going to kiss you, love."

Fiona felt something inside her crumble and feared it was her defenses. After an uncertain pause, she said, "I'd prefer that you didn't."

He understood her fear and sought to banish it. He wanted her to want him. He wanted her to feel the same emotional storm of passion that drove him. "You're mine, Fiona. You've always been mine. First my captive, then my wife. There is nothing I can do to change what happened to our child, but I can help you to forget for a time."

His mouth took hers before she could form a protest. His lips were firm, hot, persistent, demanding a response. At first Fiona was determined to withhold her response, but as his mouth worked magic on hers and his tongue coaxed her lips apart and slipped past her defenses, her body slowly relaxed.

Thorne molded her against him, one hand solid against her spine and the other tangled in her long hair. Then his hands began to roam, cupping her firm buttocks, squeezing her narrow waist, finally settling on her breasts. His kiss deepened, his tongue seeking the heat of her mouth. Fiona sighed and wound her arms around his neck. Her moan started in the pit of her stomach and worked its way up into his mouth. He swallowed it with a tortured groan as he scooped her up into his arms and carried her to their bed of straw. He laid her down gently and followed her down.

"This isn't a good idea," Fiona gasped when she finally tore her mouth free.

"Is it too soon?" Thorne asked. The startling blue of his eyes had turned dark with passion. "I don't want to hurt you."

"Nay, I am healed," Fiona said. " 'Tis not that."

"I want to love you," Thorne whispered, nuzzling her ear. "Your body wants me, Fiona. 'Tis been so long I am nearly mad with need. I never knew a man could want his own wife the way I want you."

"Perhaps you are still bewitched," Fiona taunted.

He stared at her, chuckling softly. " 'Tis a condition I welcome. I care not about witchcraft, or any spells you may or may not be capable of. I want you, Fiona; that will never change."

He buried his face in the warm hollow of her throat, kissing and licking the furiously beating pulse. Fiona's head fell back, allowing him access as her senses whirled dangerously out of control.

This man was so familiar, yet she felt that she knew him not at all. She had made love with him, slept with him, done all the intimate things a woman does with a man, and still she didn't really know him.

"What happens when this attraction between us dies a natural death?"

"By then I'll be too old to care. Have you already grown tired of me?"

"That's not a fair question. You're the one who divorced me. You claimed I had bewitched you and refused to acknowledge the child I carried."

"I was a fool," he said simply. "Forgive me, Fiona."

Fiona's eyes widened. It wasn't like Thorne to beg forgiveness. It wasn't in his nature; he was such a prideful man, this Viking she had married. "I don't know if I *can* forgive you."

"Try," he whispered against her lips.

His hands were warm, gentle, determined as he peeled away her tunic and chemise and tossed them aside. Her stockings and boots were quickly discarded. Then he stood and removed his own clothing. Fiona gazed up at him; her breath stilled and her violet eyes glazed at the sight of the most splendid man God had ever created.

He was a large, rawboned man, but there wasn't an ounce of fat on him. His shoulders were wide and his torso thickly muscled. There was implied strength in the corded tendons stretching down his long thighs and legs. His buttocks were firm and high and hard. His manhood was already full and growing harder as it rose upward against his flat stomach. Her hands curled into fists as the urge to touch him became unbearable.

He came down on his knees beside her. "You're beautiful," he whispered, awed by the dark-haired beauty stretched out before him in all her naked glory. "Unless you tell me my loving will hurt you, that you're not ready yet after your ordeal, naught will stop me from making love to you."

Fiona shook her head. She was ready. She wanted him. One couldn't turn love off and on at will. Had Thorne wanted her out of his life, she reasoned, he wouldn't be with her now, taking care of her, keeping her warm, fed and safe. She'd been a fool to believe Bretta's lies. But at the time it had all seemed so plausible, and she'd been too hurt to give the matter more serious thought.

"I'm not going to stop you," Fiona said. "I

shouldn't have been so willing to believe Bretta and Rolo. Bretta still wants you, you know."

"Bretta wants any man who will have her," Thorne scoffed. " 'Tis unfortunate, or fortunate, however you look at it, that no man will have her. Forget that bitch. In the summer we will journey to Man. Rolo and Bretta will never bother us again."

"You're going to stay with me?" Fiona asked, stunned by his words.

Thorne frowned. "I thought you knew that. A husband and wife belong together. Your island is rich and fertile, much more suited to homesteading than my own homeland. The climate is gentle. 'Tis a place where crops and children will prosper. We will begin our own dynasty on Man. The one thing I regret is leaving Thorolf behind. I will miss him."

Suddenly a picture formed in a dark void somewhere within Fiona's brain. She pulled her gaze away from Thorne as glimpses of the future rushed past her eyes. She saw Thorolf and the woman who would one day become his wife, walking hand-in-hand on the Isle of Man with their children frolicking around them. Fiona smiled as the image faded away, for she had seen the face of Thorolf's future wife.

"What are you smiling about?" Thorne asked curiously.

"The future," Fiona said, her smile widening. "You will not lose your brother."

"Is that all you're going to say?"

" 'Tis enough."

"Aye, more than enough. I cannot think beyond

the fact that you're lying naked in my arms and I'm still not inside you."

His eyes darkened to midnight blue as he lowered his head and kissed her breasts, first one, then the other. He stroked her buttocks and thighs as he concentrated on her breasts, licking and sucking her nipples until they hardened into taut buds, so exquisitely sensitive that a sigh escaped Fiona's lips.

She stretched her hand down his abdomen and curled it around his staff. He groaned and pushed his hips forward, pressing himself into her palm. Her fingers tightened. He went rigid, fearing he would shatter if he moved. Yet it was impossible to remain still. He let her stroke him for a breathless moment, then removed her hand.

Her fingers dug into his shoulders as his hand slid around her thigh and down between them into her nest of downy curls. She gave a choked moan as he stroked the moist cleft, and her pelvis surged upward into his hand. His fingers flexed, two of them sliding into her silken entrance, lavish with sweet moisture and so hot she scorched him. She tightened around his fingers and bit back a scream.

"I love the way you respond to me," Thorne whispered as he worked his fingers inside her.

"You know exactly where to touch me," Fiona gasped. "Dear God, I'm going to shatter."

"Nay, not yet," Thorne said, giving her a wicked grin as he shifted down her body. "Soon, very soon." Then he lowered his head and touched her with his tongue. She went wild as he stroked and feasted upon that intensely sensitive place. "Now," Thorne urged, giving her leave to seek the ultimate pleasure. "Now you may shatter."

The slow slide of his tongue, combined with the motion of his fingers inside her was incredibly erotic. Blood pounded in her temples, building to a climax as annihilating heat danced through her. Moments later, violent spasms ripped through her.

Thorne slid up her body and inside her while she was still climbing the heights of ecstasy. He thrust upward; Fiona's eyes widened when that small motion intensified her pleasure. He rocked against her and she responded with short, savage thrusts of her loins. His fingers dug into her thighs; he drove violently upward, raw, frantic sounds echoing from within his chest.

"Fiona!" Her name was ripped from his throat as he gave up his seed.

Not quite ready to withdraw, he rested his forehead against hers. "I didn't hurt you, did I?"

"You didn't hurt me. That . . . that was incredible. Will it always be like that?"

"Only for the rest of our lives." He rolled to his side and gathered her against him, pulling his fur cloak over them. "I have just one piece of unfinished business to take care of before I bid farewell to my homeland."

Attuned to his mood, Fiona knew exactly what he was thinking. "Forget it, Thorne. There is little pleasure in revenge."

"I cannot. What Rolo and Bretta did is unforgivable."

Fiona sighed. Life was so complicated. If only Brann were here to advise her. Then her thoughts scattered as Thorne began to make love to her again.

The next day the sun made a welcome appearance. Two days later the weather turned unseasonably mild, and Thorne made preparations for their departure. Fiona had fully recovered from her miscarriage and was as anxious as he to leave the limiting confines of the hut.

The day they left was cold and crisp; no sign of a new storm loomed on the horizon. That night they sought shelter with a friendly farmer. Overnight the weather changed abruptly from clear to gray and overcast, but no new snow had fallen when they resumed their journey. The first sign of trouble arrived unexpectedly about mid-afternoon. Thorne heard the baying of wolves in the distance.

"We have to find shelter," Thorne said, startling Fiona with his urgency.

"Why?"

"Wolves. They've caught our scent. I don't know how many there are, but I'd prefer not to be caught out in the open when they attack."

His words sent chills down Fiona's spine as she searched frantically for some form of shelter. There was nothing but trees, distant mountains and open areas of smooth snow. Then it was too late.

"Quickly," Thorne said, "into that tree." He boosted her up into the crook of the nearest tree and turned to face the wolves, who had just caught up with them.

There were four of them. They circled Thorne warily, their jaws gaping open, their mouths slavering in anticipation. Thorne displayed no fear as he clutched his battleaxe in one hand and Blood-drinker in the other. The wolf closest to Thorne crouched, then sprang. Thorne vanquished it with a single stroke of his battleaxe. The remaining wolves sniffed around their fallen comrade, then turned their glittering eyes upon Thorne. Two wolves leaped for Thorne's throat. Thorne killed one before he was brought down by the second. He tossed aside his battleaxe and reached for his knife.

Fiona screamed as wolf and man rolled on the ground in mortal combat. When the fourth wolf joined the fray, Fiona cried out a warning. Fortunately, Thorne was prepared. Slashing upward, he cut the throat of the third wolf, then he rolled to his feet to confront the fourth. The wolf must have realized he was alone and likely to end up like his hapless companions, for he turned and loped away, his tail between his legs.

Thorne stood ready to attack should the wolf return, but the forest was silent. The enemy had fled. Panting, Thorne did not relax his stance as he fought for breath. The attack had happened so quickly he was having a difficult time mastering the surge of adrenaline still pumping through his body.

Fiona couldn't believe what she had seen. Thorne had been magnificent; his strength and courage were incredible. She knew of no other man who could singlehandedly defeat four hungry wolves.

"Are you all right?" she asked, noting with alarm the numerous scratches on his arms and face and the bloodstained rip in his woolen trousers.

"These scratches are nothing. I've had worse."

"Help me down. I have some salve that will prevent infection."

He lifted her from the tree and stood patiently while she removed a small jar of salve from her pouch and spread it over his wounds.

"That was an incredibly brave thing you did," she said, reaching up to plant a kiss on his mouth.

His arms came around her, hugging her tightly. "I would slay dragons for you, Fiona. But not today, I hope. I've had my fill of wild beasts. Let us be on our way before the fellow that fled returns with his friends."

That night they arrived at a small fishing village and were given food and a bed by a widow who took in travelers. They continued on the next day and arrived in the village of Bergen before nightfall. Upon inquiry, Thorne learned they were but an hour's walk from the homestead of Garm the Black. They arrived amidst a great outcry of welcome. Tyra and Rika were so happy to see Fiona that they fell upon her, weeping with joy.

Chapter Eighteen

Garm the Black clasped Fiona's hands warmly. "I've wanted to thank you from the moment my daughter told me how you risked your life to help her. Had I known of Rolo the Bold's abusive nature I would never have allowed Rika to marry him."

A handsome, statuesque woman approached Fiona. "I am Garda, Rika's mother. My daughter is dear to us. I'd like to add my thanks to that of my husband. Welcome to our home."

"We were so worried about you," Rika said. "Tyra told us of your . . . your loss. I know it was a blow, but I'm glad to see you have recovered. When the weather turned bitter, we feared you had been caught in the storm."

"We waited the storm out," Fiona said. "Thorne

hunted for our food, and there was wood in the forest to feed our fire."

Aren, observant as always, noted the bloodstains on Thorne's clothing. "What happened? Am I right in assuming your journey wasn't without mishap?"

"We encountered a pack of hungry wolves," Fiona explained. "We escaped without serious injury, thanks to Thorne's skill with battleaxe and sword."

"Our travel was happily tame compared to yours," Aren said.

"Come, sit by the fire and tell us everything," Garm urged. "You must be exhausted."

Garm the Black was a large man whose white hair and beard presented a deceptively benign facade. He was called the Black because when he was young his hair had been black as pitch, which was unusual in a land of blond men and women. He was dressed in rich brocade robes befitting a wealthy jarl, but there was nothing soft about the hard-featured, steely-eyed man. Fiona thought he would make a formidable enemy.

Fiona accepted a mug of hot mulled wine, sipping and listening as Thorne related the trials of their journey.

"Rika told us you sold your own wife into slavery," Garm charged harshly. "Is that true, Thorne the Relentless?"

"Nay," Thorne denied. "Fiona is dear to me. I gave no such order. Rolo and Bretta lied. They feared Fiona and wanted to be rid of her. Think you I would sell my own child into slavery?"

Garda regarded him through keen blue eyes, apparently satisfied that he told the truth. "You and your party are welcome to shelter with us as long as you please," she said. "Rika has grown fond of Fiona and Tyra, and will be happy for the company."

"Thank you," Thorne said graciously. "Fiona and Tyra knew they would be made welcome when they set out for your hall. We accept your hospitality. I intend to take Fiona home to Man this summer, but first I have unfinished business with Rolo the Bold."

"Ah," Garm said, smiling. "We are of the same mind where Rolo is concerned. He sent my daughter home without her dowry. All the jewelry of silver and gold, the farm animals and land she brought with her to the marriage should have remained her personal property. There were many ells of wool and linen, bedding, even a spinning wheel and loom. Yet Rolo sent Rika home a pauper." His face hardened. "I will give him a chance to return them, but if he refuses, I intend to take them by force."

"I had to leave everything behind, Father; 'twas the only way Rolo would let me go," Rika claimed. "I promised he could keep my dowry, that you wouldn't demand its return."

"You did what was necessary to save your life, daughter," Garm said kindly. "I cannot fault you. But you had no right to speak for me. Rolo mistreated you. When you divorced him, he should have returned your dowry. I cannot allow his vile treatment of you to go unpunished."

"And I cannot allow him to go on living," Thorne said harshly.

"What about Bretta?" Aren wondered. "She is as guilty as her brother."

Thorne smiled grimly. "I will think of something appropriate for Bretta."

"Then we are in accord," Garm said.

Garm's house was larger than most homesteads, with an exceptionally large hall and central hearth. Curtained alcoves spaced around the hall served as private sleeping quarters for important guests. Thorne and Fiona were given one of the larger alcoves, while Aren and Tyra shared another. The remaining alcoves were occupied by Garm's ranking warriors. Slaves, servants and lower-ranking warriors slept on benches and the floor. Only Garm and his wife and Rika had private sleeping chambers.

Fiona was pleased that she and Thorne were to have a modicum of privacy in their bed of furs behind the curtain. She'd had her fill of sleeping on benches beside karls and thralls. She'd finally come to accept the fact that Thorne wasn't going to leave her, that he loved her and would do nothing to harm her. Brann's prophesy had finally come to pass. The sorcerer had read the stars, interpreted the runes and accurately foretold her future.

"What are you thinking?" Thorne asked one night as they lay in their bed behind the curtain. "You're so quiet."

"I'm thinking how much I love you and how dreadfully I miss Brann. He never let me forget that a Viking invader would steal my heart. I didn't want to believe him, but to my knowledge he'd never made a prophesy that didn't come true."

"I'm grateful I was the Viking who stole your heart. Tell me one thing, love. Did you really bewitch me that first day I saw you on Man?"

"Perhaps I did," Fiona teased. "Or maybe Brann placed a spell on the first Viking to set eyes upon me. Does it matter?"

"Nay, witch or no, you're the woman I want. I didn't have to marry you, you know. You were mine; I could have taken you whenever I pleased and no one would have interfered. I sought out a priest because I wanted to please you. I didn't understand it at the time, but I knew it was something I had to do. I blamed it on your black magic. I was right in one respect: you have indeed enchanted me, and I hope it never ends."

They made love that night, sweet, tender love. Thorne was so gentle it brought tears to Fiona's eyes. She was happier than she'd been in a very long time. Of course she still mourned her child, but she knew there would be another child to love one day.

Later, as they rested in one another's arms, Thorne said, "Do you recall telling me that you hated me?"

Fiona sighed. "At that time I truly thought I did. I believed you had arranged for me to be sold to Roar. I had just lost my child and blamed you for my loss."

"How do you feel now?"

"You know how I feel. I have loved you for a very long time, Thorne. Even if Brann hadn't told me I would love a Viking, I would have loved you."

"I wish . . ."

"What do you wish?" Fiona wondered.

"I wish Thorolf would relent where you're concerned. I sent Aren to inform my brother of Rolo's deceitful act and to tell him where to find me should he need me."

"Aye, Tyra is going to miss him while he's gone. What do you think Thorolf will do?"

"Naught, I hope. At least not for the time being. I just wanted to be sure he'll fight at my side when I confront Rolo."

"I wish you'd just let it go," Fiona sighed. " 'Tis enough that we're leaving this land."

Thorne's expression hardened. "Vikings do not forget."

In the days that followed, Thorne joined Garm's warriors on frequent hunting expeditions while Fiona pitched in with women's work. There was always something to do with so large a household to provide for, including spinning, making clothing for household members, and overseeing the food supplies that had to last during the long, dark winter months. Herbs had to be made into medicines and salves to cure the sick.

Fiona took charge of the family medicine chest. She spent countless hours pointing out the special qualities of herbs that were unfamiliar to Garda, for Garda was not a true healer like Fiona and had only limited knowledge.

* * *

When Aren returned a fortnight later he was not alone. Thorne was preparing to join a group of men for a day's hunting when the door opened and several men trooped inside. One was Aren, another was Thorolf. Thorne flung his bow and arrow aside and went to welcome his brother.

"Thorolf! Odin's bones, what brings you here?" They clasped arms, clearly glad to see one another. "I sent Aren to inform you of my whereabouts, not to bring you forth from your warm home."

"I was growing bored," Thorolf said with a grin. "I left Ulm in charge and decided to see what my big brother was up to."

"I assume Aren told you what occurred at Rolo's homestead."

"Aye. 'Tis a despicable thing he did to you. I never approved of your infatuation with Fiona, but I've done a lot of thinking this winter. 'Twas wrong of me to deny you access to your own home because you refused to abandon the woman you obviously love. I don't know whether Fiona bewitched you or not, but 'twas unfair of me to blame her for the ills our family suffered." He licked moisture onto his lips, wondering how to begin. Finally he blurted out, "I'm sorry about the child, Thorne. Aren told me everything. There is no longer any doubt in my mind that the child was yours."

A look of intense pain passed over Thorne's face. "Aye, 'twas wrong of you," he agreed. "Fiona never wished any of us ill. We hope there will be other children. Have you truly changed your mind about Fiona, Thorolf?"

"I will give Fiona the benefit of the doubt," Thorolf said after a long pause. "She is your wife and deserves respect."

"Come greet Fiona. Then you can tell me why you're really here."

Fiona watched with trepidation as Thorne and Thorolf approached from across the room. But this time she felt no enmity radiating from Thorolf. She sensed hesitancy and indecision, and for that improvement she was grateful. She smiled in genuine welcome, recalling the vision she'd seen of Thorolf and his family, and the fleeting glimpse of the woman he'd married.

"I'm a man who recognizes his mistakes, Fiona," Thorolf began uncertainly. "You are Thorne's wife, and are welcome to live in my hall with Thorne. As for the other"—his large shoulders rose in a shrug—"you may be a witch, and may have enchanted my brother, but it doesn't matter so long as Thorne is satisfied with you."

"Thank you, Thorolf," Fiona said. "I've never meant your family any harm. I have no powers beyond those of a healer. Sometimes I'm allowed to see things," she amended, "but my visions have never hurt anyone and on many occasions have been of help."

Thorolf nodded, his attention suddenly diverted by the approach of Rika and her parents. Fiona noted his distraction and smiled when she saw him staring at Rika with intense interest. Thorne quickly introduced Thorolf to Garm and his family.

"Welcome to our home," Garm said.

Thorolf's gaze never left Rika's blushing face. It was obvious to Fiona that the attraction was mutual. Even Garm noted the attention Thorolf was lavishing on Rika. Thorne appeared to be the only one oblivious to the couple's interest in one another.

Garm got right to the point. "How long will you stay with us, Thorolf? Must you return to your wife and children right away?"

"I have neither wife nor children," Thorolf admitted, "though 'tis long past time I took one. I will stay for a short visit. My brother and I have important matters to discuss."

"Then I will give you privacy," Garm said, guiding his wife and daughter away. Thorolf followed Rika's progress across the hall until it became apparent that he was staring.

"Rika is an attractive woman," he said thoughtfully.

"Rika may be young but she's not weak," Fiona replied. "She survived Rolo's abuse and grew stronger from it. She will allow no man to abuse her again."

Thorolf stiffened, his hands clenched into fists at his sides. "I will kill Rolo for what he did to her."

"Nay," Thorne said tightly. "You may have him only after I am finished with him."

Thorolf frowned. "There will be nothing left after you finish with him. Aren told me that Rolo abused his wife. I hadn't expected Rika to be so appealing," he mused thoughtfully.

Thorne stared at him, finally understanding. "You are smitten with Rika."

Fiona giggled. "Why are men so dense when it comes to love?"

"Love? I said nothing of love," Thorolf returned shortly. "I merely find Rika appealing. Is she promised to anyone?"

"Garm has vowed that Rika could choose her own husband next time," Fiona informed him. "She's understandably shy of marriage. If you two will excuse me, I promised Rika I'd help salt meat the hunters brought in yesterday."

Fiona moved away as Thorne and Thorolf settled on a nearby bench and promptly forgot her while they spoke together in low tones.

Rika and Tyra had already begun the salting process when Fiona arrived to help. "Thorne's brother is a handsome man," Rika said shyly.

"He admires you, too," Fiona allowed. " 'Tis time he took a wife."

A hint of red crept up Rika's throat. "I don't know if I could make a man happy after Rolo. Or if I could even allow a man to . . . to . . ."

"With the right man you could," Fiona ventured. "Not all men are like Rolo. But I truly don't know if Thorolf is a gentle man. That is something you have to find out for yourself if you're interested."

The conversation ended when Garda joined them. "The winter will pass quickly with Thorne and Thorolf here to liven up the evenings," Garda said happily. " 'Tis been a long time since we've had such interesting company."

"Has Thorolf agreed to stay?" Rika asked with more enthusiasm than was warranted.

"Your father thinks he'll stay," Garda said, regarding her daughter thoughtfully. "Does that please you?"

Rika's cheeks burned. "It matters not to me whether he stays or goes."

Fiona was not fooled, nor, she thought, was Rika's mother. Fiona had been allowed a glimpse into the future and knew what the others did not.

That night one of the last storms of the winter roared down upon them with the ferocity of a ravening demon, making travel all but impossible. While virtually snowed in, Thorolf and Rika spent their evenings in a dark corner of the hall, their heads together, speaking in hushed voices.

Rika later confided to Fiona that she believed Thorolf was not like Rolo, but she still was hesitant to commit herself. She recalled that Rolo had seemed the perfect husband until he'd gotten her alone in his bedchamber; then he'd turned into a rapacious beast.

Three weeks after the storm inundated them with snow, the sun came out and spring thaw began. It was mid-March. Though a spring storm wasn't out of the ordinary, according to Thorne, Fiona hoped to see green grass soon, and budding trees. Spring also heralded the time of serious planning for Rolo's downfall.

Fiona, Rika and Tyra were allowed to sit in on the planning sessions because they had been the ones to suffer the brunt of Rolo's abuse. Fiona listened carefully as each man contributed to the conversation.

"I will return home immediately and train with my warriors," Thorolf informed them. "They have grown lax during the winter."

"My men have passed the winter in the village with their families," Thorne said, "but they will come to my aid when I send for them. Aren can contact them and set up practice sessions with sword and battleaxe." He directed his next words to his brother. "This is not your fight, Thorolf. You need not risk yourself if you don't wish to."

Thorolf and Rika exchanged a look that hinted at private matters. When Rika nodded slightly, Thorolf cleared his throat, garnering the attention of the others. But it was to Garm that he spoke.

"I have Rika's permission to speak to you about a personal matter, Garm. I wish to wed Rika, and she is agreeable. Should you give your blessing to the match, challenging Rolo for the return of her dowry will become my right."

Garm didn't appear surprised. "I have no objection as long as Rika wishes to become your wife. What say you, daughter?"

"I would have Thorolf, Father. I am convinced he is not like Rolo."

"Then I agree to the match. The wedding will take place at the *althing* next month. Now, back to business," Garm continued once the matter of Rika's future was settled. "I have a dozen warriors at my disposal. Our combined forces will outnumber

Rolo's warriors. By law, Rika's dowry must be returned. I vow Rolo will not grow rich off of my daughter's gold and silver, nor will he use the land that is rightfully hers."

" 'Tis Garm's and Thorolf's right to fight for Rika's dowry," Thorne said. "I want naught but Rolo's life. I lost a child and nearly lost my wife because of his vile deeds. I swear he will not live to hurt another woman. Nor will Bretta work her evil upon another unsuspecting innocent again."

"Killing is against God's law," Fiona whispered, stunned by Thorne's vindictiveness.

"Vengeance is a Viking's right," Thorne claimed, scowling. "How can you argue for their lives after what they did to you?"

"I am a Christian, Thorne. Killing another human is a mortal sin."

"You need kill no one," Thorne said blithely. "I will happily perform that task for you."

"Thorne is right, Fiona," Thorolf contended. "Neither Rolo nor his sister deserves to live."

" 'Tis settled, then," Garm declared. "Thorolf will return to his homestead and whip his men into shape while Aren takes charge of Thorne's men. Thorne can train here with my own warriors. Four weeks from today we will all gather in the woods beyond Rolo's homestead. I will approach Rolo first and demand the return of Rika's dowry. If he gives it up without a fight, Thorne is welcome to exact revenge upon him and his sister in any way he sees fit.

"But should Rolo refuse to return the dowry and

initiate a battle, our combined forces will retaliate. Are we agreed?"

Before the men could voice their agreement, Fiona spoke up. "Rika, Tyra and I wish to join you."

"Nay!" Thorne and Thorolf roared at the same time.

" 'Tis too dangerous for women," Thorne added more reasonably.

Rika rose abruptly, stretching to her full height of nearly six feet. "Viking women have fought beside their men down through the ages. We are a strong and hardy lot, as fierce as our warrior husbands."

"Tyra and Fiona are not Viking women," Thorne argued. "They have not the strength of our women."

"Aye," Aren agreed. "I'd prefer that Tyra remain with Garda. And as long as we are discussing important matters, I wish to ask Thorne to release Tyra from slavery so that I may wed her at the same time Thorolf and Rika marry. Tyra is carrying my child."

Tyra flushed and studied her hands.

"Is the child the reason you wish to marry Tyra?" Thorne asked.

"Nay!" Aren said fiercely. "I love Tyra. I want to spend the rest of my life with her. We wish to sail with you to Man."

"Tyra, do you wish to marry Aren?" Thorne wanted to know.

"Aye, with all my heart."

"So be it," Thorne decreed. "I will release Tyra from slavery and dower her myself."

"That still doesn't answer our question. Will you take us with you?" Fiona persisted. "Tyra and I are not weaklings. If you do not allow us to accompany you, we will follow with or without your permission."

"Aye," Tyra and Rika agreed in unison.

The men exchanged resigned looks. "Very well," Garm said, speaking for the others. "The women can accompany us, but they will not be allowed to join in the battle."

Rika, Fiona and Tyra nodded, readily agreeing to the conditions.

Four weeks passed with alarming speed. Thorne worked daily with Garm's men, conditioning them for battle. Vikings liked nothing better than a good skirmish, and the men looked forward with relish to the pure excitement of combat. Finally the time of departure arrived. Most of the snow had melted, revealing patches of green and brown beneath a thin crust of ice. Spring arrived earlier along the seashore than it did in the mountains, making for easier and faster travel along the coastal roads and byways.

The women had been fitted with helms and light armor and provided with swords. Rika's blade was full-sized, but Fiona and Tyra received lighter ones fashioned especially for them. The night before their journey, Fiona and Thorne lay in their bed behind the curtained alcove, whispering together.

"Don't forget," Thorne reminded her. "The women are to remain behind the warriors at all times. I almost lost you once and will not tempt fate again."

"You heard Rika. Viking women are accustomed to fighting beside their men."

"And you heard my answer. You are no Viking woman. You're small and fragile and not trained to fight."

"You're going to kill him, aren't you?"

"Are you referring to Rolo?"

"You know I am."

"Don't meddle, Fiona. This is between me and Rolo."

When she started to protest, his mouth came down hard on hers, ending her words before they were formed. His kiss was fierce and demanding as he tasted, then withdrew, then tasted again, more fully this time. "I've never tasted anything as sweet as your mouth," Thorne whispered against her lips.

Her face was bathed in a halo of candlelight as she gazed up at him. "Are you trying to distract me?" she asked archly.

He kissed her again. "Is it working?"

She grinned. "Not yet."

His gaze went to her naked breasts—she had long since stopped sleeping in her chemise. Her pulse beat hard and fast beneath his hungry gaze. Her mouth went dry, aching for the touch of his lips upon hers. He happily obliged. But it wasn't his lips he diligently plied on her breasts, it was his tongue. He lapped moisture onto her nipples and then blew on them, creating a sensation so exquisite Fiona moaned aloud.

His mouth traced a path down her pale skin, stopping to explore her belly button before continuing downward to a place so erotically responsive that Fiona would have cried out had Thorne not placed a hand over her mouth to stifle her cries.

"Quiet, love," Thorne whispered. "The men sleeping in the hall will hear us. We'll have them groaning with frustration and wishing for women of their own."

Fiona's hand drifted over his face. Her breath quickened and her body tautened as her fingertips roamed over his lips. They were firm and moist from her kisses, his chin and cheeks prickly with a day's growth of whiskers. With her other hand she stroked his hair—sun-bright, thick, long, alive beneath her fingertips. He allowed her but a moment to enjoy her exploration before parting her thighs with his knee and delving his fingers into the lush thicket between her legs. Unerringly he found the hidden button and circled it slowly, oh so slowly, before moving downward to the slick crevice that was already weeping for him.

"Yes, that's how I like you," he murmured in a voice thick with desire. "Open wider, let me taste you there."

His erotic words brought a fresh spurt of moisture to her intimate flesh as her legs shifted, allowing him greater access. His head dipped into the vee formed by her legs and his tongue touched her. Forgetting caution, Fiona let out a shivering cry and arched into his mouth. He worked her with his tongue until she was drawn taut as a bow and tiny contractions began deep within her, radiating outward. Sensing her climax, he moved upward along her body and filled her with himself, intensifying the bursts of pleasure shooting through her. Control was beyond her as she writhed and twisted, pressing his buttocks, wanting him deeper, wanting it faster . . .

He surged and plunged within her, still hard and tense and struggling to achieve the ultimate pleasure. As the exquisite sensations faded away she felt him go utterly still, buried so deep inside her she feared she would burst. The pleasure was exquisite. Then his breath left him in a great expulsion of air as his body convulsed. She held onto him tightly, taking everything he had to give, content because it was enough.

Fiona heard Thorne heave a great sigh and knew he felt the same as she. If Brann could know how close they were now, he would be pleased, she thought wistfully. But of course Brann did know. He was never far from her; even now she could feel his presence.

"What are you thinking?" Thorne asked sleepily. "You're so quiet."

"I was thinking of Brann, but don't believe for a moment that I've forgotten our discussion before you distracted me. I'm afraid for you, Thorne. I'd die if anything happened to you. Rolo's reputation as a fierce and cunning fighter has been sung by skalds. What if he kills you?"

"That won't happen, love. Justice is on my side. Forget it and go to sleep."

Unfortunately, sleep wasn't easily attained. Fiona's senses were shrieking danger. Something unforeseen was going to happen but she had no idea what. Death, aye, she could literally smell the stench of death and destruction. Sharp and nauseous, it permeated the small enclosure and sent chills racing down her spine. It was a long time before Fiona's mind shut down and sleep finally carried her away. But even in sleep her dreams were fraught with images of death and mayhem.

The next day Garm, Thorne, Fiona, Tyra and Rika left in the company of Garm's highly trained warriors. The sky was overcast and the day was cool, but there was a definite hint of spring in the air as Garda waved them off. It was a six-day journey up the coast from Bergen to Kaupang. Six days of alternately being drenched with cold rain and then warmed by bright sunshine. Heavy weapons, tents made of animal hides, and furs for their beds had been loaded on pony carts and followed behind the small army.

The women had no difficulty keeping up. At night the army pitched their tents in a clearing and were off early the following morning. Meals consisted for the most part of dried or salted meat, but someone usually hunted fresh game for a welcome change. It was not a difficult journey, but Fiona couldn't help recalling that she'd lost a child along this same road, a child she'd wanted with all her heart.

They reached their destination in good time and found Aren and Thorolf waiting for them with their warriors at the designated place. Fiona counted nearly fifty men camped in the woods. The army was ample enough, in her opinion, to win any battle they chose to undertake.

Thorne had no reason to suspect that Rolo had been quietly hiring mercenaries during the winter, that he had expected Garm to demand the return of Rika's dowry and knew the powerful jarl was prepared to use force to get it. Rolo had also been suspicious of the way Thorne disappeared from his hall without a word to anyone. Being of a distrustful nature, Rolo guessed that someone in his own household had gotten to Thorne with the truth about Fiona's sudden departure, and that Thorne had hastened to her rescue.

No one would admit to the deed, so Rolo had administered severe beatings to all the thralls and karls until the guilty party could no longer stand the cries of innocent men and women and had confessed. His bed slave Mista had been severely punished for her betrayal. Rolo had beaten her himself, beaten her until she lost consciousness and two of her ribs and her arm were broken. Then he had set about hiring mercenaries in anticipation of a spring attack.

Rolo's sentries had already alerted him to the large army camped in the woods beyond the homestead. Rolo knew who they were and their numbers. He even knew there were women among the warriors.

Chapter Nineteen

Protected by six Viking warriors, Garm advanced toward Rolo's homestead. Thorne, Thorolf and Aren remained behind in the woods beyond the tilled fields where they could hear but not be seen. The women stayed close to their men, garbed like Valkyrie warrior maidens in armor and helms.

Garm and his party halted a few yards from the house. "Rolo, come out! I wish to speak with you," Garm shouted.

Several moments later Rolo appeared in the doorway, armed to the teeth. "Speak and be on your way," Rolo roared back. "Your daughter divorced me; we have nothing to discuss."

"There's the matter of Rika's dowry," Garm returned. "It belongs to my daughter and her new husband. Return it and there will be no hard feelings between us."

"Did Rika not tell you? She gave me permission to keep her dowry."

"Rika feared for her life; she had to agree to your unreasonable demands. The law is specific on this issue. Upon divorce, the dowry must be returned in full to the wife."

"And if I do not?" Rolo challenged.

"I will take it by force, if I must."

"And I will fight for the right to keep it," Rolo returned. "I am prepared to do battle. I am not stupid. I know Thorne has joined forces with you and understand why. What I do not comprehend is why Thorolf sided against me. We have always been friends. 'Tis no secret that Thorolf cast his own brother and his brother's whore from his hall."

Thorolf had heard enough. His face mottled with rage, he threw caution to the wind and strode out to join Garm. "I can speak for myself, Rolo. I've had a change of heart where Fiona is concerned. She is Thorne's wife and welcome to share my hall. As for Rika, she has agreed to become my wife."

Rolo gave a shout of laughter. "You're going to marry that cold little bitch? Now I understand why you're here. You have a stake in her dowry. You can't have it. Rika gave it to me and I'm going to keep it."

"You're outnumbered, Rolo. You can't possibly defeat the army I've gathered," Garm warned. "Prepare to die."

Suddenly Bretta stepped from behind her

brother, her tall, lithe form garbed in mail. "Look around you, Garm. We have not been idle. We are fully prepared for war and relish the opportunity to do battle with you."

Even as Bretta spoke, men began streaming out of the door and from behind the house.

"Dear God, they have their own army!" Fiona cried out, appalled by the unexpected turn of events. "Many men will die. 'Tis not worth it."

"Vikings welcome death in battle," Thorne informed her. "It has been our way since the beginning of time. Only those who die in battle enjoy the full rewards of afterlife. 'Tis straw death we fear."

"What is straw death?"

" 'Tis when a Viking dies in bed; a fearful and most shameful way to die."

"All God's people enjoy a rewarding afterlife if they live good lives on earth," Fiona responded. "I do not understand the Viking need to die fighting. If you were a Christian you would recognize the error of your beliefs."

"I am not a Christian, Fiona. Hush now and listen to what Garm and Rolo are saying."

"Do you still want to wage war, Garm?" Rolo taunted. "My army of thralls, karls and mercenaries are eager to test their skills."

"Aye, war it is then," Garm said solemnly.

"Remain here," Thorne advised Fiona. "I'm going to add my support to Garm and my brother." He strode away, a magnificent warrior armed to the teeth, leaving Fiona alone to deal with her fears.

"Ah, Thorne the Relentless," Rolo jeered when he

saw Thorne striding forward to join Garm and Thorolf. "You would wage war against me after you enjoyed the hospitality of my home?"

"You and Bretta deceived me," Thorne said. "You sold my wife into slavery and lied to me about it."

"I did you a favor," Rolo claimed. "You don't know what that witch is capable of."

"Fiona is evil," Bretta contended. "She stole my brother's manhood and will do the same to you."

Thorne's eyes turned dark with anger and his mouth flattened into a thin line. "Rolo deserved everything Fiona did to him. If you're hinting that I should abandon Fiona, forget it, Bretta. I love Fiona. She is the only woman I want. If Rolo survives the battle, I will challenge him to personal combat. He deserves to die for his betrayal."

"I look forward to our confrontation, Thorne the Relentless. You are good, but not as good as I."

"So be it," Garm said. "Prepare your men, Rolo the Bold. The battle will commence at dawn tomorrow." Turning abruptly, Garm marched off, his warriors closing ranks behind him. Thorne and Thorolf remained in place a moment longer, then both whirled on their heels and followed Garm.

Bretta and Rolo stepped back into the hall and bolted the door behind them. "Can we win this battle?" Bretta asked. "You could die, you know."

"Aye. I am aware of that. 'Tis not a bad way to die. Far better than a straw death."

"You could return Rika's dowry."

" 'Tis no longer a simple matter of returning her dowry and well you know it. Thorne will accept nothing less than my death. He is besotted with the witch."

"I have left nothing to fate," Bretta informed him. "While you've been off recruiting warriors to fight your war, I have arranged for your dragon ship to be provisioned and moored in the fjord. 'Tis ready to sail even as we speak. I hired sailors to man the ship and they are but awaiting orders."

"You've done all this without my knowledge?" Rolo asked, stunned by Bretta's cunning and foresight.

"Aye, 'twasn't difficult. I do not want to die. All my jewelry, gold and silver and items of value have been placed aboard the dragon ship while you were off hiring warriors. 'Tis but a short voyage to England. I will throw myself upon the mercy of the Viking King Ragnold of York."

"So you're going to abandon me," Rolo charged.

"Do you begrudge me life?"

"Do you think me so puny a fighter that I will die?"

"Nay, I am but cautious. Should you win the war, you will still have Thorne the Relentless to face."

"Think you Thorne will let you slip through his fingers? I think not. His vengeance includes both of us."

"I don't intend to remain behind and find out what he has in mind for me. I have a plan, Rolo."

"When do you not?" Rolo asked sardonically. "Will I be dead when you act upon it?"

Bretta flushed. Rolo had hit closer to the truth

than he knew. "Should you fall in battle, I will contrive to slip away to the fjord."

Rolo gave a fatalistic shrug. "You have my blessing, for what it's worth. I have always tried to be a good brother and do my duty by you. Should I fall in battle, make haste to the fjord and sail away as far and as fast as you can. But heed me well, sister, Thorne will find you wherever you go."

Cook fires burned throughout the campsite. Sentries had been posted and tense warriors were engaged in various activities having to do with weapons and battle. Thorne sat beside his campfire, honing Blood-drinker to a lethal edge. Fiona huddled beside him, staring absently into the flames. When she began to shudder, Thorne set his sword and honing stone aside and gave her a little shake. She appeared to be in a trance, and concern worried his brow.

"What is it you see, love? Don't be afraid to tell me."

"The stench of death is strong," Fiona whispered.

"Whose death?"

"I cannot see beyond the armor and helm. But I feel reasonably certain 'tis not you."

Light from the dancing flames made the whites of her eyes glow eerily. "Will we be victorious?"

"Aye," Fiona said slowly. "But there is something else, something I cannot see clearly. I sense danger and suffocating darkness."

"You will be safe behind the lines with Rika and

Tyra," Thorne said. "Will Garm, Thorolf and Aren survive?"

"Many will die," Fiona intoned in a voice unlike her own. "I cannot see their faces."

"I will be extra watchful of their backs," Thorne said.

"The battle will be fierce," Fiona whispered. She stared deeper into the flames. "I see . . . Bretta . . ." Suddenly she slumped against him, utterly spent. " 'Tis gone. I fear I have been of little help."

"I do not need your help, love," Thorne assured her. "I have been called a berserker in battle. Few men have challenged Blood-drinker and lived to tell the tale."

"No man is invincible."

"You said I would not die."

"I said I did not sense your death, but I have been wrong before. I love you, Thorne. The thought of losing you leaves me trembling with fear."

Thorne held her close. She was indeed trembling. He wanted her trembling, but not with fear. He wanted her quivering from passion. Pulling her into his arms, he shot to his feet and carried her into their tent, laying her gently down upon their bed of furs. Minutes later their clothing was scattered about the tent, and Thorne, now gloriously naked, knelt above her, his eyes sparkling with a predatory glint.

"I do not hold to the theory that making love before a battle saps a man's strength," he said, grinning down at her. " 'Tis my belief that pumping my seed into the sweetest vessel known to mankind can only empower me. Open your legs, wife, and welcome your husband."

Fiona spread her thighs, welcoming her Viking with a beguiling smile. She knew not what her vision had meant, but of one thing she was certain. She would not let Thorne go into battle alone. Whether he liked it or not, she would be on hand to lend aid should he need it. Then all thought ceased as Thorne's hands and lips took control of her body.

His kisses fell like liquid flame upon her flesh. He adored her with such tender care that Fiona had difficulty reconciling this gentle man with the ferocious Viking warrior who had invaded her island. Suddenly she wanted to love him in the same way he was loving her. With a strength born of need, she pushed him away.

Thorne sat back upon his haunches. "You want me to stop?"

"Nay. I want to love you." She shoved him down onto his back and promptly straddled him.

He looked at her askance, then gave her a cheeky grin. "Do what you will with me, wife. You have me at your mercy."

"I want . . ." Her cheeks flooded with color. "This is what I want," she said, leaning over him and placing tiny nipping kisses over his chest and belly . . . and lower.

Thorne sucked his breath in sharply. "Odin's balls! Are you trying to kill me, woman?"

"Would you have me stop?" she teased as she rubbed her lips over the tip of his swollen erection.

"Only if you wish to send me to Valhalla before my time," Thorne gasped.

Taking him in her hands, she opened her mouth and slid her lips over him. Her tongue explored with outrageous boldness, savoring the novelty of being the aggressor. Unfortunately, her newfound daring was short-lived. A rumble emanating from deep within Thorne's chest exploded into a menacing growl as he flexed his hips and flipped Fiona onto her back. Before she could say him nay he had buried himself so deep within her tight sheath she could feel him nudging her womb.

"Witch," he muttered. "I'm obsessed. Bewitched. Enchanted. Humbled by your love." He moved, driving himself forward. "I find myself waxing poetic. Did you know Vikings are poets who sing tales of adventure and love?" He flexed his hips, quickening his pace and wringing a keening wail from Fiona.

"I knew Vikings were barbarians but had no idea they were poets," she panted, nearly beyond simple thought now.

"Odin help me!" Thorne cried as his hands tightened on her hips, locking their loins in a duel older than time. "I would recite love poems to you now but suddenly I can recall none." Nothing mattered now but reaching that plateau where their souls joined and gut-wrenching pleasure sealed their hearts.

The hour before dawn arrived much too soon to satisfy Fiona.

"I must go," Thorne said, rising from his warm place beside her. The tent smelled of sex and pure animal lust . . . and love, but he dared not linger. "War waits for no man."

"I'll help you arm yourself," Fiona said, rising and donning her tunic.

She handed him his padded shirt, which he put on over his tunic. Then he shrugged into his shirt of mail. Once his helmet and nose plate were in place, it was difficult to distinguish him from any other Viking of his size and shape. Then she handed him his bow and arrows, battleaxe, sword and dagger. Before he left the tent he thrust a throwing axe into his belt and took up his wooden shield. He looked fierce. Had Fiona not known better, she would have thought him a demon straight from hell.

She approached him shyly, stood on tiptoe and planted a kiss on his hard lips. "Go with God, Thorne." And for good measure, she added, "May Odin and Thor bring you back to me."

Thorne gave her a wry smile. "How can I not survive? You have petitioned both our gods in my behalf. Don't forget, love. Stay here where 'tis safe. I vow Rolo will be vanquished before the day is out."

Fiona watched with trepidation as Thorne joined Garm, Thorolf, Aren and their small army. He turned but once to wave at her before he trod off through the woods to engage in mortal combat, his hardened expression no longer that of a tender lover.

The moment he was out of sight, Fiona flew into

action. Thorne wasn't going to go off to fight and perhaps die without her, she vowed as she donned her mail and thrust her sword into her belt. Though much lighter than Thorne's, the sword would give her a modicum of protection should she need it. Not that she intended to engage in battle. All she wanted to do was watch from a safe distance and make sure Thorne survived.

Fiona stepped out of the tent and froze. Then she burst into laughter despite the gravity of the situation. It appeared that she, Rika and Tyra had had the same idea. Tyra and Rika were standing outside their tents, each garbed in identical armor, their faces grim with purpose.

"Apparently we all have the same idea," Rika said, her voice bubbling with laughter.

"I wanted to be near my man should he need me," Tyra explained.

"So did we all," Fiona concurred.

Suddenly an unholy cry rent the air, followed by sounds of clashing swords and clanging battleaxes. The war had begun. As if on signal, the three women moved unerringly toward the heart of battle.

The armies met in the tilled fields surrounding the hall. Both sides were evenly matched and well trained, and fought with all the joy and fierceness attributed to Viking warriors. Men slashed and battered one another with gleeful anticipation of a happy death. They were berserkers, loyal to their chiefs, men who glorified war and death in song and poem.

Thorne wielded his sword with skill and courage. Many men had felt the bite of Blood-drinker this day, and all lay dead or dying. Sweat ran down his face in rivulets and drenched his body as pure exhilaration pumped through his veins. He was a true Viking, willing to die in battle for his cause and to reach Valhalla at the end of the battle if it was his destiny.

As Thorne slashed and cut his way through Rolo's army, he kept a watchful eye on Thorolf and Aren. Though they acquitted themselves admirably, Thorne's protective instincts were fierce. Suddenly, through a mist of sweat and blood, he saw Rolo approaching Thorolf's back. Thorne bellowed out a warning, swiftly dispatched the man blocking his path, and raced to Thorolf's aid. He knew instinctively he was too far away to save him.

Willing speed into his legs, pushing himself to the limit, Thorne feared that Thorolf was going to die. Rolo had raised his battleaxe, ready to deliver the killing blow. Then, to Thorne's utter shock, Rika appeared from out of nowhere, much closer than he to Thorolf. He saw Rika cock back her arm and let her dagger fly. Her mark was true, striking Rolo in the middle of the back. The battleaxe dropped from Rolo's hand and he spun around, his mouth open in silent horror when he saw who had thrown the dagger.

Thorolf sensed danger and whirled, his sword striking flesh and bone. When he saw Rolo writhing on the ground at his feet, he realized just how close to death he had come. Then he saw the blade embedded in Rolo's back and spun about, seeking his savior. When he saw Rika racing toward him, he knew it was she who had saved his life. He held out his arms and swept her up against him.

Thorne watched all this from afar. Though he was impressed by Rika's act of selfless courage, and admired courage in either sex, he was grateful Fiona had enough sense to remain behind in camp. Thorne was so absorbed in protecting his brother that he failed to sense danger approaching him from another direction. Rolo's lieutenant, a man who'd been with him since Rolo had become jarl, had seen his chief fall and was overcome with rage. Aiming his spear, he let it fly at Thorne.

The scene unfolded before Fiona's eyes like a bad dream. She saw Rika race toward Thorolf, saw her dagger bite deeply into Rolo's back, and winced when Thorolf delivered the killing blow with his sword. Rika had just flown into Thorolf's open arms when Fiona heard Brann speaking to her over the din of battle.

Death is near, child. You must save him.

Fiona acted instinctively, even though she had yet to spot the threat to Thorne. She moved deftly around the battling men, ducking sword thrusts and stepping over fallen bodies, oblivious to danger as she hastened toward Thorne. Then, from the corner of her eye she saw the source of danger. She cringed when she saw an enemy warrior aim his spear at an unsuspecting Thorne. She was close, so close.

Thorne saw Fiona rushing toward him at full tilt, and fear raced through him. Odin's bones! What did she think she was doing? "Go back, Fiona!" His warning was lost in the pandemonium of battle raging around him.

Fiona screamed in rage and frustration when she saw the spear leave the enemy's hand and speed toward Thorne. He was calling out to her but she paid his warning scant heed. There was a slim chance she could save Thorne's life and she didn't hesitate to act upon it. With a strength born of love, she launched herself at him. She sailed through the air and hit him squarely, knocking him flat on his back scant seconds before the spear thudded into the ground where he had been standing.

Bretta cursed long and fluently when she saw that the battle was all but lost. Rolo was either dead or dying, and the witch had somehow managed to save Thorne's life. Soon Rolo's men would realize the battle was lost and they would lose heart. Bretta had fought beside Rolo for a time, but had withdrawn when she recognized defeat. She was left with no recourse but to flee to the fjord as quickly as possible.

Carefully, she circled around the battlefield, edging toward the forest. But as luck would have it, she was seen by Tyra, who had been watching the battle from the sidelines. Tyra realized that Bretta was trying to escape and reacted swiftly to prevent it. Rushing headlong onto the battlefield, she screamed Aren's name and pointed at Bretta when she finally gained his attention.

Bretta froze. She'd been discovered! She couldn't possibly make good her escape now. Unless . . . She had but a split second to make a decision. Both Garm and Aren were racing toward her to cut off her escape. Thorolf had his arms full with Rika and at the moment presented no danger. A few paces away Thorne lay on the ground, the breath knocked out of him and Fiona sprawled atop him. Bretta ripped her dagger from her sheath and leaped with the agility of a cat toward Thorne and Fiona.

Fiona was beginning to stir from atop Thorne. When she had thrown herself at Thorne, the impact had knocked the helm from her head, dazing her. She was still groggy when Bretta leaped at her, grasping a handful of her hair and hauling her to her feet. Fiona's eyes widened with surprise when she felt the prick of a dagger against the tender flesh of her throat.

"Move away from Thorne," Bretta hissed into her ear.

Fiona obeyed. The Viking woman was stronger than she. Bretta was also cornered and desperate, and Fiona knew she wouldn't hesitate to kill.

"What do you hope to gain by this?" Fiona asked with forced calmness.

"Freedom. A dragon ship awaits me at the fjord. You're going to help me get there. Thorne is besotted with you. He'll do nothing to endanger your life."

Thorne vaulted to his feet, seeing nothing beyond the dagger Bretta held to Fiona's throat. It had all happened so fast he'd not realized what had transpired until he felt Fiona's weight leave him and saw Bretta pressing a knife to Fiona's neck. He stood very still, watching Bretta, fearing to move lest she thrust the dagger into Fiona's throat.

"Let her go, Bretta," Thorne said in a voice filled with menace. " 'Tis me you want, not Fiona."

"Fiona is my protection," Bretta contended. "I knew you'd deal harshly with me so I made prior arrangements to leave should the battle turn against us. A dragon ship is provisioned, manned and waiting for me at the fjord. I'm taking Fiona with me. She's my guarantee of safe passage."

"Let Fiona go and I'll grant you safe passage," Thorne offered.

"Nay. The witch stays with me. She's been my nemesis since the day we met." She dragged Fiona toward the fjord, the dagger pressed to her throat.

"Will you release Fiona when you reach the fjord?" Thorne called after her.

"Perhaps," Bretta said slyly. "Do not attempt to follow. If I see you behind me I'll plunge the dagger home and kill the witch."

Bretta was gaining ground as she spoke, dragging Fiona with her. When she disappeared amid the trees in the forest, Garm, Aren and Thorolf started forward. Thorne stopped them with a single word.

"Nay! Bretta is a desperate and dangerous woman. She'll not hesitate to kill Fiona if we follow too closely. I'm going after her alone. Stay here and tend to the battle."

"The battle is all but won," Thorolf said. "Rolo is dead and his army will soon join him in Valhalla. Victory is ours."

Thorne's attention was focused on the place where Fiona and Bretta had disappeared into the forest. He heard little of what Thorolf said. Never had he felt so helpless. Intuitively he knew that once Fiona boarded Bretta's dragon ship he'd never see her again. His own dragon ship was anchored nearby, but it was neither provisioned nor ready to sail.

"I'm going after them," he said with grim determination. "No one is going to take Fiona from me."

Fiona's fierce struggle to escape Bretta gained her naught but a sore neck. The Viking woman was literally dragging her along the forest path, and all Fiona could do was move her feet in an effort to remain upright. She knew that once she faltered Bretta would kill her.

"Hurry," Bretta urged as she pricked the dagger deeper into Fiona's neck to emphasize her words. "Your lover is not a patient man. Doubtless he's already hard on our heels."

"Let me go," Fiona pleaded. "Thorne will let you leave in peace if you spare me."

Bretta's harsh laughter was bitter with resentment. "You don't know Thorne the Relentless if you think that. He will neither forget nor forgive."

The path they followed was a well-trod one, used

frequently by those in Rolo's household as well as by travelers. It led directly to the fjord and the place where Bretta's dragon ship was moored.

Fiona's neck was streaming blood from numerous small cuts by the time they reached the fjord. Fiona saw the shallow draft vessel rocking gently in the surf and her heart pounded with fear. She knew that once she stepped aboard her life was forfeit.

The sailors Bretta had hired saw them and flew into action. A rope ladder was lowered into the knee-deep water and one man scurried down to hold it in place.

Bretta forced Fiona into the icy water. "Climb the ladder," she ordered.

"Nay! You no longer need me. I have served my purpose. Go while you still can."

Bretta recognized the wisdom of Fiona's words. "Aye, I no longer need you," she agreed. "Neither does Thorne."

Thorne burst through the forest just as Bretta raised her dagger to bring it down into Fiona's heart.

"Naaaay!" The wail of protest ripped from his throat in a heartrending cry of raw agony.

His cry distracted Bretta for the space of a heartbeat, time enough for Fiona to take advantage of the lapse. As Bretta swung the dagger upward and paused, the arm around Fiona's neck relaxed. A sudden twist and Fiona was free, and in that split second she ducked away and threw herself into the dark, icy water.

The bitter cold stunned her, but helped to keep her calm. She dove deep, heading away from the ship, remaining under water until she thought her lungs would burst. When she finally broke surface and dragged in a sustaining breath, she saw Bretta scurrying up the ladder. A moment later the sails were unfurled and the ship bearing Bretta slid away from the shore. Oars came out, helping the ship along as the tide took it toward the open sea. Then Fiona's heavy mail pulled her beneath the surface and she saw her life racing before her eyes.

Thorne reached the shore in a frenzy of panic. His gaze skimmed the blue-black water, searching for his love. The water was so cold he doubted anyone could live long in the freezing surf. Then he saw her, bobbing up to the surface a brief moment before being dragged down again by the weight of her mail. He had torn off his own mail and tossed aside his weapons as he raced toward the bank. He wore naught but his tunic and padded vest when he launched himself into the water and swam toward the place where he'd last seen Fiona.

Let her live, Thorne chanted over and over, pleading with his gods for her life as his strong strokes carried him through the freezing surf. Thorne was frantic with worry when Fiona did not rise to the surface again. Fearing his own gods had forsaken him, he sent a fervent plea to Fiona's Christian God, promising to become a Christian if He would but spare her life.

Chapter Twenty

Fiona sank like a rock, caught in the current and buffeted about like a grain of sand. She was cold. So very cold. The need to breathe, which had been so urgent just moments ago, no longer seemed crucial as her heartbeat slowed and nearly halted. She knew death was at hand and was surprised she did not sense the ominous presence of the dark spirit hovering over her.

Fiona didn't feel as if she were dying. But for the bone-numbing cold, she felt nothing at all. She knew she should try to save herself, and it suddenly occurred to her that she should remove her mail. The struggle hardly seemed worth the effort as she wrestled with the heavy wire-link shirt. And then she thought of Thorne and how desperately she wanted to stay with him. She struggled harder, so near to unconsciousness her numb hands and fingers simply refused to work. Suddenly she heard a soothing voice.

'Tis not your time, child.

Then hands she couldn't see were lifting the mail from her and she began to float upward through the dark, murky water toward light.

Thorne couldn't find her. She'd been under water so long he feared she was dead already. He plunged down into the murky depths again and again, until the cold numbed his reflexes and sapped his strength, yet still he refused to give up.

Then miraculously he felt silken strands of hair curling around his hand. Fiona's hair. Grasping a handful, he swam upward until her head popped to the surface. She appeared not to be breathing. Somehow, he knew not how, she had found the strength to remove her mail. It had saved her life, for he never would have found her had she remained on the bottom of the fjord.

Fiona suddenly felt warmth, sensed sunlight on her face, but could not summon the strength to suck in that vital first breath of life-giving air. She was in limbo, aware of her surroundings but unable to respond.

"Is she alive?" Thorolf asked anxiously.

"Nay, she's dead," Garm said, firmly convinced that the wan creature dragged from the fjord was no longer living.

Thorne was not ready to accept defeat. Someone

handed him a fur cloak and he wrapped Fiona in it, then lifted her so she was half reclining in his arms. Without thinking he began thumping on her back, willing her to respond. Then astonishingly she did. Fiona gasped and stirred in his arms.

"She lives!" Thorne rejoiced. "Thank the Christian God for giving her back to me."

" 'Tis impossible, she was under too long," Garm said in disbelief.

Fiona turned her head aside and spewed forth a great gush of water. Then she coughed and opened her eyes. She saw Thorne looking down at her with love and concern and gave him a shaky smile.

"What happened?"

"You almost drowned," Thorne explained. "You need a warm hearth and something hot to drink. I almost lost you. 'Tis a miracle. How did you remove your mail by yourself?"

"Aye, a miracle. I didn't remove my mail," Fiona said. Her words made no sense to Thorne. Before he could question her further, she said, "Help me to stand."

"Fiona, I don't think . . ."

"I can still see Bretta's ship, Thorne." Her eyes had a wild, glazed look to them. "There is something I have to do. Please."

Reluctantly Thorne helped her to her feet. She hugged the cloak around her and took a few shaky steps to the water's edge. Thorne started to protest but thought better of it. She appeared determined to see this to the end, whatever it was. He stood close behind her, ready to come to her aid should she require it. He was stunned when Fiona tossed aside the cloak, raised her arms heavenward and spoke.

"Lightning, thunder, rain and wind. Raging seas and violent storms. Descend upon those who disobey God's laws."

Thorne stared at Fiona in fear and awe. It sounded to him as though she'd placed a curse upon Bretta. How could that be? She'd denied repeatedly the charge that she was a witch. No one but a witch or a wizard could implore the elements to call forth storms. Fiona was a Christian. Was she more than that? He knew she was learned in the old ways of her people as well as her own Christian religion. And though she had special powers, he knew she would never use them for evil.

"What just happened?" Thorolf asked with a hint of fear.

"Naught. Fiona is overwrought and near exhaustion. She needs rest, warmth and nourishment. Return to the battlefield. I'll take care of Fiona."

Garm, Thorolf and the few men who had followed reluctantly retraced their steps back to the field of combat as Thorne retrieved the cloak from the ground and wrapped it around Fiona's shoulders. Fiona felt his warmth behind her and relaxed against him, suddenly too drained to move. Her knees started to buckle and he scooped her up into his arms.

"Are you all right?"

She looked at him in confusion. "Aye. What happened?"

Thorne went still. "Don't you know?"

"I know I nearly drowned and you saved me. How did you get my mail off without me knowing it?"

Now Thorne was truly puzzled. "I didn't remove your mail. I thought you did."

Fiona was tired, so very tired. "If I did, I don't recall. It just seemed to . . . float away. It was all so strange. I was certain I was going to die, but after a time I no longer felt the need to breathe. I could have sworn someone told me it wasn't my time to die."

"You're tired and confused," Thorne said, not knowing what to make of her strange words. "Do you remember what happened later, after I dragged you out of the water?"

She shook her head, her violet eyes wide and questioning, her brow furrowed in concentration. At length she said, "I remember naught. It seems as though I opened my eyes but moments ago and found myself in your arms. Did something of consequence happen?"

"Nay, naught that matters." If she didn't remember, he wasn't going to tell her. Better that she forget her odd behavior and the words that had sounded very much like a curse. Fortunately, he'd been the only one near enough to hear. Garm and Thorolf had been suspicious but hadn't the slightest notion what had transpired.

Fiona rested against Thorne, wrapped warmly in his arms as he carried her back through the forest toward the house. The sounds of fighting had ceased as they approached the battlefield. Bodies littered the tilled field; some were dead, others merely wounded. Rolo still lay where he had fallen, a pool of congealed blood beneath his stiffening body. Those of his men who had survived were limping away into the forest. The joyous victors were already celebrating by breaking open Rolo's best ale and wine.

Thorne carried Fiona into the house. Rika and Tyra followed close behind, wringing their hands and looking worried. Thorne set Fiona down on a bench close to the hearth and piled more wood on the fire. When he shouted for hot wine, a slave hurried to obey.

After a time, warmth and wine restored Fiona and she threw off the fur cloak so the fire could dry her wet clothing.

"Perhaps Bretta left some clothing you could change into," Rika suggested. "Shall I go see?"

"I will wear naught that belonged to Bretta," Fiona declared.

"Fiona will have new clothes fit for a queen as soon as she's able to sort through the bolts of cloth I have stored aboard my ship, or those Rolo kept here in the house."

Shortly thereafter, Thorolf, Garm and Aren entered the hall. "The dead have been dispatched to Valhalla," Garm said. "I will carry my own dead home for a proper sendoff by their families."

"Is all well with Fiona?" Thorolf asked.

"Fiona will recover," Thorne said. "Do you intend to return to your hall?"

"I'm going to accompany Garm and Rika to Bergen," Thorolf revealed. "We will return after we are wed."

"We should decide upon the disposal of Rolo's land," Thorne said.

" 'Tis yours if you want it," Garm offered.

"Nay. I have new land awaiting me on the Isle of Man."

"Since the land adjoins Thorolf's," Garm mused thoughtfully, " 'tis his to keep. Consider it part of Rika's dowry. The rest of her dowry is most likely stashed somewhere in the house."

"We will find it," Thorolf assured him.

"Let me know when you are ready to travel as I am anxious to return home. Garda will worry if I fail to return in a reasonable time."

Garm took his leave and Thorolf and Rika went off in search of her valuables. Only Aren and Tyra remained in the hall with Fiona and Thorne.

"What about you, Aren? Will you remain or take your chances with me and Fiona on Man?"

"I am for Man," Aren declared. "I have no land of my own and welcome the opportunity to become a landowner. Tyra is of the same mind."

" 'Tis settled then. We will sail as soon as my ships are provisioned and manned. Most of my men are landless and have expressed their eagerness to sail with me and settle on their own land. Those with families can return for them later if the land pleases them."

"Everything is intact," Rika exclaimed happily as she bounced into the hall with Thorolf in tow. "I found my jewelry, linens and everything else I brought with me stored in chests in Rolo's room."

Suddenly one of the slaves ventured forth and dropped to her knees before Fiona. "Mistress, if you please," she said timidly. "You remember me, I am Erica. Mista has been gravely hurt and needs attention. Would you look at her?"

"Who hurt her?" Thorne demanded.

"Rolo beat her most severely, master. We all received beatings but none as brutal as Mista. 'Twas she who came to you in the night and told you where to find Fiona."

"I will see her," Fiona said.

She turned to Thorne. "Would you send someone to Garm's camp to fetch my pouch of herbs?"

"I will go myself," Thorne said, rising. "There are personal items I wish to collect before Garm departs."

Fiona returned her attention to the thrall. "Where is Mista?"

"I am here, mistress." A small, battered woman stepped forth.

Fiona saw Mista and blanched, appalled by the woman's pitiful condition. Her right arm was swollen to twice its size. Apparently it had been broken and left to heal without proper care. The bones had not healed properly and infection had set in. Her face was flushed with fever and she appeared to be in considerable pain.

"Erica, help Mista into Bretta's bedchamber," Fiona ordered briskly. "I'll need lots of boiling water, clean rags and a sharp knife. The arm needs to be lanced and the poison drained."

Fiona set to work the moment Mista was settled, using all the skill and knowledge of healing that Brann had taught her. Unless Mista's body was purged of infection, she would die.

Fiona had done all she could for Mista. It was very late, and Erica had come to sit with Mista so Fiona could get some rest. Thorne waited for her in the hall.

"Come have something to eat," he urged. "You've been through so much today."

"I'm not hungry, truly, just tired."

Before she realized what he was about, he lifted her into his arms and carried her into Rolo's bedchamber. "Rolo won't be using this anymore," Thorne said as he lowered her onto the bed of furs and followed her down. "Have I told you how truly amazing you are?"

"I am no different from any other woman."

Slowly and with loving care he began to undress her. "You're unlike any woman I've ever known."

"Do you still think I'm a witch?"

"I think of you as the woman I love. Brann was right. Destiny created us for one another. Go to sleep, my love. You've earned it."

During the night a fierce storm blew in from the sea. A storm the likes of which hadn't been seen in Thorne's time. The wind howled, uprooting trees and shattering buildings not sturdy enough to withstand the raging gale. Thunder rattled the house and lightning created fireworks in the sky. Then came the rains. Solid, wind-driven sheets pounding into the earth. By morning the storm had moved on, leaving grim reminders of its fierce passage.

Fortunately, Thorne's flagship and two others had ridden out the storm in good shape. The other two had broken from their moorings and were smashed to pieces against the rocky shore. The next day Thorne began to provision his surviving ships and to recruit his crew for their imminent voyage to Man.

To Fiona's delight, Mista's fever broke two days later and her arm showed encouraging signs of healing. Garm and Thorolf broke camp that morning and after a lengthy farewell, left for Bergen. That same day Bretta's dragon ship mysteriously washed ashore. Its masts had snapped and its red and white striped sails were in tatters. Thorne and Aren were working aboard *Odin's Raven* when it appeared out of a thick mist. They quickly abandoned their task and climbed aboard. They hadn't expected a ghost ship, but that was exactly what they found.

There were no signs of life anywhere on the ship. Proof that it had been battered by the recent storm was visible in the wreckage they found aboard. Apparently the occupants had been swept overboard and lost. Thorne wanted to believe Fiona had had nothing to do with the misfortune, but his heart and mind told him otherwise. Even though she might not recall doing so, Thorne was convinced that Fiona had placed a curse upon Bretta.

"What do you think happened?" Aren asked curiously.

"No ship at sea could survive a storm as furious as the one that blew in two nights ago," Thorne said. " 'Tis a sad but fitting end for Bretta. She tried to destroy everything I loved and earned God's wrath." He felt a sudden need to see Fiona's sweet face. To hold her next to her heart. To tell her he loved her. He didn't bother to explain his need to Aren as he made a hasty retreat.

Fiona didn't need to be told about Bretta's demise. She'd been sorting through bolts of cloth she'd found in the house and was selecting those she liked to make into new tunics for herself and Thorne when a vision appeared.

At first she *saw* nothing but darkness. Black, suffocating darkness. She fought for breath. She felt as though she were reliving her recent near-death experience. Suddenly the veil of darkness lifted and she was allowed a peek into a dazzling light. She saw herself standing on the floor of the sea. Water surrounded her but she had no trouble breathing. Then the limp figure of a woman floated aimlessly along toward her, her eyes wide and sightless. It was Bretta, tangled in a mass of weeds and flotsam, tendrils of long blonde hair drifting around her in the eerie silence.

Fiona uttered a startled cry and fell back against a bolt of cloth. That was where Thorne found her, leaning against a bolt of scarlet silk, her face white as fresh snow.

"Fiona, what is it? Are you ill?"

Fiona shook her head. " 'Tis naught."

“You’ve had a vision,” Thorne said with sure knowledge. “Do you want to tell me about it?”

“Oh, Thorne.” He held out his arms and she went into them. “I did have a vision. Bretta is dead.”

“Aye, you’re right, love. Her battered and empty dragon ship has returned with the tide. ’Twas the storm. Everyone aboard perished. Is that what you saw?”

“I saw only Bretta. She was floating at the bottom of the sea.”

He kissed her trembling lips. “ ’Tis God’s will, love.” He meant it, though he would carry with him forever the vision of Fiona placing a curse upon the woman who had tried to kill her. God’s will or a wizard’s spell, he cared not. Either way, Bretta had been punished. And he’d never tell Fiona what he suspected. ’Twas best she didn’t remember.

Suddenly Fiona realized what Thorne had said. “Do you not mean Odin’s will? Or Thor’s will? Do you realize you just gave credit to my Christian God?”

“Aye, I know exactly what I said. When I had given up all hope of finding you alive in the cold waters of the fjord, I prayed to my gods to spare you. They chose not to reply. Then, out of desperation, I appealed to your Christian God, promising to turn Christian if He’d give you back to me. Seconds later you literally floated into my grasp.”

Fiona stared at him in numb disbelief. “Are you very certain you are willing to embrace my Christian God?”

“Aye, I always keep my promises. Now that I

think on it, perhaps that was Brann's intention. Why would I allow a lowly slave to lure me into marriage when I could have taken her at my whim if 'twas not ordained by some high authority? I would never have sought a Christian priest to perform the ceremony had it not been intended that I become Christian. And why would I leave my homeland to settle on the Isle of Man if God had not willed it?"

Fiona threw her arms around him, her face radiant. "I love you, Viking. We will have a happy life on Man. It has been promised to me by Brann."

"I love you, witch," he returned affectionately. "I have always loved you. The first moment I saw you I was enchanted. I'll never let you go. You'll have to suffer my company until death parts us."

Fiona gave a squeal of surprise when he scooped her into his arms and carried her into the bedchamber they had been sharing. He slammed the door with his foot and let her slide down his hard body until her feet touched the floor. Then he undressed her slowly, with great relish.

" 'Tis the middle of the day," Fiona said, blushing. "What will everyone think?"

"That I want my wife and can't wait for the dark of night to have her. Will you say me nay, wife?"

"I will never deny you," Fiona vowed as she removed the brooch from his tunic and let the fabric slide down his body. "I want you, Thorne the Relentless. With all my heart."

Together they fell upon their bed of furs, arms and legs entwined, hearts beating as one. They were both ready, both eager to consummate their love. Fiona opened her legs and Thorne moved between them. His hand drifted to her sweetly moist flesh, to ready her for his entrance. He groaned and shuddered when she drenched his hand with her sweet essence. With a cry of pure, gut-wrenching pleasure, he thrust into her.

He loved her tenderly, fiercely, possessively. He brought her to the brink of madness, then let her float back to reality at her own pace. Then he loved her again. When they attained that blissful place of unbearable splendor together, she screamed a single word.

"Viking!"

Epilogue

Isle of Man, two years later

Not even a gull's cry broke the predawn silence that lazy summer morning. No one was on hand to see the small fleet of dragon ships float ashore below the village. No one greeted the weary travelers as they disembarked and trudged upward along the winding path to the village.

Fiona arose early that morning, her heart soaring with joy as she stepped outside and viewed the verdant green hills and boundless richness of her land. She'd been home for two years now, and each day she shared with her beloved Viking was blessed with happiness. She'd returned to Man to find her father alive and well and her people prospering under Viking rule.

The tenuous peace between her father and Thorne had developed into a lasting friendship. It wasn't long before Adair had learned to appreciate his Viking son-in-law for his stalwart character and courage. The birth of her first son had cemented the bond between her people and their Viking conquerors. Fiona had been pregnant when she stepped ashore on Man, and bore her son, Brann, five months later. Just four months ago she had presented Thorne with another son, Bret.

The land Thorne had claimed was fertile and rich, and if he missed going a-Viking it wasn't apparent. Occasionally he journeyed to other lands for the purpose of trade, but he rarely stayed away long.

Fiona's introspection came to a halt when she spied Thorne coming from the barn. She walked out to meet him.

"You're up early this morning," Thorne said, giving her an enthusiastic kiss.

"I love this time of morning. I just fed Bret and put him back to bed. Brann is still sleeping. Are your chores done?"

He gave her a cheeky grin. "Ready to go back to bed, are you? Do we have time?"

She sent him a seductive smile. "There's always time, but not this morning. You've a surprise waiting for you, Viking, and I wanted to warn you."

His grin faded. "Surprise? You know I dislike surprises."

"You'll like this one."

Thorne blanched. "You've had a vision. I don't

think I'll ever grow accustomed to that Celtic part of you that can see things."

"Walk down to the beach with me."

"What's gotten into you, woman? There are chores . . . the children . . ."

"The servants are capable of taking care of things here. We won't be gone long, I promise."

"How can I deny you anything, love? Very well, take me where you will."

They met the landing party at the top of the hill. At first Thorne thought their sanctuary had been breached and he reached for his sword, realizing too late that he hadn't donned it this morning. He rarely did anymore.

He thrust Fiona behind him, then relaxed somewhat but didn't let down his guard when he saw there were women and children in the group. He was more than a little surprised when one of the women in the party saw Fiona and screamed out her name. Fiona stepped around her husband's bulk and raced to meet her.

Rika!

Thorne watched in growing astonishment as he recognized his brother and nearly all the warriors he'd left behind in his homeland. He caught up with Fiona and Rika where they stood in the path, hugging one another fiercely.

"Is this the surprise?" Thorne wanted to know.

"Aye, is it not wonderful?"

Then Thorolf was beside him, nearly knocking him over as they slapped backs and gripped arms.

"Am I welcome on your island, brother?" Thorolf asked.

"More than welcome, Thorolf. What brings you here?"

"We've come to settle," Thorolf explained. "Eric the Red has invaded us twice since you left, driving off our livestock and burning our buildings. I grow tired of the constant struggle to protect my land. After each attack Rika reminded me of the peaceful land beyond the sea that Fiona had described to her, and she expressed her desire to settle in a place where battling neighbors is not a way of life. Rika and the twins mean more to me than land."

"Twins? You have twins?" Thorne asked. "Fiona and I have two healthy sons."

Rika dragged forth two giggling toddlers. "Their names are Olaf and Olga, and a livelier pair of scamps you'll never see."

"They'll be playmates for our own two little ones," Thorne said. "Welcome to my home, brother. Fiona did not exaggerate, there is ample land and a peaceful existence for all on our little isle. Tomorrow you and Rika can choose the land you want to settle on. I am a Christian now," he said proudly, "but we are tolerant of all religions."

The day was one to remember. They talked for hours, catching up on one another's lives. It wasn't until they had run out of words and were settled in their beds that Thorne turned to Fiona and asked, "What kind of enchantment did you perform to bring Thorolf and his family here?"

"You're the only man I've ever enchanted," she teased.

"Promise you'll use your powers on no one but me, love."

"No one but you, Viking. Forever."

Author's Note

I found my research on Vikings fascinating. During the eighth to the eleventh centuries, all the world feared and hated Vikings, and with good reason. They were marauders, raiders, traders in human flesh, and the fiercest fighters known to mankind. Because much of their land was uninhabitable and the climate too harsh for farming, Vikings became the greatest navigators of all time. They spread out from Denmark, Norway and Sweden—west to North America, east to Russia, and south to Turkey, the Byzantine and beyond. They were traders without equal, traveling to faraway lands for personal wealth and gain.

There was another side to Vikings that is well documented but little remarked upon. They were farmers, animal herders, traders, poets and storytellers. They had no written language except for runes, but their epic sagas and poems were spread by skalds from household to household. They dressed in silks and satins for special occasions and wore fine jewelry encrusted with gems. I would have liked to include more facts in my story but felt that too much would be boring to the reader. I hope you like *Viking!* just the way it was presented to you.

Pirate is my next release. Look for it in December 1998. I hope you'll enjoy my story of swashbuckling adventure on the high seas.

I love hearing from readers. Write to me in care of my publishers at the address on the copyright page of this book. For a current newsletter and bookmark, please enclose a #10 self-addressed, *stamped* envelope and put your name on your letter in case the envelope goes astray.

All My Romantic Best,
Connie Mason

"Each new Connie Mason book is a prize!"
—Heather Graham

Spirits can be so bloody unpredictable, and the specter of Lady Amelia is the worst of all. Just when one of her ne'er-do-well descendents thought he could go astray in peace, the phantom lady always appears to change his wicked ways.

A rogue without peer, Jackson Graystoke wants to make gaming and carousing in London society his life's work. And the penniless baronet would gladly curse himself with wine and women—if Lady Amelia would give him a ghost of a chance.

Fresh off the boat from Ireland, Moira O'Toole isn't fool enough to believe in legends or naive enough to trust a rake. Yet after an accident lands her in Graystoke Manor, she finds herself haunted, harried, and hopelessly charmed by Black Jack Graystoke and his exquisite promise of pure temptation.

_4041-7 $5.99 US/$6.99 CAN

Dorchester Publishing Co., Inc.
P.O. Box 6640
Wayne, PA 19087-8640

Please add $1.75 for shipping and handling for the first book and $.50 for each book thereafter. NY, NYC, and PA residents, please add appropriate sales tax. No cash, stamps, or C.O.D.s. All orders shipped within 6 weeks via postal service book rate.
Canadian orders require $2.00 extra postage and must be paid in U.S. dollars through a U.S. banking facility.

Name________________________________
Address______________________________
City________________State______Zip________
I have enclosed $________ in payment for the checked book(s).
Payment must accompany all orders. ☐ Please send a free catalog.

Bestselling Author of *Flame*!

"Why did you do that?"

"Kiss you?" Cole shrugged. "Because you wanted me to, I suppose. Why else would a man kiss a woman?"

But Dawn knows lots of other reasons, especially if the woman is nothing but half-breed whose father has sold her to the first interested male. Defenseless and exquisitely lovely, Dawn is overjoyed when Cole Webster kills the ruthless outlaw who is her husband in name only. But now she has a very different sort of man to contend with. A man of unquestionable virility, a man who prizes justice and honors the Native American traditions that have been lost to her. Most intriguing of all, he is obviously a man who knows exactly how to bring a woman to soaring heights of pleasure. And yes, she does want his kiss...and maybe a whole lot more.

__4260-6 $5.99 US/$6.99 CAN

Dorchester Publishing Co., Inc.
P.O. Box 6640
Wayne, PA 19087-8640

Please add $1.75 for shipping and handling for the first book and $.50 for each book thereafter. NY, NYC, and PA residents, please add appropriate sales tax. No cash, stamps, or C.O.D.s. All orders shipped within 6 weeks via postal service book rate. Canadian orders require $2.00 extra postage and must be paid in U.S. dollars through a U.S. banking facility.

Name____
Address______________________________________
City______________________State______Zip__________
I have enclosed $__________ in payment for the checked book(s).
Payment must accompany all orders. ❑ Please send a free catalog

ATTENTION
ROMANCE
CUSTOMERS!
SPECIAL
TOLL-FREE NUMBER
1-800-481-9191
Call Monday through Friday
10 a.m. to 9 p.m.
Eastern Time
Get a free catalogue,
join the Romance Book Club,
and order books using your
Visa, MasterCard,
or Discover®
Leisure
Books
LOVE
SPELL
GO ONLINE WITH US AT DORCHESTERPUB.COM